BOSWELL'S FAIRIES

A novel

Peter Lingard

Reviews

Boswell's Fairies is the raucous and unapologetic tale of Paul "the Banker" Johnson's trials and tribulations as a new recruit in the elite Corps of Royal Marines in 1960's England. Paired up with his "oppo" Jack Mason, a former professional wrestler, the recruits find a kind of home in the tough but loyal squad of misfits and miscreants named after their drill sergeant, Boswell, all in pursuit of the coveted Green Beret. Equally coveted are the local women and their welcoming arms, which fast become Paul and Jack's after-hours focus, until they find themselves in the exclusive company of best friends Audrey and Jill. And for the first time, they're happy to stay there. When Boswell is charged with the murder of a gay man, the recruits' loyalty is tested and their certainty in their cause challenged, and with the guidance of Jill and Audrey, they begin to ask difficult questions of themselves, and their ideas of honour.

Funny and irreverent, Boswell's Fairies harks back to a time when the rules were clear, and the world unforgiving.

Nicole Hayes, author of *A Shadow's Breath, One True Thing, The Whole of My World, A Footy Girl's Guide to the Stars of 2017* (With Alicia Sometimes), and *From the Outer: Footy like you've never heard it* (Co-edited with Alicia Sometimes)

• • •

You won't want to put this book down. Not a word is wasted in
Boswell's Fairies. Although a work of fiction, it reads like a true account
of life in the Marines for a group of recruits training for their new career.
I was enthralled by their relationships and experiences. But most of all I
was taken in by the skillful writing that just wouldn't let me go.'

Greg Hill, co-author of *Surviving Year Zero: My four years under the
Khmer Rouge* and *Lentil as Anything: Everybody deserves a place at the
table.*

• • •

A raw and honest portrayal of life as a marine in training. A powerfully
written debut novel which takes you to another time and place.

*S.C Karakaltsas, author of Out of Nowhere and Climbing the Coconut
Tree.*

• • •

Peter Lingard has written a novel about basic training in the British
Marines in the sixties. But it is not the usual account. Often funny,
at times politically incorrect, Lingard focuses regularly on periods
of granted leave and gives an interesting insight into the minds of
young recruits in their moments of reprieve.

Stuart Reedy, publisher, Lizard Skin Press

Published by Peter Lingard

Copyright© Peter Lingard 2017

The moral right of the author has been asserted

Email: plingaus@bigpond.com

National Library of Australia

Cataloguing-in-Publication entry

Creator: Peter Lingard, author

ISBN 978-0-6481020-0-7 (Paperback)

Subject: General Fiction

Dewey Number: 823

Contents

I wish to acknowledge

my sincere gratitude

to Her Britannic Majesty,

Queen Elizabeth II,

who paid me to research this tale.

DEAL

19th February 1960

'Fancy clothes ya got there. You a faggot or sommat?'

My anger flared but I finished draping my suit jacket over the misshapen wire hanger. Then I turned to face a man who was my height but more muscular. He had incredibly blue eyes, short blond hair, and a smile that demonstrated a lack of venom in his words. There was an inch-long scar over his right eye and two of his teeth were missing. Strange lumps on his shoulders baffled me. His plimsolls, navy-blue tracksuit bottoms, and a white cotton vest made him look like an athlete.

I put out my unused hand. 'Paul Johnson. I definitely prefer bints, if it's all the same to you.'

'Parties,' the blond replied as he shook my hand.

'What?'

'Parties, not bints. It's what the Navy calls birds. Parties.'

'Yeah, but we're going to be in the Marines,' I pointed out.

'Same difference, mate,' said a second man.

'It's like this 'ere barracks is called a bleedin' concrete ship an' when we go out, we'll be goin' ashore,' the blond informed me. 'I'm Jack Mason. This 'ere is Pete Bell.'

I shook Pete's hand.

'We've bin 'ere a coupla days already,' said Pete. 'It takes a week or so for enough guys to arrive ta make up a squad.' He was a couple of inches shorter than me with dark curly hair, brown eyes, and a broken nose that gave him the look of a hard man. He appeared dirty, as if he hadn't bathed in a long while. I wondered if he'd been a miner.

'Where're you from?' asked Jack.

'Manchester. You?'

'Bradford originally, but I've moved about a bit. Pete 'ere's from Sheffield.'

I hung my jacket in the grey metal locker, decided not to take off my suit pants, then made a show of eyeballing both men. 'I guess my work suit is a little upmarket, compared with your bleeding garb.' The word bleeding was a little strange on my tongue, but I felt I had to add it, considering the other words coming out of my mouth.

'Yeah? Well, these are *my* fuckin' work clothes!'

'Yeah,' I laughed. 'What work was that, then?'

'Wrestling mate. I was a pro wrestler.'

That took me back a mental step. 'You're shitting me.'

The smile on Pete's mouth didn't match the questioning look in his eyes.

Jack seemed annoyed at my disbelief. 'Ya think so!'

'I guess you didn't make too much money at it.' I held my breath.

'No, but I can kick your arse all the way from 'ere to 'ell an' back, so watch yer mouth.' Thankfully, he didn't attempt to carry out his threat.

Pete, who was wearing a pair of old and shapeless slacks and a once white shirt frayed at the collar, rejoined the conversation. 'I used ta work in a steel mill,' so much for the miner theory, 'but it were closed down. What d'you do?'

The moment had arrived. 'I worked in a bank.'

'A fuckin' bank clerk!' Jack's derisory shout informed everyone in the room of my previous employment. 'Maybe 'e was the one that closed down yer mill, Pete.'

Pete looked incredulous, 'What the fuck're you doin' '*ere*?'

'You lose yer way or what?' Jack asked.

I was embarrassed by the show he was putting on for the benefit of everyone in the room. 'You have a problem with that?' I was acutely aware I was challenging a professional fighter.

He laughed. 'Shit, no! I just wonder 'ow long yer gonna be around.'

My anger flared again. 'Don't worry about me. I'll be here as long as you are. Now why don't you fuck off and leave me to sort out my locker!'

Jack's fist flew at my head. I ducked and aimed a shot at his solar plexus, which he side stepped. Jack grinned and I realized he had feigned the blow to my head. The pair looked at me for a second. 'No 'ard feelin's, pal. We was just gettin' to know ya,' said Pete.

Yeah. I continued to put my belongings in the locker. Two more recruits arrived and a Welsh corporal told us we now numbered twenty-three. We needed thirty to make up a squad.

A bugle blared loudly via a speaker system and Jack re-entered my bed space with Pete close behind him.

'Hey, hard on. That's the call fer food. You 'ungry?'

I closed the locker and put my suitcase on top of it. 'Yeah. Don't we get locks to put on our lockers?'

'I 'aven't got one,' said Pete. 'Neither's Jack.'

'Jesus Christ,' I said. 'Anyone could steal our stuff. Why call it a locker?'

'Fuck knows. Anyways, it's chow time. Grab yer eatin' irons and let's go.'

Galley staff kept us apart from recruits already in training. As Jack pointed out, Her Britannic Majesty was not about to let those who had already signed on the dotted line mingle with those who had yet to do so. 'They can't let us 'ear anythin' as might change our minds. Eh Banker?'

Each table was bare except for containers of salt and pepper, mustard and ketchup. We sat on long benches, twelve to a table. A Marine in chef's whites approached our group with three loaves of sliced white bread and half a pound of margarine, all of which he dumped into the centre of our table. Hands quickly reached for the bread, while I looked round for other food.

'Get what ya can while it's going,' suggested Pete. 'This is all we get tuhnight.'

I stood up, joined in the almost frenzied grab for the bread, and managed to get four damaged slices. The margarine was long gone so I made two patchy sandwiches of salt, pepper, mustard, and ketchup.

'What did we need eating irons for?'

'Ya 'ad to spread the mustard, didn't ya?'

Later, Jack, Pete and I went to the Navy, Army and Air Force Institution, better known as the NAAFI, and bought some doughnuts and bottles of pop. I also purchased peace of mind in

3

the form of a lock. After dark, we sat on beds in the centre of the barrack room and learned about each other. Many were from the Northeast where they had been unable to find work. Two had been in the army. Dusty Miller had been a sergeant in the Parachute Regiment. Ron Davis had also been in the Paras and then recruited by the Special Air Service for a three-year stint. Neither man had been able to adjust to life on Civvy Street.

Jack had lived in an orphanage and half a dozen foster homes in the Bradford area. The people at the orphanage gave him the name of Jack Mason. Jack, because he had been extremely thin, as in a beanstalk. Mason, after the type of jar containing one pound, twelve shillings and sixpence found lodged alongside him in the cardboard carton left in a church. At thirteen, his fosterers had lost or abandoned him in a crowd exiting a performance by a travelling circus. The bearded lady had taken a shine to him and smuggled him into her caravan.

'You were 'er toyboy?' asked a horrified lad.

'Nah, she just wanned a kid, that's all.' A family of circus acrobats employed him as their gofer. He learned to grapple with another circus employee and, at the age of sixteen, went on the road to earn money as a wrestler. He had never won a professional match. 'Got me arse kicked from one end of the country tuh t'other at a rate of ten quid plus expenses per beatin'. Joinin' up was the only thing I could think of.'

It eventually came time for me to introduce myself. 'So, tell us about yourself, *Banker*,' Jack demanded as he grinned evilly.

It was probably the best opportunity to get the weight of my social background off my shoulders. 'There's not much to tell, really. My father is a pharmacist who owns three shops.'

'A farmer what?'

'A chemist. My mother plays golf to fill her time. I went to grammar school and then worked in a bank. Actually, my father got the job for me. I play rugby. What else can I tell you? Oh, except to say that I'm joining up to escape my dreary life.'

'Well, if it ain't Little Lord fuckin' Fauntleroy,' someone observed.

'Hinnie, mon, you'll never make it,' one of the Geordies proclaimed.

Jack surprised me. 'Yeah 'e fuckin' will. I'll make bleedin' sure 'e does.' His words sounded more like a threat than a promise.

'Shit man, what *are* you doin' here?' asked a doubtful Pete.

I lay in bed listening to the night-noises of almost two dozen men. Hearing them grind their teeth, snore and fart was not something I'd anticipated. I thought about their reactions to my background and wondered if I was making a mistake. My parents and fellow employees had all told me that my decision to join the marines was, at best, stupid. A couple of guys at the rugby club had said they wished they had the balls to do the same and I now realized that also was a condemnation. I had been concerned that I would find other recruits uneducated and uninteresting but the truth seemed worse than my imaginings. My thoughts made me feel snobbish, which is exactly the way my parents had raised me. Being tough enough didn't concern me, but I did worry about fitting in with people whose upbringing had been less fortunate than mine.

I knew I would have to adjust; to slide down the social ladder my parents spent so much time and energy climbing. I remembered my annoyance at the recruiter who erased my self-assessed status of middle-class and substituted working-class on a form. He had told me I would thank him and I smiled in the darkness as I did so. I was done with the lies of social niceties and had no ambition to seek any rank whatsoever. I just wanted to have fun and enjoy the challenge of a physical life. Leaving had been awkward. 'I wanted to have this last breakfast with you,' my father had said. Not that we'd eaten anything.

I'd been snide. 'That's good, Dad. You sure you can afford the time? No prescriptions to be filled?'

'No, no, not now, not for a few minutes at least. I wanted to say goodbye to you properly. You're leaving home and starting a new life. I just wish you would go for a commission, that's all.'

He'd made the same speech more than once. 'It's what I want to do, Dad. I'm joining up to have fun for a while, not start a career.'

'You intend to spend nine years of your life having fun without any regard for what might come after? What will you tell prospective employers nine years from now when they ask what experience you have?' I hadn't told him I didn't give a shit. 'The day will come when you'll want to get married, perhaps have children. How will you give them the kind of education I've given you?' An education he reckoned I was about to squander.

I'd refused to let him irritate me. 'Dad, I'm about to walk out the door; can't we part on friendly terms?'

'I'm nothing if not friendly, Paul,' he'd said. 'I'm just trying to give you some fatherly advice. Nothing's written in stone until you sign on the proverbial dotted line.'

He'd had what he thought were my best interests at heart and I hadn't wanted to rile him. I'd nodded. 'Look, I'll be home for leave in a couple of months or so, so it's not like I'm leaving the planet.'

'Yes, about that,' he'd used his 'I'm superior to you' tone and the words slid down his aquiline nose, 'make sure you call before you turn up on the doorstep.' He didn't want me adversely influencing my younger brothers, or trying to reclaim my bedroom, which had already been assigned 'guest room' status.

'Yes, well.' He'd actually harrumphed. 'Mind how you go, take care of yourself. Do you have money?' I'd laughed. 'Not a laughing matter. Here's twenty pounds. Look after it. I'm sure some of your fellow marines will be liars, cheats and thieves.' Such words from a man who started out as a private in the Royal Army Medical Corps, which, apparently, is known as Rob And Murder your Comrades. But he'd read my thoughts. 'I did end up a lieutenant-colonel.'

'It was war time.'

'True, but still a fact.' It'd been a difficult moment until he held out his hand. 'I suppose it's time. In any case, I have to go. Good luck, Son. Keep your chin up, do the right thing and all that. Don't wake your mother, you know how she needs her beauty sleep.'

I'd shaken his hand. 'Thanks, Dad. I will and I won't.'

Answering two points in one sentence had confused him. 'What? Oh. I see. Yes.' He'd hesitated for a second, then strode out the door to his car.

I'd listened to the silence of the house and wondered if my step-mother was awake and had heard the conversation.

The bodies required to make up a squad arrived during the next two days. We spent most of that idle period listening to Radio Luxembourg, learning about each other, eating food in the NAAFI and speculating about the direction in which our new lives would take us.

Albert Jones was an enormous and somewhat clumsy man with stiff uncontrollable hair and teeth like a horse. He tried unnecessarily to ingratiate himself by offering to help anyone with everything.

'Want me ta make yer bed for ya?'

'Tell me when ya want somethin' from the NAFFI. I'll go fer ya fer nothin'.'

But there was little for any of us to do. He eventually persuaded us all to allow him to clean our eating irons after every meal. We relented because, as we all had identical cutlery, there was nothing he could do wrong. His sometimes laughable ignorance regarding music, sports, girls and everything else we discussed amazed us. Still, he was happy to be with us, despite the derogatory comments he occasionally received.

'It's bin a long time since I slept anywhere except in a barn,' he told us. 'My bed was straw in the loft.'

He had been consigned to live alone in barns since his eleventh birthday. He had thought it was a sign he had attained manhood. When one of the Geordies awarded him the nickname of Jonah, he boomed guffaws of pleasure and we all smiled with him.

Dave Samuels from Colchester was a short wiry youth with short wiry hair and blue/black home-pricked tattoos on his upper body. Sammy had been in and out of foster homes and juvenile detention centres and had an attitude to show for it.

'What the fuck's it to you?' he responded when asked about his background. However, once he knew someone, his manner became considerably lighter and he allowed the amusing side of his nature to surface.

'I'm Corporal Biggs and you are H Squad,' a man shouted as he walked through our door on Monday morning. 'There are now enough of you to start your training.' He led us to various stores where we accumulated everything Her Britannic Majesty decreed we would need for the next sixteen weeks and beyond. Civilian workers piled all kinds of clothing and equipment onto our outstretched arms as we paraded through numerous buildings: new bedding, denim fatigues (two sets), khaki battle dress, dress blues, a black beret, a peaked hat, and a pith helmet. Our towels were khaki coloured, as were our new socks and underwear. We received field utensils, including a metal water bottle nestled in a khaki blanket. The bottle had a khaki stopper attached to a khaki chain. They gave each of us a heavy khaki greatcoat, black fatigue boots, brown parade boots, dress shoes, khaki puttees, khaki shirts, a khaki tie, belts, badges, buttons and clips. Corporal Biggs was kept busy picking up items some of us accidently dropped.

Biggs marched us into a newly built barrack block and up a flight of stairs to rooms with polished wooden floors and freshly painted walls. Each room housed six recruits and we were allowed to group any way we wished. I shared a room with Jack Mason, Pete Bell, Dusty Miller, Ron Davis and a very impressed Jonah. 'That's it. I'm done,' Biggs shouted from the corridor which ran the length of the building. 'This will be your home for the next sixteen weeks. Someone else will instruct you further. Until that happens, square all your kit away and try to act civilized. The Provost staff will come by every now and then, so be warned.'

We spent the rest of the day stowing our new gear into our lockers. There was an advantage in rooming with the two ex-soldiers as we learned how to fold and stow our gear in an efficient military manner. I packed my civilian clothes into my suitcase and attached a label to it. Her Britannic Majesty sent it, free of charge, to my father. He had been upset when I left clothes in my bedroom wardrobe so receiving the case would send acid to his peptic ulcer. We would not wear civilian clothes again; other than when on leave, until we 'passed out' from Deal as 'The Queen's Squad' in sixteen weeks.

We paraded the following morning in our new fatigues and black berets. The two former paratroopers helped again as they showed us how to dress ourselves correctly in the unusual outfit. Jonah encountered a problem getting his puttees fastened around his ankles, but we helped him and the six of us turned out properly dressed and on time. It was obvious that no one, except the two former soldiers, had ever worn a beret before. Twenty-eight different ways to wear the strange headgear were on view. Some went for style; others pulled the objects down around their heads, presumably to prevent the black headwear from leaving their domes in the stiff breeze that blew in from the English Channel. A Corporal had us stand in ranks of three outside the barrack block. A line of trees separated us from the irrevocably committed recruits who noisily paraded on the nearby quadrangle.

We heard our drill instructor before we set eyes on him. The sharp sound of his steel-studded boots striking the concrete roadway bounced off the buildings as he marched between the barrack blocks on his way toward the parade ground. We all looked to the corner around from which we assumed he would appear. As the sound grew, I found myself impressed by a man I had yet to see.

His immaculate form rounded the corner. 'What are you lot looking at?' he screamed. 'Eyes front.' He addressed the Corporal. 'Why aren't these men at attention?'

The two-striper awoke. 'Squad, attennnnnntion!' The syllable 'ten' stretched out so we could anticipate the short 'shun' and act as one. 'H Squad present and correct, Sergeant,' he hollered at the drill instructor.

The Sergeant looked at him with disdain, 'Thank you. Dismissed.' He turned to us. 'I am Sergeant Francis Boswell. It is my job to take you through recruit training.' He had a thick Scottish accent, but was perfectly understandable. 'I will also be your drill instructor, or DI. Other people will instruct you in

9

other aspects of your training, but I will remain your squad leader. At ease.'

He approached the first man at the right end of the front rank and began to talk to him. I couldn't hear their conversation. From the corner of my eye, I saw the sergeant place a stick he carried under his armpit so he could reach up and adjust Jonah's tie. He moved to the next man and conversed with him. As he moved through the squad, I was able to get a good look at him. He was about the same height as me; six feet-one. His skin had the look of someone who suffered from acne as a child and his close-cropped hair was auburn. His eyes had a fierce look about them that I thought might be affected, until I tried to imitate the look and realised that no one could hold such a pose for long. I guessed he was in his late twenties, maybe thirty. As the sergeant moved slowly closer, I began to pick out some of his words.

He was almost at the end of the first rank when he looked up, ceased his conversation and turned sharply around. He marched ten paces away from us before again turning about to position himself in front of the squad. 'On my command, you will execute a right turn,' he said in a normal voice. He paused for a second, then, in a very loud and firm voice he commanded, 'Riiiight turn.'

We didn't exactly move with military precision, but we all managed to turn right at more or less the same time. All, that is, except for Jonah, who found himself facing the man behind him and quickly did an about-turn.

'The squad marching in front of you is G Squad and it was formed [pronounced 'forummed'] two weeks ago. They are a sorry bunch of faggots and have a mere corporal who goes under the name of Wilkins as their squad leader.' It occurred to me that if a squad formed every fortnight, Sergeant Boswell might have just left his previous squad. 'You will be ahead of that collection of miserable misfits within one month of this day. Mark my words. If I doubt you have made it, you will wish that you had never set eyes on me. Is that clear?'

We responded in unison, 'Yes, Sergeant.'

'I asked, is that clear?' he barked.

'Yes, Sergeant!' we screamed back at him.

The DI eventually arrived in front of me. 'Name?'

'Johnson, Sergeant,' I told him in an overly firm voice.

'And what brought you ta this time and place, laddie?'

I lied about my education but thought he probably already knew I used to work in a bank so I was truthful on that count. When I finished, he looked pointedly at my feet and then slowly lifted his head, working his eyes up my body, seemingly checking my balls, stomach and heart to make sure I had what it took to be a Royal Marine. His head stopped when we were eyeball to eyeball. The manoeuvre took about three seconds, but it seemed to me like eternity.

'Not exactly the commonest story for a recruit. Are ya sure you're up to H Squad standards?' I was about to tell him I was above standard but he continued and I closed my mouth. 'There is na room in this squad for anyone who canna keep up. You got that?'

'Yes, Sergeant,' I said through clenched teeth and with a judiciously weighed amount of venom.

'If ya show any, and I mean *any*, sign of falling back, I'll have you back-squadded. Do I make myself clear?'

I stared so hard into his eyes, it felt like I was flexing my eyeballs. He stared back for a couple of seconds more, and then turned to the next man. I burned with indignation and swore to myself I'd show him I was as good, if not better, than everyone else in the squad. Besides, how special was he going to make our squad when he had only just finished with his previous bunch of recruits?

That afternoon was the moment of our commitment. I don't think too many of us really thought about changing a decision effectively made some time ago. We were about to give a minimum of ten per cent of our lives to the English government – nine years' service, plus an additional three years in the Reserve. Once we signed on the dotted line, a politician could send us to our deaths and there would be nothing we, or anyone else, could say about it. A captain appeared and asked us if we fully understood the consequences of the obligation we were about to take on.

'This is your last opportunity to turn away from what is a serious and binding commitment. There will be no recriminations if you decide now to return home. However, once you sign your contract, there will be no turning back.'

In spite of the warnings, nobody bothered to inform us of what we were committing ourselves to. I thought of the stories of fellow recruits and realised we were all there to escape our past rather than to start a new life. As I waited in line to sign, it occurred to me that my decision to join the Royal Marines had been seriously questioned by a least three people within the last few days. On the other hand, if I did not sign I would have to return home to friends and family and explain why I was still a civilian. I would have to return, at least temporarily, to my old life. The thought made me inwardly shudder. However, I did have a life and a job I could return to. Others around me were probably glad to be assured of an income for the next nine years. Even the ex-Paras had joined because civilian life had not been acceptable to them. I urged myself not to become too blinkered, or I might also have a tough time when my nine years was up. What a thought! I had just signed up and was thinking about what I needed to do when my contract expired. My father would be proud of me.

A few minutes later, I exited the Captain's office a fully committed recruit in Her Britannic Majesty's Corps of Royal Marines. I sent a mental missive to my father, advising him that my commitment to join 'the other ranks' was now etched in stone.

After everyone had relinquished their civil rights, Sergeant Boswell told us a few home truths. 'Now we've got you, the molly-coddling is over. When I say jump, you dinna ask how high; ya just put one-hundred-and-ten per-cent into it. Like it or not, you are gonna be the best squad that ever passed through recruit training. If you canna make what I deem to be the acceptable grade, I will have you put back to the next squad. Hear me well. If I canna find a legitimate reason to have you back-squadded, I will beat the living shit out of you.'

I didn't doubt his ability to do just that to any of us.

'By the time you get out of the sickbay, you'll be two squads behind this one. Any questions?' Nobody could think of one. 'Good. Now, the first thing we can do to make you look like Royal Marines is give you all a haircut. You dinna have to pay for it; it's free. However, this is where you find out where the expression, 'beware of Greeks bearing gifts' comes from.' Boswell was enjoying himself. His teeth glistened in the watery sun. 'The barber is a Greek, or is it geek, I forget. As he is not charging you for his services, he will decide what style you will get,' our DI's steely gaze swept over us, 'and I have told him what style that will be. You will not find any mirrors in this barbershop, because it is none of your business what you look like. As long as the geek and I are happy, you are happy.'

'Could we offer to pay him?' Sammy Samuels called out.

Some of us laughed.

'No, but if you want to give me your money I'll ask him not to draw blood from your scalp,' Boswell fired back as he fixed Sammy with a stare.

'That was like watching sheep getting sheared,' Jonah told us with a horsy laugh. He was pleased to believe he now blended in. He was wrong, but a quarter inch of hair was a great social leveller. The change was just as radical for me, despite the conservative short-back-and-sides dictated by my previous job, as it was for those who had sported Tony Curtis and Elvis Presley 'dos'. I wondered what those I'd left at the bank would think of my new style. What would Genevieve think of it?

The civilian barber discovered a couple of guys carried head-lice and sent them to the sickbay.

'Be back in an hour, or don't come back at all!' Boswell advised them.

I was relieved to realize my hair had been cut before both squaddies. It felt strange to rub my hand over the stubble on my head. I saw others move their hands backwards and forwards on their domes as they experienced the same sensation. The black berets no longer fitted snugly.

Once we were all shorn, our squad leader lined us up in ranks of three. 'You will now see why Her Britannic Majesty, in her infinite wisdom, so designed the beret. With the wee thing on your head, pull the laces at the rear until you get a comfortable fit. Not too loose, or it will come off. Not too tight, or you will give yourselves a wee headache and end up on your face like a fairy guardsman. Now tie the laces together.'

Throughout the rest of the day, we were instructed on how to iron and fold our kit properly. We learned of the prescribed ways to make one's bed; shine boots; polish badges, blanco belts and webbing; and keep our uniforms in good condition.

Being made to change the colour of our parade boots seemed a perverse joke. What twisted person issues brown boots to recruits and then tells them to change them to black? Surely not Her Britannic Majesty! Boswell took one of Pete's boots and showed us all how to effect the change. He plastered black shoe polish over the front of the boot and set fire to it. As the polish burned, he rubbed it into the leather with the back of a spoon.

'I must warn ya that if ya get caught stealing spoons from the galley, ya will be placed on a charge.' He smiled. 'I'll also warn ya, that if anyone burrens the stitching in the welts, their boot will fall apart. Her Britannic Majesty will not provide a second pair of these wonderful parade boots free of charge.' He returned Pete's boot and took off one of his own. 'This is where the expression 'spit and polish' comes from,' he told us before spitting a gob of saliva onto the toecap and rubbing it into the surface with a cloth smothered in black boot polish. 'If ya do this long enough, and with sufficient vigour, yuh'll eventually create a toecap with such a beautiful gloss on it, you'll fight any wee bastard to protect it. You will also polish the instep of your boots to the exact same standard. Your boots must pass inspection the day after tomorrow. Any questions?' He waited for a response that didn't come. 'Good. Have fun.'

He left us worrying if we would ever get our boots to resemble the black glossy ones he wore. We spent the rest of the night only on our boots. We visited other rooms to see how everyone else was progressing and if anyone had found a secret way to easily get rid of the brown colour.

Breakfast was the best meal of the day. Marine chefs stood behind trays of fried eggs, bacon, sausages, tomatoes, and potatoes, and ladled whatever we wanted onto aluminium, all-purpose trays. When we returned to our rooms, we realized we should have spent some time during the previous evening preparing our dress for the day. The urgent need to use the ironing board caused curses and punches to fly. The ingenious among us discovered makeshift ironing boards. Some found the floor an ideal surface. Jack and I took the room door off its hinges and laid it between the ends of two beds. Unfortunately, the iron's cord was short and so we rearranged the furniture. Dusty and Ron opted out of the co-operative that Jack, Pete, Jonah and I formed, confident they could maintain their own kit with a minimum of time and effort. Jonah acted as a gofer, while Jack ironed the tunics and Pete ironed the trousers. I cleaned the badges, buckles, and clips and then assembled the belts and put the badges in the berets. My mind wandered and I realized that my leaving must have made life a little easier for my step-mother; less laundry, ironing, cooking and whatever else for her to do.

By the time Boswell appeared, we considered ourselves properly turned out. He looked immaculate. His creases had a knife-edge and his brasses shone brightly. The white on his peaked hat, together with the navy blue uniform, red sash and colourful medal ribbons, combined to give him a patriotic glow. Our drill sergeant carried a pace stick under his arm as he inspected us in the corridor outside our barrack rooms and declared us fit for the parade ground. He walked among us, making minor adjustments to our clothing. He pulled down the flap of a beret, straightened a tie, or disposed of stray lengths of cotton, which he called Irish pennants.

'Recruits as green as you,' even his brogue sounded smart, 'would not normally be allowed onto the parade ground at this stage of training. *Good God*, you've hardly started yet,' the word 'hardly' rolled off his tongue, 'but I reckon we can stand an informal inspection. What do you men think?'

'Yes, Sergeant!' we roared in our ignorance; forgetting the rush to prepare ourselves.

'Good. While on the parade ground, you will likely as not catch a glimpse of our esteemed Regimental Sergeant Major, or RSM. He is the senior non-commissioned officer and is a thistle of a man who has served our country well. You will not find it hard to afford him due reverence.'

We filed down the stairs and the sound of our boots echoed off the walls of the stairwell, making us seem more than we were. In the fresh air, we formed up in ranks of three next to the quadrangle where all other recruits were on morning parade.

Our DI faced us. 'I'm going to lead you onto the parade ground. For those of you who haven't had the benefit of a fine Scottish education, "wheel" means turn, as opposed to "turn" which means turn sharply. Got it? We'll be doing nothing fancy, just keep abreast of the man next to you and listen for my orders.' He called for Dusty. 'Miller?'

'Yes, Sergeant.'

'Change places with Smith. You are the point man. Davis?'

'Yes, Sarge,' answer Ron.

'I'm your Sergeant. There's no such thing as a Sarge in H Squad. Take up the rear of the squad and keep us together back there.' Boswell shuffled more guys around in an attempt to smooth out our undulating heights.

'By the right, quiiick march.' We set off along the side of the parade ground. 'Left, right. Left, right. Left, right.' The cadence was easy. 'Leffft wheel.' We snaked our way around the corner. 'Riiight wheel.' We turned onto the parade ground. 'Leffft wheel.' We marched into position behind G Squad at the rear of the parade. 'Squaaad, halt!' 'Riiight turn!'

Jonah started to turn left then quickly corrected himself. We stood at attention as Boswell quietly walked between our ranks, straightening a belt or freeing minute particles of dust from tunics.

A voice rang out. 'Sergeant Boswell!'

Our drill instructor and squad leader snapped to attention. 'Sergeant Major!'

'What a barrel-load of shit you've got here! Who *are* these misfits?'

'We are H Squad, Sergeant Major. We were forummed yesterday.'

'And you have the *audacity* to bring them onto *my* parade ground!' the man I assumed was the Regimental Sergeant Major screamed with incredulity. His brown, weathered face, immaculate dress, and rows of medal ribbons made him an imposing sight.

'Purely for your inspection, Sergeant Major. We do not presume to do anything but observe.'

'Thank *God* for that.' The man started to walk along the front rank. At the end, he turned and walked along the back of the line. He recognized Ron Davis as an old hand. 'Done this before, have we?'

'I was in the Parachute Regiment, Sir.'

'We won't hold that against you. At least you've managed to *end up* with the best.'

'Thank you, Sir.'

As the RSM passed along the rear of the second line, he stopped behind Jack. 'Am I hurting you, boy?' he roared.

'No, Sir!' Jack yelled back.

'Well I *bloody* well should be. I'm standing on your *fucking* hair.'

Jack didn't miss a beat. 'I wish you wouldn't, Sir. I just washed it last night.'

I almost laughed. Perhaps I did laugh. It was an involuntary reaction that I immediately knew was wrong, so all that escaped me was, I thought, an inaudible hiccup. Although we were already quiet, we seemed to become instantly quieter. I saw Boswell's eyes widen. A cloud moved in front of the sun, as if to protect it. I'm sure birds stopped singing. The fearful silence seemed palpable. Only the innocent wind could be heard blowing around us.

I watched the RSM's neck stiffen, his ears flatten. 'This man, Sergeant,' he said in a low voice that carried far more menace than his parade ground barks, 'will run the perimeter of my parade ground fifty times, all the while declaring he is a loud-mouthed arsehole. His straight man will join him, stating to the world that he is a fucking buffoon. You, Sergeant, will stay out here to make sure they don't lose count.' The man then marched crisply back to the centre of the parade ground with a parting shot. 'I'll be keeping a watchful eye out for this squad.'

Boswell turned to face us. 'Mason, Johnson, fall out and wait for me over there.' Me, I thought? He pointed out a spot with his pace stick. 'That's you, too, Johnson. Move it!' I broke ranks and joined Jack, feeling humiliated. He looked a tad chagrined. Had I have been the only one to laugh? Not even a laugh, really. I'd subdued it. 'Miller, march the squad back to your rooms and get everybody working on their boots. Do you remember where the clothing store is?'

'Yes Sergeant.'

'Good. I want you to arrange for men to visit the place, four at a time, to get measured for alterations to their dress-blues and battle-dress. Make sure they take said uniforms, without badges and clips, with them. Any questions?'

'No, Sergeant.'

'Carry on. If anyone asks, tell them you're acting under my orders.'

'Understood, Sergeant.'

Boswell seemed amused. 'What possessed you, Mason? And you, Johnson, did ya not know better than ta laugh? Well, it doesna matter now. Put it down to a lesson lerruned. The hardest part of this wee exercise is going to be the shouting. It's worth the risk of only shouting once on each side of the parade ground. Shout loudest when passing the RSM's office over there.' He nodded in the direction of a whitewashed building. 'The Sergeant Major may well have calmed a wee bit by now and could be too busy to count how often you shout, as long as he hears the pair of you when you go past him. I'll keep count of the laps. Off you go.'

'I'm a loud-mouthed arsehole,' Jack shouted.

'I'm a fucking buffoon,' I added.

Boswell was correct. Shouting out the words took more energy than running.

'I'm a loud-mouthed arsehole.'

'I'm a fucking buffoon.'

On one side of the parade ground, when we turned towards the English Channel, we felt a cooling breeze which, after a few laps, I came to anticipate.

'I'm a loud-mouth arsehole.'

'I'm a fucking buffoon.'

We saw our squaddies standing in the corridor outside our barrack rooms. They seemed to be cheering but we couldn't hear them.

'Ten!' shouted Boswell.

'Give over! Only fuckin' ten?' said Jack.

'That's twenty-per-cent gone,' I said, thinking it sounded better than the actual count.

'Thanks, Banker.'

'Dinna cut the corners, lads. The RSM doesna like men belittling his parade ground.'

Round and round we went, taking wide corners and shouting to anyone who cared to listen that we were an arsehole and a buffoon. We raised our voices when passing the RSM's office and the venom I felt seemed to make the effort more bearable. I timed my breath to coincide with my jogging – three in, three out – but hollering out that I was a buffoon complicated the procedure.

I thought of Genevieve and how upset she'd been when I told her I was joining up and therefore the best thing we could do was split up. '*But I was planning to finish with* you*!*' She'd shouted. '*You always take me for granted and now you're doing it again. Why'd you think I wouldn't want to stay your girlfriend? People can love each other even when they're separated.*' I'd been proud of myself for not pointing out her inconsistency. She'd thumped my chest and asked why it was always about me. '*To hell with you!*' she'd shouted. '*Go take a hike!*' Would she consider this a hike?

'Twenty-five!' Boswell hollered.

'Who gives a shit?' I said.

'What fuckin' per cent is that, Banker?'

'Fifty.'

'You sure? He said twenny-five laps.'

We were both panting and sweating. My legs felt heavy. The boots Her Britannic Majesty had so generously given, without caring too much how they fit, were beginning to chafe. I sucked more air into my lungs, thinking the additional oxygen would help. 'Can we stop talking?'

'Sure. It's not as if ya make any sense. I'm a loud-mouthed arsehole.'

'And I'm a fucking buffoon.'

I thought of people I used to work with. What time was it? Eight-forty-five? Judith would be filling the inkwells with red and black inks. Ink? No. Singular would mean she was mixing the colours. That'd get someone's balls in an uproar. *'How are we to differentiate credits and debits?'* I recalled wondering. I'd been in a taxi on my way to the sub-branch where most days were so quiet, I'd get through a couple of novels a week. God, it was boring, although I didn't have to run laps around a parade ground. If the Chief Cashier were to announce, *'before we open today, I want everyone to do fifty laps around the block',* old Mrs Pendleberry would say she'd be right behind him. Fridays used to be busy. Everyone brought their pay to the bank, or, if their employers had signed on for the new idea of paying employees' salaries directly into their accounts, they took it out. My brothers would be in the assembly hall. Were they having thoughts about breaking out, once they finished school?

'I'm a loud-mouth arsehole.'

'I'm a fucking buffoon,' I shouted by rote. I realized my mind had been wandering. Luckily, Jack shouted out his statement before me and thereby focused my mind, but that seemed unfair. What if his mind wandered? I needed to pay more attention.

Boswell started running with us. 'That's thirty, lads. Keep it up.'

'Are you sure you didn't lose count?' I asked.

'Positive, Johnson. Just shut your wee cake hole unless you're shouting out the buffoon message. How're ya holding up?'

'I thought you just … we used to do cross-country at school.' We'd run through fields and woods, not on concrete. It hadn't been my favourite sport, even with footwear that fit.

'I can do this easy,' said Jack. 'It's not as bad as I thought it were gonna be.'

'That's good ta hear, laddie. It's only about twelve miles in total, which is no marathon. I just need ta know you two are alright, this being so early in your training. I dinna want men from H Squad falling by the wayside, so ta speak.'

Only twelve miles! Thank God for that. I could put up with my blisters for that length of time.

'I'm a loud-mouthed arsehole.'

'And I'm a fucking buffoon.'

'That's the spirit. Isn't this what you two left home for?'

'Not exactly,' I answered.

Jack had breath enough to laugh. 'Give over.'

The blisters on my heels were a pain.

'Have ya thought how generous the RSM was in awarding you this mild chastisement, instead of putting you on a charge? He's a charitable man.'

'I'm a loud-mouthed arsehole.'

'And I'm a fucking buffoon.'

'You're doing this for all those shits standing in the corridor, shining their wee boots. If it wasna you, it would be someone else. I had Sampson down as ma favourite.'

'I'm a loud-mouthed arsehole.'

'I am a fucking buffoon.'

'You're not jogging along like a happy man, Johnson. Have some wee blisters do we? Dinna fash yerself. If they're still intact when ya return to your rooms, prick them and put after-shave on them. If they're not intact ya still splash on the foofoo. It'll sting some, but what's a wee sting to a man of H Squad? Once you've done that, yer sores'll be right as rain.'

My wellbeing improved when Boswell told us we'd finished the final lap. 'Come with me to that wee bench where I left ma pace-stick. I have a suggestion.'

We walked across the parade ground, trying to calm our breathing. I tried not to limp. 'Dinna sit doon,' Boswell said.

'Give over,' said Jack.

'Why not?' I asked with an inkling I wouldn't like his answer. I tried to work my feet forward in my boots and break contact between my heels and the leather.

'If you two men want to bond H Squad, help turn it into the greatest squad The Depot has seen, and thumb yer wee noses at the RSM at the same time, you'll do another lap of his parade ground.'

'Give over!' said Jack.

I raised my eyebrows.

'I willna order ya ta do it but it'd be a magnificent gesture, would it not?' His brogue was thick. 'I can see the RSM in his office and he can see us, which means he knows the fifty are up, and the extra lap is a measure of the men of H Squad. What do you say?'

I looked at Jack and his face creased into a grin. 'No more fuckin' shouting, right?'

Boswell shook his head. 'Nay, lad. Just give me time to leave so his magnificence can believe it's your idea.'

We stood and watched our Sergeant disappear from sight. I bent my knees a couple of times and flexed my calf and thigh muscles. 'Come on,' I said. We set out slowly, trying to gather speed. My blisters registered strong objections.

The RSM smiled benevolently as we passed his office and I realized someone from every squad was similarly punished at the start of training. Had Her Britannic Majesty, in her infinite wisdom, decreed that to bond young men, at least one of them had to run laps of a parade ground? Did a sailor run laps of a deck? Did a flyboy circle an airfield on foot? Had my father run the perimeter of the hospital grounds on his way to becoming a half-colonel? And did everyone who ran around the parade ground do an additional lap? Was it all, including the brown boots, carefully programmed bullshit, and was there more to come? Of course there was! Had the experience been merely punishment, or was I learning something that I would never forget?

We were welcomed back to our rooms like heroes.

'Fuckin' ay, Banker!'

'That were summat, Banker!'

'Hey! What about me?' said Jack. 'I were out there too, tha knows.'

'Yeah, but you was a wrestler. Banker 'ere worked in a fuckin' bank.'

I peeled off socks stiffened with blister fluid and congealed blood and sprinkled a few drops of Old Spice on my heels. It stung. Guys around me winced empathetically.

Dusty and Ron handed us our once-brown boots. Jack and I had changed the leather to black but they now had blindingly bright toe-caps. I could see my reflection in them.

'You guys did this while we ran around the parade ground?' I asked with awe.

'Give over,' said Jack. 'These're fuckin' great!'

'We wanted to do our bit,' said Ron.

Training started in earnest. Although not on parade, we still had to march everywhere, even to the NAAFI to buy an iron. We would march to the guardroom so we could march around while on guard – raw recruits with pick-axe handles to deter the IRA. When marching, we raised our straight arms to shoulder height, taking care not to stab anyone with our knives and forks when on the way to the galley to eat the abysmal food. Breakfast wasn't bad, but lunch and dinner usually tasted so foul that I wished there was no taste at all. All vegetables were severely stewed. The cuts of meats were those I would have passed on before I joined up, and were necessarily overcooked. I helped myself to copious amounts of the lumpy gravy in an attempt to mask the less than appetising flavours of everything else. I even skipped the occasional meal, believing that the hungrier I got, the more acceptable the food would become.

'What the fuck's up with you and the food?' Jack asked me in the galley one evening. 'This is good stuff. What're yer waitin' for? Get it down yuh throat, or are yuh waiting for the fuckin' pheasant to arrive? Is that what bankers eat, pheasant?' He laughed.

The next day, Boswell told us that skipping meals was a chargeable offense. 'That's why fairy guardsmen faint on parade. Anyone in this squad who fucking faints will be charged and back-squadded. Is that clear?' He looked directly at me and from then on I ate every meal.

Uniform changes occurred many times during the day but we always wore fatigues to breakfast. At morning parade, we might be required to be in dress blues or battle dress, with or without our heavy greatcoats. It was a good start to our day when we paraded in mere fatigues. As the activity of the day changed, so did the dress. We spent every night making sure that all kit and clothing was ready to wear at a moment's notice.

Most no longer needed to burn black polish into our once-brown boots but Jonah was still to be convinced. One night he ignited the polish on one of his boots while our collective attention was elsewhere. The situation became apparent when we noticed a different odour in the air. The man had his fiery boot in one hand while trying to fine-tune the radio with the other.

Pete was the first to react. 'Yer boot's on fire, Jonah!'

Jonah looked at the burning boot and was momentarily immobilised. A second later, he thrust the boot under his armpit to extinguish the flames. Jack grabbed the footwear and was pleased to report the stitching intact. There was, however, a patch of black shoe polish under the armpit of Jonah's fatigue tunic. He stripped it off and the four of us rushed down to the heads where we furiously took it in turns to scrub at the black mark. We managed to change the colour of the stain but we could not erase it.

At breakfast the next day, Jonah made himself a triple-decker of fried eggs and tomato ketchup. When he squeezed the sandwich, egg yolk and ketchup dribbled down the front of his fatigue tunic. His second fatigue tunic. 'Holy shit,' he yelled and tried to wipe the yellow and red liquids off the olive-drab jacket.

Everyone offered to let Jonah try on the tunic of their second set of fatigues, but as he was six-feet-three with a proportional body, he could not find a garment to fit him.

For morning parade, we wore battle dress and greatcoats. After inspection, we had five minutes to change into fatigues and field gear for a ten-mile route march. That was to be our only activity before lunch, at which time Jonah would be able to get to the clothing store. We began to believe his misfortunes might escape detection.

Dusty had us form up in ranks of three outside the barrack block to await our Drill Instructor. 'Tallest on the right.' As Jonah was the tallest, he was always at the edge of the squad.

Boswell arrived and Dusty relinquished command. Our DI cast an eye over us. 'Why are yee dressed in that soiled tunic, Jones? Da ya not have a second set of fatigues, Laddie?'

I watched Jonah's neck redden. 'They're both s-soiled, S-Sergeant.'

'Are they both as unacceptable?'

'No Sergeant, but the other one is w-wet. I'm gonna buy a new t-tunic at lunchtime.'

'Make sure you do. And make doubly sure this never happens again. Do I make myself clear? To make sure I do, you're on a charge.'

Boswell ordered everyone to check the equipment of the man next to him. We pulled at canvas straps, checked hooks and eyes. Our DI then marched us onto the parade ground.

The Depot's Adjutant, parading on his horse, veered towards us. He allowed us time to come to a halt and stand at attention. 'Good morning, Sergeant Boswell.'

Our DI snapped his heels together and gave the man a crisp salute. 'Good morning, Sir.'

The captain tapped the peak of his hat with his riding crop and I wondered why he didn't return Boswell's acknowledgement with the same respect. 'I understand you're taking H Squad on a short jaunt this morning.'

'That is correct, Sir.'

'Very good. I think I'll tag along, if you don't mind. My horse could do with the exercise.' He gazed at us absent-mindedly, until he noticed Jonah's fatigue jacket and then his eyes focused. He wheeled his horse around and guided it to where Jonah stood. 'What's your name, Marine?'

Jonah turned pale and stammered, 'Sir, Sir, Albert Jones, Sir.'

'Well, Sir Albert Jones, what have you done with the costly clothing we kindly provided for you?'

'Sir, I had to put out a fire, Sir.'

'I see.' To judge by the man's reaction, it was a common story. 'What kind of fire stains clothing in that unique area?'

'Sir, I had to put a flaming boot under my arm to put out the fire.'

Given recent history, it wasn't difficult to quash my laughter.

The Adjutant turned in his saddle and smiled at Boswell, causing leathers to creak. 'Am I to understand this man's boots were on fire, or do you think he's speaking down to me, Sergeant?'

'I believe his boot was on fire, Sir.'

'Mmm.' The Adjutant remained in front of Jonah while he considered the situation. The only sounds were the creaking of leathers and the jingling of brasses as the horse repeatedly dipped and lifted its head and snorted at Jonah. We stood at attention, waiting for the man to process his thoughts. He looked on Jonah with detachment. 'Sergeant.'

'Yes, Sir.'

'Put this man on a charge for negligence and/or damaging government property. I shall speak to the company commander.'

'I have already placed Jones on a charge, Sir.'

'Very good. I will however still speak to the company commander, unless you have other ideas.'

'No, Sir.'

The horse made a steaming deposit on the parade ground, as if to emphasize his rider's feelings. Would the RSM quake with anger? I wondered who would clean up the mess. Was the job given to some poor soul who'd been charged with a misdemeanour? Might it become Jonah's temporary job? There was hearsay the horse had represented England in the Olympic Games but, as Jack later said, 'That doesn't fuckin' excuse it for carrying that shit on its back.' Someone in the galley had told us the Adjutant was heir to a large gin distillery and was wealthy.

As we left The Depot, the captain rode at our head. Once the town of Deal was behind us, he cantered away and we didn't see him again. It occurred to me that my father would rather I sipped gin with the captain than share life with squaddies. I preferred to live with Jack and his 'give over's'. As my heels had hardened, the ten-mile march was nothing more than a pleasant way to pass time.

Boswell found out what had happened to Jonah's tunic and must have had a word with the company commander, because Jonah's only punishment was two hours of extra drill. The DI also loaned Jonah the money to purchase a replacement.

'You may have heard,' Boswell told us at the end of the day, 'that we Royal Marines are sometimes referred to as Bootnecks. Bootneck being a term similar in meaning to Leatherneck, the nickname given to John Wayne and the rest of the US Marine Corps.'

'Straight up, Sarge?'

'I thought I told you, Samuels, there is no Sarge in H Squad. Only the finest Sergeant this man's outfit has produced. Got it?'

'Yes, Sergeant.'

'Good. Next one to call me Sarge will be on a charge for conduct contrary to good order and military discipline, a handy coverall allowed us by Her Britannic Majesty's infinite wisdom. In short, the law is so vague, I, or anyone in authority, can have any of you for anything at all. It's a wonderful catchall. Now, where was I?' A grin creased his face. 'Oh, yes. Yes, it is straight up. On a not too distant day, you will all learn that many of the local ladies in Deal, Exeter, Exmouth, Portsmouth and Plymouth have a habit of fluttering their eyelids, dropping their handkerchiefs or, in some other genteel manner, trying to induce young, innocent Marines to follow them.' Our DI's grin was infectious. 'Having got your attention, the delectable damsels decide their favours cannot be too easily granted and they run away, sweetly crying: "Bootneck, Bootneck, can't catch me", over their tattooed shoulders.'

'Do ya think that's true?' Sammy Samuels said once we had been dismissed.

'It's never 'appened ta me,' said Ron, 'He's just telling ya to be cautious of the local women when we finally get to go ashore.'

Jack had something he needed me to read. 'I can read alright,' he told me, his eyes challenging me to make a comment, 'but sometimes I get it wrong. Russ, a guy I knew at the circus, told me I needed to read more than the first few words to know what summat were about. I try ta read everythin' but it's 'ard work and boring. This 'ere letter's from Russ and I wanna get what 'e says right.'

'So what do ya want me ta do?'

'Well, you're a fuckin' banker. Read it for me so I can make sure I've got it all down right.'

'This won't be followed by books, will it?'

He laughed down his nose. 'Books! Give over! Thems for bankers an' faggots.'

'Thanks, Jack. Are you sure you want me to read this for you?'

He threw an arm around my shoulder. 'Don't be so fuckin' touchy, Banker. I'll do stuff for you. What do ya want me ta do?'

I grinned. 'There's nothing right now but I'll let you know if I think of something.'

'Will ya 'elp me write back to 'im? Russ is the only one as writes me, an' I'd like to keep 'im as a friend.'

'Yeah, pal, of course I will.'

'That's it then. We'll be oppos. We did them fifty laps together all right, didn't we?' I wasn't sure what an oppo was or what being one entailed, but I'd liked Jack since the day we'd met. I was surprised he didn't want to pair with Pete and, despite being appointed chief librarian and scribe, was pleased he'd asked me. He held out his hand and I shook it. 'We're the perfect match; the banker an' the wrestler. We'll be famous.'

'Oppos? You mean friends?'

'Yeah, opposite numbers. We'll cover for each other when we get extra drill or guard duty. We'll inspect each other before parades, test each other on Corps history, and share all the fuckin' duties and chores. Share our women even. Oppos.'

'Share our women?'

'Well, maybe not that. I don't like smart women.'

Dusty and Ron were obvious oppos, but some pairings weren't as natural (as a wrestler and a banker). Basser (Barry) Helms and Ray Green were the least suited duo. Perhaps they had been 'the only two left on the dance floor'. It surprised us all how quickly Basser, who joined up rather than follow his father into the mines, came to hate life in the Marines. His attitude was so off-putting, we were reluctant to engage him in conversation. Consequently, he often went alone to the NAAFI where he drank beer and looked for other recruits with a similar opinion of the service. His hate for Boswell bordered on paranoia. 'I'll fix 'is arse, so 'elp me. 'E'll never see it comin'.' He was also a quitter. Whatever we did, Basser soon wanted to give up. As the rest of us held the squad above all else, we could never allow him to surrender to anything. I was shocked by how much we compounded his misery to force him to conform. We dragged him, carried him, cursed him, punched him, kicked him and did whatever we thought necessary to make him finish all we did. Being Basser's oppo put Ray in a bad situation and some squaddies were hostile towards him, believing he wasn't doing enough to bring Basser into line.

When Pete was not around, Basser tried to befriend Jonah. The big guy was too soft-hearted to tell Basser to lose himself, and there were times when Jack, myself, Ron, or Dusty had to tell the complaining squaddie to leave the room. When we advised Pete, he forcefully advised Helms to keep well away.

One night when Jack and I were on guard duty, Pete was called to the guardroom to receive a phone call from his brother, and Ron and Dusty were elsewhere, Basser sought out Jonah again. He read Jonah a letter to his local Member of Parliament, listing his alleged grievances and asking for help in obtaining a discharge. As he reached the end, Pete walked into the room.

'What're you doing 'ere?' Pete demanded. 'I told you to stay the fuck away from Jonah.' He grabbed Basser and dragged him off his perch at the end of Jonah's bed. Helms fell to the floor but Pete continued to drag him out of the room and down the corridor to the heads. 'Tell Ray to go for a beer, or summat,' he shouted.

Squaddies told Jack and me the only sounds heard from the heads were grunting and thumping as Pete handed Basser a beating. He also tore up the letter. I realized then that Pete and Jonah were oppos. They weren't a perfect pair but my opinion of Pete rose considerably. I wondered if Boswell had somehow influenced the pairing.

Nobody saw Basser again that night or the following morning. Ray dutifully searched for him but the rest of us felt the bastard's absence was a positive thing.

Boswell noticed our different formation. 'Who's missing?'

'Helms, Sergeant.'

'Anyone know where he is.'

'Probably skiving off down the sickbay,' someone volunteered.

'Green? Miller?'

'I've searched everywhere I can think of, Sergeant,' said Ray.

'No idea, Sergeant,' Dusty added.

When Basser did not appear by mid-morning, Boswell reported him absent without leave. That night, Provost Staff clomped officiously into Helm's room, emptied his locker onto his bed, rolled up the mattress and took everything away. The Duty Officer tried to ascertain if we knew where our unloved squaddie might have gone. He told us the Adjutant had notified the police of Basser's desertion. They would periodically check his parents' house. I inwardly smiled as I thought how mortified my father would be if I went over the wall.

Five days later, we were on morning parade when we heard a commotion on the far side of the parade ground. Drill Instructors brought recruits to attention and called for silence in the ranks. I fruitlessly swivelled my eyes without moving my head in an attempt to establish what was happening.

'What's going on?' someone asked in a whisper.

'What the fuck's 'appening?' queried another.

Boswell turned about to face us. 'Keep yer wee cake holes firmly shut!'

Time went by and still we stood at attention. My thighs began to numb. I wriggled toes and flexed leg muscles to keep blood circulating. The sickbay ambulance drove along the edge of the parade ground on the side I was facing.

'Ambulance,' I whispered.

'I said keep it shut, Johnson,' Boswell growled.

Eternity passed before the ambulance re-entered my vision, travelling in the opposite direction. Morning parade was cancelled but the RSM had us march around the parade ground three times, presumably to get our stiff bodies working again.

None of us was any wiser about the morning's interruption when Dusty formed us up outside the barrack block and turned the squad over to Boswell.

'No doubt you all wanna know what happened out there this morning,' our Sergeant started. 'The good news is that Helms isna guilty of being absent without leave. The bad news is the stupid wee prick has, for the past five days, been living in one of the trees surrounding the parade ground. He fell off his perch this morning and is now in the sickbay for a check-up from the neck up. If you ask me, I'd say the boy was out of his tree.' Boswell allowed us to laugh for a few seconds. 'Okay, it wasna *that* funny. We are now twenty-nine, plus me. Green! There is not a chance in hell I will become your oppo. You clue up with someone else. Make up a threesome. Ya never know, laddie, it might be fun.'

That evening, Boswell, in civilian clothes, came to the barrack block after dinner. He cleared the corridor of other recruits before ordering H Squad out of our rooms.

'As ah'm sure you all are aware, you will be allowed ashore three weeks from Saturday.' A great cheer went up and Boswell smiled like a happy parent. We were achingly aware of the fact, but to have Boswell confirm it made us happier. 'You men are shaping up well. I would go so far as to say,' he raised his voice, 'that you have almost caught up with Corporal Wilkins' squad.'

Our DI stood with a grin on his face as we listened to the comments that came out of G Squad rooms.

'Bullshit.'

'Bollocks!'

'In your dreams.'

'You should be so fuckin' lucky.'

Boswell continued to smile. 'There is just one more thing needed to fuse you together as a unit.' His smile was turning into laughter but he had no difficulty getting the next words out of his mouth. 'From now on, H Squad will be collectively known as Boswell's Fairies.'

Boswell's Fairies! He was condemning us to ridicule. We would be in more fights than a hungry scrap-yard dog. We could already hear the laughter and comments coming from G Squad.

'Boswell's bleedin' Fairies!'

'Mummy, there are fairies at the bottom of the corridor.'

'I joined the Marines and became a fairy.'

We had to do something. 'Better than Wilkins' Wimps,' I yelled as I ran into the first G Squad room. Jack was right behind me and we leapt onto the first two guys who were sitting on their beds. Other squaddies followed us and the room became very small with so many guys swinging punches at each other. Fights broke out in every room and spilled into the corridor.

I saw Jonah, each arm around a neck, banging two heads together, proudly informing the owners, 'I'm a Fairy. I'm a Fairy.'

The Officer of The Guard arrived with members of the Provost Staff and they slowly brought order to the floor. Instead of taking names and numbers, they put every member of both squads on three charges: fighting, damaging government property, and the Corps favourite charge of 'conduct contrary to good order and military discipline'. We later learned Boswell, after he left the corridor, went ashore and, on passing the guard at the main gate, mentioned hearing a disturbance in Barrack Block Beatty.

Once the Provost staff left the block, members of both squads began to tidy up the mess we had created. Not only righting beds and lockers but also scrubbing scuffmarks off walls, and rewinding the fire hose that had somehow become unreeled. We swept the corridor, cleaned up spilled drinks and washed stained bedding. I was impressed by the way fifty-nine men, who had just fought each other, banded together in harmony when necessary. While the temporary spirit of comradeship lasted, a couple of the men from G Squad told me they had so little respect for their DI, corporal Wilkins; they had dubbed him Willie Wanker.

'No,' I promised. 'It'll go no further.'

After we'd cleaned and reassembled Her Britannic Majesty's property, we returned to our rooms. Comments on our new identity weren't much different from those of G Squad.

'Can you imagine going home on leave?' started Pete. 'Friends buying pints and asking what we're doing. I'll be fucked before I tell 'em I've become a fairy.'

We laughed. Everyone had a scenario.

'Someone told me fairies are welcome in this boozer.'

'Good evenin' sweetheart, I'm a fairy. Can I take ya home and shag ya?'

One ventured his mother might see a change in him since the last time he was home. 'Yeah, Mum, I've become a fairy.'

'Give over!' said Jack.

'This is really, really stupid,' said Dusty in disgust.

'I think it's great,' beamed Jonah.

'What do you know, farm boy?' sneered Ron.

'Ease up,' Pete warned.

'Hey, there's nothing we can do about it,' I said. 'We may as well start getting used to it.'

'Jesus Christ,' Dusty shouted. 'Do you have any idea the bleedin' trouble this is going to cause wherever we go?'

'I have an idea,' I told him, 'but we're still stuck with it.'

'It's still fuckin' stupid,' were Dusty's last words.

Dusty and Ron were a few years older than the rest of us and their military experience made the age gap seem even wider. Consequently, they did not fit into our social life. Recruit training, which was new and often exciting for us, had to be little more than a mundane refresher course for them. I could understand their reluctance at being included in the juvenile collective of Boswell's Fairies. The two men were a great help to the rest of us with their knowledge of how to keep kit in good order and how to cut corners. They taught us how to separate fact from bullshit, just as they taught us how to thickly lay down our own bullshit. They, together with Pete, were probably the reason Jonah was still with us.

'Know what I found out tonight?' I told the room. 'G squaddies call Wilkins, "Willie Wanker".'

'No shit,' Pete said with a grin.

'Give over!' said Jack.

'What a floor this is,' commented Ron. 'Fairies and Wankers. Is this the Marines or a fuckin' kindergarten?'

'Will your squad disappoint me today, Sergeant Boswell?' the RSM roared as he approached us at Monday morning's parade.

'Not at all, Sir,' replied Boswell in his Scottish brogue. 'H Squad is the best at The Depot.'

'God save us,' the RSM pleaded as he glanced at the sky.

The inspection of the front rank started with Jonah, the tallest recruit in the squad. The only Non-Commissioned Officer addressed as 'Sir' stood motionless in front of Jonah and studied him for at least five seconds before he moved to the next man without a word. As I didn't hear a comment, I assumed Jonah had managed to focus his eyes on some distant object as he fought to hold his nerve. At the other end of the line, the feared man stopped in front of Sammy, the shortest recruit in H Squad and picked a loose thread off his tunic. 'Name?' he enquired.

'Samuels, Sir.'

'What have we here Samuels, an Irish pennant?' Sammy must have thought the question was rhetorical, as he did not respond. The RSM thrust his face to within a couple of inches of Sammy's nose. 'I asked you a question Samuels. I expect an answer. What are you, some kind of fairy?'

Sammy stared straight ahead. 'Yes Sir,' he shouted with pride.

Veins immediately bulged on the RSM's neck, and his face turned crimson. He wheeled about and confronted Boswell.

'During the short time this squad has been in existence, I have received adverse reports from The Adjutant, the Provost Marshall, Corporal Wilkins and other sources. The Staff Sergeant in charge of the galley believes he lost thirty spoons to this lot. You even had a man living in the trees. Now another one proudly claims he's a fairy, something I've never heard in twenty-seven years of service. Tell me, Sergeant, where on earth do you get the balls to claim that this is the best squad at The Depot?'

'I have given the squad an additional identification, Sir,' Boswell began. 'With me at the helm, I believe the squad can become one of the best. They just need to be banded together a little tighter.'

'You want to turn them into a bunch of faggots to bind them tighter together!' screamed the senior man. 'Her Britannic Majesty frowns on daisy chains in the Marines, Sergeant. She believes it has an adverse effect on the recruitment of young men.'

Boswell could not keep the smile off his face. 'My idea to have them call themselves Boswell's Fairies is, in my opinion, Sir, a way to make H Squad into a great squad. I believe that by the time they become the Queen's Squad ...'

'Doesn't that word association give you pause, Sergeant?'

'Not for a second, Sir. However, if you think the name is detrimental to the Corps, I will have them drop it immediately.'

The Regimental Sergeant Major's neck veins subsided and some of the red left his face. 'This is not an idea I agree with, Sergeant. However, if you believe what you say to be true, I will allow you to continue as you see fit for the time being. Be aware, though, I will keep an eagle eye on this Squad and if I deem things are not going well, I will intervene. If that happens, Sergeant, well, you know what that will mean. Carry on.'

'Thank you, Sir.'

As we were not allowed ashore in civilian clothes until we finished basic training, we spent the next week preparing our dress blues. We paraded in the navy blue uniform a couple of times early in the week, but we got the impression Boswell so influenced matters that from Wednesday lunchtime, we wore only fatigues or battle dress. On Wednesday evening, he told us what to expect before being allowed ashore.

'You will all be subject to inspection by the Provost Staff. If they find anyone improperly turned out, they will refuse you permission to proceed through the gates. Those same people will ask you questions on Corps history and incorrect answers will also prevent you from getting out. I suggest you spend time brushing up on how and where Marines earned Victoria Crosses, the dates of victorious battles, names of admirals, political leaders and current events.'

His warning served to kill all normal conversation for the rest of the week. Questions regarding Corps history were asked by everyone, of anyone. When was the Corps formed? How many VCs have we won? Who won the first VC? Who won a VC at the battle of Belle Isle? How did the Royal Marine colours come to be? Why do we wear a Green Beret? What units have been retired, and why?

The week was a long one. Both G and H Squads still performed the extra drill awarded as punishment for our fracas. We had not been hit in our pockets but the daily hour of drill sometimes stretched to an hour and a half and the time wasted before and after the punishment meant we lost almost two hours every night.

Rifles were issued to G Squad that week. They spent every evening stripping the weapons down and reassembling them. Their DI, Willie Wanker, toured their rooms each night, constantly testing his charges. They had to be able to strip and reassemble the rifles, while blindfolded, in less than a minute. We heard The Wanker question them on how to sight the weapon for different distances. He asked about the weapon's velocity and its effects.

On Thursday night, a member of G Squad called out, 'Where the 'ell's me bleedin' gun?'

The Wanker rushed into the corridor, trying to ascertain from which room the terrible words had emanated. 'Who said that?' he roared.

'I did, Corporal,' admitted a man, allowing his DI to pinpoint his location.

Wilkins rushed to the room. 'How many times do I have to tell you the correct name for your weapon is rifle?' The Wanker demanded.

'Gun, rifle, weapon; what difference does it make?' the man asked.

'Take out your dick and hold it in your right hand,' Willie Wanker screamed. The man must have done as ordered. 'Now take your rifle in your left hand and repeat over and over: "This is my rifle, this is my gun", for the next thirty minutes.'

I couldn't remain silent. 'This is for fighting, this is for fun,' I called out.

I heard The Wanker's boots thundering along the corridor in concert with the laughter, cheers and applause of men from both squads. 'Who said that? Who said that?' he shouted as he burst into our room.

I convulsed with laughter, lying on my bed amid brasses I was cleaning. 'I did, Corporal,' I confessed, 'but we've all read the book.'

'Stand to attention when addressing me,' The Wanker roared. His spittle flew toward me so I carefully covered the brasses with my cleaning cloth. I stood to attention, still unable to stop my laughter. 'Who the fuck are you?' he screamed at me.

'I'm one of Boswell's Fairies,' I laughed.

A cheer went up from the rest of the squad. Guys left their rooms and congregated in the corridor, wanting to witness the scene.

A protruding vein throbbed in the middle of Willie Wanker's forehead as he stood in silence, waiting for the commotion to subside. My laugher withered to a forced smile of bravado as we glared at each other for a number of seconds. I got the impression Wilkins believed his stare was as imposing as those of the RSM and Sergeant Boswell. 'A fairy is a slight and delicate thing,' he said quietly, though the vein was still in evidence. 'So delicate, it couldn't possibly lift anything heavier than a toothbrush. Therefore, you will scrub the entire length of the dirty corridor with your toothbrush. Have you got that?'

My smile died. 'Yes, Corporal.'

I was not about to disobey a direct order. I got my toothbrush, a bucket, some cleaning fluid, and went to the end of the corridor to start my chore. Willie Wanker accompanied me from the moment I left the room. He watched me get the bucket and fill it with the two liquids. He watched me go to the far end of the corridor, get on my knees and start scrubbing the floor. After ten minutes or so, he became bored.

'I'll be back later to inspect this corridor and if it isn't immaculate, you'll find yourself scrubbing it over again.'

As soon as Wilkins disappeared, the rest of Boswell's Fairies came into the corridor and started to scrub it with me. Some of the guys from G Squad also joined us. Every man used his toothbrush, not wanting to disobey The Wanker's order. It took just over an hour to complete the job. Sammy later told us he got a strange look from the woman in the NAAFI when he purchased thirty-six new toothbrushes from her. The poor woman had to make a rush order to replenish her stock.

Boswell made a surprise visit at around ten o'clock. He was not overly amused when we yelled at him for walking down the middle of the corridor. My explanation did not improve his temperament.

'Who do you arseholes think you are? Recruits dinna make smart-arsed remarks to NCOs in this man's Marines.' He eventually saw the funny side and even cracked a smile. He was making his rounds of the rooms, ensuring everybody was ready for the next day's activities when Willie Wanker returned.

'You got the job finished in remarkable time,' the Wanker observed.

'I had help from a bunch of fairies,' I risked, knowing Boswell was in the area. Corporal Wilkins stood and surveyed the corridor, seemingly turning the matter over in his mind.

Sergeant Boswell came out of Sammy's room, stood in the corridor and nodded in recognition of his subordinate. Wilkins returned the courtesy, turned about and left the building without a word.

On Saturday morning, the DI drilled us on the parade ground. The extra drill of the past two weeks had served to make us more proficient than he claimed we already were. There was to be no inspection and there was little chance of the RSM or the Adjutant making an appearance.

The only other group on the parade ground was the Royal Marine Band. Before joining the Marines, I had seen the famous band on television. They often played prior to cup finals at Wembley Stadium, rugby matches at Twickenham, or for visiting foreign dignitaries. Most people who learned of my enlistment had been unaware of the elite military force and had assumed I was joining the band. Boswell believed them to be the greatest military band in the world. He reportedly owned copies of most of their recordings and played them continuously in his spare time.

'The Royal Marine band is made up of great musicians,' he told us. 'They do not march in a dog's leg formation like the Grenadier Guards or other pongo outfits. They do not boogie-woogie down the street like American military bands. They move with precision while playing their instruments and are the envy of the worold.' He pointed to the band with his pace-stick. 'Look at them! Magnificent. When you get to march with them, you will feel the pride. Your wee toes will curul.'

'When will we get to march with them, Sergeant?'

'In good time, laddie. In good time. And while we're on the subject of the American military, when H Squad is The Queen's Squad, we will not be throwing our rifles around like a drunken Yankee drill team. You are Royal Marines and your pass-out will be a thing of exactitude. Mark my words well. This week's extra drill was easy compared with what I will put you through. When I am finished with you, you will be the greatest precision drill team in the universe and perhaps beyond. I will not allow you to be like a girlie guardsman, fainting flat on your face in the morning sun. That is why we put you through such a rigorous basic training and provide you with such fine breakfasts. And, of course, we sort out the weaklings and the ne'er-do-wells like Helms. Incidentally, I can inform you that we will not see that laddie again. Her Britannic Majesty has generously provided him with a free ticket to the funny farm.'

I had a mental image of Basser strapped on a board with electrodes taped to his temples, eyes bulging out of their sockets. He might have been a pain but it seemed cruel punishment for a guy who only wanted to escape life in the mines.

'And one more thing before we do a little drill,' Boswell cautioned us. 'While you may believe you're the toughest bunch of fairies in Deal, just think how hard you worked on your toecaps before you go kicking seven bells of shit out of all the wee greasers and skin-heads in town tonight.'

Boswell stood us easy and went to speak to the drum major. He returned within two or three minutes with a grin on his face. 'Who was the laddie wanted to know when you would get to march with the band?'

'Me, Sergeant,' said Sammy.

'Well, yee've got yer wish. The band is preparing for a function and they have agreed we can take advantage of this morning's practice session. That means H Squad will be led around the town of Deal by The Band of Her Britannic Majesty's Corps of Royal Marines. It's nae small honour. Not many squads get the band to themselves. That means the whole town, all the wee girlies and their mothers, will have nothing to look at except you. Well, there is my magnificence, of course, but they have had the good fortune to see me many times before this day. You will be on show for the first time. Make sure ya dinna let yourselves down.'

Twenty-nine chests expanded as we were called to attention. The band started with the Corps' march; *A Life on the Ocean Wave*. The sound of the drums and bugles was fantastic. Brass and silver glinted in the morning sun. Boswell gave them a few seconds' lead while we itched to take the first stride. I felt myself lean forward in anticipation. Our DI stood with his pace-stick tucked under his arm, watching the band march from the parade ground. As the rear bandsman passed, Sammy looked ready to follow him. 'Steady, laddie. We don't want any premature actions, do we?'

I eased back onto my heels. When the last musician was ten paces distant, Boswell stiffened. 'Ready, Samuels!' then he looked at the rest of us, 'Ready, men!' After one last check of the band's position, he roared, 'Quiiiicckk march!'

We strode as one in time to the beat of the march. Boswell moved between our ranks, calling out the pace and keeping an eye on the line. 'Left, right. Left, right.' We marched out of the gates, wheeled left and headed towards the English Channel. 'Left ... Left ... Left, right, left'

The buildings on both sides of the street magnified the sounds of the drums, silver bugles and brass instruments. People came out of their homes to watch as we marched by. Two or three brought out their cups of tea; one man had shaving cream on his face. Women out shopping waved to us. The police stopped traffic to let us across road junctions. Three or four small boys marched alongside us, trying to match our stride and imitating the swinging of our arms.

A lady leaned out of a window above a pub's front door and announced, 'I'll 'ave the pints lined up for ya, lads.'

It was more than fun; I experienced a tremendous sense of pride. We again wheeled left and marched along the promenade to the tune of *Colonel Bogey*. The drum major tossed his gold and silver baton into the air. People cheered and applauded.

Boswell marched backwards as he eyed us. 'Left ... Left ... Left, right, left'

Old folks taking their constitutionals raised their hats or waved. One old lady fluttered her embroidered handkerchief at us.

We were on our best behaviour, keeping our eyes looking straight ahead. However, looking straight ahead did not prevent me from seeing some of the local parties. A group of three on a street corner mouthed kisses at us. One stunning woman gazed at us as a man whispered in her ear. Another stood holding her bicycle as she waited for us to pass, bobbing her head from side to side in time with the music.

Sammy must have shortened his stride because I almost marched into the back of the man in front of me. Anyone watching our flank must have thought we looked like a concertina closing up. Boswell opened his pace-stick and marched alongside Sammy, twirling the stick along the road's surface, demonstrating the required measure of stride. Had I been in Sammy's place, I would have been mortified. More small boys added themselves to our ranks. Boswell, pace-stick back under his arm, moved amongst us again, calling out the cadence and warning the young boys to stay clear. 'Left … Left … Left, right, left.'

All too soon, the entrance to The Depot loomed and I felt disappointment. A couple of caped members of the Provost Staff marched into the street to prevent boys from accompanying us through the heavy wrought-iron gates.

As we passed the guardroom Boswell commanded, 'Eyeeeees right!' Everyone except lead-man Sammy snapped his head to the right and found the eyes of Willie Wanker. I saw his eyeballs move as he looked us over and I convinced myself that they lingered on me. Was he still pissed about the 'this is for fighting, this is for fun' quote?

We marched onto the parade ground and the band continued on their way, back to wherever it was they quartered. Boswell commanded us to stand easy.

'Nae doubt y'all saw Corporal Wilkins outside the guardroom. He is one of this weekend's duty NCOs and it could well be he who inspects you and asks you questions on Corps history before allowing you ashore today.' Just my luck, I thought. 'Keep in mind you will be observed as you return on board. Anyone considered drunk will spend the night in the cells and be in front of the company commander come Monday morning. The same applies for anyone returning improperly dressed.' He rolled his 'r's for emphasis. 'The café across from the gates is a favourite hangout of the Provost Staff, so I advise you not to use the place unless you are doubly sure you are immaculate in every sense of the word. Enjoy yourselves but bear in mind that at oh-six-hundred hours on Monday we get back to the routine of training. One last thing, I shall be touring your quarters tonight and I want to find them in good order. I do not want to come across anybody in his room. You will all go ashore and you will all have a good time. Any questions?'

There was silence for a second before Sammy daringly started to sing, 'Why are we waiting. Why are we waiting?'

Boswell laughed and dismissed us.

I couldn't get near a shower. Steam billowed out of the heads and into the corridor. Guys preened themselves like parties. Some, whom I reckoned had never heard of toiletries before they joined up, used underarm deodorants and after-shave lotions. The corridor was a constant stream of traffic as men from both G and H Squads prepared to go ashore. Sammy went to the sickbay and collared a collection of condoms from which he retained half a dozen before throwing the balance on a table in the centre of his room. Jack harvested a few for us.

'What are these for?' Jonah wanted to know as Jack handed some to him.

'Will you give over! If ya get a chance to fuck a partie, put one on your dick. It'll save you from squeezing up,' Jack advised him.

'Squeezing up what?' Jonah asked.

'Come on, Jonah,' I said. 'You must 'ave 'eard guys talking about gettin' a dose of the clap. Ya wear one of these things, you don't get anything.'

Jonah looked at the condoms in his hand and glanced fearfully down at his crotch. He stretched out his arm, trying to give the rubbers back to Jack. 'I don't think I want these. I don't know anybody I want to fuck.'

'But ya might find someone,' Jack was getting frustrated as he pushed Jonah's hand back into his chest.

'I ... I don't want to, thanks.'

'Jonah,' I asked quietly, 'have you ever fucked a partie?'

'What's it to you?' he asked as he dropped the rubbers to the floor and charged out of the room. The volume of many radios was high with owners accompanying Elvis as he sang *Are You Lonesome Tonight*, noting how the singer occasionally sang the wrong words. 'Nobody in Deal needs to be lonesome tonight,' shouted out a voice. 'Boswell's Fairies're on their way to save you, ladies.' When *The Twist* came on, guys wearing socks gyrated on the highly polished floor. Others brushed their shoes or tunics in time with the music. We needed to shout to one another above the din. Sammy flicked the end of his towel at any naked buttock that passed by. Traces of steam and the smells of different soaps and male toiletries pervaded the corridor and every room.

Worried as we were about getting past Willie Wanker, the guys in G Squad had the additional pressure of passing muster in the eyes of their own squad leader. A few of them approached guys in our squad to see if they cared to go to the guardroom gang-handed, thinking there might be safety in numbers. They also hoped The Wanker would not want to embarrass his men in the presence of recruits from a junior squad.

Jack and I decided to let the rush die down. We would see who was sent back and for what reasons. We also knew most guys would relegate sex to the evening and, as soon as they were out of the gate, head for the nearest pub to start throwing beer down their throats as if the Russians had landed at Brighton. We had different plans.

Earlier in the week we had heard Pete declare his intentions for the weekend. 'I'm nineteen years old, fer Christ's sake. Me 'ormones are ragin'. Isn't that what they say about people our age ... our 'ormones are ragin'? Doesn't 'er bleedin' Britannic Majesty, in 'er infinite bleedin' wisdom, know me 'ormones are ragin'? Being kept on board fer the last six weeks has been a cruel and unreasonable bleedin' punishment. Whatever 'appens this weekend, I'm gonna find me a female to fuck.'

After hearing Pete's words, Jonah had talked with our odd-man-out Ray, and the pair had agreed to go ashore together. But as Jonah walked into Ray's room, he accidentally kicked a pair of dress shoes at the base of someone's bed.

The owner screamed at him, 'Watch it, you fuckin' moron!'

There was an unspoken rule in the squad that nobody used Jonah's shortcomings as an insult against him. Pete left to put matters right. As he entered Ray's room, the man made an apology and promised Jonah a pint or two.

I empathised with Pete's rant about his hormones. Six-and-a-half weeks ago my goodbye sex had been ruined by goodbye tears and attempts by Genevieve to elicit promises from me to write to her on a weekly basis. I hadn't written and had no plans to contact her again. The Marines had changed me since I signed on the dotted line. I had not lost the respect for women my parents had instilled in me, but it had been tempered by also seeing them as sexual objects, at least until I found one I wanted to see repeatedly. If women saw me as a sexual object, life would be perfect.

Sunlight streamed through the windows of the corridor full of men in their dress blues inspecting one another and brushing each other down. One pair had stolen the telephone directory from the NAAFI and was searching for names of pubs, clubs and dance halls. 'Look under Ritz and Rialto,' someone suggested. A couple of sad sacks were obtaining change from everyone. They planned to make lengthy calls to their girlfriends from the privacy of enclosed phone booths. Geordie Jacobson had arranged for his wife to stay at a nearby hotel and he was desperate to get to her.

It was around one o'clock when the first group headed for the guardroom. Jack and I played cards in our underwear and waited for the imperfect to return. Dusty and Ron decided to leave.

'I hope The Wanker doesn't turn you back,' I said with a grin.

Dusty looked sourly back at me. 'The anaemic shit wouldn't dare.'

Pete returned from taking a shower, a towel wrapped around his waist and a piece of toilet paper covering a razor cut on his chin. 'What're you guys waitin' for?'

'We're 'opin' The Wanker'll wear himself out on everybody else before we make our appearance at the guardroom.'

'Yeah, that'll happen!'

Jonah walked into the room with Ray Green. 'Ya wanna check me out, Pete?' the big man asked his oppo.

Pete inspected him. 'Ya look good, Jonah. Whatcha gonna do ashore?'

'We're gonna get some decent grub, see a flick and then get a few beers before going to The Ritz,' Ray advised.

'Sounds good. See ya both later. Good luck gettin' out.'

Sammy ran in the wrong direction past our room. 'Arsehole is inspecting insteps,' he shouted.

His oppo was a couple of steps behind him. 'Bastard got me because the clips behind me badges aren't up to bleedin' standard.'

Allison and Edwards could not believe their failure to escape.

'It's a helluva comedown after that march this mornin',' Allison said. 'That was ace!'

'Yeah, but now we gotta do half our kit over again for that shit Wilkins,' Edwards complained. 'When're you two goin'?'

'After you lot've tired them out,' I answered.

Nothing could dampen Allison's enthusiasm. 'I still fuckin' say joinin' up was the best thing I've ever done. I love this fuckin' life!'

Jack and I listened intently. As we heard each reason, we checked our uniforms hanging on the front of our lockers. Our newly shone shoes with their highly polished toecaps and insteps were on the floor, under our beds. Our white blancoed belts with the gleaming brasses lay on the top.

No one had yet returned for failing Corps history. Pete concluded Jonah had passed muster and it was therefore time for him to try his luck. 'Jonah must've got an easy question,' he said with a grin.

'If yer not doin' summat else, we'll see ya in the 'Nelson Arms' around six,' Jack called after him as the two of us started to dress.

We took a clothes brush into the corridor and groomed each other.

Dennis, the ex-drummer, passed us. 'This is where bein' a drummer comes in 'andy. I've bin through all this stuff before. See ya.'

Satisfied with our appearance, we stowed our gear away, secured our lockers and set out for the guardroom. As we exited the block, we almost bumped into an angry Pete Bell.

'Why the 'ell didn't you guys tell me I still 'ad shit paper stuck on me chin?' he yelled.

'Give over! Why didn't ya take a look in a bleedin' mirror?' Jack said with a laugh.

We neared the guardroom and witnessed two guys from G Squad refused permission to go ashore. As they passed us, one of them raised his eyebrows and thereby lifted his peaked hat.

'I saw that,' screamed The Wanker. 'Don't bother coming back while I'm on duty.'

'Bastard,' Jack said.

Other recruits streamed to and from the guardroom.

We answered The Wanker's history questions as he moved behind us. 'Raise your left heel, now the right one.' I felt him pull at my belt. He came around to face us again. 'Open your tunics.' We took off our belts and obliged him. He checked our clips, took our belts from us and inspected them inside and out. Jack was not wearing a regulation tee-shirt.

'Unless standing orders changed in the last hour, I'd say that you're improperly dressed, Mason. Not good e ...'

'Corporal Wilkins!' shouted a voice from inside the guard room.

The Wanker stiffened. 'Yes, Sir.' He turned about and went to answer his summons.

Jack and I buttoned our tunics and put on our belts. A member of the provost staff who had inspected someone else and declared him fit to proceed ashore came to where we waited.

'You two been inspected?'

I nodded. 'I'd say so.'

The man checked our haircuts, fingernails, ears and chins and I wished he would hurry. The Wanker could appear at any time. He entered our names and regimental numbers in a log, which caused Jack and me to look questioningly at each other, not knowing if the notations meant good news or bad. The caped man reminded us we must return on board in a sober state and with our uniforms in good order. Then he turned away to inspect someone else. We were out!

Having marched everywhere with our arms raised parallel to the ground for the past six weeks, we continued to do so as we exited The Depot. I suddenly felt self-conscious.

'We don't have to do this outside, surely?'

'Do what? Oh, right.' said Jack as he lowered his arms.

We walked along the promenade expecting to find an abundance of oversexed parties waiting for us.

'Where the bleedin' 'ell are they?' Jack wanted to know.

'Probably doing their hair so they'll look their best for tonight.'

We turned from the water and saw two coffee bars on opposing sides of the street.

'I reckon that one,' said Jack, pointing to the noisiest.

We ordered two coffees and waited while a space-age contraption rumbled like a young monster working its way to maturity. There were hisses, spits, and gurgles.

'All I bleedin' want is a coffee,' said Jack.

When the noises ceased and a spout was wiped clean, the man behind the counter sprinkled dust over the contents of two miniscule cups before presenting them to us.

'Give over,' said Jack. 'That's not a cup.'

'It's what I serve here, son. It's Italian,' said the man.

I quickly paid for the drinks before Jack could learn how much they cost. Instead of sitting at a table, we took our coffees to the jukebox.

I thought people were politely making way for us but at one table a pimply-faced boy asked his female companion, 'What could possibly be the psychological make-up of people who volunteer to join the armed forces?'

A yob complained, 'Coffee bars used to be places in which peace-loving people gathered.'

We ignored them. Jack checked the jukebox and I turned to the counter, put down my cup and took off my hat. A partie occupied the stool to my left.

'Nice haircut there, Machine.'

I sat down beside her and gave her my toothiest smile. 'Machine?'

'It's what local women call you marines. Men call you Royal. Most of you don't seem to mind.' She smiled and her eyes lit up.

'You're not as antagonistic as some of the others here, then?'

She smiled back. 'That's because most of them have nothing going on in their lives.'

'They could always join up,' I suggested.

'That would be against the code of those who have nothing going on in their lives.'

I laughed. 'I take it you've got a lot of things going on in your life.'

'I have, plus I was married to a Machine.'

'Was?' She looked my age.

'He was killed. Got run down by a truck as he crossed the street.'

'Oh, sorry to hear that.'

Jack had made his selections and he turned to join us, breaking the ice. As there were no seats, he had to stand.

'I'm Paul Johnson. This is my oppo, Jack Mason. What's your name?'

Before she could answer, Jack said, 'He's The Banker and I'm The Wrestler. We're fairies.' His radiant smile seemed to challenge her.

I groaned.

'If you say so,' the woman said with a puzzled smile. 'I'm Diane, Diana Threlfall. Is this your first time ashore?'

'Yeah. Does it show?'

She smiled. 'You two do seem a little eager.'

'Give over!' said Jack. 'Eager? I heard they put bromide in our bleedin' tea ta stop that.'

Diane just managed to stop herself taking a sip of her coffee before she exploded with laughter. She was still seated but I guessed she had to be five-five or six. Her auburn hair fell on her shoulders; her eyes were green/brown and she had a great-looking body. Her laugh made her even more attractive, and me more eager.

'How about calling up a friend and the pair of you coming out with us tonight?' I suggested.

'Not on your first time ashore, thank you!' She laughed again. 'I'm here every Saturday until six. Why don't you come back another time?'

I was about to put my hand on her arm and plead for her company that night. If finding a friend for Jack was a problem, then I felt sure he would understand if Diane and I went out as a couple. Even if he didn't, women surely trumped oppos, didn't they? But the man behind the counter beat me to it, 'Come on, girl. There's a lot of tables be needing your attention.'

She put her hand on my knee, slid off her stool and grabbed a rag, 'Gotta work, Paul Banker,' she said with a cheeky smile. 'See you again, perhaps.'

'You woulda left me if she said yes just to you, wouldn't ya?'

'Wouldn't you?' I fancied I could still smell her perfume.

'Fuck no, we're oppos. One for all and all for one, and all that shit.'

'What? Are you suggesting we should share her? Make a threesome?'

'If that's what it comes to.'

'I'll remember that when it suits.'

Come opening time we went to the 'Nelson Arms'. The door was pegged open and Jack and I walked into a bar swarming with uniforms. There were a few drinkers in civilian clothes, but their haircuts marked them as marines. I ordered two pints of bitter. It had been a long time since my last pint and I watched the barmaid pump the swirling amber liquid into the glasses. When she put the first drink on the bar I looked at the glass for a second or too and anticipated the flavour while I allowed the liquid to settle. I handed the second pint to Jack and he too afforded the beer a degree of reverence. When my pint was still and clear, I picked it up and took a long draught. It tasted better than I had imagined and so much better than the bottles of pale ale we drank in the NAAFI.

Jonah stood on the far side of the room talking to some recruits from G Squad. Our first pints did not take long to down and Jack ordered fresh ones. With them in hand, we edged our way to where Jonah stood. The topic of conversation was Willie Wanker. Apparently, most of G Squad believed their leader to be an idiot they could live with.

'Rather him than Boswell,' offered one of them.

'Oh yeah!' Jonah became surprisingly aggressive. 'You want your fuckin' balls coming out yer ears, or somethin'? I'm one of Boswell's Fairies and I'm 'ere to tell you that man is *it*.'

'As in shit?' the antagonist pushed.

Jonah calmly put his pint on top of the piano and suggested that Boswell's detractor do the same. The man knew what was coming and he tried to steal an advantage by hurling his half-finished drink into Jonah's face. Luckily, Jonah anticipated the move and his knee landed in the man's testes as the beer hit his face. The force of Jonah's knee lifted the man off the ground and, for good measure, Jonah knuckled his ear. It suddenly dawned on me that this was a bad situation. I stepped forward and pushed Jonah in the chest and away from the confrontation.

'Enough, Jonah,' I yelled. He knew the other guy was done and he smiled like a happy puppy.

Jack stepped in front of the guy from G Squad, others were ready to hold him back. They weren't needed. The man was bent over, one hand on his ear and the other clutching his crotch.

'Any more of that and I'll be calling the shore patrol and the local constabulary,' shouted the proprietor, but he was in business to make money and so everything got back to normal very quickly.

Members of G Squad congregated on the far side of the room, consoling their buddy while shooting angry glances at us. Other squaddies returned to their pints as if nothing had happened. Pete appeared and, after we'd told him Jonah's prideful assault of a man, he, Jonah, Jack and I ordered some food from the barmaid. Fresh farm bread, cheddar cheese, butter and pickled onions were a welcome change after the food we'd eaten in the galley for the past few weeks.

We had all consumed a lot of beer before we arrived at the Ritz Ballroom. It was a cavernous hall that looked deserted, despite the presence of probably more than a hundred people – a shabby place with dim lighting, worn carpeting around the dance floor, and a terrible sound system that echoed in the vast space. The rotating mirror-ball reflected dappled light on the few dancers.

Perhaps the next set would contain more popular music, I wondered. I had been full of hope before entering the place but the drab décor and the lack-lustre patrons now dashed that hope. We headed to the bar, checking the females as we crossed the floor. I didn't see one I wanted to chat up and it seemed they felt the same way. When we'd contemplated about what we would do on our first time ashore, it had never looked as bad as this. The women bunched together on cinema-like benches along the wall or around distant circular tables on the first floor balcony. Some nodded their heads or jiggled their legs in time to the music, but overall there seemed a lack of interest.

A few stood at the bar and Jack chatted to one while purchasing four pints.

One of the women, short of a tooth, love-bites on her neck, and white dust in her hair, asked Jack, 'You gonna dance with me then, Machine?'

'After me pint,' he replied.

'What's the powder in your hair?' I asked. 'A new fashion?

She sneered. 'I didn't have time for a shampoo before I came out and it was pretty greasy, so I brushed it through with talc.' There you are Mother, I thought, grooming for the time-short woman. I pictured my father's face and smiled.

'You think it's funny?' Her attitude was suddenly aggressive.

'Give over, luv. He's my oppo,' Jack told her. 'Him an' me do everything together. Ask him if he wants to make a threesome with us.'

'Three dancing together isn't that great. What happens if a slow number comes on?'

'Give over! Dancing! I wasn't talking about dancing.'

Her eyes widened dramatically. 'What! Who do ya think you are, talking to me like that? I've half a mind ta call the Shore Patrol, you bastard!'

She hurried away to join some friends, one of whom was talking to a guy from G Squad. She went straight into a deeply hurt mode and pointed at Jack and me while she presumably told of her traumatic experience. The squaddie had a few words, then walked over to some mates.

'There's gonna be a little action comin' our way,' Jack observed.

'That's great!' said Jonah.

'If I'm not getting' any tonight, a punch up's the next best thing,' said Pete.

Jack laughed. 'All because me bleedin' oppo told me 'e was inta threesomes this afternoon.'

Pete's eyebrows went up. 'Really?'

'No, not really,' I told him. 'Jack fantasized about what he felt I owed him, as an oppo, if I got a date with a partie we met in a coffee shop and she didn't have a willing friend.'

'Oh well, that's fair enough,' he said with a grin.

We observed some members of G Squad conversing with some Teddy Boys. The civilians were dressed in long black jackets with velvet lapels and pocket flaps. Their drainpipe trousers collapsed in folds over imitation suede shoes with thick crepe soles. Some had black string ties with silver aglets. They all sported well-greased Tony Curtis style haircuts. I remembered how many of my squaddies had looked just like these guys and again realized how the past weeks had changed us.

Conversation over, the black-clad gang strode across the dance floor and climbed the three carpeted steps to the bar area.

'We 'ear you're a buncha fairies.'

'You've got that right,' Jack proudly responded. 'Why don't you give us a kiss?'

'Get their bleedin' toecaps,' shouted one piddling swine.

We all leapt forward, throwing our beer and glasses at the obnoxious bunch. Punches were thrown, heads butted, crotches kicked, eyes gouged, throats punched, and noses flattened while we hopped from one foot to the other to protect our toecaps. Parties screamed as we overturned tables and dumped bottles and glasses on the well-stained carpet.

'Watch out! 'Ere come the bouncers,' someone warned. They weren't in a hurry and it occurred to me they might be marines and tangling with them could have dire consequences when we returned on board. Perhaps they were affording us the opportunity to depart. I saw Pete split a nose with a head-butt. Jack practised a wrestling hold on a man who loudly complained his arm was broken. Jonah picked a ted up and tossed him aside as if he was a toy. One ted performed a toecap-scarring dance in front of me and I countered his every move until I stilled him by clapping his ears and prodding his eyeballs.

A man from G Squad fought with us. 'We gotta get outta here before the Shore Patrol arrives!' he shouted. We headed for a door that looked as if it might open onto the street, all the while battling the Teddy Boys. Someone banged on the release bar and the doors opened onto a car park. We forgot the fight and ran across the space, dodging the few vehicles parked there.

'Yeah, run away why don'tcha, ya fuckin' fairies,' someone called after us.

Our peaked hats! We'd left them at the bar. 'Guys, our fucking hats!' I yelled. We turned and charged back into the building to retrieve them and the Teddy Boys, taken by surprise, quickly retreated while some of the girls laughed.

Once on the street, we stopped under a lamp and checked for damages. Pete had a potential black eye and I a burst lip, but our uniforms were surprisingly intact. The man from G Squad was still with us.

Jack stretched out his hand. 'Thanks, mate. I didn't expect anyone from your squad to join in our fight.'

'It was some of the guys in my squad as set it up in the first place. There's a few who'd love to see you picked up by the Shore Patrol.'

'Tough fuckin' titty,' laughed Jonah, enjoying the use of his broadening vocabulary.

'I'm Jack. This is The Banker, Jonah and Pete.' We all nodded at the man.

He returned the nods. 'Keith Blackburn.'

The evening was finished. We could not go back to the Ritz and the pubs had closed. It was too late to trawl other parts of town.

'You know places we can go?' I asked Keith.

'Not really. This is only my third time ashore and the other two times I managed to stay in the Ritz.'

We laughed as we set out to return to The Depot. Stretching my lips caused blood to flow again. The five of us walked along the promenade in the vain hope there might be parties lined up, just waiting for us. Unfortunately, nobody had told them where we would be … or maybe they had.

As we neared The Depot, Jonah, Pete and Keith went to play pinball machines in a deserted café. Jack and I went back on board. The man on the gate was surprised to see us back so early. He noticed my lip. 'What 'appened? She lock 'er ankles too tight?' I worried I might be charged with some crime but he wasn't concerned. He asked for our names and noted our return in the register.

Our evening had not matched our fantasies and Jack kicked his locker in frustration, making sure not to damage his toecap. 'I don't fancy our chances in this bleedin' town on a Sunday. Next weekend, we do it my way.'

'Next weekend we go back to that coffee bar,' I said

'Oh yeah, I forgot. Which one of us gets 'er?'

'Diane? First off, let's see what her friend's like. If she's in the same league, I'll happily take either.'

'And if she's not?'

'Well, I guess we'll see if Diane prefers a wrestler or a banker. My money's on me.'

'Give over!'

The boozers opened at twelve noon on Sunday and those of us with perfect dress and knowledge were on the pavement outside the Nelson Arms five minutes before the doors were unlatched. As we discussed the previous night's events, the good citizens of Deal walked past us on their way home from church. Some crossed the road rather than share the pavement with us. Some parents shielded their children by putting arms around their young shoulders and turning their inquisitive faces away. They could hardly have been the same people who cheered us through the streets of town the previous morning.

'What the fuck's wrong with us?' Jack asked.

'We're not the most upstanding citizens, are we?'

'Give over.'

'Look at us, Jack. We're three deep on the bloody pavement waitin' for the pub to open. Last night we were looking for local girls ta fuck. We hardly speak the Queen's English and every other word out of our mouths is a curse word.'

'So?'

He seemed so genuinely aggrieved and I laughed. 'If you were, oh, I dunno, say a bank clerk living in a house with green lawns and a white picket fence and you had two teenage daughters, would you be keen to see us hanging about?'

'What's a picket fence?' he asked.

The doors to the Nelson Arms opened to admit us. We were not a complicated crowd and the barmaid started to pull seventeen pints of bitter.

'I don't remember seeing you lot before. First time, is it?' she said. When we said we'd been in the place the previous evening she smiled. 'First time for me, then. I wasn't on last night.'

'Here we go,' sighed a man. 'The place is only open for two hours an' I 'ave to get stuck behind a bunch of thirsty bootnecks.'

The barmaid sympathised. 'What is it you want, Ben? I'm sure these lads won't mind if I squeeze you in.'

Jack raised an eyebrow at her words.

'A gee and tee, if you will, Jill. Thanks.'

The server prepared Ben's drink. 'Will someone put some money in the jukebox?' she said.

Jonah made a move toward the machine but I got there before him. 'Here, let me,' I told him, not wanting to hear Cliff Richard, Pat Boone or songs he tried to find whenever he could get his fingers on a radio tuner.

I selected *Runaway, Shakin' All Over, My Old Man's A Dustman,* and *Shazam.* The blonde barmaid, who could have been in her late twenties or early thirties, had taken off her jacket and she started to flex her chest muscles in time to the music, all the while pulling pints of beer. Jack clapped his hands to encourage the woman. Her breasts were small, but they were finely muscled and her tight-fitting blouse served to accentuate her movements. She flexed each one individually and managed to have one rising while the other dipped to the beat of the blaring jukebox. We took Jack's cue and stomped our feet. Others joined in, clapping and whistling as the obliging woman worked enthusiastically for our benefit. Jonah stood motionless at the bar, his mouth agape.

The cabaret ceased when other customers started to arrive, but the jukebox continued to play. Although Jonah had heard the music on radios in our rooms, our first weekend ashore was apparently his earliest opportunity to hear the superior sounds of jukeboxes. He stood at the corner of the bar with his eyes closed, his body moving to the beat of the music. Frank Sinatra, Perry Como and their ilk were already ancient history. The barmaid was quite taken by the sight of our large squaddie and enquired who he might be. At closing time, we left the pub without Jonah, his services commandeered to escort the lady home.

The Sunday streets were empty. Jack and I walked into the town centre and went to a cinema. When the show finished, we found a Fish and Chip shop. We ate the tasty food slowly then paced the streets until the pubs re-opened. We returned to the pub where we'd left Jonah, but neither he nor the barmaid was there. After two pints of bitter, we returned to The Depot.

Jonah appeared around nine-thirty with a foolish grin on his face.

'So, Jonah' Pete began, 'Did you wear a johnny?'

'What's a johnny?'

'A rubber, a condom, a prophylactic. We tried to give you some. Remember?'

'I didn't need any,' defiant Jonah replied.

'Did you shag the barmaid?' Pete continued.

'No I didn't. I made love to her!' Jonah was embarrassed and getting angry.

We all laughed. 'Listen Jonah, don't get pissed. A lot of women have a different name for it but when all's been said and done, that which we call a shag by any other name would smell as sweet,' I said with a straight face.

Jack looked at me with raised eyebrows. 'What the fuck you on about?'

Pete persisted. 'She's a bleedin' barmaid, Jonah. 'Alf of every squad that passes through this place probably shags 'er.'

'That's not true!' the big man insisted, his hackles rising.

'Really! An' 'ow would you know?'

'She told me you guys would say stuff like this. She said you'd all be jealous of me. She said just because she's a barmaid doesn't mean she sleeps with a whole bunch of men.'

'She might be tellin' ya the truth, Jonah, but it don't hurt ta take precautions. Ya can always say ya don't wan' 'er to get preggers.'

''Er tubes are blocked!' the besieged Jonah shouted.

There was no way Jonah could previously have known of such matters. 'What?'

'She told me 'er tubes are blocked, so she can't 'ave any babies.'

Pete ran out of arguments. He reached up and put an arm around his oppo's shoulder. 'Listen, Jonah. You've gotta get inta the habit of wearing a johnny. You tell your girlfriend I said you've gotta wear one. If she likes ya so much, she won't bleedin' mind, believe me.'

'Okay,' said the big guy. 'I'll try.'

'One more thing, oppo.'

'What's that, Pete?'

'You're probably the only guy in the whole squad, save Geordie Jacobson, who got 'is end away this weekend. An' 'e doesn't count 'cause 'e's married. Congratubleedinlations.'

On Monday morning, the Commanding Officer appeared and announced something that we, being near the back of the parade ground, could barely hear.

When the RSM declared the parade over, our DI told us, 'We're all going to London this weekend to line The Mall for the arrival "in state" of Haile Selassie, The Lion of Judah.' The grin on his face reflected my feeling of excitement. 'I can tell from the looks on yer wee faces that you all believe it will be a grand time. It will not! I ...'

'Sergeant Boswell!' the RSM roared as he approached.

Boswell stiffened and snapped his heels. 'Yes, Sergeant Major.'

'With your permission, Sergeant, I want to tell your charges that they would not have made the party, save for the CO needing numbers. In accepting your presence, Her Britannic Majesty is scraping the bottom of the barrel. In fact, she is scraping so desperately she has come up with nothing but shit under her fingernails. Good God, you've hardly been here a dog watch. There will be no nonsense about being fairies this weekend. Do I make myself clear? There are enough genuine fairies in the guards regiments to keep the whole of London happy. They do not need reinforcements. If any of you,' he turned his head as he scanned us, 'fuck up in any way whatsoever, you will be shat on from an exceedingly great height. You all got that?' I thought he might growl but he refrained from doing so. 'Carry on, Sergeant.'

Boswell shouted 'Thank you, Sergeant Major' to the disappearing man's back. 'Take heed of what the Regimental Sergeant Major said,' he advised us. 'I think you know not to incur his fearsome wrath. A special train will take us to 'The Smoke' on Saturday. We will rehearse on Sunday and the actual event will take place on Monday. While in the capital, we will be billeted with a Guards regiment and not allowed ashore.'

I had mixed feelings. The idea of taking part in a big event in London definitely had its appeal, and next week's training would be shortened by one day, maybe two – or would Boswell find a way around that? On the other hand, we would miss what was to be our second weekend ashore. The previous weekend had been less than perfect and I looked forward to correcting the situation.

'Dinna worry about the wee girlies of Deal,' Boswell continued, as if reading my mind. 'They'll still be around the following weekend. Work on your uniforms – a lot of important people will be looking at you.'

The following morning, we paraded in dress blues but the company commander merely walked our ranks, giving each of us a cursory glance. When he departed, Boswell commanded us to stand easy.

'Come next Monday, you will understand why we are not too worried about the state of your uniforms. That doesna mean ya pay less attention to your turn-out. Mark my words well. Slackers will be severely punished. Each of you will get a haircut this week, whether you think you need one or not. I advise you to do so as soon as possible because the queues will grow as the week progresses.' The man was enjoying himself and he rolled his 'r's with gusto. 'As fairies, you are not interested in style! Get it short and clean. Remember, any part of yer head showing beneath yer peaked hat belongs ta me! Now, we're gonna have a wee rehearsal so you'll know what it's like ta line a parade route. Attennnnntion!' Twenty-nine pairs of steel-edged heels snapped together. 'Very good. You will stay here while I go for a wee cuppa. There will be no talking, whispering or farting. Anyone who faints will be on a charge for conduct contrary to good order and military discipline. I shall return in a few hours and I expect to find you all still at attention. Is that clear!'

A bloody cuppa! There were other things I'd prefer to do, were we to swap places. Sex with Dianne would do, but now it would have to wait another week. It's been seven weeks! What if she prefers Jack? I replaced Dianne's image with that of her unknown friend who, thankfully, had a beautiful, muscular, sun-tanned body. Sex with Genevieve? Chas said he would ask her for a date once I was gone. Her letters dwindled to a brief note received last Friday that accused me of being self-centred and told me it was the last time she'd write unless I replied. She'd been happy when I took her virginity; now it's become a fucking debt. She was right about me being self-centred, but I didn't care. Genevieve and her letters. She even wrote to me while we were dating, because, she claimed, it was the only way she could say things she thought important. I threw a couple away without opening them. One thing about standing at attention for so long is that it gives one time to think. I guess a lot of women would love to command men to stand at attention and remain quiet while they 'have a talk'. I resolved to write and release Gen from the bond she still believed we had. I should have done it weeks ago. Stepmother had once advised me to be careful with a girl's emotions. Telling me how a girl's emotions were different from a man's would've helped. I'll have to word it carefully but, whatever I write, I'm sure the 'debt' will accumulate interest. I recalled her screwed up face. 'Not so rough … please, not so rough'. She thought we were having rough sex, not that I've experienced it. I tried to tell her she had some sort of physical problem but she always said I was talking rubbish. 'What do you know about my body?' She didn't want to see a doctor about the problem (if one existed) without her mother being present, but couldn't tell her mother she was having sex. Thank you, Maggie, for being around when I needed an uncomplicated fuck. Would Chas be as patient with Gen? Well, it's none of my concern any more. What a fucking saint I'd been. Well, sort of. There was nothing *I* should feel guilty about! Change track. Matches at Maine Road when I didn't have a rugby game. I can picture some of the goals City scored. Ken Barnes and Roy Paul (an ex-marine) were great and Bert Trautmann, our German goalkeeper, had been between the sticks forever. You brought me a lot of pleasure over the years. Thanks, guys.

Rugby. Drinking in the clubhouse after the games. That's where I met sexy Maggie. She pretended to care about a scratch on my eyelid and cheek. 'Why don't you come home and let me tend to that.' So much for thinking I was too young for her. She put me straight on a lot of things. I would have liked to continue seeing you, Maggie, but perhaps it's a good job I joined up. When I scored the winning try against Fylde, you said I was your favourite second-row forward. Hmph! Not exactly exclusive company, but you weren't my exclusive either. All's fair in love and war, thank God. I remembered the sex we enjoyed and an erection began to rise. That was the last thing I needed. Sing a song. *My Old Man's a Dustman* …

Then it stuck like a scratched record that keeps repeating the same few notes. I couldn't get rid of it. *He wears cor blimey trousers and he lives in a council flat.* How many guys in the squad had a dustman for a father? How many had lived in council flats? *Great big hob nailed boots* ... How many of Jack's foster homes had been council flats? *He calls them daisy roots.* I wondered what my parents would think of me living, working and playing with people from council flats. My stepmother would be horrified. 'Is this what it's come to after the way we've brought you up?' Yes, Mother, it apparently is. And my father? 'What are you doing to build yourself a future, son?' Nothing. I joined up to have some fun. 'For nine years? Isn't that a little self-indulgent?' It's my life. Anyway, it's too late to go to officer school. 'You can work your way through the ranks.' Fuck off! I'm doing the nine and then I'm out. It'd probably take longer than that just to make second-lieutenant. 'So become an NCO.' What for? What good will that do me in Civvy Street? 'You don't think Boswell would be an asset to a company? He's a born leader.' Yeah, but I'm not a Boswell. 'Become one.' Become a Boswell and go back to the bank. Those wimpy bastards would shit a brick. Half of them would call in sick the next day. 'You could become a policeman.' That's almost the same as this. 'So why did you join?' I told you – to have fun. 'For nine years? You should have gone for the French Foreign Legion.' I don't speak French. 'Mmm, more's the pity.'

My old man's a chemist, Robbed And Murdered Comrades. It occurred to me I'd had a privileged life, compared to Jack. Does he see it that way?

I jiggled my thigh muscles. Could anyone see what I was doing? Nah, nobody who mattered was close enough. The muscles cooled and the discomfort drained away. I closed my eyes and felt I could fall asleep. Stop! Maybe guardsmen don't faint, they fall asleep. Is that possible? No. I blinked severely and rolled my eyeballs around which made them hurt.

He wears cor blimey trousers ... To be rid of the song I thought of books I'd read. *I Bought a Mountain* was the last book I'd finished. Who could've believed farming on a slope would be interesting? The one before that was *My Son, My Son.* That was a tale of politics, show business, and screwing your son's girlfriend. A headache focused my attention. My hat had been tightening for some time and was becoming uncomfortable. There's nothing I could do about it. I tried to think of something else. Sex? Stop it. Was this what I'd become? Wait a minute. What was wrong with thinking about sex? There's nothing in the world I'd rather do, so what's wrong with thinking about it? I might get an erection again and I don't want that. Some faggot said women are not sexual objects. Yes, they are, and I hope and pray they see us as sexual objects too. Not an original thought. Was I trying to justify the supposedly unjustifiable? Grandmother's not a sex object but my stepmother is (and wasn't that good reason for joining up!). My birth mother wouldn't be, at least not to me. Wonder what she'd look like now? Come on, change the subject. Do some maths. *The square on the hypotenuse is equal to the sum of the squares on the other two sides.* Make the length of the hypotenuse five inches and the other two sides three and four. Three threes are nine and four fours are sixteen. Nine and sixteen are twenty-five and the square root of twenty-five is five. I'm cheating. That was the example in the text book. Work out a new equation. Twenty-five and thirty-six are sixty-one – nope. Thirty-six and forty-nine are eighty-five – nope. Ah, bollocks.

I thought again of books. *He was an old man who fished alone in a skiff in the Gulf Stream and he had gone eighty-four days now without taking a fish.* I considered reciting poetry or passages by Shakespeare and Dickens. All those lessons at school had to have been worth something. *I come to bury Caesar, not to praise him.* How many guys around me could do that? *Now, I return to this young fellow and the observation I have to make is that he has great expectations.* Is that right? Something like that. Great expectations? Not exactly, Mother. *It is a far, far better thing that I do, than I have ever done.* There was a lot of truth in that, provided one saw it from my perspective. How many would want to? What was going through other guys' minds?

'This is beyond a fuckin' joke,' whispered someone.

''Ow bleedin' long's it bin?'

'Shut the fuck up!'

I heard steel-studded boots marching toward us.

'Whose squad is this?' Boswell asked with laughter in his voice. 'Oh, they're mine. It's been so long I'd forgotten all about you. How are my fairies holding up?' Nobody said a word. 'Obviously not that badly. Good. I'll be back in an hour.' The sound of his boots faded as he marched away.

'Fuckin' bastard!'

'I'll fuckin' swing for 'im, so 'elp me.'

'Put a sock in it, guys. We can do this.'

'Yeah but we don't 'ave to fuckin' like it.'

We'd have liked it less if it was raining. Would Boswell still have us out there in the rain? What would a substantial amount of rain do to our dress blues? Does serge shrink? If so, there's not a lot of time for us all to get new uniforms and have them altered in time for the show. Nah. He'd march us off to the sheds where the band practised their music. Jeez, it'd be great to march.

Ray Green was in front of me. I inspected the back of his neck and noticed an angry pimple at the edge of his collar. It had a yellow head and surrounds of red. If it's sore, it'd be a good reason for Ray not to move his head, on the other hand, if it' itchy, he might want to rotate his head a little to scratch the ugly thing on his collar. Maybe not. What if it burst? Would the pus fly back far enough to reach me? What if it splashed onto my face? Shit! It could land in my eye, or on my lips. Keep your head very still, Ray. That's fucking disgusting. I had to find something else to think about. Listen to the birds. They all seemed to be in the one tree on the far side of the parade ground; the one over Ray's right shoulder. Focus on the tree; I didn't want another eyeful of Ray's carbuncle, or whatever it was. A boil? I had boils on my neck when I was a kid. My father squeezed the shit out of them and then applied hot poultices, until stepmother told him he was doing it in the wrong order – and wasn't the chemist pleased about that! The whole routine hurt like hell. Did he derive pleasure out of my pain? Sounds like a rotten thing to come into my head but, knowing him, it was a distinct possibility. Why would all the birds be in one tree? There's gotta be a dozen or more trees around the parade ground. Why congregate in one? Does it have good berries?

My lower back ached. I flexed my buttocks but it didn't help much. I sucked in my gut and worked my waist side to side and back and forth.

'Keep fuckin' still, Banker!' a voice behind me whispered. I stopped moving and resigned myself to my backache. How bad could it get? Who was behind me? Who cared? My head hurt but there was less than an hour to go.

On Tuesday night, Jonah received a summons, via the Tannoy system, to report to the guardroom 'on the double'. He left thinking he was in trouble and Pete went with him to provide support. We laughed when we learned on Pete's return that Jonah had been called to take a phone call from 'Proud Jill' of the muscular mammaries. Jonah later told us that Proud Jill had heard about us going to London and wanted to know when she would see him again.

The following morning, the armoury issued us rifles. The Belgian Fabrique Nationale 7.062mm semi-automatic rifle weighed nine pounds. Most of us considered the weapon just another piece of equipment to be carried, cleaned and inspected. It came with khaki and white slings; more canvas and brass to blanco and polish.

The band led us to the train station on Saturday morning and, as the junior squad, we were in the rear. Every time the band turned a corner, intervening buildings and wind from the English Channel distorted the music. Boswell marched alongside Sammy, barking out the pace.

'Left ... Left ... Left, Right, Left. Dinna listen to the music ...' he shouted '... just keep pace with the man in front of you.'

Girls waved, cheered, blew raspberries and made wonderfully indecent promises to us. 'Proud Jill' stood at the pub door, her arms partially raised as she flexed her chest muscles in time to the music.

'Left, right, left, right,' Boswell shouted and Jonah's lady obeyed his every command.

LONDON

3rd April 1960

On Sunday, trucks took us to the parade route where officious men shuffled us until we gelled to their sense of form. Marines and Guards alternately lined both sides of The Mall. We stood easy all morning while army officers met in groups and tried to look imposing. There were few civilians to impress but still the officers walked around checking their clipboards. Across from where I stood, an old man sat and waited for something to happen while his dog slept at his feet. After a couple of hours, he shrugged, kicked his dog awake and sauntered off.

I noticed NCOs disappearing and reappearing but Boswell remained with us. He spoke to every member of the squad and discussed soccer teams, the qualities of parties and regional beers, our training, and our hopes for the future.

'You only need follow orders from Royal Marines. Percy Pongo, as those in the army are known, isna fit ta order us around,' he said with a grin.

'Are you serious?' I asked.

'I am today,' he said.

Army trucks arrived with lunch. An unknown Guard's captain called us to attention and cautioned us. 'You men are on public display and therefore must act only in accordance with good order and military discipline. You will not remove your hats or unbutton your tunics.' He looked around to see if any of us disagreed. 'Very good. Dismissed!'

I didn't move and I noticed other squaddies remained in place. It was a nervous moment. The guards rushed to use the portable toilets positioned some distance behind us.

Boswell beamed with pride at our refusal to be dismissed by a mere army captain.

'H Squad dismissed!' he roared.

Jack and I put tepid soup and stale bread before bladder relief.

By mid-afternoon, the officious seemed even more superfluous. Boswell allowed us to remove our hats and the relief was wonderful. After wearing my peaked hat for seven hours, what hair I had was soaked with perspiration and I had a throbbing headache. Ten minutes later, we were ordered to don our hats again and my headache returned, but the break had been welcome.

When organisers realized it was time for gee and tees in the mess, trucks picked us up and returned us to the barracks where we were pleasantly surprised to discover Percy ate tastier food than Marine recruits.

We returned to The Mall early Monday morning. Eager spectators were already gathering behind the wooden barriers situated at our backs. We stood at ease and waited.

Civilian police acted as a deterrent to the small number of troublemakers who were correctly of the opinion that people in the armed forces had no jurisdiction over them. Boswell roamed, telling us to ignore abuse shouted at us and alerting police to problems. We remained silent and motionless while the crowd behind us swelled. Bored children darted into The Mall and police officers chased them back. One young boy scrambled between my legs, making me wish we were at attention. People constantly jostled me as they moved around. Adults pushed children to the front of the crowd so they would be able to see 'Er bleedin' Majesty'. When the youngsters tried to sit in front of us, the police arrived to send them back.

One mother asked me to keep an eye on her daughter. When I didn't respond, she said to someone, 'Bleedin' stuck up lot, aren't they? Don't even answer me.' I felt a finger poke me in my back. 'You too bleedin' good to look after my Annie? You lot are supposed to obey us civilians. I know, 'cause my Arnie told me.'

A police officer came to my rescue. 'Leave the young man alone, ma'am. He isn't even allowed to speak to you, let alone look after your children.'

When the man left to take charge of another situation, the woman continued to mutter. 'I swear I don't know what this bleedin' country's comin' to. They must know 'ow difficult it is fer us to 'ave to stand all the time an' 'old our bags of food an' drink. 'Ow're we sposed to look after our bleedin' kids as well? It's our taxes as pays for the police an' the army. You'd think they'd show a little appreciation now an' then. It's them toffs as gets all the appreciation, sittin' in the stands and 'avin' all sorts of food and drink served to 'em.'

'What stands?' somebody wanted to know.

'Oh, there'll be bleedin' stands somewhere, mark my words.'

'I can pretty much see the whole of The Mall and I don't see any stands.'

'Then they'll be somewhere bleedin' else, won't they? What're you arguin' wiv me for?'

Another woman demanded to know where her companion had been until the early morning hours. 'I called your work, but there was no reply.'

'I had to go and see a customer. It's because I worked late last night, that I'm able to be with you today.'

'You were with a customer until two in the morning?'

'Yes. Are you saying you don't believe me?'

'It is a little hard to swallow!'

'Well, hard or not, that's what happened. A factory was at a stand-still until I was able to deliver a new machine part and install it.'

'Oh, so now you're an engineer, as well! Will you be getting a raise?'

'It's not likely.'

'If it was so easy to replace, how come it took you until two in the morning to get home?'

'Go to hell, Enid. I'm fed up with your nagging. I'm going for a drink. I'll see you later.'

'Don't bother!'

'Fair enough.'

A couple of women discussed what their excuses should be for taking time off from the office.

'Ah've just about wiped out me 'ole bleedin' family. Ah can't possibly 'ave to go to another blessed funeral,' bemoaned one.

''Ow about 'aving to pick up some relation what's just returned from overseas?' her friend suggested.

'Maybe, but 'ow come I didn't know about it before 'and?'

'Cause someone else were supposed to do it, but they got sick an' you 'ad to go instead.'

'Yeah? Oh yeah, that's not bad. I like that one. You could give the same story to your boss an' all.'

'I don't 'ave to worry about 'im. A little slap and tickle termorrer lunchtime and 'e'll forget today ever existed.'

'Jesus, Jill and Joseph, you are *so* lucky. I wish I 'ad a boss like that.'

'You could 'ave. All you 'as to do is let 'im know it's available any time 'e wants it.'

'You wanna come an' work fer me, luv?' a male voice asked hopefully.

As the morning wore on, I began to hear the rustle of sandwich wrappers unfolding. I heard the escape of compressed gas as people opened bottles of pop. The aroma of hot coffee followed the sound of a flask top being unscrewed. There were the smells of oranges and bananas and I realized I was hungry and thirsty. We had eaten a breakfast large enough to sustain us, yet small enough to prevent the need to visit a bathroom.

When, peripherally, I saw two Guardsmen pitch over onto their faces, I knew they had not eaten enough. An army sergeant, together with Boswell, used hands to indicate we should move to fill the space left by those who had been unceremoniously carted away. I stepped a pace to my right and wondered if Her Britannic Majesty or The Lion of Judah would notice the breaks in the sequence of the two very different types of servicemen.

People bumped and prodded my back throughout the day. Some apologised and others ignored me. At one point, a mother admonished her child for smearing something on my tunic.

'Give it a good soak when ya get 'ome, luv,' the youngster's mother told me. 'It'll come out all right.'

My main concern was for my boots, specifically the toecaps. I, plus Ron and Dusty, had put a lot of time and effort into achieving a blinding black surface on the once brown footwear and I didn't want the spectacular result ruined by some careless yob.

The crowd behind me must have shifted; voices and conversations changed. A woman told her friend about a recent date.

'We were necking in the back seat of his car for what seemed like hours. I was horny as hell, so I started to feel him up. He got all righteous on me and declared it was time to take me home.'

Two parties giggled and then a second voice said, '*He* definitely didn't rise to the occasion, did he?'

I thought they were still talking about the first partie's date until she replied, 'Maybe, maybe not. He'd probably get into trouble if he said, or did anything. Here's my name and phone number, Haircut.'

I felt a hand inserted into the right pocket of my trousers and I started with concern and excitement. The hand moved to the left and I prayed to any God that might be listening to prevent me from getting an erection. None were listening.

A loud voice called out. 'Keep your hands to yourself, if you don't mind, Madam.' The policeman smiled as he walked over to where I stood, 'You okay, Royal?'

I didn't say a word but the erection withered as fast as it had risen. Boswell arrived. 'I would say, constable, that the man has not suffered any permanent damage. Thanks for intervening.' I saw him look over my shoulder and grin. 'I know he's a fine specimen of manhood, ladies, but I have to ask you to keep yer wee hands ta yourselves.'

I heard giggling as Boswell and the police officer departed and left me in my vulnerable position. Then the second woman spoke in a whisper, 'Elizabeth! I can't believe you did that!'

'Did what?' Elizabeth asked in her normal voice. 'You got any complaints, Haircut?'

I remained silent.

'See! It was okay by him. The permanent damage will come when you get to know me better, Haircut.'

Thankfully, we were called to attention at that point and my mind was able to focus on our reason for being in The Mall. I realized I could hear music from bands still a long way off. The crowd also heard the sound and started to pack away their personal items. Parents called out to their children and told them to be good.

'Here, blow yer nose,' I heard one mother tell her child. 'The Queen's coming.'

When the leading band came into view, people started to cheer and wave their miniature flags. The music got louder and I pushed out my chest and flexed every muscle. The cheering of the crowd almost drowned out the sound of the horses' clip-clopping on the road's hard surface. The colourful, ornate carriages passed more quickly than I had imagined. The Queen gave her insipid wave and her people cheered. The Duke of Edinburgh, Captain General, Royal Marines, obligingly smiled for the minions. Haile Selassie showed a little more enthusiasm, but it was still condescension to the masses. I wondered if all royalty forever taught their offspring to wave in such a disparaging manner to the people who kept them on the throne. I had heard the wave became an anaemic flutter because it was too tiring to offer anything more energetic for prolonged periods … or perhaps they practised by lazily flicking at flies.

Once the procession passed, the crowd started to break up. I silently willed the two parties behind me to stay around until I could get a look at them, possibly even speak to them. Surely they must be inquisitive regarding my own appearance.

'How long's it going to be before you're relieved, Haircut?' asked the now familiar voice. Everyone within my peripheral vision was still at attention. Even those whose job was to clean up horse droppings had passed, but Boswell still paced The Mall and I remained silent. 'Oh, what the hell!' she exclaimed and she must have ducked under the barrier because she appeared and took up position in front of me. She was probably five-five or six, looked to be in her mid-twenties and was gorgeous.

'Smile for the birdie.' She laughed as she took my photograph. Her eyes sparkled. Unfortunately, her friend was becoming nervous and wanted to leave. Cecilia B. DeMille put her camera away in its case and stepped up to me so that our faces were inches apart. 'My number's in your pocket, Haircut. I expect to hear from you soon.' She leaned forward and kissed me on the mouth and I could not repress a smile. 'That's my man!' Elizabeth laughed as she turned and walked down The Mall, arm in arm with her friend. After they had gone twenty yards, she turned and blew me a kiss. 'See you soon, Haircut.'

As we broke from our positions and started to get into the trucks, we noticed almost everybody's tunic was filthy. Many belts were missing sliced-off buckles. The backs of tunics had been smeared with what looked like mustard, ketchup, HP Sauce and other substances not readily identifiable. Apart from the apologetic mother, it had not occurred to me what might be happening while I was brushed and pushed by the people at my rear. I unbuckled my belt and discovered one of my back buckles hung from a few threads. Perhaps the culprit had been frustrated when we closed ranks to cover for the fainting Guardsmen.

I saw Jack and we headed for the same truck. 'Summa these people are real arseholes,' he said with a derisive laugh. 'The Perce next ta me 'ad a guy be'ind him piss on 'is leg. 'E just let fly where 'e stood an' splashed everythin' in sight.'

'Give over,' I said with a laugh. Jack looked stunned. 'What?' I said. 'You the only one who can use that expression?'

He hesitated for a second, and then smiled. 'It doesn't fit ya,' he said. 'Any road, people in the crowd were pretty disgusted but nobody did nowt about it. 'Ow'd you go?'

'Not bad. A party pushed a piece of paper in my pants pocket and told me to call her,' I said as I fished for it.

'Give over! 'Ow far into your bleedin' pocket did she go?'

'Pretty much all the way. She might have gone further but a cop and Boswell came and told her to leave me alone.'

'They're always around when ya don't need 'em! She 'ave a friend?'

'She did.' I unfolded the paper. 'Here it is. It's a London number.'

'What bleedin' good is that to us? We're goin' back to Deal. Was she good looking?'

'She was.' I laughed. 'Look, we have to take a train to London to go to wherever we go on leave. We can see them then.'

'Good one, Banker. How old was she?'

'I would say mid to late twenties.'

''Ow old?' he said with alarm.

'Don't worry, Jack. They aren't looking to mother us. Mind, she was a bit shy. Look, enough of that. Take a look at my back.'

I turned around and heard him laugh. 'You've got shit all over the place. Take a look at mine for me.'

We both turned around and I saw a swathe of what looked like salad cream across his back. Someone had spelt out the name 'Jim' in the creamy stuff.

'Your name's Jim.'

'What?'

Boswell grinned at us, 'Now you're getting to know the people whose rights you have sworn to defend. Buncha fuckin' animals, aren't they!'

'What about our gear?' someone wanted to know.

'Dinna fash yerself, laddie,' Boswell put on his best Glaswegian accent. 'I'll inspect you all tomorrow morning and anyone with damaged issue will be given a free replacement. How about that, men? Her Britannic Majesty's generosity knows no bounds. May God bless her and all who sail in her.'

Had Boswell made a mistake or had he let the information slip out on purpose? That night, back in our Deal barracks, we relieved the galley of several bottles of Ketchup and mustard. We spent some entertaining moments in our rooms smearing, staining, cutting and ripping. The Lion of Judah was going to cost Her Britannic Majesty a lot of money.

DEAL

5th April 1960

On Thursday morning, the Adjutant honoured us with an inspection. He reined in his horse when he saw Jonah.

'Sir Albert Jones!' His voice had the sound of a smile. 'Tell me, Jones, what does D.S.O. mean to you?'

Jonah didn't hesitate. 'The Esso sign means happy motoring.' He sang the words proudly, then added, 'Sir.'

The Adjutant could not keep a smile from his face. He attempted to hide it by leaning down on the far side of his horse's neck and giving the animal a couple of friendly pats. Leather creaked and brass jingled as he straightened. 'Do you know who the Prime Minister is, Jones?'

'No, Sir.'

'Who, in your opinion, is the most important person in England, Jones?'

'Sir, Elvis Presley, Sir,' said the man who had been learning about the music that was so new to his life.

The officer paused and I knew whatever was going through his mind wasn't good. 'I don't believe said gentleman is an Englishman or a knight, Jones, but you are the proof that he undoubtedly has influence here. Anyone else?' Jonah kept his mouth closed. 'Tell me, do you read a newspaper, Jones?'

'No, Sir.'

'Hmm.' The Adjutant turned his attention to Boswell. 'See me after parade, will you, Sergeant.'

'Very good, Sir.'

The man wheeled his horse and left, presumably to encourage someone else to make a fool of himself. Boswell waited until the horse was out of hearing distance, then moved to where Jonah stood. 'Jonah, Jonah, what was that shit about the Esso sign, laddie?'

'I thought that's what he meant, Sergeant,' replied our forthright squaddie.

'Haven't you ever heard of the Distinguished Service Order?'

'Oh. Yeah I remember you said something about it, but I thought the Adjutant was asking about the advert-song on the radio.'

Boswell shook his head. 'How're we gonna hide the fact you're a fucking ignoramus, laddie? Ya know you're being watched, and now you've just given them another nail for the lid of yer coffin.' Jonah said nothing but he must have dropped his gaze because Boswell suddenly shouted at him. 'Look me in the eye!'

Jonah shouted back at Boswell, 'I know I'm not as smart as the others but I'm holding my end up, same as everyone.'

Boswell took the edge off his voice, 'It's not enough, son. We dinna have the same chain of command as the Army, so there won't always be someone around ta tell ya what ta do. A Marine has ta reason things out and then act on what he has deduced. The point of being here at The Depot is learning – how ta work as a squad, ta understand and inwardly digest all the academic stuff. The instructors here are trying ta teach ya everything we know so you'll have the information ta make the right decision at the right moment. I'm trying ta help you all I can, laddie, but it's up ta *you* ta understand what's being taught and to commit it ta memory. If ya don't, it might cost your oppo his life one day. If ya cannot keep up, ya will be gone. Not just from this squad, but from The Corps. Do I make myself clear?'

When we paraded after a lunch during which we tried to figure out how best to help Jonah, the RSM came over and spoke quietly to Boswell. He then marched up to Jonah. 'The Adjutant tells me you're less than a genius, Jones. Is he correct?' Jonah said nothing and I thought his silence might ignite the RSM's wrath. However, the senior NCO didn't seem to require an answer. 'Let me tell you what's going to happen here, son. You have until the end of the month to prove to me you can make a good Marine. If, by that time, you have not convinced me of your worth, I'll have you discharged. Do you *want* to go back to your cows?'

'No, Sir.'

'Well, the ball's in your court.'

After dinner, we held a squad meeting and decided to pound the theoretical stuff into Jonah at every spare moment. The big guy's happy head swivelled as he listened to what everyone had to say. He was, at first, happy to be the centre of attention but as the reality of the situation dawned on him a look of terror appeared in his eyes. Guys who were good at different subjects were to act as main tutors, but we were all to assist whenever possible. Everyone fired questions at him.

'What does SHAPE stand for?'

'What are the stages of radiation?'

'Why is the word "Gibraltar" written above the "globe and laurels"?'

'How do you judge distances when sighting a rifle?'

'How many VCs has the Corps been awarded?'

'When was the battle of Belle Isle?'

'Who is the foreign secretary?'

'When and how were the Royal Marines formed?'

'Why do we wear the Green Beret?'

'Who's the Prime Minister?'

And on and on and on … We got him so flustered, I wondered if we were doing more harm than good.

The grilling didn't cease until Saturday lunchtime.

With the evening approaching, like everyone else, Jack and I went through the anxieties of self-inspection hoping to be allowed ashore at our first try. Having been part of Jonah's coaching team all week, we were confident we could handle any questions.

Once again, Sammy was the first man to try his luck at the guardroom, and the first to return.

'What'd they get you on?' Jack asked.

'Who's the duty NCO?' Pete wanted to know.

'I dunno; never seen 'im before, but the bastard sent me back 'cause I have soap behind my *fuckin'* ear.'

'Give over!' Jack laughed. 'You 'aven't used soap since Monday.'

He gave Jack a look. ''E asked one of Willie Wanker's lot who was 'ead of the royal family, an' the dozy prick said the Duke of Edinburgh.'

Jack burst out laughing again. 'Give over! Who said that?'

'I dunno. One of the wankers, an 'e were sent back for it. I tell you, I'm not going back 'til the prick's off duty!'

A couple of guys stripped off their uniforms and began to re-clean and re-press. We wondered if all questions would be about government, royalty, and the like.

Jack and I inspected each other once more and declared ourselves immaculate. 'If we're not back in ten minutes, you'll know we made it out.'

The situation was beginning to resemble a low-budget escape movie.

When we got to the guardroom, Boswell strode out of the door and paced in front of us, seemingly admiring the sky behind us. He made an awesome sight in his dress blues, medal ribbons, and red sash. Two members of the Provost staff took our names, regimental numbers and barrack block details.

'What squad you in?' one of them asked.

'They're mine,' Boswell told him, 'and as mine I know they'll be immaculate.' He gave us a steely grin. 'Isn't that right? The Wrestler and The Banker, huh? Who would've thought?'

Jack and I looked at each other but said nothing.

'Take your belt off, Johnson. Who's the Prime Minister, Mason?'

'Harold Macmillan, Sergeant.'

Boswell looked at my belt, turning it over and inspecting the fold-back. 'Foreign Secretary?'

'Mr Lloyd, Sergeant.'

Boswell gave Jack a surprised glance. 'And without a prompt from your oppo, laddie. I'm impressed.' He moved behind me. 'Show me your insteps, Johnson.'

I lifted my right heel and then my left. 'We didn't know you were on duty today, Sergeant,' I risked.

'That's because I'm filling in for someone who just succumbed to the dreaded lurgy.' He moved in front of us again. 'You'll do. I'm still reeling from your political knowledge, Mason. Well done. Okay, that's it. Off you go.'

'If I go back to the room, will I have to go through another inspection when I get back?' I asked.

'Why not? Any number of mishaps could occur in that time. What's it to be? Go ashore now, or run back and tell your wee squaddies that I'm the one on the gate?' He smiled. 'Tell everyone they'd better be ship-shape or make out their last will and testament.'

I turned to Jack. 'Why don't you wait here for me?'

He looked at Boswell. 'Nah. I'll be in't café across the road.'

I ran back to H Squad rooms and told everybody that the duty NCO was Boswell and what he'd said.

Sammy wasn't happy. 'Jesus fuckin' Christ! What time is it? I'm waitin' until the four o'clock change of the duty NCO.'

'The Pubs'll be closed by then, Sam.'

'I don't give a monkey's.'

Pete accompanied me when I returned to the guardroom. Boswell smiled. 'Told all yer wee squaddies, have you? Put them in a state of panic? Go on, get outta here. Make sure you're sober when you come back on board. Now, Bell, take off yer belt and tunic and tell me what a bowline is.'

As Jack and I walked toward the town centre, we heard Pete call and we waited for him to join us.

'You made it through! Did Boswell have something else to do?' I said.

'Yeah, I couldn't believe ma bleedin' luck. The Officer of The Day came to talk to 'im. 'E just handed me the stuff I'd stripped an' told me to be'ave.'

'We're off to a coffee bar to see this partie, Diane, that me an' Banker fancy,' said Jack. 'Ya wanna come along?' Pete had heard Jack and me kidding each other about who was going to end up with her.

'What 'appens if this bird wants to clue up with me, insteada one of you two?'

I laughed. 'That'll never happen!'

'Give over!' Jack bellowed as he put his hand on Pete's shoulder. 'Banker only chats up parties with class.'

'Bullshit,' Pete replied with a grin. 'You wait an' see.'

'Bullshit? Ya think? You try cashing in on this partie an' 'you an' me will 'ave a serious fuckin' chat. Got it?'

Pete shrugged Jack's hand off his shoulder. 'Don't get yer knickers in a twist. Anyways, whatever 'appens, do ya think this 'ere Diane can rustle up a coupla fuckin' friends?'

'We plan to ask,' I said.

'Yeah, but while you're askin', make sure ya stress the word *fuckin'*, okay.'

'We might put it a little differently.'

'No dogs allowed, either.'

'You know you don't have to come with us.'

We entered the coffee bar and heard the first comment: 'Bloody Royal Marines. Bring down the tone of any place.'

We ignored it but Diane must have heard the remark because she immediately hurried across the room, weaving her way between tables, to confront the unkempt pacifist. 'Tell me, Fred; what makes you so special? You draw your dole money and then look to the world to do you a favour. Why don't you look for a job?'

'What's it got to do with you?' the man asked.

'Plenty! You think buying one coffee allows you to sit for hours and carp at people who actually spend money here. We're not a charity so please, do us all a favour, and take your business across the road.' Fred looked embarrassed but didn't move. 'Well, what are you waiting for? Go on, get out!'

The man rose to leave: 'Bloody typical! Put down a man who's out of work.'

'The only thing you're out of, Fred Dawson, is ambition!'

I turned and smiled at Jack and Pete, proud of the partie who was going to be mine. Unfortunately, they also were smiling and Jack was actually nodding. Diane returned to the serving side of the counter, while we sat on stools at the paying side.

'Hello. Paul and Jack I know. Who are you?'

'Pete. Pete Bell. Pleased ta meet ya,' said our unusually charming squaddie, as he rose halfway off his stool and smiled.

Diane returned the smile. 'Three coffees?'

'Please,' Jack agreed. 'You remembered my name,' he added, sounding hopeful.

'That was some speech,' I said with admiration.

'It's always been the same. I heard it directed at my husband often enough.'

Pete's head lifted sharply. 'You're married to a machine?'

'I was. He's dead.'

'Oh. Sorry to hear that. Where'd 'e get it?'

'Crossing the road in Deal.'

'Crossing the road! Death before dishonour, eh?'

'Not very funny, Pete.'

'I'm sorry. I opened me mouth wi'out thinkin'.'

And thereby killed his chances. Once we had our coffees, Diane turned to the man who seemed to run the place, 'I'm going to take a break, Dad, if that's okay with you.'

'Go ahead girl, you deserve it.'

She came around to our side of the counter and perched on the stool next to me. Pete mouthed 'bollocks' and immediately surveyed the place for alternatives. Jack sipped his coffee.

'I thought I'd see you last weekend,' she said to me.

'I was hoping to see you too, but we had to go to The Smoke to line The Mall for Haile Selassie. Didn't you see us on the telly?'

She laughed. 'Of course I didn't. Was it a speaking part?'

'Can't say it was.' I grinned. 'Are you free tonight, or am I still too unaccustomed to life in the company of genteel civilians?'

Jack's eyebrows rose.

She laughed. 'It wasn't your relationship with the general public I was concerned about. Did you find a girl last weekend? Or the one before?'

'Unfair. I'm damned if I did and damned if I didn't.'

Her eyes were still laughing as she rubbed the stubble on top of my head, 'Don't look so disappointed. I'll see you tonight.'

That put the grin back on my face. 'Would you happen to have two friends for my sad-sack oppos here?' I asked.

'I'll make some calls and see.' She grinned at Jack. 'Can you wait here for a while?'

She returned in about fifteen minutes, 'My friends Carla and Judith will be here at seven.'

Jack beamed at her. 'Thanks, Diane.'

'Me too,' added Pete.

'Look, guys. My dad owns this place and I don't want to leave him alone, so I'm going back to work. See you later?'

'I hope you guys don't end up with a couple of dogs,' I joked as we stepped onto the pavement.

'As long as she's easy, I don't give a shit,' said Pete with a Yorkshire man's directness.

'I'm takin' the best-looking one,' Jack said. 'If she's also the easy one, you're outta luck.'

Pete gave Jack a look but said nothing.

We found a café and attacked homemade steak-and-kidney pies, chips, peas, bread with real butter, and large mugs of strong tea. At five-thirty we walked to The Nelson Arms. I thought we'd be the first customers, but Jonah was already roosted in what had obviously become his place of honour at the end of the bar.

'Hey, Jonah. How'd you get here before us?' I asked.

'He has a special arrangement with the management.' Proud Jill gave a knowing wink.

'Ya got out without a problem then?' Pete said. 'See 'ow I look after ya.'

'It wasn't that,' Jonah protested. 'Boswell didn't bother to inspect me or ask me any questions. 'E said it was probably my last time ashore as a member of H Squad, so I could just go.'

We quickly changed the subject, but I did notice Proud Jill's secretive smile. The three of us limited ourselves to a couple of pints, not wanting to load up too much before picking up our dates. We took our time returning to the cafe, buying the sports edition of the evening paper to find out Manchester City had won their game.

Diane's friend Carla looked like one of Max Factor's best customers. She wore so much dark make-up around her eyes, I thought she must be consumptive. The girl saw no reason to close her mouth as she chewed gum. However, she did have a couple of good points that she proudly displayed for all to see. Her hair, faux-leather jacket, blouse, broad plastic belt, socks, shoes and handbag were all black. She softened the image with a pink brooch on her lapel and a pink gadget to imprison her long, frizzy auburn hair.

Judith looked like a librarian. Her beige sweater and cardigan matched and she had a string of pearls around her throat. She wore a tartan skirt, nylons and flat shoes. There was little evidence of make-up but her grey eyes and mousy hair shone. I hoped Jack would find her attractive because Carla seemed perfect for Pete's stated requirements.

We all shook hands.

'There's one thing you need to know,' I said. 'The three of you are dating fairies tonight.' Carla laughed nervously, Judith raised her eyebrows, and Dianne smiled knowingly.

'What The Banker means,' said Jack, 'is H Squad, our squad, are a buncha fairies. Boswell's Fairies.'

'Bankers, fairies, it's all too much for a sheltered girl like me,' said smiling Judith.

We discussed what we wanted to do. Pete, Jack and I knew exactly what we wanted to do, but even Pete was reluctant to state it openly. The Ritz was out as far as Diane and Judith were concerned. We could not agree on a film to watch and the idea of roller-skating didn't appeal to us. We ended up in a glass-and-plastic pub that played music by Mantovani. The women ordered drinks that featured fruit and veg while we men stuck to pints of bitter.

'We 'ad a great time in London last week,' Jack told Carla. 'Why don't you tell 'er aboud it, Pete!' His eyes showed he was not making a request.

'I'm tellin' Judith aboud it, so *you* tell Carla what we did.'

Jack's voice matched the look in his eyes. 'Remember what I told ya?'

Diane and I finished our drinks and left them to it.

As we walked hand in hand through Deal, Diane and I told each other about our backgrounds. She had impulsively wedded Michael Threllfall when he joined up and been married for a mere five weeks when, seven months ago, he broke a leg during training. He was on crutches when he left hospital in the rain, and foolishly started to cross a road in front of a stationary bus when a speeding car appeared and flipped him. She had no children and lived with her parents above the coffee bar. That news depressed me, as I had assumed that a woman who had been married would have a place of her own. Then I felt a twinge of guilt. Yes, Father, I thought, I'm becoming as shallow as the liars, cheats, and thieves you think I live with. We walked and talked and I took in the beauty of Diane. She was lovely to look at and seemed to have a beautiful personality. It made me happy to realise my supercilious parents would highly approve of her, save for her father owning a coffee bar.

She slowed to gaze at a dress in a shop window. I suggested she step into the shop's recessed doorway for a better view of the garment. Once we were in the somewhat secluded space, I folded her in my arms and kissed her. It had been three months since I had kissed someone and the way Diane responded made me believe that she was as needy as I was. My hands were about to start an exploratory journey when she broke away and fiercely whispered, 'Let's go down to the beach.'

It wasn't the quiet, romantic spot I'd anticipated. White hats and belts lay on the pebbles near shadowy forms, some of which moved rhythmically in the moonlight. A few cigarette ends glowed and we could hear noises lovers made; giggles, moans, slaps, sighs and calling on God. There were peals of laughter, and someone crying. As bodies moved, displaced pebbles clinked together. Snatches of conversation were borne on the slight breeze that blew in from the English Channel. I tried to gauge Diane's feelings. She looked at me, shrugged, and gave a thin smile that said, *'it's this or nothing'*.

As we searched for a remote spot, the crunching of pebbles beneath our feet drowned all other sound. We walked to the water's edge and turned west. After a while, we stopped and kissed.

'Is the tide coming in or going out?' Diane asked.

'Well, the moon's waning and …' I had no clue what, if anything, that meant. 'I've no idea,' I said. 'We'd better go up the beach to make sure we don't have to move later.'

'Really? I thought Marines knew everything.'

We found a reasonably secluded spot and I redistributed stones in an attempt to make the area comfortable, but there were so many it was a pointless exercise. I took off my belt and hat, and unfastened the clips and buttons of my tunic. Diane spread her coat on the pebbles so we could lie on it. We wriggled around in an attempt to make the makeshift bed less lumpy. The circumstances were not ideal but they were tolerable. We started with a rush, then restarted more slowly. Diane asked me to stop moving; to lie still on top of her. I felt her stomach spasm a couple of times and tasted the saltiness of her tears. I wasn't sure if she'd experienced some sort of orgasm. Except for my gentle kisses, given mainly as impetus for her to move, we stayed immobile. After several minutes, she started to stir beneath me and I took up the rhythm her body dictated. A short while later she climaxed, urgently whispering 'Michael, Michael, Michael, oh God, Michael.'

Michael! What was it with the women I clued up with? One was in denial about a physical problem and one calls for her dead husband. Why can't they all be like Maggie? You rotten bastard, I told myself. She's hurting and you're being a prick. What am I supposed to do, I asked the voice, pretend I'm Michael? No, arsehole! Just keep going as if nothing happened. I soldiered on.

'Stop. Stop it,' Dianne suddenly urged as she squirmed away and tried to eject me.

'What the fuck!'

'If we go on, I'm going to scream.'

'Nothing wrong with that.'

'On a beach full of people there's lots wrong with that.'

We were done. I rolled away and started to feel for discarded clothes.

'I can't find my undies. Help me look for them, please,' she said. The catch in her throat wasn't because of missing undies.

I found them. 'Here.'

'Well done. Now, wrap the condoms in them and I'll get rid of them at home. We don't want to leave them for kiddies to find.'

'So I'll be walking you home while you have no undies on?'

'That's right. Are you shocked?'

'Not so much shocked as turned on. About taking the condoms home; is that what everybody does?'

'I hope so. If not, I suppose it's because some guys take undies back to the barracks as souvenirs. You forget I was married to a Marine.'

'Not guys from H squad,' I said loudly and proudly. 'We're a bunch of Fairies.' Pebbles along the beach jangled as people twisted to see who had made such a statement.

Somewhere to our far right a voice said, 'Give over.'

A concerned voice asked, 'What's she doin' to ya, mate?'

A woman giggled and said 'Shhh.'

Diane asked. 'Was that Jack?'

'Who else?'

'Judith always said she'd never have sex on the beach.'

'Needs must, I suppose.'

'That's a great line. I'll use it on her. *Needs must, Judith*?' She giggled, then quietened. 'Sorry about before. I promise it won't be like that again. I'll get my folks out of the house and we'll do it properly.'

'You know you called me Michael?'

She paused. 'Yes, now I think back. You're the first since him. Sorry.'

Jack was on his bed playing solitaire. 'How'd you get on?' I asked.

'Fuckin' ay!' A broad grin broke out on his face. 'I clued up with Judith and ended up doin' her on the beach. What about you?'

'Yeah, the same. We heard one of your "give overs".'

Pete arrived. 'Hey, how'd it go?'

'It were a bit funny at first but it all worked out in the end,' he said.

'How funny?'

'Well, me an' Carla went for a poxy walk and came to this 'ere bus shelter. She said the busses on that route stopped at nine and we could 'ave a bit of a cuddle there. I started to pull 'er knickers down an' she got all righteous, said she didn't 'ave sex with guys she'd only known a couple of hours. I pissed off ta the Ritz. An' then, wouldn't you know it, she turns up there. I was getting' cosy with a right looker when she comes up an' makes a bleedin' scene. Tells the girl I was wiv, if she didn't plan on 'aving sex wiv me, I'd dump her somewhere. This girl looks at me like I'm Jack the fuckin' Ripper or summat, slaps me face, and runs off. Carla laughed and I shouted she was a right shit, an' she shouted summat back, and then't bouncers come over an' tell us ta leave. When we was outside Carla bursts out laughing, says we're a pair an' takes me to the flat she shares wid two girls. They was out, so we 'ad a couple of shags, an' 'ere I am. Decent night, really.'

When we reached the guardroom late Sunday morning, there was no one outside, so we entered our details in the shore-leave register and left.

We strode into The Nelson Arms and found Jonah in his place. Proud Jill pulled three pints. Jack bought the round, but the barmaid refused to take payment for Jonah's drink.

'His drink is on the house. You just make sure you never tell him it's his shout, seeing as how you never have to buy him anything in here,' Jill quietly warned us.

'What about when we're drinking elsewhere?' I asked with a grin.

'He won't be drinking anywhere else, unless it's with me.'

Diane and Judith walked into the place five minutes later. Jack ordered their fruity concoctions while I introduced them to Jonah and Proud Jill. Once the drinks were on the bar, I encouraged the versatile barmaid to demonstrate her muscular prowess. She switched on the radio and tuned to Family Favourites. The barmaid raised her arms and started to flex her breasts in time to the beat of *Volare*, swaying her hips at the same time. Judith and Diane tried emulating the barmaid but didn't have enough muscle control and they burst into peals of laughter. Jack nudged me, nodded, and moved his eyes to indicate I should look around the bar. Every Marine who had arrived after us was watching the cabaret intently. Some must surely have been entertaining the idea of separating the two beautiful and playful women from their recruit escorts. Jack and I finished our pints and almost dragged our dates out of the pub.

Diane invited the three of us to her place for the afternoon.

'Judith and I can listen to records while you two watch the footy on TV.'

'Footy?'

'You know exactly what it is and if you don't want to watch it, you can always listen to records with Judith and me,' Diane threatened as she punched me in the ribs.

'Give over!' exclaimed Jack. 'Footy's a great word! I'd rather watch the news than listen to a partie's records. Cliff Richard and that wanker Pat Boone, right?'

'Don't forget Ronnie Carrol and Ronnie Hilton.' Judith laughed at us.

Diane was equally amused. 'Not to mention David Whitfield.'

Diane's parents greeted us warmly, then apologised for having to leave.

'We're off to your gran's. No need to come along; we'll tell her you send your love.'

We waited for a short while in case her parents might have forgotten something. Then Jack and I started to take off our uniforms.

'You have no idea how hard we work to keep our things in good shape. It'd be criminal to get them creased or dirty. Why don't you take off your outer clothes too? That way no-one will feel awkward.'

Diane screamed with laughter. 'Paul Johnson, I'm ashamed of you.'

'What?' I didn't see anything wrong with the idea.

'That is *so* feeble. Couldn't you come up with anything better?'

'I tried, but I couldn't think of anything else.' I grinned.

'Come on,' she took me by the hand and led me to her parents' bedroom where everything came off, and Michael did not intrude.

Jack and I returned to The Depot around ten and found Pete already on board.

'You guys 'ave any cash?' he asked.

'Yeah,' I said. 'I've got a little. Why?'

'I took a partie down the beach. When I got back 'ere, I found oil on me bleedin' blues. I gotta buy a new uniform before the next time we 'ave to parade in full dress.'

'When's that?'

'Fuck knows. Tomorrer mornin' we're in battle dress, but I dunno after that. Ya know Boswell. 'E could send us away ta change just 'cause 'e needs a piss.'

I gave him four pounds and some change. Jack added three and change.

'Thanks guys. I figure Dusty an' Ron'll probably 'ave summat. I don't think I can take anythin' from Jonah. 'E'll probably be gone before I can pay 'im back. Pity, 'cause 'e must be loaded. 'E just bleedin' sits at the corner of that bar and drinks all night for free.'

'There's always the other guys in the squad.'

'Yeah, I know. I'll wait for Dusty and Ron and then see 'ow much I still need. Ya know what time the bleedin' clothin' store opens?'

We couldn't remember but, as civilians staffed it, consensus was it would be at eight. We waited up with Pete, listening to the stories of guys returning on board. There had been a fight at The Nelson Arms but no-one in H Squad had been involved. Apparently a Marine took offense when someone asked his girlfriend if she'd been one of the parties who had attempted to emulate Proud Jill. It seemed everyone had heard about Judith and Diane's attempt at copying the bouncy barmaid's party piece.

'Leddus know when ya finish with oitherer dem two judies,' a Scouse requested.

Jonah returned around two, 'in case you guys wanna teach me more stuff'. He heard about Pete's problem and insisted his oppo accept the ten pounds he thrust at him. I could tell Pete didn't want to admit to his oppo that he might not be around long enough to get the money back. He must have reasoned he could always give the money to Proud Jill, given it seemed the two of them were going to be together no matter what, and he made Jonah happy by accepting the money.

After parade the next morning, we learned how to roll away from an opponent during unarmed combat or to quickly regain our feet after being thrown or tripped. We learned to hold our arm in an arc and to ensure that initial contact with the ground was with the back of one's hand, wrist or forearm. The arced arm then turned the fall into a shoulder roll and momentum brought one to one's feet again. Once everybody got the knack of it, we rolled all over the gymnasium.

The afternoon was devoted to a fifteen-mile route march. Pete had made it through the day without having to parade in his blues. He purchased the new uniform at lunchtime and immediately had himself measured for alterations. The finished garment would be ready at five-thirty. It would then down to him to get it up to scratch by the next morning. Those of us in the room helped in any way we could. That evening, everyone practised rolls. Men in fatigues rolled in their rooms, in the corridor and in the NAAFI. We rolled to and from the galley and anywhere else we travelled.

I started a roll as I went to the guardroom. Too late, I saw a young lieutenant approaching. As I came out of the roll and gained my feet, I whipped my hand to my head in salute.

He returned the acknowledgement. 'Nice manoeuvre, Marine. We'll have to have that incorporated into the manual. Carry on.'

'I used ta think the army was a kindergarten,' Dusty said with disdain, 'but at least the Paras 'ad the dignity to act like grown men when they first learned the same manoeuvre.'

We continued to pound information into Jonah's head. The poor guy got so punchy, he called out answers in his sleep. It was frustrating for us to find that, after hearing something ten or twenty times, Jonah still did not remember or grasp its meaning. On Thursday night, Boswell came to our barrack rooms to check on Jonah's progress.

'What's the DSO, laddie?'

'The Esso sign ... no. Wait, Sergeant ... just a minute.' Boswell stood and waited while Jonah searched his memory. 'The Distinguished Service medal. No! The Distinguished Service Order.' Jonah beamed with pride.

'What does SHAPE stand for?'

'Er, Special ... no ... SHAPE ... Oh, Supreme Head and...'

'Supreme Headquarters Allied Powers Europe?'

'That's right, Sergeant! You said it too soon ... before I could say it.'

Boswell remained silent, and Jonah knew his excuse was lame.

'He's getting' ta know stuff, Sergeant,' said Pete.

Our DI said nothing but turned about and walked away. As he left, we all fell silent, worrying about what would happen to our largest fairy.

After all, save G and H Squads, left the parade ground on Friday morning, the last day of the month, Boswell ordered Jonah to report to him.

'Marine Jones,' he started. 'The Adjutant has directed me to decide whether or not I should keep you in my squad. I propose a ten-lap race around the parade ground. If I win, you're gone. If you win, you get to stay, at least for the time being. Fair enough?'

'Yes, Sergeant,' Jonah said nervously.

'Bell?'

'Here, Sergeant!

'You are in charge of H Squad until I relieve you.'

The two men handed their peaked hats to Pete, then, at Boswell's prompt, jogged to the corner of the square. We had paraded in dress blues that morning, and were therefore wearing our studded parade boots. As Boswell neared the corner, he slowed down to keep his purchase and Jonah had the sense to do the same. Both men still had difficulty staying on their feet, their boots refusing to take a solid grip on the parade ground's concrete surface. Pete stood us easy and we turned slowly around as we watched the race. We all cheered for Jonah and the noise of our encouragement grew with each lap. It was obvious Boswell was allowing Jonah to win and we began to think our friend's troubles were temporarily over. As the two competitors passed the RSM's office during the eighth lap, the senior NCO emerged to watch the race.

G Squad had paraded in fatigues as they were about to go on a route march. Willie Wanker stood them easy and allowed them to watch Jonah run for his life.

Jonah was a step ahead of Boswell as they started the tenth lap and G Squad cheered our big guy on.

'Let's make a finishing tape,' Pete suggested. 'Scouse, Taffy, hold your arms out.' Then he changed his mind. 'No, I'll do it,' he said and he pushed Taffy aside and touched knuckles with Scouse.

The racers were neck-and-neck as they turned the last corner and headed toward the finish. I urged Jonah on as loud as I could. Everyone was shouting some form of encouragement.

We so concentrated on willing the big guy to win; we were oblivious to anything else. The nearer the pair got to the finishing line, the louder the noise became. The squad broke ranks and formed a vee into which the two contestants would run as they neared the end of the race. With ten yards to go, Jonah was ahead by a stride. His open mouth stretched down and back in a grimace as he put his final effort into reaching the finishing line.

'Come on Jonah.'

'Fuckin' run, Jonah!'

'Come on!'

He charged across the line ahead of Boswell, bursting the outstretched arms aside as he did so. Everyone then milled around him, congratulating him and slapping his back and shoulders while he put his hands on his knees and sucked in great gulps of air.

'Sergeant Boswell!' the RSM yelled out, as he approached.

'Regimental Sergeant Major!'

'Restore order on *my* parade ground *now*!'

We scrambled to form ranks of three before Boswell could bark the order. He gave us a few seconds to measure an arm's distance between each man, while he calmed his breathing. The RSM meanwhile paced to and fro in front of the squad, the veins on his neck pulsating as he waited for Boswell to present us to him.

'H Squad at your disposal, Sir,' Boswell shouted to his superior.

'What the fuck did I just witness?'

Boswell explained the reason for the race and the RSM moved to where Jonah, still gasping for breath, stood at attention.

'Do you accept the conditions of the race, son?' he asked.

'Yes, SIR,' Jonah punched out in a happy, if breathless voice.

'Umm, it seems to me that the difference in ages between you and Sergeant Boswell gave you a distinct advantage. Don't you agree?'

'Not really, Sir.' Trepidation entered Jonah's voice.

'Not really?' The RSM turned away. 'Corporal Wilkins.'

'Yes Sir!'

'Send me your fastest man. On the double.'

Boswell started to protest. 'If you will leave matters to …'

'Leave matters to you! Your fairies were jumping up and down and whooping like a women's' hockey team on *my* parade ground! It seems matters have gotten out of your control, Sergeant. You will now allow me to put things right.'

The Wanker did as ordered. 'Right away RSM. Blackburn! Report to the RSM on the double.'

Keith Blackburn ran up to the RSM, and halted. 'Marine Blackburn, Sir.'

'Blackburn, you will race against Jones here. Let us assume that you two are the representatives of your respective squads. You are to race ten laps around the parade ground. If, at any time, I believe you are not putting your all into the race, I will charge you with malingering, conduct contrary to good order and military discipline and anything else I can think of. Do I make myself clear?'

'Yes, Sir.'

'Good. Sergeant Boswell, Corporal Wilkins.'

'Sir,' both men responded.

The RSM was in full flow, his voice crisp and clear. 'You will see to it that silence is maintained in the ranks at all times. There will not be an outbreak such as I witnessed just moments ago. Both squads will stand to attention throughout the race and you will put any man who moves or flaps his lips on a charge. Have you both got that?'

The race commenced behind us and so we were unable to witness its start. We could, however hear the sharp strikes of Jonah's steel studded parade boots and the dull thuds of Keith Blackburn's composition-soled work boots. Jonah didn't stand a chance. Not only had he just run the race against Boswell but also, as he approached every corner in this new race, he had to reduce speed in order to stay upright while his opponent hardly slowed. I didn't want a charge for moving my head, but I did swivel my eyes so far to the right that after a while they began to hurt. Keith Blackburn came into view first, followed by an already ailing Jonah. Once they passed beyond my sight I listened to the sounds of the boots hitting the ground and attempted to assess how Jonah was faring. The thuds of the rubber boots grew louder as they passed behind us and then faded. When Jonah followed, not only did I hear his boots, but also his laboured breathing. I again swivelled my eyes in their sockets and waited for Keith Blackburn to come in view.

Jonah was falling further behind and would soon be lapped.

The RSM walked between our ranks. 'Eyes front,' I heard him yell at someone. I now had to be aware of where the man was before I swivelled my eyeballs but, as Jonah was so far behind, there was no longer the compelling need to follow the race.

'Your man's not doing as well against someone his own age.'

Boswell had taken up a position just behind the RSM, possibly out of a fear that someone might take a swing at the seemingly hateful man. There was an almost tangible feeling of anger in the air that grew as the race progressed and Jonah's life in the Marines trailed away.

The RSM marched out of our ranks with Boswell in tow. The two men stopped at a point where the RSM must have thought they were beyond our hearing distance.

'I am surprised, Sergeant, that a man of your experience chose this inappropriate way of trying to sort out a problem that should have been dealt with more decisively. Did you think matters would improve if you delayed for yet another week? Jones has to go. That is an unfortunate, but undeniable fact. Your circus act has done nothing but foster false hopes in the man and his squad-mates. They may be 'Boswell's Fairies' but they are still worthy of respect. I trust you will find some way to build something positive here?'

'I will try, RSM.'

By the time the race came to its end, Jonah's pace had slowed to a weary jog and Keith had lapped him twice. The man from G Squad quietly resumed his place in the ranks and Willie marched his squad off the parade ground.

'You know what to do, Sergeant Boswell.'

'Yes, Sergeant Major. Jones!'

'Yes, Sergeant.'

'Report to the guard room immediately.'

When we returned to our rooms at lunchtime, the Provost staff had already stripped Jonah's bed and emptied his locker. We heard later that Boswell somehow fixed matters so that Jonah would train to be a navy chef. He was too large for a ship's galley, but at least our friend would not revert to tending cows.

Our ranks increased to thirty again. Spike Kielly was a Geordie who had once been in G Squad. 'I joined up 'cause I couldn't getta job fer love ner money,' he told us as we sat on our beds and watched him put his things in what had been Jonah's locker. 'Left the wife wid me parents so as she could keep 'er job but the bitch started to run around with anythin' in pants. I've bin back 'ome on compassionate leave ta kick 'er out de 'ouse and get divorced from 'er. She wanned shut of me as much as me of 'er, so it weren't any big deal getting' legally split.'

Tommy Sargent had broken his arm during unarmed combat instruction with D Squad. His limb mended, he was able to continue training.

Both men had the weekend to move into our barrack rooms, bring their gear up to scratch and be ready to resume recruit training the following Monday.

Pete had been able to settle most of his debts but was consequently so broke he planned to stay on board for the weekend. He handed me ten pounds and asked me to go to the Nelson Arms and give it to Jonah or Proud Jill.

On Saturday, Judith borrowed her father's car and the four of us travelled through the Kent countryside. When the women agreed Jack and I had shown enough restraint, we left the car and took up horizontal positions in two convenient fields. As the hedge between us didn't provide enough privacy for the women we had to move to the opposite ends of the meadows.

'It's your job to keep an eye out for any cows,' Judith told Jack who was mumbling about having to move.

'Cows! Give over,' he said. 'It's what they leave on't ground we 'ave ta worry about.'

The coffee bar was closed on Sunday, so Judith's parents drove to an exhibition in London and we used their home for activities they would probably have frowned upon.

Pete lined the squad up outside the barrack block on Monday morning, ready for Boswell's arrival. The man, as always, looked immaculate as he marched to where we waited.

'We seem to be more today, Bell. Bring out the new meat.'

Pete ordered Spike and Tommy to march up to the DI, and brought them to attention.

Boswell moved a step to his right. 'Name?'

'Sargent, Thomas Sargent, Sergeant.'

'Never in a million fucking years!' Boswell roared at the man. 'I'm the only sergeant this squad will ever have or need. Change your name, laddie. I mean NOW. No, forget it; I'll change it for you. John. That's your new surname as far as this man's squad is concerned. John comma Thomas. Anyone with the name of Sargent deserves to be called a prick. Fall in John, Thomas.'

Tommy turned back to us with a grin on his face.

Boswell took a step to his left and faced Spike. 'Tell me your fucking name is Major and you'll die where you stand!'

'Kielly, Sergeant.'

'A Celt?'

'Geordie born and bred, Sergeant.'

'You are no fun, Kielly. Fall in.'

Boswell took up his position in front of the squad. 'The first thing you two need to learn is you are fairies. The whole squad is a bunch of fairies. You will wear that distinction with pride. You will tell your girlfriend you are one of 'Boswell's Fairies'. You will tell your mates back home in squalorville you are a fairy. You will tell any Percy Pongo or three-badge stoker you are unlucky enough to meet, that you are a fairy. Do I make myself clear?'

'Yes, Sergeant,' the two men replied.

Boswell beamed and the sun glinted off his teeth. 'I said the *whole squad* is a bunch of fairies!'

'Yes, Sergeant!' we all roared. I imagined my father being told to declare to the world that he was a fairy.

'Furthermore, you two new men have the distinct honour of joining one of the best squads ever to pass through recruit training at this august establishment. Any previous squad that could measure up to this gang also belonged to me. That means I am the greatest Drill Instructor in the long and glorious history of Her Britannic Majesty's Corps of Royal Marines. I am justifiably proud of that fact and I will not tolerate anything from anyone that might spoil my enviable reputation. Anybody who fucks up, dies. Do I make myself clear?'

'Yes, Sergeant!' we all roared again with pride and happiness.

Every Saturday morning, the Officer of the Day made an inspection tour of recruits' barrack rooms. If he found a room below standard, he cancelled the inhabitants' shore leave until the area had been successfully re-examined. The residents also received two hours of extra drill to be performed on Monday night. Once a room was ready for the second inspection, its occupants were at the mercy of the officer's workload and whim. Our room failed an inspection once when the officer found some clean but unpressed items of clothing in Jonah's locker. It had happened before shore leave was a weekend option for us, and so the failure did not hit us too hard. Thereafter we reluctantly took turns to press Jonah's kit, telling him of our displeasure as we did so. Spike had taken Jonah's bed and locker and, since we did not have to look out for him as we had for Jonah, we found it easier to keep our quarters in pristine condition.

Ray Green's room had once failed inspection for a number of infractions and when the officer departed, Ray and his roommates set about putting the wrongs to right. They were still working on the problems when the officer, who was on his way out of the building, stepped into their room for the second inspection. The man realized their predicament and told them he would return later in the day, provided he found the time. The guys stood by their beds, waiting for the officer to return, until the 'last post' sounded over the Tannoy system.

We pressed, folded and stowed every item of kit in a prescribed manner. We displayed toiletry items on a clean khaki towel folded into an exact nine inch square. A clean, dry razor had to be in the 'open' position with the clean blade lying beside it. Clean, dry soap had to centrally rest in its clean, dry container. Tubes of toothpaste squeezed only from the bottom and a parallel toothbrush completed the grouping. Any other items could be subject to forfeiture. A flunky from the Provost Staff followed the officer with a rubbish bag into which the man dropped forfeited items. Young officers were generally sympathetic to recruits having a bottle of aftershave or an under-arm deodorant in their locker but older lieutenants, men who had worked their way up from the ranks, believed real men had no need of such items. Some guys hid their illegal products in the water closets at the end of the corridor. Jack and I originally put such items on the corner of the window ledge that extended beyond the sides of the windows, out of sight from anyone in our room. Unfortunately, the trick had been used by others and we forfeited our unessential toiletries on the first inspection. After that, we put the items in the pockets of our greatcoats and hoped we would not be ordered to turn them out. Others, once they were ashore, paid a threepenny piece at a civilian barbershop for a squirt from a choice of aftershaves or colognes.

Inspecting officers wore clean white gloves and ran their fingertips along ledges, locker tops, chair spindles, bed frames, and other surfaces on which dust might collect. The man with the rubbish bag also carried a supply of white gloves, handing a new pair to the officer whenever requested. Some officers ordered the occupants out of the room whilst the inspection took place. If the inspector found unadvised infractions, the occupants had to reclean the whole place to ensure perfection. As six men could easily keep a room spotless, it was a mental error that usually caused an inspection failure, such as forgetting to dust the underside of the air vent, or the unobserved entry of a leaf or feather through an open window just as the inspecting officer entered the room. Some officers seemed to view the routine with tedium; others took on the job with gusto.

Two weeks after Spike joined us, we read in Monday's company orders that our room had been adjudged the 'best in barracks'. The honour entitled us to the coveted prize of an ice-cream cake. After dinner on Tuesday, Spike reported to the galley to collect our reward. A large aluminium serving tray held vast quantities of variously flavoured ice creams, surrounded by mounds of synthetic cream. Junior squaddies came out of their rooms to catch a glimpse of the sought-after prize. They crowded around Spike as he swaggered along the corridor. The oblong tray was so large, Spike had to turn sideways to get it through the door to our room.

Once inside, he placed the tray on the central table. Six of us picked up our spoons and attacked the already melting dessert. It did not take long before all of the different coloured substances on the tray became a quagmire of confection. After consuming about a quarter of the dessert, we decided we didn't want any more. Jack volunteered to take the tray to the heads to clean it and then return it to the galley. Some of the junior squaddies were aghast that we should even consider such a wasteful action.

'Come on, you guys. Led us 'ave what's left. We'll clean the tray off for ya. We'll even return it to the galley, if ya want.'

'Give over! Win yer own fuckin' tray,' Jack yelled at the guy.

Spike had other ideas, ''Ang on a sec, Jack.' He walked into the corridor and addressed the crowd, 'What's it worth to ya?'

'We'll clean your boots for a week,' offered one whose boots must still have been brown and had yet to realise how paranoid a Marine can become over his toecaps.

'We'll press your uniforms for a week,' another naïve recruit offered.

'We'll do your next watch on guard duty.'

Bingo! Spike pointed to the man, 'Are ya all 'ere or in yer room?'

'Yeah,' the man looked about him. 'I think so.'

'Right. Lead the way.'

The guy was from K Squad and he started along the corridor and down the stairs, followed by Spike. Jack trailed them with the tray. Pete and I left Ron and Dusty in the room and set out behind Jack. Spike called the six recipients of our largesse into the corridor while Jack entered their room and placed the tray on the central table.

'D'ya all accept the trade of the ice-cream against standin' in fer us on our next guard duty?'

'Yeah,' the six chorused.

'Ya gotta finish what's on the tray, otherwise someone from another room will say they woulda done so. Agreed?'

'Agreed,' said six salivating mouths.

'Right. I want everyone's name and number so we can arrange the guard-duty-swap with the Company Sergeant Major.' The ice cream continued to melt as Spike wrote down the six sets of details. When he finished, he gave them a curt nod. Six spoons flashed in the artificial light as the lower caste of recruits dug into the brightly coloured mire. After about half of the tray's contents disappeared, a couple of guys stopped eating.

'Way-ey! What the fuck's up with you?' Spike demanded of them.

'I've 'ad enough, thanks,' one of them replied.

'Bollocks. You all agreed ta finish everythin' on the bleedin' tray. Ya gonna leave it for your mates to finish it for ya? What kind of squaddie are you?'

The guy still didn't get it. 'Yeah, but I'm full now. If I 'ave any more, I'll throw up.'

'I don't give a rat's arse. Get that spoon goin'.'

The other quitter did not need any such urging. He reluctantly started to gorge himself again.

The man with the full stomach lowered his spoon in the general direction of the tray, but he was not moving fast enough for Spike. 'Haway mon, get on with it then.'

As the reluctant spoon headed for the tray, vomit exploded from the man's mouth. He tried to turn aside and shower the regurgitated mess on the floor. Unfortunately, he was not quick enough and some of it fell onto the surfaces of the table, tray and a nearby bed cover. The five remaining eaters straightened up like jackrabbits and took a step away from the table.

'Who the fuck told ya to stop?' Spike shouted, 'Ya gotta eat *all* that shit.'

One eater's eyes bugged out in disbelief, but he carefully scooped up a spoonful of untainted ice cream from the tray. The rest remained motionless.

'Forget it, guys,' I intervened. 'Show over, Spike.'

Pete led the laughing Spike out of the door. 'Jesus aitch Christ! What's up with you lot? I was gonna 'ave them eatin' their own puke.'

'Yeah, but we might 'ave to depend on 'em to save our bleedin' lives one day,' I reminded him.

'Ah, come on! We was just 'aving a bitta fun. They wouldn't 'old it against us.'

'I sure as fuck would,' Jack said.

'Not if someone's life depended on it.'

'Maybe not. But by the time I'd thought about it, you might already be dead.' The guys returned the spotless tray to us fifteen minutes later. We still insisted they stand our next guard duty.

Our time at Deal was nearing its end. G Squad was now the Queen's Squad and we would assume that senior position in two weeks.

Dusty was not happy at the thought. 'Isn't this just fuckin' great. Joinin' Her Britannic Majesty's bleedin' Corps of Royal Marines 'as caused me to become a fairy and a member of a Queen's Squad. I just hope I don't run into any of my old mates from the Paras.'

In four weeks, we would depart for fourteen days leave before moving to Poole and water training. Our courses completed, we were going over much of the material again, especially drill. Boswell was a Drill Instructor after all and he was in his element when on the parade ground. However, he did give us a break by allowing us to parade in fatigues on many occasions. We were already practicing manoeuvres for our final parade.

We often occupied the parade ground with Willie Wanker and G Squad, now the supposed top recruits. On Thursday afternoon, Boswell marched us towards them as they stood at attention in rows of three, listening to whatever The Wanker had to say. Sammy was point man and he waited for the order to right-wheel, or to make an about turn, but it never came. He told us afterwards how he readied himself for the punches that would fly. But nothing happened. We marched through G Squad's ranks and not a word was uttered, nor a punch thrown. We were the top dogs.

'My apologies, Corporal Wilkins,' Boswell roared with a grin on his face. 'Ma wee fairies must be feelin' a tad frisky.'

Pete and Spike became oppos from the moment Spike joined us. Jack and I still saw Diane and Judith. A bird in the hand is a lot cheaper than one chased. Home-cooked food and sex every weekend were good reasons to keep up the relationships, but we also spent time ashore with our squaddies. Proud Jill kept us up to date on Jonah's new life. The big man was in Portsmouth, taking a cooks' course. He rode the train back to Deal every weekend, unless duty prevented him from doing so. On a couple of occasions, we found him sitting on his stool at the corner of the bar and we brought him up to date on our lives. He told us about peeling potatoes and slicing onions and how happy he was at the way his life had changed. However, he was no longer a fairy and a small gulf had grown between us.

Tommy Sargent, known as Comma, became Ray's new oppo. Their friendship was not as solid as most pairings in the squad, possibly because they had been thrown together by circumstance.

The Adjutant was on foot one morning and decided to make us one of his targets for the day. He walked along our ranks, stopping every now and then for a brief chat. He enquired what our thoughts were on different subjects, from life as a recruit to the cold war. I wondered if the man believed every answer given was an honest one, or did he realise we gave him replies we thought were expected, yet calculated to be the least engaging. The sooner he passed on to the next man, the better.

He stopped to talk to Ray. 'Tell me, Green, if there was some sort of serious incident and a number of stretchers were needed to transport the badly injured, what would you do?'

'I'd take doors from the barrack rooms and use them, Sir.'

'Good, very good.'

The Adjutant's groom appeared, leading his boss' horse to where we stood.

'Now, Green, can you find anything here that can be construed to be of a superstitious nature?'

'Yes, Sir. Your horse's shoes.'

'I meant something of a permanent nature.'

'Metal is pretty permanent, Sir.'

'Granted, but the horse is likely to disappear at any time, is it not?'

'The horse is not the lucky charm, Sir.'

'The two are irrevocably attached, Green.'

'I believe I answered your question correctly, Sir.'

'Come now, Green. If you didn't understand the question you should have said so.'

'I thought I did understand the question, Sir. You didn't say anything about permanent.'

'I think I amended the question.'

'I didn't hear that, Sir.'

'Then I put it to you Green that you need time to reflect on the matter. Sergeant Boswell!'

Boswell was standing at the man's elbow. 'Sir!'

'Give this man four hours of extra drill, during which time he can think the matter over.' He stormed away from our ranks, leaving his groom and horse wondering what to do next.

'Very good, Sir,' replied Boswell as he saluted the man's back.

Once the man was out of earshot, Boswell addressed Ray. 'You did well to keep your cool, Green. You showed me something there. Well done. I canna do anything about the extra drill, but at least ya have the consolation of knowing ya caused the Adjutant to show us all what an arsehole he is. Not that he needs much help.'

Ray completed the punishment in two nights. Comma took care of all his laundry and gear, making sure his oppo had everything he needed for the next day. The new respect both men felt for the other cemented their friendship.

We constantly received extra drill throughout our time at The Depot. Hours of it were handed out as punishment for any infraction not covered by a specific regulation. One would receive two hours for having an Irish pennant (Marinespeak for a piece of lint or cotton thread) adhering to his uniform. Being fractionally late, i.e. not five minutes early for any appointment, was also worth two hours. Speaking out of turn in Boswell's vicinity got the speaker two hours of pounding the parade ground in all weather. Part of one's face missed when shaving, insufficiently cleaned boot cleats, a tube of toothpaste with a depression in the middle, or not swinging one's arms high enough when marching around The Depot, earned the miscreant at least one hour of extra drill. Dumb insolence could get you innumerable hours, plus a physical beating behind some building. Anybody from a corporal up had the power to hand out the punishment. If some horny man's wife had a headache one night, it was a sure bet a recruit would get a beating or some unwarranted extra drill the next day. If any trained Marine suffered a hangover, he shared his distress with a recruit.

Wherever we were in The Depot, the threat of extra drill was omnipresent. If a recruit objected to an officious corporal jumping the NAAFI queue, he would likely be found to be guilty of some clothing infraction. The punishment was handed out so frequently, we accepted it as part of our training.

Rumour had it a corporal from the motor pool desired a partie who preferred a certain recruit. When the mechanic by chance espied the recruit under inspection outside the guardroom prior to going ashore, he dug some dirt out of his nose and smeared it on the back of the lad's tunic. He then reported the dirty tunic to the Provost Corporal who refused the recruit leave and awarded him four hours of extra drill.

There was very little drill involved in the punishment. Some DIs required a uniform change every ten minutes but most were happy to stand in the middle of the parade ground and watch everyone jog around the perimeter with their rifles held above their heads. If the weapon became too heavy and one let it rest on top of his head, no one cared, as the resultant headache was punishment enough for that minor offence. Spare rifles were always available for those too new to possess one.

Recourse existed for anyone who believed his punishment unjust. However, the convoluted rigmarole bore numerous risks, so it was easier and safer to suffer the drill.

As The Queen's Squad was excused Saturday morning room inspection, we stood by our beds for the last time with the belief that our room was immaculate.

A young Officer of the Day breezed into our room with his white gloves and clipboard. 'H Squad?'

'Yes, Sir,' Pete replied.

'I take it your room is clean. Kit and effects stowed as required.'

'Of course, Sir.' Pete flashed the man a smile.

'Indeed. Enjoy the weekend. I for one am looking forward to see how you men perform as The Queen's Squad.'

We all went ashore that weekend, but we also spent time on our uniforms, equipment, and boots. A few guys loaded up on Saturday, but on the following day we were all models of what the conservative civilians of Deal believed recruits in Her Britannic Majesty's Corps of Royal Marines should be. Being sober wasn't too tough, as many of us had a partie with whom to spend time. Everyone was back on board relatively early on Sunday night and the banter and horseplay was subdued.

On Monday morning, after inspections were over, the complement of recruits marched out of The Depot and around the town behind the Royal Marine band. As the senior squad, we were the first behind the musicians. We pounded the road's surface as one in time to *Men of Harlech, Colonel Bogey* and other familiar marches.

Boswell marched at our flank, not needing to call out the cadence or make corrections. We were The Queen's Squad; the greatest precision drill-team in the world. To show our prowess, we wore white lanyards on our left shoulders. We kept our rifles firmly tucked into our right shoulders. Peaked hats were pulled low over our eyes and we stared only ahead, not bothering to catch the eyes of the local females.

As we rounded a corner, the road surface changed from tar-macadam to concrete and flint. Boswell turned and marched backwards at our right flank, 'Come on, Queen's Squad, make the sparks fly.'

And we did. The band struck up the Corps march, *A Life on the Ocean Wave* and we drove our heels into the pavement. Thirty pairs of steel-tipped boots crashed into the flint, creating sparks.

'You've stopped the town, men. All eyes are on you. Keep it up!'

I heard people applauding.

A partie shouted, 'Hey Royal, you can come and spark me anytime,' and earned squeals of laughter from other women within earshot.

'Go Machines!'

Some sang the well-known words of the march.

Boswell had taught us to be arrogant and that is exactly how I felt. I remembered my banking friends and knew they would never feel the emotion of that moment.

We marched past the Deal Coffee Bar and I heard Diane call out, 'Let's go, Boswell's Fairies.'

We returned to the parade ground and the Adjutant rode to where we stood at attention. 'Have your squad stand easy, Sergeant.' His horse leathers creaked as he leaned forward in his saddle, and he seemed to relax in front of us. 'You men have made it to your last two weeks at The Depot. As The Queen's Squad, you are probably the best drill squad in the world and you have every right to be proud of that distinction. Your sergeant will plan a display which you will practice and use to demonstrate your prowess when you make your final parade. At the completion of your pass-out, you will enjoy two weeks leave, during which you can let off as much steam as you want. Each of you will receive a train ticket to the destination of your choice. You will have two weeks' pay, plus any savings you have accrued. Enjoy yourselves. Spend some time with your families as well as girlfriends. When the two weeks are up you will report for further training to Poole, which is in Dorset. In the meantime, I strongly urge you to act in a manner befitting your status as a member of The Queen's Squad. Every recruit in The Depot will look at you as an example of what he is striving to achieve and you must act accordingly. To date, you have made an impression on those of us who rate, as a better-than-average squad.' In the corner of my eye, I saw Boswell bristle at the perceived insult and I had to suppress a smile. 'Make sure we still have that impression when you leave in twelve days' time.' The polished leathers creaked again as the man straightened in the saddle, 'Carry on, Sergeant Boswell!'

The captain waited until we were all standing at attention again and then saluted us. He wheeled his horse about and, as he set off for the stables, rode toward the RSM who was approaching. He raised his riding crop to tap the peak of his hat. The RSM halted and snapped the officer a crisp salute.

'Good morning, Sir.'

'Morning, RSM. Good squad we have there, wouldn't you say?'

'They could do with a little more discipline, but overall they're not too bad, Sir. We don't want automatons.'

Boswell greeted the RSM. 'Good morning, Sergeant Major.'

'Good Morning, Francis. No need for formalities. Stand the men easy.'

Once we were again relaxed, he continued. 'I must tell you that I had serious doubts about the title of Boswell's Fairies, but it has had better results than I anticipated. If I know your sergeant here, he will have future squads assume the same identity. Therefore, I am taking this opportunity to tell you that you are the original Boswell's Fairies. That is something you will always remember. Who knows, ten, twenty years from now you might be speaking to someone who will boast that he was once a Fairy. How good will it feel to be able to reply that you were a member of the original squad of Fairies? You lost two members of your squad along the way, but it was for the good of you all, whether you believe it or not. Their replacements have made you a full unit again.' To my surprise, the man smiled. 'I'm wandering a bit here. I just wanted to remind you not to relax because you are The Queen's Squad. Now is the time to bear down even harder. You have completed the training here and now have two weeks to perfect yourselves on my parade ground. It is generally accepted that most Queen's Squads, on their pass-out, are the best drill team in the world. Although a squad matures every two weeks, you should not take the distinction lightly. To be the best in the world, for even a day, is something in which one should take great pride. The American Marines have enviable drill teams but they cover lapses in discipline by being flashy. That is not our way. We are men so well trained; we can depend on each other at all times. Because of that training, we have a thin chain of command; something you'll understand more when you join a Commando. What we have done here is instill pride and self-discipline in you all. The marching will be over when you leave here, but you'll be learning a serious craft for which your time at The Depot has been preparation. Use the next two weeks well. Make us remember you.' He smiled and nodded to us. 'Carry on, Francis.'

It was in the following week that Boswell revealed his plan for our final parade. Jack and I believed he was making it up as he went along. We learned what he taught us and tried to imagine what our final routine would be. The first practice after the Adjutant and RSM had spoken to us involved marching from one end of the parade ground to the other. Our DI then split us in half and the separated groups marched in opposite directions, passing between each other's lines before turning about and reforming. Boswell changed the formation of the squad. We practised with our rifles, slapping the brasses of the slightly loosened slings against the wood and metal of the weapons.

Since our first day on parade, we had counted the beat in our heads ... tup (pause) three, as Boswell had taught us. We counted aloud again for a day to ensure we had perfect timing. Whenever we clicked our heels, slapped our slings or slammed to a halt, we made but one sound. When the band rehearsed in our vicinity, Boswell had them play for us. He discussed with the musical director what music they would play during our pass-out. Drummers punctuated some of our moves. We made others in complete silence, save the bangs, slaps and clicks of our equipment.

'What're ya doing while we're on leave?' I asked Jack.

'I dunno,' he said. 'I know a few decent pubs where they'll put me up and I'll try an' drink 'em outta beer.'

'Nobody ya wanna see?'

'Nah. The fosters were all a bunch of pricks an' I never made any real friendships in the wrestling or the circus.'

'Why don't you come home with me?' I suggested. 'We could stay at my folks' house and use it as a base. We'd save money and have more to spend on good times in Manchester.'

'Give over! I'd be like a spare prick at a prossie's wedding.'

'Hey, if it doesn't work out, we'll take off.'

I kept at him, and in the end he agreed to my plan.

The day of our pass-out arrived. We all rose before dawn, and after an early breakfast went to the stores where we returned items belonging to Her Majesty which we would no longer need. We then dampened and smoothed the blanco on our slings and belts. We checked our white lanyards for smudges. We breathed on brasses we had cleaned the night before and gave them a final rub. When we were satisfied, we assembled the equipment and laid it out on our bare bedsprings. We washed the whites of our caps with soap and water, then breathed on and wiped their shiny black peaks. Everyone had purchased a new pair of white drill gloves and so we wore the old ones as we prepared our uniforms.

We stood in line in the head, waiting to ensure a call of nature would not occur while we were on parade.

At nine-thirty we started to dress. Boswell came to our rooms to go over the routine for the umpteenth time. Our drill instructor looked impressive in his dress blues and red sash. His medals and ribbons added panache. We inspected each other in the light of the sun that shone through the corridor's large windows. Boswell had arranged the postponement of our receiving pay and rail tickets until after the parade to ensure we had empty pockets. 'Listen up, Fairies,' he yelled. 'Today is the day and now is the hour. Does any man have a problem?' He searched faces as silence reigned. 'Okay. You men are H Squad. You are also Boswell's Fairies. You have become the squad I wanted and this is the culmination of your time at The Depot. Let's go out there and show the world something they will never see the likes of again; absolute perfection on the parade ground.'

Boswell lined us up in ranks of three at the rear of our barrack block. As we waited to hear the band, he walked along our ranks giving us the benefit of a friendly pre-inspection inspection. He asked us what we intended to do while on leave. He told us of times he had spent when on leave overseas.

I heard him talk to Dennis. 'Beats the shit out of banging a drum, eh Potter?'

'This is the best day of my life, Sarge,' Allison risked.

Boswell growled. 'I'm still a Sergeant to you, and ya need ta get a life, laddie. Have ya never heard of sex?'

After a short while, we heard the band play itself onto the parade ground. Then there were a few minutes of silence while the musicians prepared themselves and waited for some sign that we were ready.

When we heard the first notes of *Life on the Ocean Wave* Boswell brought us to attention. 'This is it, lads,' he said. He looked us over once more then barked, 'By the right, quiiiiiiiiiiick march!'

My chest swelled. We marched around the block, across the perimeter road, and made two circuits of the parade ground before coming to a precise halt in front of the reviewing stand. There were a number of minor dignitaries seated on the platform and I tried to pick out anyone I might know without moving my eyes too much. The commanding officer, the Adjutant, and, judging by the enormous chain around his neck, the Mayor of Deal, descended three steps and approached us. As the group reached each recruit, Boswell reported the man's name and then stood aside as one or other of the trio asked a question.

'Where are you from?'

'Is life in the Royal Marines all you expected it to be?'

'What hobbies do you have?' Oh, golf, collecting antique silver bowls?

'Do you intend to make the Royal Marines your career?' asked the mayor. In my head, my father again asked the same question. Did the man know we were a bunch of fairies? Did he think nine years was a holiday?

'I made that decision when I signed on, Sir,' I said.

The C.O. said, 'I suppose you're looking forward to seeing your family.'

I pictured my father and Jack shaking hands. 'Yes, Sir.'

It took about thirty minutes to complete the inspection during which time I caught sight of Diane and her mother. Both were dressed for church on Easter Sunday. I saw Judith with her twin-set and pearls. Carla was there, as ever in black. Even Jonah had somehow managed to turn up, Proud Jill hanging on his arm. There weren't many more; perhaps a total of twenty. Evidently, word of our prowess on the parade ground had not been loudly broadcast.

The three-man inspection team returned to the reviewing stand.

Boswell roared 'Left turn' and, after we'd turned and slammed our left heel into the right as one, 'Quick march!'

Our chests were out and our chins were in. We fixed our eyes on the head of the man in front. There were no wisecracks. Our timing, tup three, was exact, especially when the band stopped playing and we stressed the stamping of our boots and, tup three, the slapping of our rifle slings. Boswell didn't give a single order as we worked our way through the well-rehearsed routine. We slow-marched and quick-marched and performed adroit about-turns. We halted and re-started; all the time in harmony. We were thirty minds and bodies acting in perfect unison. The sun glinted off our brasses and peaked hats, and caused us to perspire under our blue serge tunics as we marched, turned, and wheeled around the parade ground.

I knew the routine had ended but it was still a disappointment when Boswell gave his solitary order, 'Squaaaaad HALT!' and the band started playing again.

It was over. People applauded us. There were a few immediately forgotten words about there being a field-marshal's baton in every knapsack from the CO. The mayor, thinking of all the money Her Britannic Majesty's Corps of Royal Marines brought to his town, said we were the pride of Deal. Then Boswell marched us off the parade ground and around the back of our barrack block. I felt a growing excitement at the thought of being free for two weeks. Jack and I would have sixteen days in which to do nothing but have fun. Then, after the break, we would report to Poole and then to Lympstone where we would be treated more like men than raw recruits.

'Did we make any mistakes on the parade ground, Sergeant?' Sammy asked.

'None that I could see, laddie.'

'So were we perfect, then?' Ray probed.

'Dinna push it, Green. Recruits'er never perfect but ya came mighty close. Let it go at that. You were near perfect fairies. That, in itself, is a unique distinction.'

Our drill instructor marched us to the armoury where we handed in our rifles, and then back to the barrack block. 'I'll see you all in Poole,' he said. 'Make sure you arrive there on time. Dismissed.'

We ran to our rooms as fast as our studded boots allowed. There we changed into our shoes and finished packing our kitbags. Not having civilian clothes, we would leave The Depot for the last time in uniform. We received our pay and tickets and then the Scots, Irish, Geordies and others with comparatively long journeys piled into a truck waiting to take them to Deal railway station.

Jack and I ate one more free meal in the galley before departing. Jonah was there and we shook hands and asked how he was, but he was no longer a fairy and we soon descended into an awkward silence. He told us he'd like to buy us a pint, if we turned up at the Nelson Arms, but Jack and I said we had other plans and wished him luck.

We gave our kitbags to the left luggage clerk at the station and went to the coffee bar to say our goodbyes to Diane and Judith.

Mr and Mrs Smethurst – Diane's parents – tended to their customers while the four of us went upstairs.

'Will we see each other again?' Diane asked.

'It's not likely,' I admitted. 'We still have a few months of training and then we'll be posted overseas.' It had occurred to me to promise to see her again, but I felt better telling the truth. 'I've had a great time with you,' I continued, 'and I thank you for your love and generosity. I'm sorry we have to split up, but there isn't much either of us can do about it.'

'It's okay. I know,' Diane whispered into my shoulder. 'We both knew this is the way things would work out. I have to say you're the last marine I'll ever date. I've had a good time and I'll be happy knowing you're alive and in one piece. You might drop me a letter or a card sometime.'

I pushed her away so I could look into her face. 'No, I won't, Diane. It's no good me making promises I won't keep. I mean, I haven't written to my parents since I joined up, so I can hardly claim to be a letter writer.'

We made love, but I was excited and she was depressed and it was over too quickly. We dressed in silence. I walked out of her parents' bedroom and banged on Diane's bedroom door.

'You ready, Jack?'

'Be right with ya, Banker.'

Diane joined me on the landing and I put my arm around her shoulders, 'Take care of yourself. Don't hang around with any more Fairies.'

Jack came out of the room without Judith. I heard her sniffle. He squeezed Diane's upper arm and headed down the stairs. I gave Diane another quick kiss and followed him.

'Look after yourselves, boys,' said Mrs Smethurst as she pressed a bag of sandwiches into my hand.

Dianne's father shook hands with us. 'Will we see you again?'

'Probably not,' I said, as Jack was saying 'Maybe.'

'You two should get your stories straight.' He smiled. 'It's been good knowing you. You're a couple of grand lads. Make sure you stay that way. Now off you go before the girls break down completely.'

Peter Lingard

LONDON

10th June 1960

During the journey to London, Jack, five other squaddies, and I tried to exhaust the bar car's beer stock. An inspector asked us for our tickets.

'What? You reckon we've flogged 'em, or what?' said someone.

'Just doing my job, guys. Going to delight the ladies in The Smoke, are we?'

His comment reminded me of the two parties from Haile Selassie's procession. I got my kitbag from the rack and blindly rummaged in it until I found the paperback I'd been reading. It was a boring novel but a handy place to keep odd bits of paper, including the one stuffed in my pocket by the partie who dubbed me 'Haircut'.

'Whaddya looking for?' Jack wanted to know.

'If I can find the paper with that older partie's number on it, we could look 'er and 'er friend up when we get ta The Smoke.'

'What partie? 'Ow old?'

'The one from London who put 'er number in my pocket when we lined The Mall. I told you about it.'

'Give over!' he said, as he grabbed my kitbag and prepared to dump its contents on the floor.

'I bleedin' found it already!' I yelled as I grabbed it back from him. I showed him the book. 'The number's in here.'

'Lemme see,' Jack shouted. 'I wanna see the bleedin' number before I get me 'opes up.' I unfolded the paper and gave it to him. He smiled. 'We're in 'ere. When we get tuh't Smoke, let's grab a room at't Armed Services Club an' call the number.'

Jack had purchased some civilian clothes during the day, but I wanted to see what, if any, of my clothes still existed at my parents' house. Consequently, we wore our dress blues. As I couldn't remember either of the two women's faces, we were dependent on them approaching us and our uniforms would mark us. We'd arranged to meet in a West End pub.

Most of the drinkers in the packed place were older than us. Jack ordered two pints of bitter. When the barman asked for payment, my oppo loudly said, 'How much! Give over. You must be bleedin' jokin'.'

The barman smiled. 'Your choice to drink 'ere, mate.'

We stayed at the bar, thinking we were more outstanding. A couple of queers tried to turn on to us, but when Jack growled at them, they smiled sweetly and left us alone. 'Every bleeder knows we're fairies,' he said with a grin.

Two parties further along the bar indicated an interest that we tried to maintain with the occasional smile, in case our dates failed to show. I ordered two more pints and we raised them in a toast to the two women.

'You two haircuts hedging your bets?' asked a voice behind us.

Jack and I turned to face our dates. I recognised Liz and was more than pleased to see the well-displayed body that had been so effectively hidden at our previous meeting. Her breasts jiggled slightly as we shook hands and I forgot the three-second rule.

'Down boy,' she said with a laugh. She turned to her friend. 'This is Caroline.'

Jack was drinking in his date's equally stunning appearance and I had to slap his back to break the trance.

'This is Elizabeth, Jack.'

Jack had already shaken hands with Caroline, so the four of us made a knight's cross of our arms. Two men who had been sitting at the bar offered their stools to our dates.

'What'll you have to drink?'

'A gin and it, please,' replied Caroline.

'It?' said Jack. 'What's an it when it's at 'ome?'

'It's a dry martini and I'll have the same,' said Liz. 'Two lumps of ice and just show the label to the glass,' she told the barman.

'It's no secret what we do for a living.' I said. 'What about you guys?'

'We're teachers, and definitely not guys,' Caroline advised.

'Just an expression,' I said. 'What do you teach?'

'I teach Latin, biology and hockey,' said Liz.

'Latin! Ugh. I was in hospital and missed my first week of Latin. Snowy never bothered to help me make up the lessons, so at the end-of-term exams I put my name on top of the paper and put my pen down. Nobody cared. Next term I took music instead. What a laugh that was.'

'Who was Snowy, the Latin teacher?'

'Yeah. Latin and chemistry.'

'Sounds like you might have had a bad teacher in a good school. I guess you didn't do so well or you would have signed on as an officer.'

'That's what my father wanted. Maybe I joined the ranks just to thumb my nose at him.'

'Kind of like cutting off your nose to spite your face, wasn't it?'

'You know ...' I stopped and drew a breath to control my anger, '... Jack and I just completed the first part of our training and have no wish to be analysed. Can we just have fun?'

Jack and Caroline had been discussing their respective backgrounds.

'Jack used to be a wrestler,' an impressed Caroline told her friend.

'She teaches maths and physics, as well as hockey,' an equally impressed Jack told me.

'What happened about your uniform that day?' Liz asked. 'By the time we got behind you, you were already a mess. Made me want to clean you up, but I got control of myself and left you my number instead.'

'Her Britannic Majesty gave us free replacements, but never mind about that. You really got me going when you squeezed my balls. I was worried I would still have the erection when the boss went by in her carriage.'

'I did *not* give your balls a squeeze!' Liz insisted loudly.

One of the men who had given up his barstool turned his head at the remark.

Liz looked icily at him. 'I didn't!'

'It wasn't for the lack of trying.' I grinned.

'Bend down a little, will you Jack,' Caroline commanded. 'I want to feel the top of your head.'

'Our two haircuts,' Liz said with a laugh as she ran her hand over my near hairless skull.

'You're a little different from the men we usually date,' Caroline commented.

My hackles went up. 'You can be sure I won't be anything like the guy in the car.'

'The guy in the car?' Liz frowned as she tried to work out to what I was referring. 'Oh, him! That was just something I made up for your benefit. I was teasing.'

'Teasing's out from now on.'

She threw me a mock salute. 'Yes Sir, General!'

'What's this different? 'Ow different?' Jack wanted to know.

'Well,' said Caroline, 'we generally date people in our own social circle; professional men, business men and the like. They're usually mid-to-late thirties, mainly because Liz and I are ten years, or so, older than you two.'

'Captains of industry,' Liz said with sarcasm.

Both women laughed.

Jack's hackles also rose. 'Paul used to be a fuckin' banker. Will that do?'

I tried to change the subject. 'So what made you agree to meet us tonight?'

'Well, I *did* put that paper in your pocket and you *have* come all the way from darkest Kent to see me, so I suppose I owe you a date.'

'We thought it'd be an adventure,' added Caroline.

'You don't owe 'im anything,' Jack said, ''im or me.'

Caroline laid a hand on Jack's cheek, 'Take it easy, Jack. We just want to have fun. Isn't that why you're here too?'

Jack's mouth opened and closed twice, as he weighed the situation. There was anger still in his eyes. Things were not going well. I turned around to see if the two women we had noticed earlier were still at the bar.

'Too late,' said Liz. 'Somebody already moved in on them.'

I had to smile. 'You don't miss much, do you? What would you like to do for the rest of the night?'

She paused for a couple of seconds. 'You've some pair on you, Haircut. You switched from me to them and back to me without missing a beat. Moreover, after you are caught doing it, you want to know how I would like to spend the rest of the evening. Presumably with you?'

'That *is* the plan.' I gave her my most disarming smile.

The quick smile she returned was humourless. 'I have heard tell that a bird in the hand is worth two in the bush, so to speak.' She caught the barman's attention, 'Another round please.' After the man acknowledged her order, she turned back to me. 'And on top of it all, you let me pay for the drinks.'

I'd been caught off-guard again. 'Relax. I'll pay for the round.'

'No, that's all right. I'm sorry; I was annoyed for a moment. I'm happy to pay.'

Jack started to tell a couple of stories from his wrestling days and I resigned myself to the belief that the women would remain with us until closing time and then say goodbye.

Liz put her glass on the bar and shifted her position on the barstool, effectively cutting us off from the other two. She grasped my hand to maintain her balance as she twisted around, then said, 'Tell me about yourself, Haircut. Forget the bravado. Just tell me about – well, tell me your name again and then you can carry on from there.'

'It's Paul. Paul Johnson.'

'That's right. Tell me all about Paul Johnson.'

Jack interrupted us to offer another round, but Caroline said she wanted to pay for it.

We left the pub shortly before closing time and took the underground to Swiss Cottage. We walked to a large building that seemed to be a block of flats. I anticipated a goodnight kiss and a farewell wave.

'This is it, Paul. It's been nice meeting you.'

I was right, but I wasn't having it. I backed her up to the wall of the building, cupped her chin in my hand and pulled her face toward me. She offered a slight resistance, but then she relented and wrapped her arms around my neck and a leg around my back.

'Are you the rough sort?' she breathed.

I thought it wisest not to answer. I pulled her to me again and continued kissing her. She lightly bit my tongue and then our tongues had a sparring match. I thought I was supposed to pin her tongue until I half-choked in the effort. She laughed.

After a couple of minutes Caroline spoke. 'Fun as this is, I need more. Let's invite these two in.'

'Damn it, Caroline!' Liz broke into laughter. 'I had this one wondering whether or not I wanted rough sex. What would you have done, Haircut?'

'I don't know. How rough?'

'I'll let you know as we go along. It won't be anything radical. By the way, this is Caroline's place. Her folks are in Spain on holiday.' She smiled evilly. 'You thought my mother was in there waiting for me, didn't you?'

'Something like that,' I mumbled. I noticed Jack looking at Elizabeth with a questioning eye and realized he was pondering the 'rough sex' comments.

In the flat, Caroline produced a bottle of wine with some cheese and biscuits. 'You two ever make a foursome?' she asked, as if she were talking about a doubles match at the tennis club. She didn't sound at all like the shy woman I'd heard at The Mall.

'Not lately,' said Jack.

Liz kicked off her shoes and pulled down a zip at her hip. 'Come on. Let's see how entangled we can get.'

MANCHESTER

12th June 1960

Katie, the Irish landlady, was cleaning tables as we walked into the public bar of 'The Jugged Hare'.

'Will ya look and see what the wind has just blown in,' she announced in her rich brogue. She wiped her hands on the dishcloth resting over her shoulder, brushed aside a wisp of hair and gave me a hug and a kiss. I introduced Jack who received a handshake.

'That's some bloody haircut you two have. Just don't be asking me out 'cos I wouldn't be seen dead wid oider of you.'

'I'll buy a wig,' Jack offered.

'Oh sure. And they all come off in moments of hot passion, do they not. It'll be me with me legs in the air, calling on the good Lord for his help, when the skin of a rat falls on me face. Can't yee just imagine that now? Will you boys be havin' a pint, then?'

The whole place burst out laughing, except for Jack, who only managed a smile. I could see he was considering the possibility of getting horizontal with the lovely landlady.

A couple of regulars made sure Katie was aware they had a full head of their own hair.

'Now what would be the point of me sleepin' with any fella that's already giving me money just to supply him with a beer or two?' the landlady said with an impish laugh.

'Two pints of bitter would be great, Katie. Thanks.' I left a pound note on the bar and put my kitbag in a far corner of the room. I removed my hat and belt and placed them on the top of the canvas holdall. I unbuttoned my tunic as I returned to the bar. Jack did the same.

'Don't yee dare insult me again, Paul Johnson, leaving yer money on the bar like you was a stranger in here.'

I picked up the money and put it back into my pocket. 'Thanks, Katie.'

'So where are you from?' she asked Jack.

'In and around Yorkshire; Bradford mostly. Ya bin there?' 'Now why would I be going so far from home?'

'Ta see me?' Jack tried with a smile.

'Well there's no need for that *now,* is there?'

'That's right. I'm here an' reportin' for duty, ma'am.'

'Oh will you listen to this one.' Katie laughed. 'He has as much opinion of himself as I do of me.'

Peadar Powell, a guy I often drank with when I was a civilian, bought Jack and me refills. 'How long are you in town for?' he said.

I went over to shake hands with him and his friend Sean Town. 'Coupla weeks. How's it goin'?'

'Sean and me opened a nightclub. 'Powell's Town', we call it. Make sure you come by one night while you're here.'

The clock said two and so Katie dutifully closed the pub's doors as mandated. It did not occur to anybody to leave.

'Never let it be said that a man in uniform had to leave his hard-earned money in this fine establishment,' Katie declared as she served Jack and me another pint of her best bitter each and, from that point on, we were unable to buy a drink. Every time one of the other customers bought a round, they added two pints for the 'Bootnecks'.

Two men who I knew were detectives drank at the end of the bar. One said he felt slighted. 'They've got a great racket goin' there. Let's you and me go home and put our uniforms on.'

'Oi'll tell you two what,' Peadar interjected. 'Come down our new club an' Sean or me'll stand ya a pint or two.'

'What about me?' asked Tommy, the postman.

Katie exploded. 'Jesus, Jill and Joseph! Are yee comparing yourself to a Royal bloody Marine?'

The man reddened. 'Jesus Katie, I was only bleedin' jokin'.'

'Well just remember where you are, Tommy Flanagan. It's not every pub that'll allow you ta spend all afternoon drinking. I could be upstairs doing something else, ya know.' She smiled at the raucous laughter from some of her customers.

Katie put some food on the bar and invited everyone to help themselves. Jack and I hadn't eaten in almost twenty-four hours, so we gratefully tucked into the pickled eggs, trotters, cheeses and wedges of different pies. I felt a little guilty at the amount of food we ate and offered to pay Katie for it. When she refused to take our money, Jack suggested that we should stay at the pub for the rest of our leave.

We stayed and drank and ate our way through the whole day. When Katie's last 'after hours' customers departed around one in the morning, she kindly told us we could sleep on the benches. We would have to leave once the cleaner arrived so she could re-lock the doors after we departed. One of Katie's daughters found a couple of blankets. We said our goodnights and promised to be back.

The elderly cleaner, her hair in rollers and a net, woke us. ''Ere, you two. Wake up. It's eight o'clock already.'

I saw the woman through a haze. My head hurt and my mouth tasted like a barmaid's armpit. I tried to lift my head from my wooden pillow, but the effort was too much. I could see Jack struggling to come to grips with the day. If I looked as bad as he did, I must have been a terrible sight.

'Come on then. Move yerself. I've got to clean this place,' the cleaner chided us. We roused ourselves and started to dress. 'Two young lads like you. You should be ashamed of yerselves on a Monday mornin'.'

When the taxi turned into the road where my parents lived, Jack shifted, as if uncomfortable. 'Give over! Ya live *'ere*?'

The driver stopped in front of the house. 'I used to. Ya mind?'

'Nah. I shoulda known, you being a banker an' all.' We got out of the vehicle and waited for the driver to open the trunk. 'You 'ave ta know nobody in't squad 'as an 'ouse like this.'

I paid the driver and we hefted our kitbags. 'It's not mine, oppo. It belongs to me dad.' Saying 'me' for 'my' made me realise how much I'd changed in sixteen weeks.

'Same difference,' said Jack.

The first words out of my stepmother's mouth were, 'My God, Paul. What are you doing here?'

'We're on leave and I thought I'd come and let you see I'm alive and well.'

'I see. Well, we certainly wouldn't know from the letters that failed to arrive. How long are you home for?' It sounded more like how soon before you leave.

'Just a few days. This is my friend Jack Mason.'

She took the cigarette out of her mouth, smiled to reveal lipstick on her teeth and shook Jack's hand. 'Pleased to meet you, Jack. Where are you from?'

'In and around Yorkshire, mostly,' he said.

'Oh, I love Yorkshire. Are you undergoing training with Paul?' Jack gave me a look. At least she didn't make a fuss about me not letting her know I was coming home, or for bringing a friend with me. 'Your brothers are away at camp and your father and I had planned to go to France until something came up. You're lucky to find us at home. I'm off to the shops now, but I'm sure you can show Jack the guest room.'

We went to unpack and hang up our gear; Jack to the guestroom and me to my old bedroom which, despite my father's departing words, hadn't been converted for other use. I tried on some of my civilian clothes. Those that had been snug no longer fit me. However, there were enough miscellaneous items to keep me decent until I could buy something new. We put our dirty laundry together and used the washing machine in the larder. My step-mother was still out and so we walked to the local pub for some 'hair of the dog'.

Stepmother must have phoned father because he took my return, accompanied by Jack, in stride. After shaking hands and stiffly welcoming us, he disappeared until dinner was served. The atmosphere around the table was strained. My stepmother tried to make it special by lighting candles and bringing out the best silverware. Whatever she did, it didn't cover the fact that I'd left home and they'd settled into a reworked life without me. I felt like an intruder and wondered how Jack felt. Conversation often lulled into long, embarrassing silences that my father relieved at nine by switching on the television news. My stepmother cleared away the dishes, and brandy materialised while we waited for the weather forecast. She returned from the kitchen with a 'gin and French', switching off the television as she walked past it. I knew her intentions were good, but it led to more silences. The harder my stepmother and I worked to get conversation going, the harder it became to say something intelligent.

My father decided to join in. 'How long before you go to Officer Training School, or whatever they call it these days?'

Jack took it well. 'I have no plans to do that,' he said.

'My question was directed at my son,' father said matter-of-factly.

'Yeah,' said Jack, 'but I know what his answer is and I thought I'd help break the ice.'

'Are you going to allow your friend to answer for you?'

'No, Dad. I will not be applying to attend the Officers Training School. I have no plans on making the Marines a career. I just want to have fun.'

'You think it's fun to put your life on the line.'

'No, but the time spent doing that will be a small percentage of my total time.'

'And how long is your so-called total time?'

'Nine years plus three in the reserve, but that doesn't count.'

'What doesn't count?'

'The three years in the reserve.'

'So you intend to do nothing but have fun for nine years?'

It didn't sound good when put like that. 'It's not all fun, Dad. The training is pretty intense and then we'll be going overseas to join a commando unit. Hopefully, that'll be active service.'

'You hope for active service?'

'Yes. That's the point.'

He sighed and rubbed his throat. 'I can hardly chastise you for wanting to serve your country, even if your reasons are extremely juvenile. However, when you return to civilian life, you'll have fallen a long way behind those who put similar thoughts of fun aside. Having been a soldier ...'

'Marine,' Jack interjected.

My father nodded at him. 'Having been a Marine will not stand you in good stead for any of the top jobs. What will you do then?'

'I dunno, Dad. I guess I'll find out when the time comes.'

'Yes, well, don't expect hand-outs from your mother and me.'

Stepmother reached out to cover my father's hand. 'Your father's right. You've made your bed and when the time comes you're going to have to lie in it.'

I felt my face flush and swore to myself that I would be well prepared when I walked away from the service.

On Wednesday morning Jack and I went to the rugby club where I assumed I was still a member. The groundsman remembered me and opened the gymnasium so Jack and I could use the equipment. We knew the way we were living meant we had to work at keeping fit, or we would suffer badly when we returned to training. We finished with the weights and then ran thirty circuits of two rugby pitches. After taking a shower, we went to a pub for a couple of pints plus meat and potato pies smothered in a mess of pickled onions. Lunch over, we shopped for clothes. We purchased shirts, jackets, trousers and socks and were happy to discover a shoe shop next door.

We arrived at Powell's Town around eight-thirty. Peadar was 'setting up' behind the bar. 'With dose haircuts, you two look a lot better in yer uniforms.'

'Thanks fer those few kind words. The sales assistant at the clothes shop agreed with you,' I said. 'Thankfully it's the birds' opinions that count, not yours.'

'True. You wanna pint of Guinness? We serve the best in Manchester, if I do say so meself.'

'No thanks,' said Jack. 'That stuff's too heavy. Can I have a pint of bitter instead?'

'Me too,' I told Peadar. 'What happens here at night?'

'The place'll fill up pretty soon an' we'll likely stay open 'til one er two, dependin' on 'ow busy we are. Tonight's entertainment is a filthy comedian who's funny as all hell, anudder one who isn't, and a Welsh singer.'

'Good for you. We're more interested in the skirt situation.'

'Really! Well, I'd say with dose haircuts, yer gonna have a problem getting a bird to talk to ya. Ya look like ya just escaped from Strangeways. If ya do yer drinkin' at the bar, I'll try an' break de ice for ya, but it's not gonna be easy.'

At nine, the regular barmaids arrived and Peadar joined us. The place was filling and Jack and I would gladly have put the word on a few parties, had not Peadar cautioned us to hold our patience.

'You'd be wastin' yer time. Most o' dese young tings are just waitin' fer deir boyfriends ta leave da boozers and come an' re-attach demselves.'

Sean joined us. 'Hey. Glad to see you guys. Our accountant says we need some more tax write-offs. Have anudder round on de 'ouse.'

The comedian came on stage and immediately got everyone's attention. After his turn, while we were laughing and applauding, Peadar tapped me on the shoulder.

'I'd like ya ta meet a couple o' friends o' mine; Penelope and Susan. Dis 'ere is Paul and Jack.'

I was still guffawing as I took in the two parties. They would not make Sunday-School teachers. Penelope had to be five-nine-plus with gaudy make-up and dark brown roots at the base of her blonde hair. Her perfume was not exactly a 'come-on', but her smile was. Susan looked pretty much the same, except she had red hair instead of blonde. She also wore boots that stopped six inches below her knees.

Penelope was the first to speak. 'Hi. Peadar tells me you just got out of prison. Is that true?'

I looked over at Peadar, whose eyes smiled over the rim of his glass.

'Not exactly. We just escaped, and now we're looking for a place to hide from the Old Bill. Peadar told us he knew someone who might help. I guess that must be you.' I stood up and offered my stool to Penelope, 'What'll you have to drink?'

'Brandy, please.' Thankfully, Susan wanted lemonade.

'On the house,' said the barmaid as she served the drinks, together with two more pints of bitter.

Penelope was impressed by the free drinks. 'Peadar told me to use the prison line. You're not offended are you?'

'I think you might have misunderstood Peadar. We really *are* on the run. Was I wrong in my assumption that you are the ladies that will hide us for a short time?'

Peadar got a long look. 'What did you do?'

'Gun running.'

'Gun running?!' Her eyes widened in what was probably disbelief.

'Sssshhhhh. Not so loud. We don't wanna broadcast it.'

'You mean you sell guns to people? Who?'

Jack had been listening and picked up the line without missing a beat. 'Couple of African nations. Can't tell ya which ones, but if ya keep your eye on the news you'll be able to figure it out sooner or later.'

'Wow!' said Susan with a gaping mouth and widened eyes.

'Yeah, well, let's change the subject. Where do you live?'

'Didsbury,' said Penelope. 'Do you know the area?'

'Somewhat.'

'What do you do?' Jack asked Susan as she linked her arm with his.

'Nothing as exciting as you. Pen and me load cartons of cereal boxes onto trucks.'

'Well, it certainly keeps you both in good shape,' I said.

The second, less funny, comedian had finished. Sean walked onto the stage and introduced the singer.

'Oh, this guy's great!' exclaimed Susan. 'Can we turn around and watch him?'

We took a taxi to a flat where Susan dragged Jack straight into her bedroom.

Penelope indicated the door to her room and left to get a 'night-cap'. The area was a mess, but perhaps my time in the Marines had made me a clean freak. Five months ago, I might not have noticed the unmade bed, the overflowing wastebasket, clothes and shoes scattered around, and a dirty glass on the bedside table. Genevieve kept a tidy bedroom, but then, she lived with her parents.

Penelope entered and put a large brandy next to the dirty glass. 'Sugar! I should have taken this to the kitchen.'

She undressed and joined me in the small bed. After we kissed for a couple of minutes, she broke off for a sip of her drink. We eventually performed some mechanical sex before I left her to her brandy and went to sleep.

The next morning, she awoke me with a glass of orange juice and a different personality. 'I'm sorry I got drunk last night. Can we start again tonight, after I get home?'

Her words didn't impress me as much as her body. As she bent to kiss me, her negligee gaped and I saw a pair of magnificent breasts on an otherwise tight body. Her clean face was a lot prettier without her black eye-makeup. Her breath smelled of toothpaste.

'It's a thought, but I'll have to talk to Jack first.'

'Oh, don't worry about them. They're in love already. Why don't you get your head down for a while? Help yourself to whatever you want.'

'Do either of you have a car, by any chance?'

'Susan has a rust bucket she keeps round the corner. Why?'

'I was wondering if we could borrow it today. I've got some things to do and then we could pick you up after work. We could go out for a meal, if you want.'

'Maybe. We work only a few blocks from 'ere, so we don't need the car. I'll go an' ask her.'

She returned and told me while she dressed that Jack had the car keys and the address of where they worked. She kissed me again and then departed, taking a bag containing a change of clothes.

Jack drove the temperamental car to my parents' house where we started another load of laundry, picked up our clothes and left a note for my again absent stepmother. I told her not to expect us, but that we would see her and my father at some unspecified time. I knew my comings and goings would annoy them, but I justified my actions by thinking of all the years they'd annoyed me. We went for another workout at the rugby club, then found a decent pub for lunch. A couple of elderly regulars got quietly but happily drunk because of our ineptitude at dominoes.

At five, we sat in the car across the road from the cereal factory and watched a commotion. A man stood on the bed of a small truck to address a crowd of agitated workers. He was having a difficult time getting his message through to the men and women who chattered amongst themselves. I wound down the window to hear his words.

'Comrades, I beg you ta listen. Unless we pull together, we'll not be an effective force against the management of this factory.' The workers still argued with each other. 'Quiet!' the man roared over his portable loud speaker.

'Ya do know the pubs are open, don'tcha?' a man shouted.

There were calls of, 'Justice!'

'Throw the machines out with the management,' shouted others, but the crowd quelled sufficiently for the man to say his piece.

'Comrades, the employers can't arbitrarily get rid of a coupla dozen workers just because they've brought in machines to do their jobs.' The crowd cheered. 'Alternative employment must be found for these workers. They 'ave families ta support.' More people cheered, as if on cue. 'We must band together and show these arrogant Yankee employers they can't treat the British working man like some southern darkie.' The crowd warmed to his words and their cheering was accompanied by a sustained round of applause. 'We must act.'

The crowd swelled as workers from a recently finished shift left the factory. The cheering grew louder.

'There's a meeting at seven tonight in the car park of Manchester City's Maine Road ground. At that time, we'll take a vote on whether we should strike in support of our comrades what 'ave been put out of work by our callous American managers; the American managers who care more about money than they do about British workers. Be there, comrades. We're in the cradle of unionism here in Manchester. Remember the

Easter Sunday march. Make your voice 'eard. Make your vote count.'

Voices in the crowd yelled, 'Strike, strike.'

Helpers wandered through the throng and handed out leaflets.

'Tonight at seven,' the speaker called out. 'Pass the word.'

The meeting seemed to be over so I wound the window up.

'Wonder what would happen if *we* went on strike', Jack mused.

'We'd get umpteen hours of extra drill.'

He laughed. 'Give over!'

The girls knocked on the window before sliding into the back seats. Both had re-dyed their hair during the day and the ugly roots had disappeared. They looked a lot better.

'What's going on?' I asked Penny.

'Some blokes got laid off and the union wants ta strike. I would've learned more about it but Sue an' me wanted to dye our 'air at lunchtime, which is when it first blew up. We took so long, we got into trouble when we went back to work.'

'Oh, we were in such trouble,' Susan said. 'We woulda got the sack if all this other stuff wasn't goin' on. We're lucky. I don't think they want to sack anyone right now.'

We ate Chicken Tandoori. Penny and Susan declined to drink alcohol, so it was up to Jack and I to keep the barman employed. Once the meal was over, the women wanted to go to Maine Road and find out what had happened at the strike meeting.

People were streaming away as we arrived. Susan rolled down her window. 'Whor 'appened?' she asked a passing woman.

'We're on bloody strike,' the disgruntled female informed us. 'And me wid a sick 'usband and three nippers.'

'What're we supposed ta do?' Susan asked.

'I dunno. There's another meetin' outside't factory tomorrer morning. We'll find out then.'

Penny's grin was infectious. 'Isn't that great? Now we can spend all our time together until the strike is over.'

'Whoa. Let's not rush it,' I said. 'We've got to see how we get on first.'

'Oh, we'll get along just fine, you'll see.'

'We're getting' on fine,' said Jack.

Back at the flat, Jack and I watched the second half of a football game while the two women cleaned the place. They considered the job finished five seconds after the referee blew the final whistle.

Penny closed and locked the bedroom door, drew the curtains, and draped a flimsy red scarf over the lamp on the bedside table. I was undoing my shirt buttons but she playfully slapped my hands away and took over the task. I had already taken off my shoes, but she made me sit on the bed while she knelt before me and slid off my socks. I hadn't known getting one's socks off could be so pleasurable. I felt a little self-conscious doing nothing, so I leaned forward to pull her blouse up over her head. I unclipped her bra and released her breasts. We stood to ease the undoing of garments covering our lower halves. As soon as we were naked, I was eager to enjoy her fabulous body.

'Not so fast Paul. I want to take it slow. Let's take the time to discover each other's bodies.'

'We can do that later. Come on.'

She laughed at my impatience and raised her hands. 'No! I mean it. Trust me. If we take a little time to find out about each other, the sexual tension will mount and we'll enjoy the sex much more.'

My erection was almost painful. 'Bollocks! Sexual tension's for old folks and those who need help to get it up. I wanna mount you now.'

But she was determined. I did as asked and started to inspect the body I urgently craved. Even in the dim light I could see not a scar, bruise or wrinkle anywhere. There were no warts, evidence of inoculations, skin eruptions, or other blemishes. Penny had the most luscious body I had seen and I wanted to bury myself in it. Not merely be inside her, but to lie on her, to touch her, to lie under her, to touch her, to lie next to her and to touch her. I wanted to inhale her.

I weighed her breasts, one in each hand. They were identical. I similarly assessed her buttocks. The flesh on the inside of her muscular thigh was unbelievably soft and smooth. There was however one small deficiency; she was as white as snow. A little sunshine would have made her perfect. As her light touch rose on the inside of my thigh, Penny said, 'You have a nice body, Paul, but it could use a little colour.'

The strike enabled the four of us to spend Thursday together. We went to a pub in Salford known for its food. We ate hot meat pies with homemade coleslaw and washed it down with Tetley's Best Bitter. Susan took Jack on an inspection tour of the multitude of knick-knacks that adorned the walls.

Penelope took advantage of their absence. 'So. How are we getting along?'

'Bleedin 'orrible,' I told her.

'What's wrong?' she asked quietly. 'I promise I'll take it easy with the drinking. You seem to enjoy yourself in bed, so what more do you want?'

I put my hand on her knee. 'Nothing. Nothing's wrong.' I smiled at her. 'I was joking. I think you're really something. By the way, we're not escaped prisoners. We're in the Marines and we're only on leave until a week from Sunday.'

She grinned. 'I know that. Jack already fessed to Susan.'

'How'd it be if Jack an' I moved in with you two for the rest of our leave? Or is that asking too much?'

'Seeing as 'ow you're just about livin' with us already, it wouldn't be much of a change, would it?'

'Is that a yes?' I asked.

'Of course it is,' she murmured as she nuzzled my neck.

We dropped the girls off at their flat, then drove to my parents' house to pick up our kit. We left a bunch of flowers and a bottle of scotch that Jack had purchased, together with a note thanking them for putting us up. They would probably be as happy not to see me, as I was not to have to say goodbye to them.

Jack and I went to the rugby club on Friday. As Saturday was game day, I wanted to keep away from the place in case Maggie was there. Jack said I was stupid. On Saturday afternoon, Penelope and Susan went to the laundromat and grocery store. We offered to go with them as bag carriers, but they were enjoying playing homemakers. Perhaps it was fortunate that Jack and I would only be around a few more days. At Susan's request, we spent the night at Powell's Town. She specifically wanted to see a group called 'Freddie and The Dreamers'.

Penelope drank four brandies during the five hours we were in the club, and was no more drunk that I was when we went home.

The strike at the cereal factory continued, allowing us to spend the rest of our leave together. Jack and I tried to give the women some money in an attempt to make up for some of their lost pay, but they said they were affronted by our offer. They said as we paid for most meals and drinks, we contributed more than our share.

Every night, Penelope and I heard Susan scream out threats to Jack.

'I'll cut your fuckin' balls off if you don't take this blindfold off me!' Another time I heard, 'Don't you dare go to sleep tonight, Jack Mason, because I'll smash your brains in with a poker.' She was once plaintive. 'You have to untie me Jack before I wet the bed.'

'Should I be worried?' I asked Penny.

'No. She loves bondage and screaming out her curses. Her threats are really terms of endearment.'

'If you say so.'

The next day I asked Jack if he was worried. 'Give over! She 'as a grin a mile wide when she's cursing me.'

There wasn't a night when we didn't hear Susan promising Jack every kind of gruesome retribution once she got free of her restraints. I wondered what neighbours thought, but the girls seemed not to care.

Starting Monday, Jack and I went daily to the rugby club for a work out. As the week progressed, our alcohol intake decreased. At the end of the week, Penny and Sue each had a photograph taken. They scrawled erotic messages on the reverse side of the professional pictures before presenting them to us as a memento of our days together.

On Sunday morning, they drove us to the station. They did not wait to see us onto the train, or try to extract promises regarding future plans. As I kissed Penny goodbye, she handed me a brown paper bag containing sandwiches for Jack and me.

'That's for the journey. Take care, won't you. We had a lot of fun.'

Jack and I had left most of our remaining cash in the flat to help the pair through the strike. Perhaps they wouldn't be offended again.

Peter Lingard

POOLE

26th June 1960

Boswell stood on the platform of Poole railway station, hands clasped behind his back, pace stick under his arm and a red sash across his bemedalled chest. He looked at the few civilians who alighted from the train as if they were a lesser form of existence.

'Welcome back to the good life,' he grinned. 'There's a truck in the station forecourt. As another train is due in fifteen minutes, we shall wait and see if any wee fairies arrive on it before we depart for our new home.' His peaked cap, teeth, medals and toecaps shone in the watery sun. 'Parade is at nine a.m. tomorrow.' He delighted in rolling his 'r's. 'Dress of the day is fatigues. Make sure you are properly turned out.'

Hamworthy Camp where we were to spend the next two weeks was on an island situated on the shoreline of the English Channel. It looked almost deserted. . When we drove through the gates, the sentry seemed indifferent. The truck stopped outside a trio of wooden huts and we carried our kit into our new quarters. Once unpacked, I went to find an iron and we set about ridding our clean kit of wrinkles gained in transit. We polished our boots and brasses, blancoed our webbing and stowed our gear. By the time we were done, we would have passed inspection by any of The Depot's duty officers. At 'lights out', a third of the squad had yet to report. Late arrivals made a racket finding their way around the unfamiliar quarters. They stubbed their toes on the ends of bed frames and walked into tables and chairs as they looked for an empty bed. I recognised Pete's voice and told him where to find an iron and, after unpacking his kit, he left to find a lighted building wherein he could press his fatigues and otherwise prepare for morning parade. The rest of his kit would have to wait until the next night.

A while later, Spike arrived and searched in the dark for somewhere to sleep.

'I never want to be on night patrol with you,' a voice called out as the Geordie stumbled into furniture.

'Screw you. Why doncha put a fuckin' light on,' he said.

'There are no light switches, mate, and the night light's 'ad it. We're at the mercy of the guard room.'

'Helluva way to run a fuckin' ship.'

The next morning, Pete lined us up in ranks of three on the dirt track in front of the huts. Boswell, dressed in fatigues, walked amongst us, asking how we had enjoyed our leave while he checked our turnout. He then returned to the front of the squad.

'Just about every one of you miserable men is in need of a haircut. Make sure you get one today! The commanding officer will be here in a couple of minutes to welcome you and give you the low-down on this place. A bus-ride down the road is a holiday resort called Bournemouth. It is full of old ladies and young French girls just waiting to help suckers like you spend your money on them. Be warned and be careful. Now, you will find discipline in this camp very lax but you will not succumb to this disease. I am here ta make sure you do not succumb. *Each* of you must ensure you do not succumb. I will shit all over any man who *does* succumb. You will all remember that word – succumb. Remember it well and dinna do it. Do I make myself clear?'

'Yes, Sergeant,' we roared.

'A word about the Special Boat Service, or SBS. They are a special unit. In peacetime, they swim around the world taking photographs of every coastline that exists, noting the best places for water-board assaults. In times of conflict, they often work on their own or, at most, in pairs. If you are happier in water than you are on land, they may be interested in you. You'll also need a pair the size of the dome of Saint Paul's Cathedral. You cannot volunteer but they might ask you to join them once you've done a tour with a Commando. Here, dress of the day, every day, is fatigues. That means you will have ample time to ensure your entire kit is immaculate by the time we get to Lympstone. I will put you over an assault course every morning while we're here and we'll be going for a wee swim or two but, other than that, there will be no physical training. Make sure you work off all the fat you've picked up in the bars and brothels of this fair land during the last two weeks. Any questions?'

'Yes, Sergeant,' Sammy piped up, 'What's "I love you" in French?'

We stood at ease for half-an-hour while we waited for the commanding officer. Boswell made Sammy chant 'Je t'adore' repeatedly. He also tried to convince us that whispering, 'Ma petite Chou' in a French girl's ear was a sure way to win her heart. Another recipe for success, he assured us, would be to ask the women from across the Channel, 'Voulez vous couchez avec moi ce soir'.

A man with water dripping from his wetsuit wandered over to speak with our leader. He was in bare feet and had goggles pushed up onto his head. A removable armband displaying three stripes was wrapped around his upper arm.

'How's it hanging, Francis?'

'Thick and long, Bob. You?'

'Same as always.' He nodded his head in our direction. 'This your latest lot?'

'What else?'

'Don't you ever get tired of wet-nursing these sorry bastards?'

'This lot's no too bad. Fairies, the lot of them.' Sergeant Bob smiled. 'How were Willie and his brood?'

'Fuckin' shambles. They gotta kick that guy upstairs or something. Trouble is, he'll be a sergeant then, an' I, for one, don't wanna socialise with the prick.'

He turned his attention to us. 'Welcome to Poole. The next two weeks is probably the only time you'll ever be here, so don't lie in of a morning. While you wimps wander around the world pulling your plonkers, one branch of Her Britannic Majesty's Corps of Royal Marines is actually working. We're the SBS. The only word of our title you need to remember is Special. You've probably heard of the SAS who are also special and are our land-based equivalent. We live in the water. We're so fucking good, sharks shit themselves when they see us coming. While you're here, we'll show you a little of what we do. We'll also be lookin' to see if any of you have the ability and the balls to join us. Now Her Britannic Majesty, in her infinite wisdom, has nominated this lovely island be the place where you learn to fight fire – as in throwing water on flames. Course, if you join the SBS, you'll be able to take to the water while some shit-for-brains takes the water to the flames. That's up to you. The CO doesn't have time to come and talk to you; it's his coffee break. So I'm it. Don't ask me any questions 'cos I won't answer them. That's what your DI is for.' He turned to Boswell, 'Back to you, Francis.'

The wetsuit headed back to his beloved water as Boswell addressed us. 'Basic training at Deal being over, you now are expected to become self-dependent. I'm making Dusty Miller squad leader and Ron Davis his back-up. I do not want any flak from anyone over this. Right Turner?'

'Right, Sergeant,' said Pete.

'Given their experience, they are the two logical men to help get you through the rest of your training. Get together and sort out responsibilities for other members of the squad. I'll give you a coupla days to work on it and then you'll be flyin' solo.'

Each day's instruction finished around four and we had little to do to prepare for the next day. We laundered our fatigues and underwear as we showered. It took less than five minutes to clean and polish our boots. We ironed fatigues washed the previous day and were then ready to step ashore. For the first time since we joined up, we went ashore in civilian clothes. No one inspected us or cared what we knew about Corps history. The camp gate was open and we just walked through it. Jack and I both regretted our departing gesture in Manchester, as we now had to borrow money. Bobby, the squad's financial genius, lent us ten pounds each.

Boswell had told us to start at The Ritz bar situated in the basement of one of the large hotels in town. He assured us we would progress from there without further help from him. Over twenty of us stepped off the bus and descended the steps to the bar. A jukebox blared out 'Apache' by the Shadows as we walked through the swinging doors. The place was full of smoke, parties, and hardly any men. The barman was kept busy for a few minutes, pulling the pints we ordered. Jack and I took a draught of our beer, made faces at the insipid taste, and set out to inspect the premises and customers.

I heard a slap and turned to see a red-cheeked Sammy glare at a young thing, then return to the bar. We watched Pete, who was learning what 'Voulez vous couchez avec moi ce soir' meant.

'You might as well ask if a girl wants to fuck,' said the partie with a sexy French accent. 'I think you will find somebody 'as 'ad a joke at your expense. Did your instructor per'aps tell you these words? Yes?'

'Yes,' Pete admitted.

'There is no need for you to try to speak the French. We all students who learn the English and workers who know already the English. Every second Monday we come 'ere at zis time to see new Marines. We all looking for same thing, no?'

Pete smiled. 'We sure are, luv. Can I get you a drink?'

'Oui. Un Pernod et l'eau, s'il vous plait.'

'Er, you said we should speak in English.'

'Ah, oui,' the woman laughed, 'A Pernod and water, please.'

Spike managed to convince a partie to stick with him, despite his opening line.

Jack tried Boswell's words on a partie but stumbled over them. The girl knew what he was trying to say and she flounced away with an impudent flick of her shoulder-length hair.

'Fuck it,' he scowled. 'I'm trying something else.' He bade me follow him to a table. 'Hi,' he said with his best grin.

The two parties smiled sweetly at us. 'Hi,' they responded.

'We don't speak French,' he said. 'Can you teach me an' Banker a few words?'

One of them nodded and slid her empty glass across the table. 'Oui monsieur. We 'eared what you say to Simone.'

'What?'

'I think she said buy me a drink.'

'Give over!'

We pulled a couple of stools from under the table and sat.

'I'm Jack and this 'ere is Paul, bedder known as Banker.'

'Bon soir. Je m'apelle Francoise. That is, Hello, my name is Francoise.'

'Francoise?' Jack hesitantly reached across the table and shook her hand.

'Mercie,' the other partie said as she looked at me.

'Thanks?'

'Non.' The woman burst out laughing, 'Je m'apelle Mercie. It is my name.'

I felt about three feet tall, but still tall enough to reach out and shake her hand.

Mercie pushed her empty glass forward.

'Would you like a drink?' Jack spoke slowly and the effect was charming.

'Mais oui. Of course. We both like Pernot and water, please,' said Francoise. Both girls smiled.

When I returned with the drinks, Jack was explaining, 'Yeah, well, we were told what ta say by someone. It didn't work fer me, so I 'oped you'd speak English, seeing as 'ow we're in England.'

'Of course. The words you used were 'ard to recognise because of your accent. Jacques, yes?'

'Jack.'

'Oui, Jacques. You are a funny man, Jacques.'

'Paul is your real name?' asked Mercie.

'Yeah, but some people call me Banker.'

'I think is strange,' mused Francoise.

Her friend agreed, 'Why do you change your name? Do you not like the name your parents give to you?'

'It's not a matter of liking or disliking' I tried to explain, 'It's just that lots of people acquire what we call nicknames. Sometimes it's just a shortened version of their real name, like Rob for Robert. Mine is Banker, because I used to work in a bank. Don't you have nicknames in France?'

'Not the people we know,' Mercie announced with a measure of indignation. 'Don't you ever call me Mer!'

Francoise smiled. 'Too close to Merde, n'est ce pas.'

Mercie also smiled. 'My friend Frank.'

Both girls broke into peals of laughter. Our financial situation dictated we resort to a less expensive pastime. 'Where do you live?' I asked.

'We are at the college on an exchange program and so we live in a college dromedary,' said Mercie.

'Dormitory?'

'Ah, oui, dormitory.'

'How many other girls sleep in the same room?' Jack inquired.

'Oh, it is a large room with perhaps ten girls.'

Jack and I looked at each other in disappointment. Francoise interpreted our facial expressions correctly.

'We are a little inconvenient for you, yes?'

'Give over!' Jack lied.

'Do many people go down to the beach at night time?' was out of my mouth before I realized how transparent the suggestion was.

'Some do. But first we should learn more about each other, do you not agree?'

Francoise' words allowed Jack and I to shift our seats to get respectively closer to Francoise and Mercie.

I guessed Mercie to be three or four inches over five feet, but as she had yet to stand in my presence, I couldn't be sure. Her navy-coloured woollen smock covered most of her body, but when she propped herself up with her forearms, I could see a pair of petite yet nicely rounded bulges. Her thin wrists and small hands led me to assume the rest of her body was similarly slight. Her short, dark-brown hair gave her an elfin look, and a presumed fake beauty spot on the right side of her chin was a definite attraction.

'Why you only stay at Poole two weeks? It is not much time to be soldiers.'

'Marines,' I said with indignation. 'We're only 'ere to get some experience in the ocean and allow the instructors to assess us. Some guys might come back 'ere in a coupla years.'

'My last Marine boy was Keith and he said he was going to another place to learn more training. Is he true or is he telling me a lie?'

'Keith Blackburn?'

'Oui. Keith Blackburn. You know him?'

'Hey, Jack. Mercie here dated Keith Blackburn for the last two weeks.' I turned back to Mercie. 'Yeah. I know him. He's a pretty good guy.'

Jack bought a round and then I again took the plunge. 'We need to get outta here. I don't know about you ladies but if Jack and I have much more to drink, we'll be drunk.'

Jack followed my lead. 'That's true. Why don't we go for a walk along the beach?'

Mercie grinned at us both and her face took on an even more impish look. 'If you want to make love, we go to your camp.'

'Give over! You'll get us inta all sortsa shit!'

'No shit. We've been to your camp many times with other Marines,' Francoise said. 'We know all good places to go,' she said with a look of such innocence I had to stifle a laugh.

Mercie spoke again; 'Please what is "Give over"?'

'Uh? Oh, it's just an expression. I stress it different, dependin' on the situation.'

'Different situations? It is a blanket?'

'Yeah. Ya could say that. It's a blanket expression. How many times 'ave you been tu't camp, then?'

The two parties looked at each other and Francoise shrugged her shoulders before replying. 'I do not know. It is not something that a person would count. Many times.'

My face must have registered my shock, because Mercie laughed at me. 'You Marines! You always think you should be a girl's only lover. Inside your 'eart, you must know that is not so, eh? We are the gooses and you are the ganders. Do we not both have same rules?'

Jack smiled like the lecher we both were. 'Come on oppo, let's take 'em back to the bleedin' camp, fer Chrisake. Boswell's shacked up with some married fad an' you know the place is almost empty.'

'Yeah, but it's still a bit risky.'

'Give over! Let's do it.'

We alighted from the bus one stop before the camp. The girls took our hands and led us to an open area where we could gain access to a boatshed. Mercie led me to a corner while Jack and Francoise made their way to another spot.

Other couples tried to enter the boat-shed during the night but we dissuaded them with our screamed instruction to find another location.

'Fuck off!' Jack shouted.

'Get the fuck outta here,' I added.

'Occupe,' one of the girls would call to their French friends.

'Pas de chance,' Mercie added and then laughed.

'What does that mean?' I asked.

'For you, it means "no chance",' she explained between giggles.

There were a few acknowledgements in French, proving the foreigners knew more about our camp than we did. I briefly wondered if the Irish Republican Army knew our security was so lax.

The next afternoon we stowed pillows, blankets and condoms in the shed before we caught the bus into town. We worried someone would take advantage of our foresight and so we planned an early return. After some discussion, Jack and I agreed to concentrate on the women from across the channel and leave home grown talent until we reached Lympstone. We met the girls, bought some ice cream and took the bus back to Poole. The items we had left in the boat-shed made the place a lot cosier than the previous night.

During our time at Deal, everyone had passed a swimming proficiency test that in no way prepared us for the manoeuvres at Poole. Boswell's friend Bob, whose name we learned was Myerson, had us participate in a silent approach from the sea under the cover of darkness. Two tables set on the beach were covered in rubber suits. 'Find one that fits you and put it on,' said Myerson. 'Don't be too fussy with how you look, it's a one-time exercise. If it's a bit tight, use the talc to help squeeze into it.'

The suits had no size markings and so we scrambled to find good fits. Dennis and Sammy found a couple of smaller suits, but the sameness of the black rubber made it difficult to determine sizes, so we stretched, pushed, and pulled the suits on. Some guys had ankles and even heels well covered while others, including me, showed a good length of their legs. It was similar with wrists.

'Come on,' Myerson urged. 'You guys take more time to suit up than a bunch of parties. Is that why you call yourselves Fairies?'

Once suited up, we smeared our feet, faces, and hands with black camouflage cream. Sammy dropped to one knee, threw his arms wide and started to sing 'Mammy', but Myerson's boot on his backside was the only appreciation he received.

'You will all swim toward France for a few hundred yards, or so,' said Myerson. The words 'few hundred' got my attention. 'If you haven't come across a couple of pontoons in that distance, you've missed them. In which case, you can either keep going for France, or start searching. Communication is the key. Let others know once you're clutching a wooden platform. There'll be a couple of men from this unit to help, if needed, but they're not supermen; they can't be there for everyone. Right, off you go.'

We swam into the English Channel to where I was relieved to find another sergeant 'homing' with a powerful flashlight. The men from the SBS swam out with us to ensure Her Britannic Majesty didn't lose any of her precious recruits and I tried to copy their energy-efficient swimming style. I noticed Jack study them, also. Although it was a fine August night, it didn't take long before I felt cold and I thought how much fun the exercise must be for the squads that passed through Poole in the winter. When we reached our destination, we held on to pontoons and rested while the Sergeant made a head count.

'Right, you've all made to this point. Now you will swim back to shore in complete silence. That means you use the breast stroke. We have no time for idiots who think the crawl is the way to go. Silence is the key. Remember that at all times. The water lapped gently against the pontoon, making only the slightest sound and I realized how difficult the task would be. 'If detected by the beam of a flashlight, you will turn back out to sea before attempting another approach. My two assistants and me will be watching you. Not until we give you the okay will you turn around and make another attempt. The only way you can leave the water is by doing so undetected.'

The beam of light picked out Jack and me on our first run. We swam back out to sea for what seemed a long time before someone told us to turn around and make a second attempt. Our re-approach was so slow, it seemed at times the tide carried us back out to sea. We made landfall eventually, but my heart sank when the beam of a flashlight settled on us as our feet made contact with chattering pebbles.

'You've made it lads,' said Myerson. 'Unfortunately, the enemy heard the noise of the disturbed pebbles and killed you with fire from a machine gun positioned on top of the sand dunes. Nothing wrong with that, of course. As long as fifty percent of you make it to the base of the sand dunes, you'll be able to take out the machine gun post. Then all you'll have to worry about are the snipers with their infra-red sights.'

We joined guys who had already left the water, and gladly received a cup of hot soup. A half-hour later, two squaddies had yet to make it back. Ray Green and Tommy the Comma were missing. Myerson organised a head count, then another. Being still two short, he got on a field telephone and called for all available SBS personnel to report to the beach immediately.

'We've lost two of these shitheads,' he told whoever was on the end of the line.

Suddenly Ray Green's voice called out. 'We're here, Sergeant'

Myerson barked into the 'phone, 'Belay that. The pricks are here.' He put down the receiver with studied calm and called for Ray and Comma to approach him. 'How long have you fucks been here?'

'I dunno. Maybe fifteen minutes,' Comma told him.

'Come 'ere.' Comma stepped forward a couple of paces and Myerson grabbed his head. 'You're lucky your hair's still wet.

How come nobody heard you walking through the pebbles on the beach?' Myerson demanded.

'I dunno, Sergeant. It was pretty sandy where we came up the beach.'

'Sandy my arse. We use this beach specifically because it has wall-to-wall pebbles. Did you have any of the hot soup?'

'We didn't want any, Sergeant.'

'Of course you bloody didn't. That would have meant having your name checked off on the roster, wouldn't it? You two miserable fucks thought you could outwit us by swimming away from this beach and getting back onto this man's island at another point. Am I right? Fess up, son. Come daylight we'll find your footprints somewhere. It'll be easier on you if you tell me now.' There were a couple of silent seconds. 'Well?'

'Yeah, Sarge. We made a couple of approaches here and then decided we could swim to another beach, land and get the machine gun from the rear. That way we might save our squaddies.'

'From the rear, huh? That how you two faggots take it – from the rear? Back into the water. Now! Keep fucking going until you see lights on the French coast. You will then turn and finish this exercise the way you were instructed. Only now, there's just the two of you and I'll be concentrating on nothing but you. You better not let me detect you until you're lickin' my fuckin' boots.'

While we waited for Ray and Comma to make it to the beach, I thought how they'd shown initiative in what they did. I also saw how dangerous the exercise could become if recruits decided to make landfall elsewhere. There was safety in having a restricted approach zone. Myerson probably went through some worrying moments when he realized we were two short. Having to call out reinforcements to find his missing charges could not have improved his mood. It was one thing for Boswell to teach us drill at Deal but these instructors had a lot more responsibility. It would probably be the same at Lympstone.

Myerson had sent Ray and Comma back to sea twice. 'How much longer do we 'ave to put it to these pricks, Sarge?' asked one of Myerson's assistants. 'I'm on a promise tonight.'

'Yeah, bring 'em in this time. Make sure you fit a boot up their waterlogged arses.'

We continued to see the French parties. It wasn't difficult to convince them it was more economical if they took a bus to Poole, rather than us going into Bournemouth to pick them up. Jack and I still left camp at five every afternoon but we boarded a bus in the opposite direction to a pub where the only drinks we had to pay for were our own. Men in the public bar played darts for drinks and we added our names to the list of challengers. When our turn came, I discovered Jack was a good player and we remained unbeaten until we had to leave the pub to meet our dates. On the first night, we each left with credit for two pints behind the bar and we didn't pay for another drink for the rest of our time in Poole.

We had to get to the boatshed earlier every night. The competition for desirable space was increasing and the thought of having to wander around looking for an alternative site was not appealing. Nor was the idea of someone else using our pillows and blankets. At the weekend, the four of us spent some time together doing things that did not involve sex. We became so familiar with one another that Jack and I suggested to the women that we swap partners. They were a little reluctant when we first broached the idea, but they eventually agreed. After that, Jack and I swapped places in the boatshed on a couple of occasions and the parties pretended not to know with whom they had spent the night.

One day, Myerson split us into groups of four and assigned each group an inflatable rubber dinghy with an outboard motor attached. He and a corporal took a couple of hours instructing us in the care and maintenance of the Gemini and its portable engine. Thereafter, we spent the day in the water getting acquainted with the craft. As the hours went by and we became more accustomed to handling the zippy little vessels, we increased speed. We zigzagged around the bay, skilfully avoiding each other.

As we grew in confidence, there were a couple of white-knuckle occasions. A head-on collision caused one Gemini to leave the water and skim over the heads of those in the other craft. One guy hit the deck. Others dived over the side to avoid decapitation by the whirling outboard motor. The flat-bottomed Gemini landed on the oggin, a word we'd learned was marine-speak for sea or ocean, with a jarring slap, and we heard the occupants shout, 'Shit'. Her Britannic Majesty must have been relieved there were no casualties. Once we saw the fun of becoming airborne, we all attempted to do the same. Our total number being thirty, one craft contained two guys and, due to the relative lightness of their Gemini, they enjoyed more flying time than anyone else. We played until dusk, at which time we had to haul our newfound toys out of the water. We separated the dinghies and motors for cleaning and return to the boat-sheds. The two-man team who had enjoyed themselves so much in the water now realized the advantage of being a four-man team. 'Just remember what it's like to carry this stuff,' Myerson told us. 'You'll undoubtedly get the job one day, when you're on patrol in a God forsaken corner of the world.'

The rest of our time at the SBS camp passed without mishap. We learned how to set fires and put them out, and spent more time in the oggin. In the end, we were glad to leave. We were eager to get to Lympstone, with its Devonshire girls, its scrumpy, and the coveted Green Beret.

LYMPSTONE

10th July 1960

It was drizzling when our train pulled into Exeter station. Waiting there were trucks with tarpaulin tops to take us to Lympstone. No girls waved to us during the hour-long journey along Devon's country roads. As we neared our destination, the lorries geared down to climb the steep hill to the unimpressive gates of our new home. Inside the camp, the vehicles stopped close to wooden huts wherein we would live for the next few months. Pete, who had been at the rear of the truck, left his gear for Spike, Jack, and me to pick up as he ran to the far end of the nearest building and reserved the last four beds. We unpacked our kit, arranged our living spaces, pressed our fatigues, shone our boots, stowed our gear, drew our bedding, and made our beds.

Willie Wanker's squad was in the huts next to ours, so Jack and I went to find Keith Blackburn. He was on his way to the NAAFI to buy some thread but we convinced him to show us around the camp.

''Ow come Boswell ain't showin' ya this stuff?'

'Since 'e made Dusty squad leader we 'aven't seen much of 'im,' I said.

'I wonder if 'is day of glory was being the DI of The Queen's Squad?' Keith said. 'There's not much drilling done 'ere. Maybe 'e's gone off the boil.'

'We all 'ad a relaxed life in Poole,' Jack offered in defence of our admired leader. 'We goofed off mosta da time. Musta bin same for you. Maybe 'e'll be 'is old self again, now we're 'ere. Anyways, me an' Banker 'ad a good time with two French parties called Mercie and Francoise.'

Keith grinned. 'Francoise and Mercie, huh? That Mercie gives a man an 'ell of a tongue lashing.'

'She sure does. 'Ave you been here long enough to experience everything we 'ave ta do?' I asked.

'Pretty much. We've bin over the assault course, Tarzan course and endurance course. The PTIs seem ta be allowed ta smack anyone around. Don't retaliate or they really go ta town on ya.'

'Give over!'

'Straight up. There's unarmed combat. Oh, make sure ya got yer arm rolls down pat. The instructors take pleasure in throwin' everyone around. They know we learned the roll at Deal, so they figure everyone's an expert.'

'Yeah, we're okay with that. You been ashore yet?' I asked.

'Yeah. Exeter, or Executor as some call it. I didn't reckon it much, but some guys swear it's the best. I prefer Exmouth. Mind, it's only been two weeks. You'll 'ave ta see fer yourselves.'

The next morning, Boswell inspected us. 'Thought I'd deserted ya, didn't ya?'

'You wouldn't give up on such a good thing, Sarge,' Sammy called out.

'Don't put your life on it,' Boswell shot back at him with an edge to his voice. 'You might have been top dogs at the end of your time at Deal but your back down to the bottom of the pit now and working your way out is what's gonna make you Marines. I won't be wet-nursing you sorry bastards any more. I'll be around to kick your miserable arses, and I mean that literally, whenever I think ya need it, but for the most part you'll take your orders from the PTIs or physical training instructors. Be aware that life here is different. There's no extra drill, or such mundane stuff, but if you put a foot wrong you could get a beating – not enough to put you in the sick bay, but enough so you get the point. When you're swinging through the bonny trees, I'll be inspecting your lockers and kit. I'll be keeping you up to scratch on the parade ground and giving instruction in field craft and the like. However, and mark my words well, it is up to you all to read company orders everyday and to be where required, when required, in the dress required. You'll see me around but I won't protect you from yourselves anymore. You listening, Miller?'

'Yes, Sergeant.'

At eleven, Boswell took us to the assault course, stating we would do ourselves a favour if we became physically acquainted with it before PTIs made the formal introduction. He started us off in sets of three at thirty-second intervals. Dennis, Sammy and Ray ran up a slight incline and leapt over a wide ditch full of water. Ray almost got a soaking but Sammy looked over his shoulder in time to grab Ray's outstretched hand before he fell backwards into the brackish pond. Dennis stood by, waiting to give assistance. The three then ran to a six-foot wall whereat they leapt for the top and hoisted themselves up and over. The wall prevented us from seeing what lay beyond.

Bobby made our third man and, once over the wall, we ran for three sets of monkey bars, then a set of free-swinging logs suspended over an open ditch. Next came a set of high ropes to climb. Twenty feet further, we hit the deck, and crawled through an underground tunnel. Back in daylight, we ran at a rope, swung over a gaping hole, and hit the ground running. We climbed a fifteen-foot wall with the help of a cargo net, dropped to the ground, then up a rope ladder to a thin plank that stretched some twenty feet. I needed to wave my arms about to hold my balance but made it to the end and sprinted the couple of hundred yards to end the course.

When the last trio finished, Boswell had us gather around him. 'Not bad for a bunch of Fairies, but you were all sucking wind at the end. The real test will come when you have to do it with full kit, tin hats, rifles, and in the early mornings when dew coats everything. And, of course, you'll have to do it at the same speed.'

After lunch we visited a pool of stagnant water, over which was a hawser (a thick rope) we were to crawl halfway along, fall beneath while maintaining a hand-hold, then regain the position back atop. It sounded chancy. Boswell was in fatigues and he gave us a demonstration. He lowered his body onto the rope and stretched his arms and upper body along it, causing it to creak as it took his weight. His left leg dangled over the water. He bent his right leg so his knee pointed at the water from the other side of the hawser, but his ankle remained hooked over the rope, which ran under his right shoulder and to the left of his crotch. He pulled with his arms and pushed with his right ankle until he reached the middle of the tank. 'This is how one crawls along a single rope. While this wee exercise is not about transporting yerself along a rope, ya need ta know how ta do it.' He allowed his body to slip from the rope, then dangled above the water, his boots almost touching the surface. Once he was still, he bent his arms, kicked up his right leg and hooked his ankle over the rope. He paused momentarily, then swung the rest of his body up, smoothly regained his original position, and pushed/pulled himself toward the end of the tank.

'That, men, is how the regain should be done. If ya swing up too robustly, you'll flip over and come down the other side. Johnson, why don't ya give it a shot!'

Jack laughed. 'Give over. 'E'll get soaked.'

I worried he may be correct as I settled carefully onto the rope before crawling hesitantly along it. At what I judged to be the hall-way point, I rolled off the rope and ended up swinging like a pendulum over the water.

'Well done, laddie,' said Boswell. 'Now make your regain.'

I took a second to recap what I'd seen Boswell do before I swung my legs up and got my right ankle over the rope. I stretched myself in preparation to complete the regain and my cigarette lighter and loose change fell from my pocket and splashed into the dark liquid below.

'Jesus fuck!' I shouted.

'Lesson number one,' Boswell put on his best Scottish brogue, 'is ta always remember ta empty yer wee pockets before attempting a regain.'

'Hah fuckin' hah,' I said.

'Dinna fash yerself, laddie. What's a few paltry pennies to a banker?' I heard everyone laugh. 'We do but learn from our experiences,' said Boswell haughtily as everyone deposited the contents of their pockets on the grass.

Mindful of Boswell's words about flipping over the other side, I gingerly swung myself back above the rope. When I was confident of my balance, I inched my way to the end while the rest the squad queued to practice the manoeuvre.

'When bullets are whistling past yer earhole, laddie, you'll have to move a bit smarter than that. Plus you'll have a full pack an' your rifle on yer back and a tin hat on yer wee head.'

Three guys slipped into the murky water. 'Lesson number two,' said our DI. 'This tank is never cleaned, so, if ya wish to avoid contracting typhoid, make sure ya complete the exercise successfully. Either that, or convince the Banker to clean it out so he can reclaim all the pennies that must be lying on the bottom. Bear in mind that this was a demonstration of what is to come. The PTIs will have you doin' it with a full kit and at ten times the speed.'

The first dinner at Lympstone was awful; undefined meat, potatoes, and French beans, all coated with brown, lumpy gravy. Someone ventured it was like soggy cardboard, though why they knew how cardboard tasted was a mystery. The meal was odourless but Sammy speculated the food might be off, until someone, who had presumably once eaten rotten food, assured us it had not tasted as bad as the stuff on our trays.

As we still owed Bobby money, Jack and I declined Pete and Spike's invitation to join them for egg, chips and beer in the NAAFI. We stayed in the hut with a bunch of squaddies and told each other lies about sexual and sporting exploits. There was an ambience I hadn't experienced. We formed a wide circle around the unlit stove in the centre of the hut, turned up the volume of the radio, sang songs and told jokes. As guys joined us, the circle widened. Sammy amused us with stories about his time in Borstal. Dennis told about being a drummer.

'Hang Down Your Head Tom Dooley' came on the radio and we loudly did it proud.

Scouser John told of how he'd seen The Beatles when they were The Quarrymen.

'What d'ya mean beetles?' someone asked.

'Beatles as in beat – ya know, beat music.'

'Seems strange ta me. What were wrong with The Quarrymen?'

'I dunno, but The Beatles is good, it's a name you'll remember.' He looked deflated when most shrugged and said they'd not heard of the group.

Spike and Pete returned and, as the circle had reached its extremes, climbed on top lockers as if they were balcony seats. Others returning from the cinema did the same. Eventually, the whole squad was present, swapping stories, telling of ludicrous sexual escapades and generally bonding.

Geordie bragged of having a threesome with a mother and daughter. 'Of course ya did! We all know 'ow parties like ta keep it in the family,' Pete said.

Chris claimed he'd had a threesome with 'a coupla lesbos'.

'That were kind of ya,' said Ron. 'They probably wanted proof their way were the best way.'

We all laughed.

Ray tried to convince us Tottenham Hotspur had scouted him and asked him to report for a try-out at White Hart Lane. 'My old man reckoned I weren't good enough for the first team and I'd be better off joining up.'

'Bollocks!'

'An' ya never gave it a shot? Loada rubbish.'

'He coulda been,' said Hank. 'I was on Liverpool's books.'

'Yeah, right! Me too,' shouted Spike and we all laughed raucously.

'Straight up,' Hank insisted.

'And ya only just remembered it now!'

'Well, we 'aven't 'ad a chat like this before, 'ave we.'

'Still an' all, mate, if you'd been on Liverpool's books you would've told someone before now.'

'I didn't wanna brag,' said Hank.

Steve saved him from further embarrassment. 'Me an' this Tar picked up two parties when we went 'ome after passing out at Deal. They was really up for it an'...'

'That's nothing,' Jack shouted. 'Me an' Banker went to see two school teachers in The Smoke. They taught us ...'

'Where the fuck would you meet two bleedin' teachers?'

'One of them was 'er as put 'er name and number in Banker's pocket when we lined the Mall. You 'eard about that. They were 'ockey tea ...' He looked at me. 'What were they, oppo?'

'Games mistresses,' I said.

He laughed. 'Yeah, that were it, games mistresses. They was games mistresses. Anyways, when we went back to their place, Banker's partie acted like she wanted some rough sex an' ...'

'That's a bit iffy wiv parties ya don't know, ain't it?'

The same look that had been on Jack's face that night, as if he had learned something, appeared again. 'They seemed all right to us ... they 'ad this bottle of wine ...'

'Bottles of wine, games mistresses, rough sex! You're as bad as 'Ank.'

'Give over! This is straight up an' ...'

A couple of guys waved his words away. 'Fuckin' rubbish!'

I saw a dejected look on Jack's face. 'It's true, guys,' I said.

'Fuck off, Banker. True my arse.'

Parade next morning was in full battle dress. Being the new squad, the Adjutant and the RSM honoured us with a visit. Both men welcomed us to the camp and promised us the next few months would prove to be the hardest of our lives.

'This is where you will become men. We're going to turn you into Royal Marines, *whatever* it takes.'

The Adjutant strolled away and the RSM marched off with Sergeant Boswell. Dusty took a position in front of the squad and we waited for the PTIs.

Bert Stephenson marched silently in his plimsolls to where we waited. He wore a white vest with red piping and a crossed-Indian-clubs motif, white shorts and socks. He had curly blond hair, baby blue eyes, flashing white teeth and a lot of veined muscle.

'Good morning, men,' he said. 'Welcome to Lympstone. The two Corporals behind me are my assistants and we're going to take you through most of your training during the next few months. The first thing you must do is forget about being The

Queen's Squad. You are now starting at the bottom of the pile again and it is going to take a lot of pain and sweat and probably blood before you regain the dizzying heights of that relative stardom. To put it bluntly, everyone here regards you all as a pile of shit. The one thing you have in your favour is me. I'm the man who's going to turn you into Royal Marine Commandos. Do not draw any wrong conclusions from my plimsolls. I can, and will, kick the mother-loving-shit out of each and every one of you if you piss me off.' The two Corporals, who were dressed like Stephenson, stepped around him and wandered through our ranks. 'Word is,' the sergeant continued, 'that you call yourselves Fairies. Let me just say that if you don't move fast enough for me or my assistants, you'll find a foot so far up your arse, you'll start talking like a fairy.'

'He's a mean fucker, ain't he,' one of the Corporals mocked.

Sammy let a chortle escape.

The second Corporal was in front of him within two seconds, 'What's so bleedin' funny, arsehole?' he screamed, his face a couple of inches from Sammy's nose.

'Nothin', Corporal.'

'Oh, you laugh at nothin', do ya?' Sammy kept his mouth shut. 'I'm waitin'!'

'I laughed at the other Corporal's joke.'

'Hey, Dinger. This Fairy thinks yer funny.'

Dinger felt flattered. 'The guy's gotta good sense of 'umour. What'dya want from me?'

Corporal number two turned back to Sammy. 'Are you trying to start trouble between us, ya shit?'

'No, Corporal.'

'You're a fuckin' troublemaker. What's your name?'

'Samuels, Corporal.'

'Well Samuels, I'm going ta be keepin' my eye on you. I don't like trouble-makers.'

Stephenson broke in. 'Are you done, Corporal Tucker?'

Tucker slammed a fist into Sammy's mid-section. 'I am for now,' he replied, his eyes still on Sammy. I was impressed by Sammy's refusal to bend to the blow, although he exhaled a noisy breath.

Stephenson turned to Dusty. 'You the squad leader?'

'Yes, Sergeant.'

'Good. Have the squad lined up and ready at the assault course, dressed in fatigues, in ten minutes. You know where it is?'

'Yes, Sergeant.'

Corporal 'Dinger' Bell split us into groups of three and set us off at regular intervals. Sergeant Stephenson wandered over the course watching our progress and Corporal 'Tommy' Tucker waited at the end, making a note of everybody's time. As the last trio completed the course, Stephenson arrived with them.

'I can see why you call yourselves Fairies. How come so much huffing and puffing? And what was all that at the little wall? You're all near enough the same height as the fuckin' thing. If you can't get your arse over an obstacle of your own height in a hurry, you may as well lie down and die right now. Most of you went through the underground tunnel like pregnant nuns. From now on, we'll drop a few thunder flashes in there. Maybe that'll convince you to move your fat arses. When you get to the open ditch, you will dive for a rope without hesitation. If one isn't waiting, tough shit. When you get to the top of the fifteen-foot wall, you immediately drop down on the other side. We didn't build it so you can view the fucking scenery from up there. Any man who can't complete this Boy Scout's course to my satisfaction will be sent home to his mother.'

Dusty marched us over to the 'regain' tank where we stood and waited.

Sammy was not happy. 'I'm gonna get that Tucker.'

An anonymous voice said, 'Sure, Sammy.'

Dusty called for silence. Making a member of a squad its leader was one of Her Britannic Majesty's better ideas. We were not about to cause trouble for a squaddie and so it was easy for Dusty to maintain order.

Our instructors finally arrived. Stephenson had us break ranks and watch a 'regain' as demonstrated by Corporal Tucker. The man made the manoeuvre look easy.

'Okay. Now it's your turn. Anything falls into the tank belongs to Corporal Bell and me,' Tucker announced.

But we had learned Spike's lesson and our pockets were empty. Two squaddies who stayed dry on our first attempts took a dip and it dawned on us that it was not always going to be easy. Tucker acted like a fairground barker, insulting us and occasionally jerking the rope. As Stephenson said nothing, our overall performance was presumed acceptable. When we had all made a regain, he gave us ten minutes to change into full battle dress and report to the parade ground.

That night Jack and I drew our first guard duty at Lympstone. For the hours between ten and two, we wandered the camp perimeter carrying axe handles and fighting boredom. When we returned to the guard room, we found the tea was stale. I thought I would have no trouble sleeping through what remained of the night but I was wrong. The comings and goings of duty personnel and their whispered conversations prevented me from sleeping for what seemed like an age.

Boswell inspected our kit on Saturday morning. 'You men aren't doing badly,' he said after someone complained about the PTIs. 'Believe me, if Sergeant Stephenson thought you needed it, you would be going over the assault course and regain tank this weekend. Having said that, those of you who know you need more practice should use the weekend to bring yourselves up to scratch.'

Jack and I stayed on board Saturday and Sunday. We had a couple of beers in the NAAFI, went to the camp cinema to see 'To Hell and Back', and repaid the money borrowed from Bobby.

After the Adjutant inspected us on the Monday of our third week, he strode to the front of our formation, Boswell and Stephenson at his rear.

'I am informed you are to go over the assault course in full gear today. Well done. A squad at your point of training would normally wait another week before doing that. It would appear the reports we got from The Depot regarding H Squad might be correct. That means you will have to double your efforts if you intend to live up to your reputation. It is one thing to impress when marching around like toy soldiers.' I saw Boswell raise his eyebrows. 'You'll have to do a lot more than that to impress the people hereabouts.' He turned to the Sergeants. 'Good work. Keep it up.'

The man saluted us, turned briskly about, and left. Stephenson dismissed us and sent us to change into fatigues with full gear.

As we were fastening our packs, Spike mumbled, 'Keep up the good fuckin' work, 'e tells 'em. It's *us* what's runnin' around like idiots.'

We lined up in threes at the start of the assault course wearing steel helmets, packs stuffed with kit, ammunition pouches full of empty magazines and our rifles slung across our backs. Our gear seemed heavier than it probably was. The first ditch seemed considerably wider and the six-foot wall had definitely grown a few inches. As I entered the underground concrete tunnel, the tip of my rifle, which was slung over my shoulder, hit the lip of the tunnel's entrance and for an instant I wondered if Tucker was trying to hold me back. Once in the burrow, I took the opportunity to tighten the strap of the helmet that had been bouncing on my head with every step. As soon as I was out and running again, I realized I had not tightened the strap enough. The pounding of the head protector was not in tune with my body and so I found a new rhythm with which to pace myself. I eventually figured out a beat that was a combination of my feet hitting the ground, the rifle pounding on my back and the helmet jumping up and down on my head. Tucker waited at the end of the course and took great pleasure in telling us how our times had deteriorated.

'Over two minutes longer, Johnson. You're gonna 'ave to do a lot better than that.'

'Yes, Corporal,' you petrified turd.

'And by the way,' he added. 'Take better care of your rifle in future. Let me see if ya damaged it when you careened inta the concrete pipe.' I took it off my back and handed to him. He made an exaggerated inspection of the weapon. 'You're lucky. I don't see anything wrong. Be more careful in future.' He slammed the rifle into my midriff and I let out a grunt. 'What did you say?'

'I didn't say anything, Corporal.'

'Bollocks! I distinctly heard something. What was it?'

'I grunted when you forced the rifle into my stomach.'

'Forced? Are you one of these fairies I've heard about?'

'Yes, I am, Corporal. I'm one of Boswell's Fairies.'

'Really! You sound proud of the fact.'

'Me, too,' I heard Jack say. 'I'm one of Boswell's Fairies.'

'An' me,' said Sammy.'

Spike made the same declaration, and then everyone announced they were Boswell's Fairies.

'What *is* this world coming to?' Tucker said. 'Fuckin' Royal Marine Fairies.' But he wore a smile as he said it.

Stephenson made no comment.

At the regain tank, eleven of us took a dip and Tucker seemed so pleased he folded his arms and whistled, 'A Life on the Ocean Wave'. Still Stephenson kept silent.

Spike, Pete, Sammy, Dennis, Jack and I dressed again in full gear and went over the assault course several times that evening in an attempt to improve our times. There were bods there from other squads and they paired with us to pace us. At Dusty's suggestion, we had filled our packs with building bricks, wedged into place with bits of wood or anything else we could find. 'That way, if ya go in the water, ya' 'ave less dhobi ta do.' We went to the regain tank and practised getting back onto the rope, realising Dusty's idea of the bricks had been brilliant.

Apart from the food in the galley, life was going well for us. We had grown to enjoy sandwiches made of mustard, ketchup, salt and pepper. Breakfast was the best meal of the day but the chefs occasionally erred at lunchtime and made an acceptable soup. Tucker was an irritation, but we derived pleasure from planning his downfall and ridiculing him at every opportunity. He became the symbol for anything ridiculous. If we heard news of a building collapse, we assumed Tucker had been in the area. If a football player scored an own goal, we knew he'd taken lessons from Tucker. Any kind of disaster reported on the radio was greeted with, 'That fucker Tucker's done it again.' Training was going well and none of us was in trouble for any major infractions. There were just two problems in our lives.

Pete Edwards and Jimmy Allison decided that life in Her Britannic Majesty's Corps of Royal Marines, as experienced at Lympstone, was not to their liking. They had done well enough at The Depot, while keeping a low profile. They now complained loudly and long about everything. They hated the food (they had a point). They hated Corporal Tucker (another point conceded). They thought all training was without purpose, other than to cause them pain and frustration. There was too much kit to maintain, too much violence (mostly from Tucker) and too much guard duty. The work was too physical and there was too much of it. Our pay was insufficient, as was our free time.

One night, when their carping was louder than Radio Luxembourg, Spike exploded.

'What the 'ell did you guys think you were joining, the bleedin' army?'

When the pair realized nobody was paying attention, they feigned illness. Medical staff knew the two were malingering and charged them accordingly. Both received four hours of extra drill, which they saw as evidence of persecution. They spent most of their free time at the cinema or in the NAAFI and the maintenance of their kit suffered.

When both men's turnout was below par, Boswell awarded the entire squad four hours extra drill and his message got through to us. After completing the first two hours that night, we were disgruntled. As we started to prepare our kit for the next day, Edwards slammed his webbing onto his bed.

'This is fuckin' rubbish!' he exclaimed.

'Rubbish?' Pete exploded. 'You're the fuckin' rubbish that got us extra drill!' He grabbed Edwards by his collar and half led him; half dragged him down the hut's central aisle towards the exit. The space narrowed at the stove and Sammy had to make a quick re-alignment of the chimney pipe knocked out of kilter by the floundering Edwards. Comma grabbed Allison by the front of his tunic and set out after Pete.

'Look out for the chimney pipe,' Sammy implored him.

'Look out for the fuckin' chimney pipe,' Comma gruffly told Allison.

Those of us present followed. When Pete reached the heads, he kicked open the door. 'Anyone not in H Squad get outta here now!'

'Hang on mate, I'm in the middle of a bleedin' dump,' came from one of the stalls.

'In that case, stay there 'til someone tells ya to come out.'

Attention reverted to the two malingerers.

'What's with you two? You intent on screwin' all of us?'

'Piss off!' Allison spat into Comma's face.

Comma wiped the saliva from his cheek, grabbed Allison and kneed him in the groin. Pete drove his fist into Edward's solar plexus and he too doubled over, desperately trying to suck air into his lungs.

'You two guys gotta smarten up fast,' Pete told them. 'We don't fancy getting extra drill because of ya, so if we 'ave ta, we'll kick the shit out've ya every night. If ya still fuck up, we'll beat you so bad, you'll spend a coupla weeks in the sick bay and get back-squadded. Ya got it?'

'Bollocks!' said Edwards and so Pete kneed his testes.

Comma straightened the still-bent Allison. 'You got anythin' ta say?'

'Shove it up yer arse.'

Comma whipped his forearm under the man's chin and smashed his head into the tiled wall behind him. 'Your arse mate, not mine!'

Dusty and Ron ran into the heads. 'What the hell's goin' on? Let these two alone right now. Everyone out of here. Now! What the fuck did ya think you were doin'?'

'These two aren't gonna screw us anymore,' shouted Pete.

'I hear ya Pete, but splittin' their heads open is not the way ta go about it.'

'Who gives a shit?'

'We all do! We're H squad. Remember?'

Comma said to Jack, 'Thanks fer teachin' me that forearm smash. It works a treat.'

Edwards and Allison had disappeared. The rest of us filed out of the door.

'Okay to leave now?' the man in the stall asked.

We went to Exeter gang-handed on Saturday afternoon. As we exited the station and strolled around the city, more than a few people gave us apprehensive looks. We left the cathedral, castle, museums, art galleries, gardens, and old houses to those who appreciated them, and concentrated on other sites. The first pub we entered was in the city centre. It was a cavernous place with a stage and dance floor, but it felt dark and dirty without bright lights and dancers. It was obvious that nothing much would happen until later, so we made a note of the location and set out to find something livelier.

Jack and I split from the rest of the group and ducked into a restaurant Keith Blackburn had recommended. The food was wonderful, but the ancient waitresses didn't hide their belief that we should dine elsewhere. They didn't get a tip.

We found a pub wherein we could wash down lunch. Two thirty-something barmaids wore blouses cut so low one could see aureoles straining to burst free. I let Jack negotiate the purchase of a couple of pints while I concentrated on the orbs of flesh.

'What time ya get off?' Jack ventured.

'Closing time,' was the curt reply. 'My boyfriend picks me up. Why?'

'Oh, just wonderin'.' Jack smiled as he handed the money to the woman.

I bought the next two pints from a different barmaid, although she could have been the identical twin of her co-worker.

'What time you get off, then?' I asked.

'I date Marines, not recruits,' the sweet-natured woman advised me.

'Really? Why's that?'

'They have more money. Take it somewhere else, love. There's plenty of girls your own age just waiting for the likes of you two.'

At the next pub, Jack tried the line Peadar had used in Manchester. 'We've just gotten outta the nick and after doin' two long years inside we really need some female company, if ya know what I mean.'

'You're two bleedin' recruits. Don't give me that rubbish.'

When we later returned to the first watering hole, we found it starting to fill with customers. A few of the early birds were unattached. We found out why when they pointedly told us they would remain virgins until the day they married. It became easy to recognise parties who went to dance halls to listen to the music and wait for the pubs to close and their boyfriends to join them. We'd learned at Deal they were anti-servicemen because their mothers correctly advised them we could easily escape their clutches. Braver ones flirted with us for drinks. However, when their drunken, belligerent boyfriends finally appeared, the women usually smiled and feigned pleasure at seeing them. Some recruits became angry when ditched for some unwashed drunken civilian. Embarrassed parties occasionally asked if buying them drinks meant one could expect sex. When they were told 'yes', the fights started.

We usually waited until after eleven-thirty before attempting to separate a girl from her friends. Those still waiting for someone became immediately skittish and looked over their shoulders in fear, or just got up and quickly walked away. Others looked impatiently at the time and the door, becoming more irritated as the minutes ticked by. Those were the ones to grab. They became angry when their dates failed to materialise and would leap into bed with handsome young Marines out of spite. The only remaining problem was to find said bed.

Betty was such a girl. She stood at the junction of the stage and the passageway to the toilets. I watched her tap her foot, more with impatience than to the beat of the music. Jack was trying to convince some young thing he was a professional wrestler whom she could see on the television almost any Saturday afternoon.

'Oh yeah, so how come I didn't see you today, then?'

'I got injured on Wednesday night in Plymouth. The quacks won't allow me ta fight fer another week so I'm 'ere in Exeter takin' it easy.'

'How did you get injured? I mean, what happened? What did you hurt?'

I left Jack to persuade the young redhead that tender loving care would soon straighten him out and went to offer my support to the thin blonde woman still tapping her foot.

'Hey. I saw you standin' here and wondered if you'd like to 'ave my seat at the bar. Perhaps I can buy you a drink?'

'I'm waiting for someone.'

'He's not turning up now, is he? The pubs shut an hour ago.'

She stared at my face for a couple of seconds. 'I'll wait a while longer if it's all the same to you.'

'Okay. I'll be at the bar if you change your mind. My name's Paul. You?'

'Just go.'

I returned to the bar in time to hear Jack's intended conquest giggle. 'That can't be true!'

'Cross me 'eart,' said Jack with all the sincerity he could fake.

'Come on then.' She was still laughing as she picked her shawl and handbag off the back of her barstool, 'This I've gotta see.'

'Nice talking to ya, buddy. See ya around,' the professional wrestler said to me as he departed. 'Good luck with the Marines.'

'Yeah. Good luck.'

'Don't need it ma friend. I'm a pro!'

I was ordering another drink when I felt a tap on my shoulder.

'Can I have a Bacardi and Coke, please?' asked the blonde-haired woman as she climbed on to the barstool.

'Sorry about your boyfriend. You and *I* can still have a good time.'

She said, 'I hope so,' without enthusiasm.

Betty lived on the outskirts of the city and it occurred to me I might have trouble finding my way back to the railroad station. We didn't bother with the usual face saving games at her front door.

'You can come in if you like, but please be quiet. My parents live here.'

I took off my shoes and followed her up the stairs in my socks. When the fourth step creaked under my weight, I inwardly cringed and waited two or three seconds to see if Dad would appear above me.

Betty took me to 'the spare room'. We stripped and lay on a mattress covered with a cool plastic sheet. The only movement the woman made was to repeatedly cover my mouth with her hand while she whispered 'Shhhh' to me.

The next morning, she awoke me with a hand over my mouth again. 'Shhh,' she said her eyes wide with emphasis.

I pushed her hand away. 'What are yer parents gonna do?' I whispered. 'Throw you out?'

'Shhh.' Betty gestured again for me to be silent and cocked her head, listening for any noise or movement elsewhere in the house. 'I lied to you,' she whispered. 'I was waiting for me husband at the dance hall last night. My parents aren't here but he's asleep in the next room.'

'He's what!' Then I realized, 'You knew the set up last night!'

'Shhh,' she said, pointing to the wall behind her. 'He says he got too drunk to meet me and came home in a taxi. Sorry.'

'Fuckin' sorry!' The fierce whispering was making me hoarse.

'Shhh.'

'How do you know all this?' I asked.

'Shhh. I got nervous during the night so I went into the other room to make sure he didn't get up.'

'Is this a joke?'

Her eyes said it wasn't. 'Shhh. Please don't make a scene.'

'Don't worry lady, I'm gone.' I dressed as quickly and silently as I could, picked up my shoes, and quietly descended the stairs. When the fourth step creaked, I threw caution to the winds and ran out of the house, leaving the front door open. Betty's husband could close it. Only after I had turned a corner did I stop to put on my shoes and adjust my clothing.

As I entered the hut, Dusty approached me. He breathed on his brasses, then rubbed them. 'Boswell came in around six last night an' made a surprise locker inspection. 'E found three days of unwashed laundry in Allison's locker and told Edwards 'is rifle was dirty enough ta grow potatoes in the barrel. Each of 'em received two 'ours extra drill. They reckoned it was unfair to 'old locker inspections when so many guys 'ad gone ashore. Boswell took off for the stratosphere. Told 'em those who'd gone ashore did so because their kit was up ta scratch. Said as they spent money in the NAAFI every night, they probably couldn't afford to go ashore. Anyways, there's gonna be another locker inspection at eleven-thirty this mornin'. Ya better make sure yer stuff's all shipshape.'

An hour later, Jack walked in the door, together with half-a-dozen guys who had caught the same train. Dusty, polishing his boots, began the story once more.

I was reading a book when Jack joined me.

'How'd ya do last night?'

'Ya wouldn't believe me, if I told ya!' But I told him anyway.

'Give over!' He laughed. 'You sure 'er old man wasn't watching ya through an 'ole in't wall or summat?'

I grinned. 'How'd you get on?'

'Worse than you. Bitch lets me take 'er 'ome, then stands on 'er front doorstep an' tells me she'd love to see me again and can she give me her bleedin' number. Writes it down with some make-up pencil thing on the back of me 'and.'

I grinned. 'That was nice of 'er.'

'Give over! Fuckin nice! I wiped the back of me 'and down the sleeve of 'er jumper. Keep yer bleedin' number, I told 'er.'

'She must have loved you for that.'

He shrugged. 'I started to walk 'ome but I was tired so I slept on a sun-lounger on someone's front lawn. Woke up stiff as a bleedin' board this morning. Anyways,' he continued, ''ow're we supposed ta dress for this 'ere locker inspection?'

'Any way we want, apparently. It's a locker inspection only, so how we're dressed doesn't matter.'

We stripped off our clothes and headed for the showers. We laundered our under clouts, socks and shirts and hung them up to dry. When we re-entered the hut wearing our towels sarong fashion, we found Edwards and Allison had returned.

'You pricks ready for a locker inspection?' I demanded.

'What's it to you?' Allison shot back.

'I'll tell ya what it is ta me.' Jack moved menacingly toward the man. 'I don't like extra drill or extra guard duty, so if you and your bleedin' oppo cause me to get any, I'll kick your arses from 'ere to Exeter.'

I grabbed Jack's arm. 'Leave it. This isn't the time.'

Jack shrugged my arm away and took a mock swing at Allison's head. The guy ducked, then turned crimson as he realized Jack's intention. We returned to our space and were putting our personal gear away when Boswell entered the hut.

'Attennnnnnnnnntion!' Dusty barked.

Boswell wore a serious face. Most guys were present but we were all dressed differently. Some were ready to go ashore as soon as Boswell dismissed us. Jack and I still had our towels wrapped around us. We stood by our open lockers, not sure how to behave during the informal inspection. Standing to attention in bare feet and dressed only in an olive green towel made me a little self-conscious. Boswell progressed down one side of the hut, making thorough inspections. He found a trace of dust on top of Ray's locker.

'You won't be going ashore until that has been properly cleaned, will you, Green.' It wasn't a question and Ray knew to remain silent.

Boswell arrived at my locker. 'Your soap dish is a tad wet, Johnson. Why is that?'

'I've just had a shower, Sergeant. It would have been dry, but you turned up a little early.'

'Early?' Boswell looked at his watch. 'So I am, laddie.'

He moved to Jack's locker. 'You shower with Johnson, Mason?'

'At the same time, Sergeant, yeah.'

'Semantics laddie, pure semantics.'

Jack didn't respond.

Half way down the other side of the hut, Boswell arrived at Allison's bed space. He used his pace-stick to poke around the bottom of the locker.

'It appears you havena done your laundry, laddie. Why is that?'

'You said to go ashore, Sergeant. I didn't have time to do dhobi *and* go ashore.'

'Dinna be a smartarse, Allison. You're in a 'no-win' situation here, so cut the bullshit.'

He moved to Edwards' locker and took out his rifle. He stripped out the working mechanism and held the weapon up to the light so he could see inside the barrel. 'I see you've attempted to clean your rifle, Edwards. Unfortunately, you've done such a sloppy job, it's now swimming in oil.' He used one of Edwards' clean towels to wipe oil off his hands. As he did so, he caught sight of the man's razor and picked it up with the tips of his thumb and forefinger, seemingly not wanting to touch the object. 'What have we here, laddie? Has Her Britannic Majesty invented a razor that not only cuts the whiskers from a man's face, but can actually grow the stuff as well? Don't *you* tell me I arrived early, because I can see this wee tool hasna been used in a while.' Boswell dropped the razor onto Edward's bed and turned to face the rest of us. 'Except for some minor infractions, the inspection has gone well ... with two exceptions. I leave it to you as a squad to sort things out. One of you is getting crabby, so ya could all be in danger of playing hosts to the wee beasties. As today is Sunday, we will pretend this inspection never took place. However, as you all are aware, tomorrow is another day. If I, or anyone else, find anything amiss tomorrow, you will *all* feel the wrath of God. Do I make myself clear?'

'Sergeant!' shouted Dusty in acknowledgement.

As soon as Boswell left, we grabbed Allison, Edwards and their laundry and dragged them off to the heads where we gave them brutal scrubbing until their bodies were bright red and lined with bristle marks from head to toe. 'That's how ya scrub summat. Now do yer dhobi.'

Dusty, Ron, Spike, Pete, Jack and I walked down the hill to a pub called 'The Pig and Whistle' for lunch. The place had a low ceiling from which hung bric-a-brac. Sawdust covered the floor. At the rear of the room, a skittle-alley ran across its breadth. Jack and I ordered pints of best bitter but the landlord convinced us to try 'scrumpy'. The liquid appeared cloudy and foreign bodies floated in it, but the man assured us they were signs of a good pint.

Jack screwed up his face. 'This shit tastes like apple-flavoured vinegar!'

'That's the way it should taste. You'll not find a better pint anywhere.'

We accepted his word and the price was right, so we decided to see if we could get to like the rough cider. We all ordered homemade French bread, cheddar cheese and pickled onions before taking a table near the skittle alley where we put our names on the game board. The food was tasty and, while devouring it, I tried to pick up tips on how to play the game.

Spike put some money in the jukebox and played 'Locomotion' by Little Eva.

When our turn came, the opposing team had won seven straight games and we did nothing to endanger their run of success. Next to fall were Pete and Spike, but then Dusty and Ron surprised the four of us by winning.

'This ain't the only pub in the world with a skittle alley,' Dusty said with a grin.

Bobby Pearson sat alone at the hut's only table, making entries in a journal. 'The sport of kings isn't played on Sundays,' he explained. 'I'm updating me records on the 'orses I follow.'

It seemed like serious work. ''Ow much you make this week, Bobby?' Pete asked.

'That's fer me ta know. By the way, bloody Edwards and Allison flipped their lids while you were out. They mixed a bottle of aftershave with some rum they'd bought ashore an' drank the stuff.'

Dusty raised his eyebrows. 'You're shittin' us, right?'

'Straight up! I went down the sick bay and told the duty SBA what'd happened. He and another guy ran up here and hauled the two of them away.'

'Jesus Christ,' Spike whispered.

'Give over!' my oppo laughed. 'What'd they wanna do that for?'

'They're trying to work their ticket,' Ron said.

'What's 'work their ticket'?' I asked

'Trying ta work their discharge. They'll probably claim they're nuts, or a couple of faggots, or somethin'. Guys in the Paras did the same thing. Right, Dust?'

'Yeah. I remember a couple of shits who tried it. I don't think they were successful though.'

Twenty-eight of us paraded in fatigues on Monday morning. No one mentioned the absence of Edwards and Allison. The Commanding Officer said a concerned father of two young girls had reported a man, presumed to be a Marine recruit, had spent Saturday night sleeping on his garden furniture. The practice was to cease forthwith.

After parade, we stood in line behind other squads, waiting for our turn to go over the assault course before doing a regain. From the tank, we went to the rifle range for a brief introduction to some foreign weaponry. We all fired a few rounds with three different weapons, but did not learn much about them. The chances of us having to be proficient with Russian rifles were slim, but it was conceivable we might one day need to use the American 'armalite' rifle.

Edwards and Allison re-joined the squad, having had their stomachs pumped. Their churlish attitude was dulled by embarrassment. The company commander had fined them each a month's pay and restricted them to camp, pending further review – whatever that meant. We all envisioned more trouble.

Pete discussed the situation with Dusty. 'Why don't we ask Boswell ta 'ave 'em back-squadded so they can 'ave a chance with a new squad?

'No can do,' Dusty replied. 'We do that an' we admit to a lack of unity in H Squad.'

'Yeah, but there *is* a lack of bleedin' unity.'

'Then it's up to us ta put things right.'

'Ya mean we 'ave to cover fer the two of 'em, or put 'em in the sick bay?'

'They'd rat us out if we put 'em in the sick bay.'

'So we 'ave ta carry these guys 'til the end of training?'

'Or change their attitude,' Ron joined in. 'There 'as ta be guys in every squad who're a pain one way or another. It's part of our training ta 'andle situations like this. We 'ave ta show we can take care of our own shit.'

'Tell ya what,' Dusty suggested. 'Me an' Ron'll take Edwards, an' you an' Spike take Allison. Jack and The Banker can follow up. That way, we'll cover the assault course and stuff. The whole squad is gonna have to keep an eye out for their equipment and whatnot. We'll give 'em an inspection at nine every night an' make sure their kit and dress are ready for the next day. That way, anythin' we find amiss can be put right before lights out.'

'But they get too much extra drill and guard duty for that to work.'

'If we keep 'em clean, they won't get the extras, will they? We've gotta help 'em over the next coupla days, or until they've worked off any drill or guard duty they still 'ave against them.'

'Jesus Aitch Christ! Ya know what yer saying?'

'Yep. But we gotta do it.'

That night the squad got together and cleaned, ironed and stowed the kit of the two malcontents while they polished and repolished their footwear.

'You two'd better get it together, 'cause I'm not enjoying this one bit,' Comma told them. 'You screw up again and you'll be takin' a nasty tumble off the top of the 'igh wall.'

The following day, Stephenson had Bell and Tucker give a demonstration of their expertise on the Tarzan course. To begin, one climbed a rope some twenty-odd feet to reach the web-like circuit strung between trees in a wooded area. The web began with a single rope along which one had to crawl to the next tree. Said rope stretched for more than fifty feet and made us grateful for our experience at the regain tank. Next came three ropes strung together in a vee shape. We walked on the bottom rope and steadied ourselves with one hand on each of the other ropes. Then there were two parallel ropes along which one crawled on hands and knees. On his first time across, Ray allowed the ropes to widen and he became splayed out like a four-pointed star.

'Pretend you're a virgin and pull your legs together,' shouted Tucker.

Other ropes dangled from above, enabling us to transfer from one tree to another. We had seen Johnny Weissmuller perform similar manoeuvres on film and many could not resist aping his call as we swung through the air.

Stephenson wasn't amused. 'This ain't Hollywood. Behave like Royal Marines, not swishing film actors.'

Two parallel ropes came next. We walked sideways along the bottom rope and held onto the one above. The descent, called The Death Slide, was, we were told, the most popular part of the course. As we left the ropes, we came to a single line attached to the tree. The hawser slanted down and away to a distant trunk where it was secured at a point about eight feet above the ground. The rider picked up a toggle, immersed it in water, and then put his right hand through one of its loops. He slung the figure-eight-shaped device over the hawser and put his left hand through the second loop. All one needed to do then was step off the platform and slide down the hawser. At the base, another rope pulled the slide sideways and down and provided a makeshift brake.

As each of us prepared to take the death slide, Stephenson advised us, 'The brake is not always reliable. Keep your legs together and when you come to the end of the slide, make sure you direct both legs to one side of the tree or the other. Failure to do so might ensure a permanent end to your sex life.'

The first time we went 'round the course, the instructors pushed and prodded us. However, as no two people were ever on any section at the same time, it was somewhat easy. Our second assault was a different experience. We set off at twenty-second intervals and found the actions and weight of others on the ropes took away our control and balance. We realized why we had spent so much time at the regain tank. The first reaction was laughter, which Stephenson stifled.

'You think it's funny to look like a bunch of spastics?'

Amusement gone, frustration and anger took over. That made Stephenson happy and so we set ourselves to make him eat his words. We finished the course in an average time of seven and a half minutes.

Tucker smacked Dennis on the back of his head. 'Before you pass out of here, you have to reduce your time to less than four minutes. That's while wearing full battle gear, tin helmets, and carrying rifles. Think you can do it?'

We spent the rest of the week under canvas on Exmoor. Edwards and Allison didn't give us trouble, but their surly attitude made it unpleasant to be near them. Being August in England it rained for the entire three days as we trekked from one compass point to another. We spent Friday night and Saturday morning cleaning our wet and muddy gear. By mid-afternoon on Saturday, the only items not dry were our sleeping bags. The sodden objects hung from the ends of upper bunks and the tops of lockers, causing so much steam we could hardly see one end of the hut from the other.

'We've got to get outta here before we get tubercufuckinlosis,' Jack announced. ''Ow's about Exmouth? I wrestled there a coupla times and I know a place or two ta go. Whaddya say?'

Jack assured me that a particular Italian restaurant was 'the best place to eat in Exmouth'. The owner remembered my oppo and sat us at a wall table under a signed photograph of Jack in his wrestling vest and tights.

I nodded my head at the photo. 'I'm impressed,' I told him.

'Give over,' he said with self-conscious pride.

We stuffed ourselves with pasta, sausages, a tasty sauce, fresh parmesan cheese and a doughy bread. Although the meal cost more than expected, it was worth every penny.

As we were too bloated to drink pints of beer or scrumpy, we decided to have some scotch in the cocktail bar of a large hotel. 'Ya never know, oppo, there might be teachers there.' The only other people in the bar were two middle-aged adults with two passable parties who were the right age as far as Jack and I were concerned.

'You two from Lympstone?' the man asked.

As I was ordering drinks, I let Jack answer.

'Yeah,' was all he said.

'I don't remember seeing you around,' the man persisted.

His observation annoyed me. 'I 'aven't seen you around, so why should you 'ave seen us?'

My attitude didn't deter him. 'We live in the area and have a soft spot for you lads, don't we?'

The woman recognised her cue. 'We certainly do. We're very proud of the Royal Marines. Do you boys get much mail from home?'

'None at all, missus,' said Jack.

I wondered if there was a full moon.

'Deidre and Belinda would love to correspond with you, if you like, wouldn't you, girls?' the woman offered.

'Yes, Mother,' the two girls said flatly.

'Why don't you let us have your names,' the clucking hen persisted.

'Recruits Mason and Johnson.' Jack's interest was growing. 'H Squad,' he added.

I had reservations. 'We're both Fairies, actually,' I said with a false smile as I kicked Jack's foot.

'Oh, how wonderful.' The woman beamed with joy. 'We'll address the mail like that, shall we?' she asked her brood.

I put my now empty glass down on a table next to the door and Jack followed suit.

'Sorry to rush, but we have to meet our dates in five minutes. It's been nice talking to you. Bye.'

As I ushered Jack out of the door, he called back over his shoulder. 'Perhaps we'll see you again.'

'I do hope so,' one of the young parties shouted as her sister, outside her parents' view, mouthed a kiss at us.

When we were on the street, Jack turned to me. 'Are you fuckin' crazy, or what? We were in there. Mother wants us to screw 'er daughters, while 'er bleedin' 'usband fantasies about 'is time as a machine. People're going to believe we really are fuckin' fairies.'

'Fairies, Jack; not fuckin' fairies.'

'What?' Then he got it and burst out laughing. 'Give over! Let's go to a regular boozer.'

Our stomachs were already a little lighter and we went in search of the type of place we knew and preferred. The air in the Black Swan was thick with smoke, cheap perfume and a smell I couldn't identify. No one in the place was ever going to want to write letters to anyone else. Jack bought a couple of pints of scrumpy, which we drank at the bar while we stood and surveyed the crowd. One partie was single-handedly rolling a cigarette while drinking from a pint glass. Another tried to dig something out of her scalp. My father would be tut-tutting. We walked past them and their friends and into another room. It was already around ten and we had to meet someone quickly if we didn't want to go the dancehall route. Three young and seemingly unattached parties caught our eye and we were about to introduce ourselves when we were rudely interrupted.

'You machines smoke?' asked a woman with an impish grin on her face.

'Yeah, sure,' said Jack as he fumbled in his pocket for his packet of Senior Service.

'No no no. Not cigarettes, you silly man. Grass. You wanna smoke some grass?'

'Uh, no. I've never tried it. I mean yes.' My friend looked very sheepish.

'How about you?' the woman asked me.

'Me neither, but I'm willing to try it,' I admitted.

'Well, this is your lucky day. Let's go to the car park and blow a little weed.'

A couple of civilians accosted the girls at the exit.

'Get lost. You had your chance.'

'Screw you, Jill,' said one as he gave Jack and me the once over.

'In your dreams,' the woman told him with a laugh. I gave him a look that told him what I was prepared to do if he continued to be a nausea. Jack feigned a head-butt at him.

'Let it go, man,' his friend advised him.

The two women smiled at each other.

In the car park, Jill took what looked like a hand-rolled cigarette out of a Players packet and lit it. She inhaled the smoke deeply and held it in her lungs. She passed the joint to her friend who also sucked in a lungful of the stuff.

'Here,' she said without breathing as she offered the joint to me. I drew deeply on the stick and had to repress a cough as I inhaled the rough smoke. I passed the joint to Jack and he did the same before passing it on. Jill exhaled and was ready for another hit.

'I guess you're Jill,' I said to our benefactor. Smoke escaped me and I felt like an amateur. 'What's your name?' I asked the second female as she released the smoke from her lungs in short spurts.

'Au' exhale/sniff 'drey.'

It seemed out of place to shake hands. I breathed out our names. 'Paul and Jack.'

Audrey exhaled, 'I've not seen you around here before. You knew?'

'Yeah. We've been at Lympstone for three or four weeks. This is only our second time ashore. We were in Exeter last weekend.'

'Well, welcome to beautiful Exmouth.'

The joint reached me again and I inhaled a second time, before passing it to Jack. I copied the women and tried to suck in additional air. After two attempts, my lungs reached their limit.

'You should inhale less grass. There's only so much you need to hold in at one time. Just hold it in for as long as you can,' Jill jerkily advised me between exhales and sniffs.

'I've bin 'ere before,' Jack squeaked as he let some smoke out. 'I wrestled at some 'all near 'ere.'

Jill put the tips of her thumb and forefinger to her tongue before she nipped the lighted end from the joint. She blew on it to make sure it was out and put the inch long stub in the cigarette packet. 'Well, mister wrestler, how about you and Paul here buy us ladies a drink?'

I felt very happy and my mind had never been clearer. We walked into the pub and the lights dazzled for a moment before I re-acquainted myself. I swayed a little and Jill put her hand on the small of my back.

'You okay, Royal?'

'I have never felt better in my entire life,' I assured her.

Her smile looked so incredibly warm and friendly. 'Why don't I give you a hand with the drinks?' she said.

'What do you and your friend want?'

'Two halves of cider will do.' She was still smiling with her eyes.

The barmaid set the four glasses on the bar and we carried them over to the table where Jack and Audrey waited. As Jill walked in front of me I watched her lovely posterior undulate.

'Audrey 'ere's an actress,' Jack told me as I handed him his pint.

Jill produced sprigs of parsley obtained from a server. 'Here, you two need to chew on some of this stuff. You reek of garlic.'

Audrey responded to Jack's announcement. 'An aspiring actress, really. I don't get many parts except for a pantomime at Christmas and the occasional 'walk on' gig here or in Exeter. But you're not really interested in hearing about my life, are you Paul?'

She was correct. Chewing on the parsley like a lunatic and gazing at Jill made me very happy. She was about five-feet-five with brown shoulder length hair, thick eyebrows and hazel eyes. There was a dark mole on her left temple and a fuzz of hair grew on her cheeks in front of her ears. At the base of her throat was a hollow, the likes of which I had never seen. She had nice breasts, well, nice was a dreary understatement because, although they were covered, I knew they would be firm and soft and wonderful. Her slim waist and long, lovely legs were equally alluring. Sex with her would be terrific. 'You're really beautiful,' I told her.

'Now you're embarrassing me, Royal. Can we change the subject? How about you explain Einstein's theory of relativity.' Her smile reappeared.

I felt I could, if only I knew it! Maybe I could figure it out for them, 'Well, you know the symbol E ...'

'Stop this right now,' laughed Audrey. 'Don't tell me you're a bloody talker.' She turned to Jack. 'What are you, my lovely wrestler, a muncher?'

'What's a muncher?' he asked.

'Someone who can't stop eating when they're stoned.'

Jack thought about it. 'I might be. We'll 'ave ta see.'

'Do you know,' I started, 'the food we get at camp is unbelievably bad. The only meal worth eating is breakfast. It's served buffet style and we can eat as much as we want. This morning I had three fried eggs, three sausages, three rashers of bacon, two slices of fried bread, a whole bunch of mushrooms, some grilled tomatoes, some black pudding, and some fried potatoes. Oh, I had a mug of coffee as well. But the food at other meals is terrible. The boiled potatoes have black parts in them and the vegetables are cooked so much, they're like mush. Or nearly mush, anyway. You know how they get when they're cooked for too long. Mind you, I suppose they keep cooking to a certain extent when they're put out in those trays with the heat underneath them. What do you call that system? Never mind, I'll think of it later. The meat is always very gristly and is overcooked too. We get beef and pork mostly, oh yeah, and lamb. But I think it's really mutton. You know how bad mutton smells when it's cooked. My friend back home's mother, used to cook mutton for their dog, Trixie, Trixie? Yeah, her name was Trixie and that's what she ate all the time ... mutton. I'd say fresh mutton but it can't be fresh after it's been cooked for so long. You could always tell when they cooked some, because the house had that smell. You know what I mean? Well, that's how the so-called lamb smells at camp. All Jack and I eat mostly is the desserts and fresh fruit. Not at breakfast, of course. At breakfast we get fried eggs, sausages ...'

Jill gently put her hand over my mouth and smiled at me. 'Okay Paul, we've got the picture. Let someone else get a word in, will you.'

I would do anything for one of her smiles.

'Phew,' Audrey sighed.

'All this talk about food has made me hungry,' said my pal. My best pal in the world. I put my arm around his shoulder. 'You're the best mate a guy could have,' I told him. Jack laughed, said 'give over', and reciprocated by putting his arm around me.

'You know,' I said, 'I never invited anyone home before. Well, that's not quite true. My mother once threw me a birthday party when I was about six or seven. I think I was probably seven. Maybe eight. But, anyhow, my mother had on this string of pearls and one of the kids, I don't remember his name, I'll think of it later, grabbed the necklace and the string snapped. Bloody pearls rolled all over the floor. She had us on our hands and knees, picking up the fucking things, she did. Screeching at us, "my pearls, my pearls, get my bloody pearls". Well, she might not have said bloody, but then again, maybe she did. I can't really remember.'

'Very interesting, Paul,' Jill said with an indulgent smile.

'Hang on. That's not all of it. She did use the word when she was agitated. Anyhow, we picked up all the pearls we could find, but she made us keep looking. Stupid woman didn't know how many pearls had been on ... should that be in ... in or on? I don't know ... in or on the fucking necklace, so we 'ad to cover every inch of the room. Then she had us looking under chairs and the settee. Kept saying we had to find every one of the things, because the cleaning woman was coming in after the party to Hoover up. She needed every one of the pearls to take to the jeweller so he could restring her precious fucking necklace. So, that was it. She never allowed any of my friends in the house again. When anybody called for me, they had to stand at the back door. Nobody except special people were allowed to knock on the front door. I wonder how anybody knew they were special. Maybe it was just anyone who knocked on the front door became special in my mother's eyes. I mean, whenever I went to call for a friend, I always went to the back door; never really thought about it. Wonder how that was ingrained into us – always use the back door. Wouldn't think about it now, I'd just go to the front door. Must be something to do with children knowing their place. Seen and not heard, and all that shit. You know what I mean?'

'Are you done?' Audrey asked.

'Well, I just wanted to tell my pal, here.'

'Tell him some other time. While you've been gabbing away here the rest of us have been drinking and now your best pal feels hungry. I think he may be a muncher. Any suggestions?'

'Well ...'

'That was a rhetorical question as far as you're concerned.' Jill smiled at me again. I wondered if there was a way to save her smile. Keep it in a clear-glass bottle so that every time I shook it, the smile would appear and make me feel good.

'How about some fips an' chish,' Jack suggested.

The women took us to what they considered the best fish and chip shop in Exmouth. Jill and I held hands as we walked and she let me prattle on about the Labour Party being a bunch of socialists while the Tory politicians had no idea how people like us lived. When we arrived at the chip shop, we added ourselves to the end of a small queue. The odour of the fried food made me realise how hungry I'd become. Jack looked with such intensity at the shelves displaying the already cooked food, that he seemed unaware of Audrey at his side. He licked his lips in anticipation.

'Please tell me you've eaten today,' Audrey pleaded.

'Uh? Oh yeah. I had a breakfast just the same as Paul and then we ate at that Italian joint on Sunderland Place, just before we met you guys.'

'You ate just two hours ago! Anyone looking at you would think you haven't eaten in days. Get a hold of yourself!'

'Uh? Yeah, sorry. It's just that I'm really hungry.'

'We never got fish and chips at camp,' I told Jill, but then I realized I had to amend the statement because we did get fish and chips in the galley. 'Where I was mistaken was that we never get them at the same time and the fish isn't fried. Plus, the chips are nothing like the ones in this chip shop. Or any chip shop. In fact, I know a chip shop in Liverpool that is run by a Chinese couple that....'

My three companions all shouted at me at the same time. 'Shut UP!' In fact, Audrey said, 'Shut the fuck up,' and Jack said, 'Will you please shit'n it?' I suppose Jill was the only one to actually say, 'Shut up.'

Jill laughed, but Audrey told her, 'I never want to be around this man after he's smoked grass.'

'Oh, keep your nickers on,' said Jill. 'It's not as if you're tight-lipped. You're just jealous because he out-talked you.' She laughed and Audrey smiled. Jack continued to be mesmerised by the food.

Then it was the turn of Audrey and Jack to give their order. 'Three fish and three large chips, please,' Jack told the man behind the counter. 'Oh, and a coupla servings of mushy peas.'

He turned to Audrey, 'What'll you 'ave, luv?'

Audrey beat him on his upper arm and shoulder, 'What do I want? What do I want? You big galloot. You think you're going to eat three large servings of fish and chips on your own! You've ordered enough to feed the whole cast of War and Peace, including the extras.'

Jack laughed so hard, tears rolled down his cheeks. 'I know that. I thought you might like some pop, or somethin'.'

'Oh,' said Audrey, suddenly deflated. 'Thank you. I'll have a Tizer, please.'

'What're you smiling at, Johnson?' asked Jill.

'Me? Oh, nothing. It's just that I see my oppo has a need to exceed an elegant sufficiency.'

Audrey screamed, 'Jill! Don't you let him start again.'

I laughed so hard, I had trouble ordering a steak and kidney pudding with chips for me and rockfish with chips for Jill.

We walked for a while, eating our food. Jack inhaled his portion and then tried to pinch some of Audrey's chips.

'Do they give you extra rations when you're out in the field, or wherever it is you people go?' the aggrieved woman asked. 'Do you have to carry additional food on your back? That'd make me cut down on what I eat, wouldn't it you, Jill?'

'I suppose they don't smoke a joint before they go in the field. Imagine trying to keep this one quiet while waiting in ambush!'

I didn't find her remark amusing, but the other three almost collapsed with laughter. The hot steak and kidney pudding was proving difficult to eat with my fingers, so I used my chips to transport the meat to my mouth.

'The food keeps him quiet. I would save some of my chips, if I were you, Jill. They'll come in handy if he gets another case of verbal diarrhoea.'

There were more peals of laughter.

We finished the food and put the leftover papers in a rubbish bin. I slowed my pace to allow Jack and Audrey to open some distance between us. When I judged them to be far enough ahead of us, I stopped and drew Jill to me.

'I've wanted to do this for a while,' I said as I bent my head and kissed her. It was a great kiss. Everything was perfect. When I put my arms around her, she moved into me and the fit of our bodies was just right. Her soft lips felt wonderful. They were neither too wet nor too dry. Her tongue was combative. I raised my head and looked at her face. Jill stepped back and took my hand.

'Come on,' she said and we set off after our now distant friends. As we walked, Jill fished in her handbag and found two sticks of chewing gum. 'You want?' she asked.

The explosion of mint as I worked the gum in my mouth was tremendous and created rivers of saliva.

Jack and Audrey were in an embrace when we caught up with them.

'This is it,' Jill announced between chews.

I mistook her meaning, 'Oh. You mean goodnight?' I was more than a little disappointed and it must have been evident.

'Not unless you want it to be. I was actually hoping that you would make it so.'

'Huh?'

'A good night ... never mind. This is where I live and I'm inviting you up for a proverbial coffee.' Jill grabbed my jacket and strode, with me in tow, toward the house entrance. I left the door open for Audrey and Jack and we ascended the stairs to the first floor flat.

'You picked the right girl, Machine. As I'm the only one working right now, I get first dibs on the only bedroom. Your pal's going to have to make do with the settee or the floor. Got good knees, has he?'

I laughed. 'I dunno. It's not something that comes up in conversation.'

Jill put the kettle on the stove and spooned instant coffee into four mugs.

Jack followed Audrey into the flat and we sat on the floor of the living room, drinking coffee and sharing a joint.

'Listen to me, Royal,' Jill whispered in my ear. 'You have to stop yourself from talking. Do you think you could channel that compulsion into something else?' She lightly bit my earlobe.

The other two were engrossed in each other, so we left them with the joint and our half-empty mugs and went to the bedroom.

Jill slid my jacket off my shoulders and let it drop to the floor. I undid the imitation-pearl buttons of her blouse and was peeling it back from her shoulders as she was pushing my unbuttoned shirt down my back. We restricted each other's movement.

'We can't do it like this,' Jill breathed.

We sorted ourselves out, except for her hose. I attempted to roll a stocking down her leg with my tongue, but stopped when the sensation of having the underneath of my tongue caught between my teeth became too uncomfortable. Jill had the tanned and muscular body I had envisioned. We embraced and Jill turned us around so I could drop to the bed with her on top of me. We kissed and ran hands over each other's bodies until Jill raised herself to a kneeling position and cautioned me not to move again until she gave me permission.

'Anything you say.'

'I didn't think I'd get an argument,' she laughed as she twisted her body one hundred and eighty degrees and bent to envelope my penis with her mouth. I ignored her orders, lifted her thighs off my lower chest, and stretched her body out toward my head until she lay flat on top of me. I opened her legs and used my tongue to search for her clitoris. It took me a couple of seconds, but then I worked her clit with the same rhythm that she worked my cock until she said, 'Chewing gum.' I took it out, stuck it on the bedpost, and resumed. If she wanted to be licked and sucked at a different pace, she could easily let me know. Jill started to move with some urgency and I had to wrap my arms around the small of her back to hold her still. Suddenly, she struggled free of my embrace.

'Time to stoke up,' she grinned as she produced another joint. Two tokes later we resumed our activities in a missionary manner. I entered her as slowly as I could and we moved like a pair of sloths, languishing in every stroke. The grass gave me an intensity of sensation that allowed me to feel every lump, crevasse or wrinkle inside Jill's body. We seemed to go on for hours, alternately grinning and grimacing with the fantastic pleasure. I rose above Jill and grasped the bed's headboard as I repeatedly entered and left her as slowly as I could.

After an age, she beat her fists on my chest, 'Come ON, Machine. Speed it up.'

'Shit, no. This is great.'

She took another tack and started to buck beneath me. I let go the headboard and lay on top of her in an attempt to calm the movement and maintain a rhythm. By necessity, the rhythm became speedier and more violent. After a while, I was slamming myself into her.

She wrapped her arms around my head, her legs around my waist and cried out, 'Way to go, Royal.' I continued to slam myself into her. She looked up at me with her teeth clenched and her lips pulled back in an expression that could have been pleasure or pain, or was it just the concentration of trying to hang on and move with me. Then she closed her lips, as if to suppress the little noise starting to escape from her throat. Her eyes squeezed shut and beads of perspiration appeared on her forehead. The guttural sound from within her grew louder and still I pounded myself into her.

I lost my grip with my right knee and foot and moved quickly to find it again without breaking the rhythm. Jill had a problem suppressing her scream and she thrashed her head from side to side. I noticed a perfume bottle on the bedside table fall over, roll, and then drop to the carpet. Then I felt the climax start in my toes and scalp and begin to travel along my body towards my cock. Jill grabbed a pillow with one hand and stuffed part of it into her mouth. She entwined the fingers of her other hand in my hair, seemingly trying to grab my scalp as she abandoned control. The climax reached my balls and progressed along my cock with an uncontrollable urgency. Jill opened her eyes wide and gave me a look close to panic as I exploded inside her. We writhed, squirmed, and kept the movement going. We kissed so hard, we bruised our lips.

The kisses softened as we slowed our bodies and our pounding hearts did the same. I experienced a feeling of tenderness for Jill such as I'd never felt for anyone before. She stroked the side of my face and smiled up at me.

'Good job, Royal. You can finish the chewing gum now.'

Late Sunday morning, as I stretched and started to yawn, I realized I couldn't move my jaw. I shook Jill by the shoulder and she enveloped me in a stretch, thinking I had amorous intentions.

'You 'roke my 'uckin' yaw,' I told her.

She lifted herself up on her elbows. 'I did what?' she asked.

'You 'roke ...' the words tailed off as I realized my speech was unintelligible.

'Oh you dummy,' she laughed. 'Chewed yourself to a standstill, did you? Don't worry. It'll go away in a few hours.'

'A fu ours!' probably sounded like a cat meowing.

Jack had no sympathy. He covered his large breakfast plate with fried eggs, bacon, tomatoes, and potatoes. Fried bread lay on a side plate.

'This is real good, oppo. You should 'ave some.'

'Uck you fal,' I said between sips of orange juice sucked through a straw. I couldn't even use Jill's toothbrush to clean the insides of my mouth.

'Don't worry, pet,' Audrey consoled me. 'It'll wear off before the day is done.' She turned to Jill. 'How could you let it happen?'

'Let's just say it was in my interest to maintain the status quo last night.'

'Yeah, we 'eard,' said Jack with a grinning mouth that displayed potatoes.

'Ya mean ya knew dis was gonna 'appen?' I managed to verbalize.

'Yes and no.' She grinned

'Whad th'ell tha mean?'

'Well, if I'd thought about it, I might have realized what was going to happen. Fortunately for me, you kept my mind on other things. I did tell you to take the chewing gum out.'

''Eah, but you said …'

By the time we reached Lympstone, I had gained enough jaw movement to swallow a couple of pints of scrumpy at the Pig and Whistle. Dusty ordered drinks when he saw us walk through the door. Drinking was not quite the easy exercise it normally was, but I managed, without spilling too much of the rough cider.

'What 'appened to you?' Dusty asked.

'Bleedin' partie crushed me ' ead between her thighs last night.'

'If you say so! Same thing 'appened to me when I was in the Paras. Unfortunately, when she slammed 'er thighs over me ears, she imploded me brains. That's 'ow I'm 'ere today.'

Someone at the back of the room must have noticed the antics I performed with my pint glass. 'I always knew fairies couldn't 'andle their booze,' a voice called out.

I spun around and decided the man with a smirk on his face was the one who had made the remark. I appreciated him offering himself as an outlet for my frustration and charged across the room, threw my glass and its contents into his face, and dived across the table at which he sat, taking us both to the floor. A couple of tables and a few stools tumbled over. Glasses fell to the floor as we rolled around trying to get a grip of each other. People grabbed their drinks and cleared the area to give us room. I got to my feet and had time to measure the loudmouth as he straightened up. I knuckled his temple and kneed his face before Dusty, Jack and a couple of others pulled us apart.

The landlady was not happy. 'We always make recruits welcome here and there's not many pubs do that,' she said. 'This place is like a second home to some.'

Dusty placated her, while everyone else righted the furniture, picked up the broken glass and generally tidied the place. Loudmouth and his friends departed. I brushed the sawdust off the front of my clothes and Dusty took care of my back. Jack bought three pints of scrumpy and we retired to a table.

'Bloody Edwards acted up again last night,' Dusty began. 'I went to the 'eads around two and found 'im with a saturated towel wrapped around 'is left forearm. 'E was beating on the towel with a length of wood. I asked what 'e was doing and 'e launched into this tirade about 'ow I should mind my own business. 'E went on about 'ow the rest of us were always poking our noses into matters that didn't concern us and if we'd let 'im and Allison alone, they'd be out of our lives in no time.'

'What was 'e trying to do?' I asked.

'Well, 'e was pretty drunk. Turns out, 'e got ossified so as 'e could find the courage to break 'is arm and work a medical discharge.'

'Give over! Does that work?' Jack found it hard to believe.

'I dunno, but I shouldn't think so. I told the prick I was takin' 'im up to the guardroom. 'E resisted at first. 'E even started for me with the lump of wood, but I took it away from him and then 'e just seemed to accept the situation and walked next to me as calm as ya like.'

It was my turn to be surprised. 'He went for you?'

'Yeah, sort of, but 'e was real drunk and didn't exactly pose much of a threat. Anyway, we got to the guardroom an' I told the duty sergeant what 'appened. 'E told the duty officer and they threw Edwards in a cell. They'll parade 'im in front of the company commander in the morning.'

'Let's 'ope we get rid of the bastard,' said Jack.

'Maybe. I dunno. I feel like a real prick. When all's said and done, 'e *is* a member of our squad.'

'Come on Dusty. The guy's an arsehole. You think ya should have left him to break his arm?' I said.

'Truthfully? Yeah. We would've been shut of him, wouldn't we?'

'I wouldn't lose too much sleep over it,' Jack said. 'I'd 'ave done the same as you.'

'Thanks, Jack. Doesn't stop me feeling like a shit though.'

The landlord called time and I went to the bar to apologise for my behaviour and to get three refills.

We spent the rest of the afternoon cleaning our now dry gear and watching a football game on the television. I was able to eat food by dinnertime.

Allison returned to camp, despite his ban on shore leave. The Provost Staff charged him with being AWOL and put him in the cell next to Edwards. He too would be in front of the company commander on Monday morning. I wondered what had happened to them since Deal. When we were marching everywhere and learning basic infantry skills, they had been proud to be part of H Squad. Now we were earning our Green Berets, they had soured on life. Most of us had grown bored at Deal with the endless extra drill and constant inspections. At Lympstone we were treated with more respect and, despite

Boswell's waning influence, enjoyed life more. Could it be the pair had joined the wrong service? Would they have been better off in the army?

Boswell was absent on Monday, so Dusty presented us to the RSM. The senior NCO gave us a casual once over, then instructed our unpaid leader to take us down to the assault course.

At lunchtime, we learned the fate of our two reluctant squaddies. Edwards was to move into the guardroom, where he would spend all his time when not training and where he would be under constant surveillance. He moved all his kit into a cell that was to become his home until someone reviewed his case in two weeks. Provost staff would deliver his meals and I wondered what they might mix into his food before he took delivery of it. Every night, he would do two hours of extra drill and have his locker inspected by the duty officer. The boss remanded Allison for a court martial and he had to report to the guardroom whenever not under instruction. It would be up to the Provost Staff to keep him employed, which meant he was going to be keeping the cells in immaculate condition until the court assembled. At least he would have Edwards for company.

In the evening, Ron returned from the company office with the mail, which included a letter each for Jack and me. As I ripped open the envelope, I smelled perfume.

'Get a whiff of your envelope,' I suggested to Jack.

He beamed at the smell. 'What she do, spill 'er perfume?' he asked.

'I think they did it on purpose oppo. Mine smells too.'

'Give over! Why would they do that?'

'I think it's supposed to be a hint of things to come.'

'Oh yeah? Now I'm gonna smell every letter I get.'

'Yeah, that'll keep you busy.'

Both letters were pretty much the same in content; hoping we were getting along all right and wanting to know if there were any home comforts we might need. The signatures were of

Deirdre and Belinda Simpson. We assumed they were the two youngest members of the family in the hotel in Exmouth.

Boswell came to inform us about Allison and Edwards and to give us a pep talk. After he had spoken to us collectively, he wandered through the hut, talking to anyone who wanted to chat with him. Jack and I spoke to him together and asked if he knew of a couple of parties named Simpson.

'Deirdre and Belinda?' he asked.

'That's them, Sergeant. We each just got a letter from 'em.'

'So you're the two this time round, eh?'

'This time round?'

'That's what I said, laddie. Johnny Simpson is the camp mailman. Has been for twenty-seven years, and then some. Technically, he still is. Rumour is the man has a third daughter in the WRNS. If she's in pay and records, they could be working a nice racket.' He smiled. 'But about Deirdre and Belinda. They're adamant they're going to marry a Marine. Dad thinks that is just great and conspires with them and their mother. He uses his position in the mailroom to keep tabs on anyone in whom their daughters' have an interest. Checks to see if they get mail from other parties. Steams open letters from parents and that sort of thing.'

'Steams open letters? Give over!' Jack seemed stunned, despite the fact he never got any mail.

'Nah, probably not,' said Boswell. 'You know what rumours are like.'

'Yeah, I suppose.' I grinned at Jack's horror.

I told Boswell, 'We were in a boozer in Exmouth, Saturday, when we ran into the whole family. The mother wanted to know if we got any mail and when we told 'em we didn't, she said her daughters'd love to write to us.'

Jack recovered from his shock. 'I knew we were in there.'

'You might be in better than you thought,' Boswell said.

'How so?' I asked.

'Well, first off, these two young things are determined to go to the altar as virgins.'

'Give over! 'Ow the fuck is that better?' Jack asked.

Boswell was enjoying himself. 'The way I understand it, laddie, is the two girls refuse to get into a situation wherein they run the risk of becoming pregnant. However, they know that a healthy young recruit with raging hormones is not going to settle for holding hands at a picture show.'

A frown appeared on Jack's forehead. 'Yeah. So?'

'Haven't ya got it yet, laddie?'

The light went on behind Jack's eyes. 'Give over!' he whispered, looking around to see if anyone was listening.

'Just one thing. Johnny Simpson has many friends both inside and outside this camp. Don't either of ya do or say anything that will embarrass him or his family. Ya got that?'

'We'll be souls of discretion,' I promised him.

Boswell smiled and moved on. Jack and I sat down to compose a couple of letters.

Allison and Edwards had a different attitude on Tuesday morning. Living in the cells must have had an effect on them. They pulled their weight on the assault and Tarzan courses, thereby helping the squad to complete both in the allotted times. As no one took a dip at the regain tank, we were happy, but Tucker turned mean and slapped a couple of guys.

We spent the next day at the range, where we learned to handle and fire machine guns. Stephenson was so relaxed; he even tried to work on his tan. Six men took up prone positions at the firing line while Bell and Tucker paced behind them, observing and making corrections. A few hundred yards away, six other squaddies were below ground level in the spotter trench. They changed the targets and used long pointers to indicate where shots hit the charging Russian paper soldier – or missed him, as was sometimes the case. We had plugs in our ears and tin hats on our heads.

A truck delivered our disgusting lunch. Thankfully, an enterprising civilian arrived in a food wagon and sold us dripping sandwiches, chips, meat pies, steak and kidney puddings, mushy peas and sticky buns for very reasonable prices. Before she departed, Stephenson walked over to the van and collected his commission.

After lunch, six men, including Sammy, took up position behind the machine guns and were surprised to see three sheep wandering across the range. Sammy could not resist the temptation and he opened fire on the woolly creatures. The other five joined in, causing bits of wool and mutton to fly in all directions.

Tucker ran up and down the line, kicking everybody's feet and screaming. 'What the fuck are you crazies doing? Those sheep belong to someone. Cease-fire at once. Do you hear me? Cease-fire!'

Sammy and the others continued to blast away at what remained. The irate Tucker used a stick to bang on the shooters' steel helmets while he continued to scream out the cease-fire order. The guys did stop firing, but whether it was because there was nothing left to shoot at or whether they were obeying the order was unclear. Spotters' heads cautiously emerged from the trenches to see what had caused the blood and guts to splatter the paper targets. Two of them wore red debris and were trying to finger-comb it out of their hair.

'Now ya know what your tin hat is for,' Stephenson joked over the telephone to the spotters' trench. 'In future, you will keep them on your heads until I tell you differently.'

Spittle flew from Tucker's mouth. 'What the fuck did you bastards think you were doing? Samuels, you started it. I hope you'll still be amused when the cost of those animals is deducted from your pay.'

The man looked long and hard at Sammy, but it must have occurred to him there had been no word from Stephenson and he let the matter drop. He walked out of earshot, probably to regain his composure.

'What's a sheep worth?' Sammy asked of no one in particular.

'I understand you can get two women for one in Oman,' Dusty grinned.

'Sounds reasonable to me,' Ron added.

The trucks stopped outside the company office and we piled out, still laughing and joking about the sheep. Boswell stood on the veranda, talking to the Quarter Master Sergeant who was alternately sucking, exhaling and tamping as he tried to get his pipe going. Tucker jumped down from the cab and proceeded to relate the sad tale of the slaughtered woollies. The QMS had a fire going by the time Tucker finished and he waved his hand in front of his face in an attempt to clear the smoke.

'Not to worry, Corporal Tucker. This has happened before. Local farmer's a bit of a lad. Every time he has a couple of sick or infirm animals, he herds them out onto the range and our trigger happy recruits make believe they're John Wayne taking Iwo Jima single-handed. The old man pays the going rate for the animals to the farmer, who then donates about ten times that amount to our widows and orphans fund when we have the drive every Christmas.'

Tucker nodded once. 'So there's no harm done then?'

'Nothing to lose sheep over, as they say.' The QMS disappeared into his office with a cloud of blue-white smoke trailing after him.

Boswell strode into the hut. 'How do you guys manage it? You sleep on civilians' garden furniture. Yes, Mason, we know who it was. Then, just when you're in the middle of this bloody kerfuffle with Allison and Edwards you go and ... you two Einsteins here?'

'Yes, Sergeant,' they answered unenthusiastically.

'Good. As I was saying – you picked the wrong time to screw around. More than a few people are taking a look at this squad. They're waiting to see how you handle yourselves and this stunt with the wee sheep doesna help. Does it, Samuels?'

'I guess not Sarge ... Sergeant,' a subdued Sammy agreed.

'Come on, Sarge,' argued Dusty. 'There must be some kind of ordinance or something that prohibits civilians and their animals from trespassing on government property.'

'You're right, Miller. However, in the interest of our relationship with the local community, we refuse to hide behind it. Many of the civilians hereabouts are a mite concerned about what would happen if any children accidentally wandered onto one of our ranges. You men have just brought those worries to the forefront of their minds again and the CO is going to have to give interviews to local newspapers to allay their fears.'

After a light, fluid lunch on Saturday, Jack and I purchased four bottles of wine, several Indian 'take out' dishes and went to Jill and Audrey's flat. The two women had arranged the place in such a way that life would be a little more comfortable for the couple using the living room. There were new scatter-pillows. Heavy curtains were drawn and two table lamps, over which thin scarves hung, gave the place a blue and red hue. Incense sticks smouldered in a vase on the mantle-piece, filling the room with an odour I tried to convince myself was pleasant. Both women wore colourful embroidered dresses, and smelled of soap and perfume. Jill wore a red carnation in her hair and a necklace of white and pink coral around her throat. Audrey had a thin black leather strap around her neck from which hung an Egyptian ankh of green jade.

We didn't linger long on greetings before Jill and I went to the bedroom.

After a while, I wanted to eat. Jill knocked on the bedroom door. 'Can we come out?'

'Just a sec,' said Audrey in what sounded like mild panic.

The four of us lounged on the floor and smoked some grass. The women made me promise not to talk too much and Jack vowed to control his food intake. Audrey got up and turned on the oven.

''Ow long's that gonna take?' Jack asked.

'Twenty minutes, maybe. Then we'll have to wait for the food to warm up.'

'Give over!' said my oppo. 'I'm bleedin' starvin'.'

'Ah,' Audrey said, 'Deal with it.'

The women laughed and I, seeing Jack's craving, reminded myself not to start talking. I got up and opened a bottle of wine to occupy my mind. I became engrossed in the procedure.

'Having a problem with that task, are we?' Jill asked as she kissed my ear and stroked the back of my head.

'Not at all. I ...'

She placed a finger on my lips, then crossed the room to the record player. She stacked half-a-dozen platters on the machine and twisted the start button. The music of Adam Faith filled the room.

'We have Elvis and The Everly Brothers,' said Audrey. 'Did you put them on, Mare?'

'I did. And on that note, as they say, Johnson and I will again take our leave.' Jill smiled at Audrey. 'See you in thirty minutes.' She got to her feet and took my hand.

''Ow're the prospects on the job situation?' Jack asked Audrey.

''Not good, lover. Cheer up though. Look at all these lovely cushions.'

The Adjutant rode up to inspect us on Monday morning. 'You seem to be a man short, Sergeant.'

'Yes Sir, recruit Allison has his Court Martial scheduled for this morning.'

This was news to all of us. How did The Adjutant not know? Allison spent so much time at the guardroom, we rarely saw him. On the occasions when he joined us, his sullen silence killed all attempts at conversation. After dismissal, we urged Dusty to find out what was going on. Edwards seemed more animated than usual and so we figured he must know something.

'What's the story, Eddie? You know what's happening?'

'No. I heard he was in the shit the other day but that's all. 'E wouldn't tell me anything. Said 'is life is fucked.'

Stephenson refused to discuss the subject with Dusty, so we waited until mid-morning to isolate Corporal Bell and ask him what he knew.

'There's a rumour,' he told us, 'that the Provost Staff got fed up with Allison's belligerent attitude and took him to the exercise yard behind the cells to perform extra drill. Two of them ordered Allison to 'about turn' for so long, they were in danger of losing their voices, so they ordered your squaddie to continue the manoeuvre until someone told him to stop. They allowed as 'e could reverse direction if 'e got dizzy. They left him alone in the yard while they went to take care of other matters. The surface of the yard is cinders and every time Allison performed the manoeuvre, his boots caused said cinders to spit out from under him. They reckon he made a small hole in the ground. Sometime later, a sergeant went into the exercise yard and found Allison had cleared a patch of cinders and was working on the clay underneath. He asked him what he thought he was doing. Your man took on an attitude and said he was trying to tunnel out. The sergeant charged him with trying to escape, destruction of government property, and conduct contrary to good order and military discipline.'

Edwards heard what Bell said and turned ashen. 'That's ridiculous. They can't get away with that! I'll write to the newspapers.'

Bell threaded his way through the squad until he came face to face with Edwards. 'If you're in the glass-house, your outgoing mail is censored. How do you propose to write to the newspapers then?'

'I'm not in the glass-house,' our white-faced squaddie replied.

'You sure as hell will be if you go around spouting off. Next thing you'll wanna do is write to your MP. We've seen it all before. Do you know who your MP is?'

Eddie's shoulders slumped. 'No.'

Bell shortened the distance between them to three or four inches. He then spoke to Edwards in such a low voice, most of us strained to hear his words. 'If you don't wanna be a part of this squad or this man's Marines, why don't you do us all a favour and piss off? You wanna know what I think? Ya don't have the balls to go AWOL. Ya don't want the military and civilian police after your arse. You want to go home to your mummy and live the soft life. If ya go AWOL, ya won't be able to do that, will you?' Eddie knew better than to respond. 'Let me tell ya some home truths, Edwards. If ya don't knuckle down, you're gonna be in big trouble. Be aware Her Britannic Majesty allows us a margin of three per cent fatalities during recruit training. That's almost one per squad an' we haven't had nary a one in years. You push your luck too far and you'll make the newspapers all right. You'll get two inches of print on page thirteen of your local rag. Ya got that?'

In the afternoon, we piled into a couple of trucks and went to an area of Dartmoor to learn how to climb up and abseil down some miniature cliffs. When we arrived at the base of the instruction site, we saw three ropes dangling from the top. The three NCOs instructed us on how to scale the bluffs by wrapping the rope loosely around us and walking up the cliff-face while holding the line. I was relieved to accomplish the exercise with relative ease.

We were relaxing at the top when Stephenson advised us it was time we returned to the base of the bluffs. 'A demonstration, if you will, gentlemen.'

Bell and Tucker each picked up a rope, wrapped it once around a leg and over a forearm, then leapt over the edge. We formed in lines behind the anchored ropes and waited for more detailed instruction. I felt nervous about jumping out into fresh air. Would the rope prevent me from taking the fastest way to the bottom? I had to make sure I wrapped it around me properly. Would I blister my banker's hands? The skin on my palms had hardened to a degree but not enough to prevent a rope burn or blisters if I slid for too long. Sammy, Ray and Pete were at the front, holding the ropes and waiting to learn how to curl them around their bodies.

'Hold it,' Stephenson called out. 'Edwards, did you see Corporals Bell and Tucker go over the edge?'

'Yes, Sergeant.'

'Good, then you know how to do it. Why don't you give us a demonstration? Take Samson's rope.'

The colour drained from Edwards face for the second time that day. 'I didn't, I didn't see how they did it, Sergeant. I just saw them go over the edge.'

'Don't worry about it. A wise arse like you should be able to figure it out. Get the fuck down that cliff. NOW!'

I had no reason to like Edwards but I felt nervous for him. How could Stephenson take such a risk? What would I do in

Eddie's place? I'd ask for another demonstration and refuse to move until I got one. The cliff was maybe fifty-something feet high, too high to jump off and expect to land safely at the base.

'You must be kidding,' Edwards' voice cracked in his dry mouth.

'Go. That is a direct order.'

'You can't give me an order like that,' Edwards protested.

'Sonny, I'm a Sergeant in Her Britannic Majesty's Corps of Royal Marines and you're a fuckin' recruit. That makes me God. Now grab hold of that rope.'

During the confrontation, Ron had quietly walked up to Pete and taken the rope from him. Pete took Ron's place in the line.

Edwards' voice cracked. 'No. I won't. You can lock me up or whatever you want but I'm not goin' over this cliff until somebody teaches me 'ow ta do it.'

Ron quietly spoke to our petrified squaddie. 'Take the rope an' wrap it around your leg and under your crotch like I'm doing.'

Stephenson looked on in silence. It took a couple of seconds for Edwards to realise Ron was helping him out of the situation. The tension eased. I heard people release pent-up breath. Eddie stared at Ron and regained his composure. Ron unwrapped and then slowly re-wrapped the rope around his body. He nodded to urge Edwards to follow his lead. 'That's it. Now lightly grip the rope in your elbow. That'll be your brake.'

I absorbed every word Ron said. I mentally practised arranging the rope around my body. Eddie copied the one-time paratrooper. 'Okay, now what?'

Ron smiled at him. 'You're not going to believe this, but now we jump out backwards and begin our descent. Watch me and then do exactly the same. If I were you, I'd follow me down. The alternative is Sergeant Stephenson.' The smile on Ron's face widened as he looked at the three-striper. He looked back at Eddie, 'Ready?'

Eddie gave a nervous nod.

'Let's go.' Ron sprang up and out into space. Eddie watched him fall about fifteen feet before he used his elbow to brake and land feet first on the face of the cliff.

A voice called out. 'Go on, Eddie. Take a jump!'
'Do it Eddie,' another voice encouraged.
'Yeah!' several other voices joined in.
'Go on, Eddie. Jump!'
'Stick it to 'em, Eddie.'

I wondered if Eddie accepted the words as encouragement or hopes for his failure. He bent his knees and jumped out just as Ron had shown him. Cheers and whistles rang out as the rest of us moved toward the edge of the cliff to see his descent. Unfortunately, he braked far too soon and landed about four feet down the face of the cliff. His head and shoulders were still visible to us, his confidence visibly shaken.

Dusty grabbed the rope out of Ray's hands. 'Don't squeeze on the brake on so fast,' he told Edwards. 'Watch me.' He leapt out and landed some twenty feet down the cliff.

'You had to go further than me, didn't you?' laughed Ron.

'All for the good of the squad,' Dusty replied.

Eddie saw Stephenson advancing and sprang from the cliff face. He resisted the temptation to brake long enough to almost land on Ron's head.

'Easy there, Eddie. You gotta watch where you're going.'

I was relieved to see how easy it was. When my turn came, I completed the descent without hesitation.

Corporal Bell told Ron and Dusty to wait at the bottom of the cliff while the rest of the squad scaled it for the second time. Tucker climbed up with the last duo and Sergeant Stephenson abseiled down to speak to the ex-Paras. I was the last recruit at the base and I excused my nosiness by asking if I should wait for Ron and Dusty to make up the last ascending trio go up as one. Stephenson seemed not to care.

'Just because you two learned how to abseil in the Paras, didn't mean you had to interfere up there. I thought you fairies wanted rid of this guy.'

'We do, but we don't want him dead,' Ron replied.

'Come on you two, wise up. I wasn't going to let anything happen to the man. He would have got his discharge as not being able or suitable to complete his training. My report would have ensured that.'

Dusty spoke up, 'I figured that, but I have a problem with it.'
'A problem?'
'I was the one who took him up to the guardroom on the night I found him trying to break his arm and I've been feeling lousy about it ever since.'
'To hell with that. You made the right decision then. Today you made the wrong one. You of all people has to know if you want to rise through the ranks, you have to make the right decisions and stick by them, no matter what your inner feelings might be.'
'Maybe, but there is another way. We could pull Edwards through and have him pass out with us. He can't be happy right now and it'd probably do him the world of good if he could get more of his self-esteem back.'
'I can live with that, as long as I feel it isn't doing any harm. The day I think Edward's presence is having the slightest detrimental effect on any other squad member, he's gone. Francis was right about you people. You're a strange fuckin' bunch.'

Given the day we'd been through, we anticipated a visit by Boswell that night. When he didn't appear by nine, we had an informal squad meeting about his absences. He had always been around at Deal but that was no longer the case. Our training schedule at Lympstone was such that we no longer expected him to be in constant attendance. However, he was our DI and still, we believed, supposed to be with us at morning parade, for drill instruction and the occasional field exercise. Importantly, he was the man who had formed the squad, the man we could talk to when we had a problem. The craggy Scot had turned us into a bunch of fairies and we were extremely proud of that distinction.

Jack and I received another letter from the Simpson sisters. Both girls sympathised with us for having to eat camp food and offered to send us some home-baked victuals as an appetiser for a meal they would prepare for us on the coming Saturday. They would pick us up outside the camp gates at three, should we decide we wanted to see them. Jack took our letters of acceptance to the post box while I called Jill to tell her we were assigned guard duty on Saturday and would be unable to see her and Audrey. Jill regretted not seeing me, and assured me we would make it up to each other the following weekend. The huskiness of her voice carried as much promise as her words.

Tommy Sargent was becoming a minor celebrity. During an inter-squad boxing tournament, the PTIs found the guy we called Comma to be a promising fighter with considerable ring savvy. One PTI, who had been an amateur national champion, took to training our fellow fairy in his free time and many people were quietly hopeful that our squaddie might achieve the same amount of success. Jack sparred with Comma once but became so frustrated by the Marquis of Queensbury's rules, he refused to do it again. There was a tournament soon in Portsmouth that would test Comma's ring prowess. The PTIs at Lympstone believed he could win and made bets with the PTIs at Eastney barracks. Bobby made inquiries around the squad to see if we wanted to make a collective wager, thereby affording him the chance to negotiate better odds.

As promised, the Simpson parties picked us up on Saturday afternoon. Their parents were on hand to welcome us to their home and I feared they would be around for the duration. Renata Simpson insisted on taking both of us on a tour of her house. As we entered each room, she pointed to camphorwood boxes, wooden masks, carved horns, supposedly ceremonial knives, spears, shields and other items the couple had garnered from around the world. Posters advertising The Beating of The Retreat, Searchlight Tattoos and concerts by the massed bands of Her Majesty's Royal Marines covered the walls of the girls' bedrooms.

Johnny and Renata left at six to attend a bingo game. 'We'll be back around midnight, girls. Be good now.'

Deirdre and Belinda waved farewell to their parents, then switched on the television, plumped up the cushions and told Jack and me to relax while they prepared dinner. It dawned on me I did not want to be in the gloomy house alone with the desperate daughters. The reality of the situation was a long way from the fantasy that got us there. Ten minutes later, they both re-appeared with fresh beers and a bowl of crisps and their buoyancy increased my discomfort.

When they returned to the kitchen, I turned to Jack. 'This is bad. I don't wanna be here.'

'Give over,' he said. 'What's so bleedin' bad? We're gettin' a free, slap-up meal with a bit of oral to follow. That's good in my book!'

'Come on, Jack. We're leadin' 'em on.'

'Seems ta me they're leadin' us on and, in any case, what's wrong with that? We lead all parties on; they wanna be led on.'

'Yeah, but these two 'ave the camp postie for their dad, for Christ's sake!'

That hit home. 'Okay. Let's get outta here before they come back. Come on.'

We put down our beers and walked out of the house. We were outside their neighbour's house when we heard a voice call for us. We ran all the way to the Pig and Whistle.

At a change of watch in the guardroom, a member of the Provost Staff discovered Eddie Edwards had vacated the premises. The result of Allison's court martial was unknown to us, but we knew he was no longer a member of our squad. We were down to twenty-eight for the second time.

The following week, we took on the endurance course with its miles of waterlogged fields, underground tunnels and various other obstacles. Guys from senior squads had told us the route was aptly named.

We were sucking wind when we completed our first assault of the course. The ever cheerful Tucker advised us we would have to cut our times in half. 'Practise on your own for a few nights,' he suggested. Jack and I joined with other guys and we went 'round the course several times.

We spent the rest of the week on the moors. As with our previous trip, it rained all the time. Our kit got so thoroughly soaked, we didn't bother to put up our ponchos at night.

On Wednesday night we went to a range to practice night-time firing using night-scopes and tracer bullets. Unfortunately, there were only four firing positions and we spent a lot of time waiting in the pouring rain. The range's red warning lights gave Sammy some diversion; he shot them all out. Boswell, Stephenson, Tucker and Bell were present and surely one of them should have noticed the absence of the warning to the general public. It made us wonder how sincere Boswell had been when lecturing us about the incident with the sheep.

The next day we took a twenty-mile hike across the moors in boots that got as wet inside as they did outside. Strangely, my feet felt comfortably warm. When we took our boots and socks off that night, we found our feet wrinkled like prunes. We so worried about rust forming in the barrels of our rifles and on the blades of our bayonets, we cleaned and oiled them several times.

We returned to camp around midday on Friday and heard from Stephenson that our time was our own until oh-eight-hundred the following Monday. We washed our kit, hung it any place we could find, and waited for it to dry. The steam in the hut formed beads of condensation on the metal bed frames and lockers. We re-cleaned and re-oiled our rifles and bayonets and then wrapped them in our bedding to ensure they remained dry.

After dinner, Boswell visited the hut. 'So how are things with the wee Simpson girls?'

'We gave 'em a miss,' I said.

'I heard from a reliable source that you two fairies were eating with them last weekend.'

'Well, yeah, that's true, but we sorta lost our appetites. We're seeing these parties in Exmouth and decided it's best not to take up with anyone else.'

'Oh, the delights of civilian companions. Ya probably made the right choice. Ah hope ya let the girls down gently?'

'Yeah, pretty much,' Jack said hesitantly.

'Pretty much?'

'Yeah, well, we was in their 'ouse, sipping a brew when my oppo 'ere suggested we should leave.'

'So you legged it?'

'Yeah, sort of.'

'What a courageous pair you are. Two big, tough Royal Marines running from some wee girls' clutches. Her Britannic Majesty need not tremble,' said our leader as he moved across the aisle.

'We're better off with the parties in Exmouth,' I reminded Jack.

'Give over! I'm fed up of shaggin' on the floor. 'Sides, Audrey's too straight for me.'

'As in she hasn't done what you expected the Simpson girls to do?'

'Right.'

I smiled. 'So give 'er the news. Maybe, if you take the initiative, she'll follow suit.'

'What d'ya mean, take the initiative?'

'Give 'er a little tongue and she'll probably reciprocate.'

'Give over! Really?' The idea seemed to fill him with awe.

'You've got nothin' to lose.'

'Yeah, but, I never did it before,' my friend said shyly, looking around the hut to make sure nobody overheard him.

'Neither did I, until the first time.'

'What? Oh. How was it? Did ya wanna puke?'

'Nah, it was fine. I mean, I don't know 'ow clean Audrey keeps herself, but it was great with Jill. Just make sure you don't shove your nose up 'er arse!'

He looked relieved. 'You're a crude fuck, Banker. Did anyone ever tell you?'

'And you're not?'

'I used to be a wrestler, not a lily-white banker. I got an excuse.'

'Of course you do, Jack. What did it say on the photograph in that restaurant in Exmouth, "White Shoes Mason"? All right, let's date Jill and Audrey this weekend and I'll see if I can

influence matters for ya. I'll try and convince my girlfriend to
convince your girlfriend to give you a tongue lashin'.'

Audrey and Jill met us at Exmouth station and suggested we go
to the beach and walk for a while. Jack and Audrey stayed too
close to allow me to bring up the subject of my oppo's current
sexual preference.

Once in the flat, I offered to help Jill in the kitchen while
Jack and Audrey watched television.

'I don't quite know how to word this, but we have a
problem,' I started. 'Jack thinks some girl who's been writing to
him is gonna indulge in a little oral and as Audrey doesn't seem
willing to perform the same act, 'e's thinking of dating this
other bird. Seeing as how I'd like to carry on seein' you and
seein' as 'ow Jack is my oppo, I have a bit of a conflict. Think
you could talk Audrey into taking the plunge – so to speak?'

Jill stopped peeling the potatoes and looked at me with eyes
alive with anger. 'You two can go and play your games with the
mailman's daughters all you want. Where do you get off trying
to blackmail me, you miserable shit?'

I laughed. 'You know about those parties?'

'Every girl in every pub from Exeter to Exmouth knows
about them. They've been trying to get some arsehole to marry
them for over two years now. You two might just be their
ticket.'

My laugh was dying. 'I don't think so.'

'Shut up. I should kick you both out of here after what
you've just said. Let me tell you something, Johnson. Audrey
and I date you recruits at weekends because, on the whole,
you're a lot of fun to be with.' I opened my mouth to speak, but
she brandished the potato peeler to silence me. 'During the
week, when you're all tucked up safely in your barrack beds,
we're out dating civilians. I don't make any excuses for our
behaviour. One day I'll end up marrying a civilian, because he'll
provide me with constant companionship, a house in the
suburbs, one cat, two cars, and three kids. All you'll ever
provide will be food stamps, long absences and other Marine's
wives for social contact.'

'Yeah, fine, but in the meantime will you have a word with Audrey?' I managed to duck in time to miss the full impact of the potato peeler that sliced through the air toward my eyes. The implement hit my shoulder, which I grabbed dramatically as I staggered back a pace.

'You got me!'

'Ah, poor diddum,' she purred.

I laughed at her insincerity, knowing the two relationships were safe for a while.

Jill had picked up some éclairs for dessert and a special coffee to accompany them. After Audrey poured the coffee, her friend picked up one of the éclairs and made a big production out of forming an 'O' with her lips, then slowly advancing her mouth toward the pastry and finally enveloping it. She tightened the grip of her lips on the éclair, closed her eyes and then slowly began to withdraw it. She repeated the move a couple of times and I watched her with growing excitement. Nobody spoke.

Jill looked across the table at her flatmate. 'I'm told there are certain Marines who will only go out with women who are very adept at eating éclairs and their like.' Jack blushed as Jill purposely turned to face him. 'I also understand that these Marines, whoever they might be, are themselves very adept at eating an éclair.' As she spoke, she separated the two halves of the pastry. She raised one of the halves to her mouth and rapidly flicked her tongue several times at its upper end. When she was done, a small blob of white cream sat at the tip of her tongue.

Audrey laughed to hide her embarrassment and turned to Jack. 'Do you always get a woman to do your dirty work for you?'

My red-faced oppo didn't know what to say. He opened and closed his mouth a couple of times, spread his hands wide, and shrugged his shoulders.

Jill slowly withdrew her tongue, closed her lips, raised her chin and swallowed dramatically while giving Jack a hard stare. 'He thought he was going to get someone to lick his stamps at the post office, didn't you Jack?' she said. Audrey looked at each of us, searching our faces for a clue to Jill's meaning. 'A couple of ladies, who shall remain nameless, have taken to writing to these two charmers,' Jill explained to her friend. Audrey's facial expression changed to amusement. Jack fidgeted on his chair.

His date reached out and lightly scratched his head. 'You couldn't wait, could you? I was waiting for our turn in the bedroom before making like we had éclairs.'

'You didn't get a job, did you?' I asked with trepidation.

''Fraid so, Paul.' Audrey smiled. 'It's you two for the living room tonight. You can revel in the delights of the floor, or whatever else takes your fancy.'

Jill grinned like a Cheshire cat, 'You should have been here last week. I was still the only one with a job then.' I wondered if she somehow knew what we had done last weekend and the blood rushed to my face. 'Don't worry, Johnson, we'll think of something to protect those precious knees of yours.'

'Let him skin the bleeders,' Jack urged.

'That's the last favour I do for you pal,' I shot back jokingly, relieved that the subject had apparently been dropped.

'What favour?' Audrey inquired.

'Another time.' Jill jumped up from the table and I was again relieved. 'You two can help with the dishes before you disappear on us.'

We met some of the guys in the Pig & Whistle on Sunday night. Bobby handed me a piece of paper on which was a telephone number. 'I was in the guard room on duty last night when some partie from Manchester called. Said you'd know who she was and will you please call her back.'

Jack had enjoyed a great weekend with Audrey that included the sharing of imaginary éclairs. 'Who needs 'em?' he beamed.

'Last I 'eard, you liked 'em,' Bobby said with a grin.

'Yeah, well, I've got enough on my plate, right now.'

Bobby changed the subject. 'Have you guys seen the photos on the wall in the snug?' he asked. 'Alan bleedin' Ladd made a film 'ere about life in the Corps. The arsehole was so bleedin' short; he 'ad to run around on planks raised off the ground. Guy was two bricks shy of a knee-trembler.'

'Why'd they use a Yank actor to play a Bootneck?' Jack asked indignantly.

'I dunno. What English actor could play the part? Sir Laurence Olivier?' Bobby laughed at his own humour, almost spilling some of his scrumpy.

'How about Dirk Bogarde?' Jack half shouted, half laughed.

'How about the one that played Douglas Bader? What was 'is name? You remember that film. "Reach for the Sky", or somethin'.'

'Kenneth More?'

'That's 'im.'

'Give over! That guy couldn't reach for 'is dick.'

'When you consider all the jokers there are in this outfit, I should think Peter Sellers would fit the role nicely,' said Dusty, who had just arrived.

The following Saturday, we drew guard duty. We thought of paying someone to do it for us, but realized we needed the money for ourselves. Not paying someone else and not paying to go ashore would bring us back to healthy economic shape for the following weekend.

Three days later, as Jack and I returned from a visit to the Pig and Whistle, a member of the Provost staff advised us there was a message for us in the guardroom. The duty sergeant was elsewhere when we arrived, so we sought and obtained permission to see Jimmy Allison while we waited for his return. Jimmy was serving thirty days in the cells and would resume training with K Squad when he got out. We walked down the corridor to his cell and peered through the barred window in the door. A single bulb encased in a protective wire mesh dimly lit the area. I could see a wooden bed attached to the wall on the right. On the left was a stool and a small table on which lay two books. In one corner there was a dull aluminium toilet bowl not attached to any plumbing system while in another corner stood a locker in which Allison's gear was stowed.

He saw us standing at the door. 'What're you bastards starin' at? The fuckin' zoo's closed fer the day!'

'Hey, Jimmy, ease up. We only came to see if there's anythin' we can do for ya.'

'Don't make me laugh. You were as glad to get shut of me as I was to be shut of you. You wanna do somethin' for me? Here, grab this pumice and boot polish. That's what they give me to clean up my own shit.' He grabbed the bowl in the corner, ran toward us and smashed it up against the cell door. 'Here. Why don't you fuckin' clean it for me?'

'Cut it, Jimmy. Your bein' in here is your own fault. You don't want to see us, we'll leave. Go shit in yer bucket, arsehole.'

We walked back down the corridor; Jimmy's screamed insults trailing after us.

We went to a bank of public telephones that stood permanently to attention just outside the camp's main gate.

'Hotel Royal. How may I help you?' asked a tired female voice as she tried to stifle a yawn.

'Two one three, please.'

'One second. Putting you through now.'

I heard a ringing tone for the second time. 'Hello,' said a vaguely familiar voice.

'Hello. This is Paul Johnson. Who's this?'

'Paul, how are you?'

The four words were enough for me to detect the Mancunian accent. Penelope! What could she be doing in Exmouth? 'Is that you, Pen?'

'Of course it is. Who did you expect?'

'Not you …' was out before I realized how bad it must have sounded, '… but it's a nice surprise to hear your voice again. How are you? Is Susan with you?'

'Yeah. Jack with you?'

I looked out of the booth to where Jack stood absent-mindedly digging dirt from his nose. 'Yep. Same as ever.'

Pen laughed happily and said something to Susan. 'We have two weeks holiday, so we came to the nearest resort to you and Jack. Aren't you pleased? When can we see you?'

'Not until the weekend, I'm afraid. Hang on a second; I'll put Jack on the phone.'

I pushed the door open with my shoulder. The squeaking of its hinges brought Jack out of his reverie and his finger out of his left nostril.

'Hey, pal. Guess who's on the line.'

''Ow the fuck should I know?'

'Yer Manky maiden.'

'Give over! You're shittin' me, right?'

'Nope.' I backed out of the booth and offered him the receiver on the end of its taut line.

His eyes widened questioningly. 'Susan?'

I nodded my head in assent. Jack took the receiver and squeezed past me into the booth. A couple of minutes later he hung up.

'Susan brought the curtain cords, so it looks like we'll 'ave ta pull guard-duty again as far as Audrey and Jill are concerned,' he said with a grin.

The next day, we each got a letter from a Simpson sister. They wondered what they could have done to make us disappear and were disappointed they had not heard from us. Would we like to go for dinner again on the coming Saturday?

'Would ya believe it?' laughed Jack. 'We've both got three dates for this coming Sat'day. When was the last time that 'appened?'

'Yeah, but we're only going to make one of them, so what are we going to do with these two teasers?'

'We'll write to them, of course,' said my friend.

'Okay. You write to Deirdre and I'll write to Belinda.'

'Yeah, well, you're gonna 'ave ta make up somethin' for me to copy from.'

'Piss off. Do your own dirty work.'

''Ang on a minute, oppo. You know we 'ave to go easy an' not embarrass the old postie. You're better at this stuff, seeing as 'ow ya used to be a banker.'

'Fuck off, Jack. This was your idea. Write your own bleedin' letter.'

'Yeah, but 'ow do I know what you're putting in your letter? We 'ave to get our stories straight, don't we?'

'All right, all right. I'll draught you a letter. But I'll tell ya somethin' right now. I get to fuck every partie we meet who 'as an IQ of over one hundred, okay?'

'Shit, yeah. I don't even know what that means.'

I wrote and told Belinda I would be unable to see her for the next two or three weeks because two friends from Manchester were vacationing in the area and I wanted to see them. Jack wrote a similar letter to Deirdre. As I wrote, it occurred to me that, save for Jill and Audrey, I was dating women I would not have met in the days before I joined the Marines. My standards were slipping but I valued my friendship with Jack and that thought made me smile as I also realized he was in a reverse situation. He would never have dated someone like Audrey when he wrestled. So, although my standards were slipping, I was still a snob. Job well done, Dad.

Before signing on the dotted line all those months ago, we underwent a thorough physical examination. For reasons known only by Her Britannic Majesty, she had waited until now to pay any attention to the physical state of our mouths. On Thursday morning, the whole squad stood in line outside the dentist's office, waiting to have our teeth and gums inspected. If anything was found amiss, the offending mouth's owner went to another part of the building with written details of the treatment required. As we stood waiting, we watched people leave the room with blood on their faces and, in some cases, chests. Most of them held a handful of gauze over their mouths in an attempt to contain the bleeding. Not many escaped the attentions of the enthusiastic butcher. We all became a little apprehensive, knowing that as we inched closer to the building's door, we were getting nearer to receiving similar treatment. When Bobby was at the head of the line, Jack shouted out to him.

'Whose name is painted on that bleedin' door? Mengele?'

I sat in the dentist's chair, and 'opened wide'. The man made a circuit of my mouth, tapping each tooth with the base of his metal stick. No further examination was necessary for him to know I needed two extractions. He thrust the written instructions into my hand and I went down a corridor to the surgery. Once I settled in another dentist's chair, a naval Sick Berth Attendant (SBA) put a vice between my front teeth, placed a mask on my face, and turned on the gas.

I awoke with a painful mouth and blood on my face and chest. I took another piece of paper (this time bearing instructions to stitch up my wounds) to another part of the building where I joined another line. Jack wasn't around, so I assumed his mouth had not needed repairs. After a ten-minute wait, it was my turn. The SBA behind the desk seemed to find the situation amusing.

'Join the Marines and get state of the art dentistry, eh Royal?' said the grinning sailor. He put eight stitches in my gums and called for the next patient.

Stephenson saw no reason to change anything because of the morning's activities. 'You'll have ta deal with worse things than that when the Chinese 'ordes are comin' at you in waves.'

We went over the assault course, the Tarzan course and finally, the regain tank. My gums protested with every step. Three squaddies returned to the sick bay to have their wounds re-stitched.

Jack and I caught the ten o'clock train to Exmouth on Saturday and went straight to the hotel to meet the Mancunians. When we got to their room, we tried to get down to the basics of a lovers re-union, but the girls had a different agenda.

'Why didn't you write to us or call us?' Susan wanted to know.

'Didn't anyone tell you we called a couple of weeks ago?' Penelope asked.

I had forgotten about Bobby's message. 'I don't know anything about any call,' I lied. 'Anyhow, didn't we agree we wouldn't write?'

'What did I tell you?' Susan said to Penelope with exasperation.

'Come on, girls,' Jack pleaded. 'We might've neglected ya a bit, but time's too short to be bleedin' complainin' about it. If I say I'm sorry, will ya forgive me?'

Susan put her arm around his neck and gave him a long and seemingly forgiving kiss. I looked at Penelope, spread my arms and shrugged my shoulders in what I hoped was a charming admission of guilt.

'All right this time, but you'd better make it up to me, Paul Johnson. I love you.'

The words made me pull back but I was able to cover the move by telling Penelope what the dentist had done to cause the pain in my mouth.

'You two must know this town quite well by now, so you can take us out and show us around. The other stuff can wait 'til later,' Susan firmly insisted. 'We all need to get re-acquainted.'

'Give over!' Jack cried out, laughing at the same time. 'We 'aven't 'ad any of the 'other stuff' since Manchester.'

'Yeah, and I heard pigs can fly down here,' Susan said with a grin.

'No, he's right.' I backed up my oppo. 'It's the same for me.'

'Well, if you've waited this long, another couple of hours won't make any difference now, will it?' Penelope said.

I nearly asked why someone who loved me needed re-acquainting, but thought better of it. 'Well, it's almost lunch-time so Jack and I'll be 'appy ta take ya to a little Italian restaurant where my oppo is well known.'

'Sounds great. Let's go.'

The girls looked better than expected. The sea air and summer sunshine made them look healthier and sexier. Penelope already possessed a great body, but the tan made it look even better. Both wore skirts that were definitely shorter than I remembered. The eighty-degree temperature allowed them to wear flimsy, revealing tops that ensured us great service from the Italian waiters.

'Stick to the food, pal,' Jack informed one of them as he flipped open Susan's linen serviette and placed it across her lap. Both Jack and I played along with the game that the four of us were not getting together for purely carnal purposes. We lingered over Sambucas with fresh coffee beans while we told them of our lives.

When they started to relate the troubles at the cereal factory, Jack called for the bill, paid it promptly, and suggested we all retire to the hotel.

'Just a sec,' said Penelope, causing Jack to grunt and to sit again. 'We only have the one room at the hotel and we thought it would be fair if we tossed a coin to see who gets to use it first.'

I gave Penelope a half-crown piece and she flipped it in the air. 'Your call, Jack,' she told him.

'Tails never fails.'

The coin came down with a queen's head on view. I grasped Penelope's wrist and dragged her to her feet.

'Have fun,' we chorused as we made for the door.

'All change at six?' suggested Jack.

'Bloody 'ell, pal. It's almost three now and we've still got to get back to the 'otel. Besides, I 'ave a bad mouth.'

'Come on, oppo. Ya can always use the room again later on.'

'Okay, see you then.'

'I'll be the one trying to knock down the door.'

The telephone rang at five minutes past six. 'What the fuck're you doing?' Jack demanded.

'Hold your water, oppo. We'll be down in ten minutes. You in the bar?'

'That's right. There's a drink waitin' for ya, but if yer not 'ere by six-fifteen, I'm downing it meself.'

'Hey, make sure you don't choke on it. I'd 'ate ta lose ya.'

I took Penelope to an Indian restaurant just down the road from the hotel. We passed a newsagent and I bought the evening sports paper. We ordered food, then split the paper so Penelope could check what was showing at the local cinemas as I read about City's win over Blackburn Rovers.

'If this is how Marines spend their time on guard duty, I think I'll join up myself,' said Jill's scathing voice.

I felt my testes shrivel and head for cover. I rejected the idea of introducing Penelope as my sister. I lowered the newspaper, lifted my head and saw a man hovering at Jill's shoulder. I was off the hook! My balls came out of hiding and gained some heat in my scrotum. I stood up. 'Hello, Jill. I'd like you to meet Penelope. She's a friend of mine from back home.'

'I'm sure she is.' Jill ignored Penelope's outstretched hand. 'Where's your partner in crime?'

'I dunno. He's in town somewhere. I expect we'll meet up somewhere tonight. Audrey with you?'

The waiter arrived with poppadums and accompanying dishes of dips. I could have hugged him for his timing.

'Jack is at the hotel with my friend Susan,' Penelope blithely blurted out.

'Really! Let me guess; they're playing Monopoly?'

Penelope blushed. 'Probably not.'

Jill tipped back her head so she could look down her nose. 'No, probably not.'

Penelope kept her eyes on her hands as they twisted the serviette on her lap. I saw a tear land on the back of her right hand. She quickly mopped it up with the crumpled square of white linen.

'So, lover.' Jill turned back to me with a false smile. 'What to do?'

Why was she having so much fun? She had the silent civilian with her. Surely, we were guilty of the same crime. 'I guess the best thing would be for you and your date to enjoy your meal, while Penelope and I get on with ours.'

'Convenient for you, but not what I had in mind. By the way, this is Michael.' We nodded slightly in recognition of each other's presence. 'He's not my date, he's my brother.' Of course he is. Use of the weak story I had abandoned, gave me a feeling of superiority over the woman I much preferred to be with. 'Michael, say hello to Paul. He's the Marine recruit I was telling you about. See what a good judge of character I am.'

Penelope quietly placed her serviette on the table, picked up her handbag and departed for the Ladies' Room.

'Okay, Johnson, time to make a decision. What's it to be? You can pay for the meal, explain to your friend just what a louse you are, give her money for a taxi back to her hotel and then come with me. On the other hand, you can kiss my sweet rear-end goodbye. I'd advise you to stick with me though, 'cause you'll never, and I mean never, find another like me.' Michael was studying the pattern in the carpet, possibly worrying about what he would do if his supposed big sister told him to smack me for being such a shit. He wasn't up to the job, but I sent him a telepathic message telling him to relax. I knew what I was going to do. 'I'll wait ten minutes, Johnson.'

The two of them strolled to the bar and I sat down to wait for Penelope's return. I snapped off a piece of the large, oily poppadum and scooped up some green dip. I didn't enjoy the taste.

The waiter arrived with the main courses. He re-arranged items on the table so he could fit all the additional plates and dishes on it. The man knew all was not well and he deliberately avoided eye contact. He put the warmed plates down, placed the silver serving dishes containing the aromatic meats in front and to the right of the plates, the steaming bowls of rice to the left. A third plate containing flat bread almost teetered at the edge of the table. A carafe of iced water and two glasses took up the remaining space. When he finished, he turned and left without a word or glance in my direction.

I tore the naan apart and dragged a piece of it through the dish of beef vindaloo. The sensation of the hot sauce reacting with the wounds in my mouth wasn't too pleasant. I dropped the bread onto my plate and picked up my glass of iced water and, as I raised it to my mouth, I found I was looking over its rim at Michael and Jill chatting to each other at the bar. Jill turned her head and looked at me for a couple of seconds that seemed like an eternity but I couldn't interpret her expression. The cold water felt worse than the vindaloo. I sampled Penelope's mild vegetarian dish, but I didn't even like the stuff on a good day.

My ten minutes had to be up and Penelope hadn't returned. Had 'brother' not been at the bar with Jill, I would have gone over and humbled myself to win her back. However, I was not about to let her fake sibling see me grovel. I was amazed he was still with her, talking and laughing as if nothing had happened. Presumably, he was the weekday date and had to be elated to witness the weekend stud's predicament. On the other hand, what kind of man sits and chats with a woman who has stated he is second in choice to another man in the room? Perhaps he knew the ranking was only temporary. Could he be happy to let Jill have her fun with the likes of me at weekends because he knew, when the time came, she planned to marry the likes of him? When commando training at Lympstone was done, I'd be moving on. On the other hand, if Jill and I were merely using each other as playthings, how was it that she was giving me another chance and I was prepared to do almost anything to get her back?

A different waiter arrived and handed me a note. 'Don't worry too much, Johnson. I will only start the clock when your friend returns.'

I looked up at Jill, then saw Penelope returning to the table with red-rimmed eyes. 'You must think I'm a real fool,' she whispered.

I felt bad. 'Not at all, love. Jack and I were made up by you and Susan decidin' to take your holidays down 'ere. We thought you'd go back ta livin' the way you used to; dating other guys and stuff. When you called, Jack and I thought we could burn the candle from both ends. Unfortunately, we've been caught in the middle. I suppose we were selfish, but we didn't want you to think you'd wasted your money by coming 'ere.'

'It's all right,' she said with a sniffle. 'We were stupid ta think we could take up where we left off. To be honest, I knew this afternoon that things weren't the same as before. I'm sorry I told you I love you. Please forget I said it.'

'I'm sorry too, Pen. I never meant to hurt you.'

'I know. I just wish things had been different, that's all.' She wiped her eyes with her already soaked handkerchief. 'I'm going to leave now. Sorry about all this food.' She managed a watery grin. 'You should try and make things up with the bitch at the bar.'

I had to smile. 'Good luck, Pen. I hope everything works out for you.' I put my hand in my pocket. 'Here, let me give you some money for a taxi.'

'Don't be silly. The hotel's just down the block.'

I watched her walk out of the restaurant before I hurried to find a telephone, mentally kicking myself for not having done so while Penelope was in the bathroom.

The rings seemed to go on and on but Jack's voice eventually came through the line, 'What?'

'We got caught, pal. I'd get out of there before Pen gets back if I were you. I'll explain everything to ya later.'

'How long 'ave I got?'

'I'd say she's walking inta the lobby right now.'

'Shit. See ya at the Lamb and Packet,' he said.

The waiter stood on the other side of the restaurant, his hands folded. I pretended to scribble in my palm and he nodded his head. I put on a smile and walked to the bar to join Jill and her escort.

'Had to phone your oppo to warn him of the pending disaster, did you?'

'Something like that,' I admitted.

'You'd better hope he hasn't lost any of his wrestling or unarmed combat skills, 'cause Audrey'll try and kill him when she finds out about today.'

'What? You're going to tell her!'

'She's *my* oppo, Johnson. What do *you* think?'

Michael finished his Kingfisher beer in a gulp, put his hand on Jill's shoulder, said 'Ciao,' and walked away.

'Did you and whatshername spend time together in the hotel room too? No, don't answer that. You just make sure you get it up later, Johnson, or I'll make your life even more miserable.' Instinct kept me silent. 'Wondering if we made the right choice, are we? Well, you did. I wouldn't put up with shit like that if I didn't think you were special. Just make sure you don't fuck up again.'

Jack was already at the Lamb and Packet when we arrived.

'What did you tell Audrey?' he asked Jill.

'Just that I'd run across you two and we'd meet her here. It's up to you to explain about your so-called guard duties.'

'Yeah, but I don't want to hurt her feelings,' Jack mumbled.

'Listen to me, you louse,' Jill advised him. 'We've only known you two for a short while and the facts won't be as devastating to her as your ego would have you believe. Tell her the truth before we leave this pub, or I'll tell her my version of what went on today.'

'You 'inted I should lie to 'er.'

'That was a joke, Jack; a joke and a test of character. I've a feeling if we hadn't had this conversation, you would've failed the test.'

'Nah. I was only gonna lie to 'er if ya thought it were the best way to prevent 'er from getting 'urt.'

'Of course you were!'

I changed the subject, 'So 'ow did you deal with Susan?'

'Er, well, I uh told 'er Pen would be back in a couple of minutes to explain everything.'

'And?' I prompted.

'I left.'

'Just like that?' Jill was flabbergasted. 'Without any explanation or goodbye? What did she do?'

'Uh, nothing really. She was tied to the bed-frame.'

Scrumpy sprayed out of my mouth. I swallowed what was left and then nearly choked as the descending liquid met more ascending laughter. Jill thumped my back, but I could still see her horror-filled eyes.

'You left her tied up?' she said. 'Did you at least throw a sheet over her body?'

'Uh, no. See, she was blindfolded and I thought it'd be better if I just left.'

'My God! I hope whatshername got there quickly. The poor woman must have been terrified. You really are a prick, Jack. Call her to see if anyone answers the phone. If they do, hang up. If they don't, you'd better get over there fast.'

Later in the evening, after I proved to Jill that I had not spent all my energy in the hotel room, she graciously informed me, 'You just saved your miserable arse, Johnson. And listen, I want more oral from you in the future. Tell that excuse for a dentist to take more care next time.'

Back at camp, I noticed Jack's body had several lacerations on it.

'A good time was had with Susan, huh. How'd you explain those to Audrey?'

'Give over! It were Audrey as made these marks!'

Tommy Sargent competed in a boxing tournament at Portsmouth during the weekend and triumphed in his weight class. We won our even-money bet and now needed to re-invest the doubled pool on him to win his division in the Armed Services Championships at Plymouth in a month's time. Tommy's winning of the title put another feather in H Squad's hat. We knew Stephenson was aware of Tommy's win, but he made no mention of it. Some of us were a little upset that Boswell was not around. We felt sure he'd be proud of John Comma Thomas' win.

With just over two months left in our training at Lympstone, we started to believe again that, despite some setbacks, we had re-established ourselves as a better-than-average squad. Everyone's times on all the courses were equal to or better than the acceptable level. None of us had trouble with the academic side of training, and we all completed the long marches in far less than the maximum time allowed. Everyone was proficient in unarmed combat and the use of the different weapons that we would someday fire in anger. We knew what various military and political acronyms stood for, even though we did not see the need to retain much of the information. We learned to recognise the flags of various countries. Most importantly, we learned to watch our oppos' backs.

We honed daily routines to a fine art. At day's end we showered, then laundered our underwear. We pressed our uniforms, or re-pressed them if not worn for three days. We scrubbed our webbing and, if necessary, applied blanco. We cleaned and polished our boots, shoes and brasses.

The food offered by the galley did not improve, but we learned to pick out and eat great quantities of what was edible. We occasionally visited the NAAFI to eat mouth-watering egg and chips, and drink a beer or two. We went to the camp cinema if the film wasn't too old, or we hadn't already seen it too many times. Other nights we remained in the hut, watched television with the sound turned off, listened to Radio Luxembourg, and discussed football and females.

We rose at six, checked the dress and equipment needed for the day and went to breakfast. We returned with mugs of steaming tea and placed them on the tops of our lockers while we carefully dressed in the uniform specified in the previous day's Company Orders. The twenty-eight of us always arrived on the parade ground fifteen minutes before eight. The smokers, who were half the people in the squad, carried one cigarette and two matches. They struck a match on the parade ground's concrete surface and, after lighting their cigarette, put the used match into their trouser pocket. If the second match was unused, it remained in a different pocket. Smokers always stood with their backs to the wind to ensure no ash fell on their uniforms. When finished, they ground their cigarette butts into the concrete and scattered the remaining tobacco. Members of Her Britannic Majesty's Corps of Royal Marines do not smoke filtered cigarettes.

At five to eight, squads formed up in ranks of three. In our case, nine rows plus Dusty. Our informal leader stood apart, in charge of us until one of the NCOs took over. The ex-paratrooper then made up a tenth row consisting of one man. When not in the field, we cleaned rifles, ammunition magazines, and bayonets at lunchtime. We also rechecked the scheduled afternoon gear. Just as at Deal, certain guys were good at cleaning, pressing, or polishing and groups of four or six formed to share the work. We wrapped cleaned brasses in a cloth to keep the air from dulling them. Guys checked their oppo's haircut regularly and if the slightest doubt about the need for cropping existed, a man took his head to the barber. Some oppos tried to cut each other's hair but horrendous results soon killed the practice as a botched haircut adversely affected one's sex life. Generally we visited the camp's tonsorial artists on a weekly basis. There were those of us who thought Boswell probably cut his hair on a daily basis.

The rail fare to Exeter or Exmouth was a nominal amount, but so was our pay and most of us saw no reason to buy a ride on a train going to its destination regardless of our involvement. One weekend, Pete and Spike exited the rear door of a carriage to avoid an approaching ticket inspector. They somehow managed to get themselves on the outside of the canvas and rubber sheeting that covered the walkway between coupled pieces of rolling stock. No ticket inspector would find them there. Unfortunately, they were drunk. Both men lost their footing and ended up in a patch of blackberry bushes. As the train had been slowing for a signal at the time, neither of them was seriously hurt. They did, however, rip their clothes and suffer some nasty scratches on exposed flesh. Spike failed to see any humour when a couple of guys asked if they could play noughts-and-crosses on his face.

Sammy was dating a partie in Exeter who had champagne tastes on a beer income. One Saturday, she told him she no longer wished to live like a pauper and planned to return to prostitution. Sammy told her it was a good plan. He would try to find her additional customers and provide strong-arm protection at weekends in return for a commission and some free action. He stressed the word 'free'. The lady Sandra was so overjoyed at Sammy's acceptance of her situation, she agreed our man could share in the earnings from clients he solicited for her. So we had a pimp in the squad.

Dennis had joined the Marines at an early age under a program that provided orphans with a basic education. He also learned to read music and play various instruments, especially the drums. He gave up the idea of joining the Marine band and, on his seventeenth birthday, volunteered to join the active part of the

Corps. Musicians sometimes latched onto a partie, but young drummer boys are not at the top of most girls' wish lists. Dennis was due to turn eighteen shortly and Sammy thought it time to initiate the lad in the ways of the flesh. Because Dennis was a fellow fairy, Sammy planned to use his influence with the lovely Sandra and get him a free lesson in the joys of the delightful deed.

Dusty attempted to persuade our youngest squaddie to decline Sammy's offer. 'Find your own girlfriend,' he told Dennis. 'You'll feel a lot better for it.'

Dennis turned a deaf ear. 'Next weekend'll be great,' he agreed with Sammy.

When we returned from Exmouth the following Sunday, we found Dennis already on board.

'How'd it go, Den?' Jack asked him. 'Think you'll do it again?'

'Yeah, sure. It was great,' Dennis replied, but without enthusiasm. He then went to bed and was asleep within minutes.

About an hour later, Sammy breezed into the hut. His oppo, Ray Green, was in bed, but still awake. 'Poor ole Dennis,' Sammy started to tell Ray. 'He gets to Sandy's place, strips off his clothes and is getting on the bed, when she takes his balls in the palm of her 'and an' Dennis shoots 'is load all over 'er bleedin' arm. She burst out laughin' and poor ole Den grabbed 'is clothes and ran out the place.'

Jack got up from his bunk and walked to Sammy. 'You tell that story again and I'll squash you like a fuckin' bug. Ya got that?'

'Hey, relax Jack. There was no 'arm meant. I did somethin' similar *my* first time. It's no big deal. He coulda stayed around for more, insteada running off.'

'I don't give a rat's arse what *you* did on yer first time. Just don't go repeatin' that story to anyone else. Okay?'

'Okay this time, Jack, but don't ever talk ta me like that again.'

Jack gave Sammy a hard look before returning to his bed space.

The next day, Jack called Audrey and asked her to line up a date for Dennis the following weekend. He was to call back on Thursday to see if she had been successful.

Bobby Pearson hardly went ashore, unless to settle with one of the bookies with whom he maintained telephone accounts. Mind, he was not what I considered a lady-killer. I didn't think he was queer, just someone who couldn't be bothered to chase women and it was unlikely women would chase him. He rarely paid a bookie. His trips ashore served to collect money and put it in his bank account. He scanned the racing sheets on a daily basis and transferred relevant facts to several exercise books that he constantly updated and studied. The books contained details of track conditions, handicaps, times, jockeys, trainers, histories, lineage and other pertinent information. Whenever horses he followed were scheduled to race, he calculated their chances of success and made exotic bets. On a good day, he might fancy nine horses and so combine them to make eight triples. If all nine horses ever won, he would collect a lot of money. His main income came from straight bets and was steady, if not spectacular. We never knew how much he won, but Jack and I thought he must have an enviable bank account.

Bobby listened to the stories of squaddies' adventures ashore and realized most men needed a place where they could have sex. The majority of parties our age lived with their parents or shared a flat with one or two other females. It was impossible to bring a partie back to camp and so most sexual activities took place on beaches, in parks, graveyards, darkened doorways and alleys. The restrictions tended to put a limit on the parties available. Most women were unreasonable – they wanted to enjoy their sex in privacy and comfort. Bobby purchased a used van and fitted it with a miniature dry bar, curtains, lighting and a wall-to-wall mattress. He hired the vehicle out for five pounds a day or twelve pounds for a three-night weekend. As he also required a ten-pound deposit to cover petrol and any necessary cleaning, most guys took their sleeping bags along to spread over the mattress.

Members of H Squad had first refusal on the vehicle's hire. Jack and I didn't want Dennis and his weekend date to interfere with our current arrangements, so we decided to hire the screwmobile. On Thursday, Audrey confirmed she had found a girl for Dennis who was as sexually naïve as he.

'Hey, Bobby. We need the screwmobile for the weekend.'

'Too late guys. Paddy Phelan's already hired it.'

Paddy was not exactly a 'tear-about'. He volunteered to act as substitute on guard duty most weekends and sent what he earned home to his girlfriend. We checked company orders to see the scheduled guard list for the next weekend. Sammy's name appeared under 'Saturday'.

'Hi, Sammy,' said Jack. 'Whatcha doin' this weekend?'

'I'm on fuckin' guard duty. What else?'

'So why don't you get Sandy to finance a sub for you?' I asked.

Sammy looked at me with such malice I thought I'd miscalculated. 'Who the 'ell wants to do a sub on a Sat'day night?'

'What about Paddy?'

'I already tried 'im, but 'e's goin' ashore. Bastard's even 'ired the screwmobile. Why would 'e want the thing? All that talk about 'is girlfriend back 'ome and the bleedin' money 'e keeps sendin' 'er.'

Jack saw our opening. 'Listen, you pay 'im ta sub for ya on guard-duty and we'll take the van off 'is 'ands. We'll even pay 'im an extra quid over what he's given Bobby. If you pay 'im a little extra as well, 'e'll be able ta send a nice amount 'ome ta the little lady.'

'What d'you need the screwmobile for? Finished with them parties from Exmouth, 'ave ya?'

'Sammy, Sammy, we're just tryin' to do you a favour.' I grinned.

'Yeah, right. Okay. What've I got ta lose? I'll go an' talk with Paddy.'

Ten minutes later, he returned to tell us we had the van for the weekend.

Handling Dennis was not easy. His experience with Sandra had convinced him to leave sex alone for a while. We told him Ellen was just a regular, eighteen-year-old girl, who had never had sex.

'Oh, she just came out and told you that, did she? What would make her volunteer that kind of information? You pricks tell her what happened to me last weekend?'

'No, Dennis. You've got it all wrong. To be honest with ya, we don't know she's never been fucked before. When you see her, you'll understand. She looks like a virgin. Ya know what I mean?' I mentally crossed my digits and hoped I was right.

Jack tried a different line. 'Look, Den. We told Ellen you wanted a date with 'er and she was just as reluctant to date someone she 'adn't met. It's a matter of bleedin' 'onour now. Ya can't let 'er down after she's gone against 'er better judgement an' agreed ta go on the date with ya. You *'ave* to see her on Sat'day.'

He finally agreed under the proviso we not leave the two of them alone together, unless, of course, he told us otherwise.

On Saturday morning, Bobby gave me the keys to the screwmobile and the three of us set out for Exmouth. The set-up of the van impressed Dennis, although he had no inkling the vehicle was for his exclusive use. We arrived at Jill and Audrey's flat and found Ellen to be a slight girl with blue eyes, blond hair and hardly any make-up. She really *did* look virginal. As the small talk began to die, I handed the keys to Dennis.

'Here you go, pal. Have fun. See you back at camp tomorrow night.'

Dennis turned scarlet. 'I ... I can't drive,' he stammered.

'Can you drive?' I asked Ellen.

She shook her head. 'No. My dad's teaching me but I don't have a license yet.'

Jack and I flipped a coin and he and Audrey took the screwmobile.

I bought a newspaper and we went to Jill's local for lunch. Ellen took the Entertainment Section and checked what films were playing. She was an avid film fan and knew enough about every flick to tell us something about it. After we finished our lunch of hot meat pasties and coleslaw, during which time Jill stretched out a leg beneath the table and discreetly teased my testes, Ellen and Dennis left hand-in-hand to go to the cinema.

When they returned to the flat three hours later, I was asleep and so Jill played the gracious host for a couple of hours. I walked into the lounge around six to hear complaints of hunger. Dennis and I agreed to share the cost of some Chinese 'take-out' food, which, in keeping with Oriental logic, was delivered in. A magnet kept a menu from 'The Golden Bamboo Restaurant and Take Out' attached to the refrigerator door. We selected our dishes and Jill called the eatery to place the orders.

While we waited for the food to arrive, Jill put on some records and then rolled a joint. After lighting it and filling my lungs, I offered the joint to Dennis. He stared at me as if he had suddenly seen a monster and slowly shook his head. I dramatically swung my arm in an arc and offered the joint to Ellen.

'No thanks, I'm high on life,' she sweetly informed me.

I burst into laughter and coughed up the smoke I'd been holding in my lungs. Jill gave me a look of disapproval.

'When I was a bandie, they showed us a film about what can happen to someone who gets hooked on drugs,' Dennis said 'You really shouldn't smoke that stuff. You could end up a junkie.'

'Dennis, smoking the occasional joint at the weekend isn't exactly the same as mainlining heroin.'

'Maybe not, but that's how everyone starts out. Once you decide you need a bigger kick, you have to progress to the more dangerous stuff.'

'Dennis, you've seen too many fuckin' films.'

'If you insist on ruining your life with drugs, you should at least do it in private,' Ellen admonished me. 'And I'll thank you not to use foul language when I'm in your company.'

'Ellen, we're all guests of Jill, but you're more of a guest than I am. And if you don't like my language, then it's up to you not to be in my company.' I quickly held up my hand as all three of them started to react to the statement. 'Okay, okay, I'm sorry. I didn't mean to say that. It's just that ...' I couldn't think of the words I needed, '... you're going to be in mixed company from now until the day you die. You might not like all the things you see and hear, but you either have to accept that people are different, sometimes annoyingly so, or change your life completely. Live and let live as someone said. Ever think of becoming a nun?'

I ducked and the magazine thrown by Jill sailed harmlessly over my head. 'Pompous prick,' she said.

I realized the joint had been in my fingers all the while and I offered it to Jill.

'You know that I never touch the stuff, Paul,' she said, eyebrows raised.

'And pigs don't fly!' I roared with laughter. 'You're the one who rolled this joint and you were the one who turned me into a junkie in the first place.'

Jill managed not to laugh, but she couldn't keep the smile out of her eyes.

Ellen looked at both of us. 'I don't see what's so funny.'

Gallant Dennis stood up and grabbed Ellen's wrist, dragging her to her feet. 'Come on, Ellen. We don't have to stay here and be made fun of.'

Jill tried to stop them. 'The two of you are far too touchy. We're not making fun of you ... well, not much. You make yourselves into targets by getting so worked up about things. It's okay if you don't want to try the grass, but ease up on the recriminations. You'd be pissed if someone criticised you for drinking. This is just the same.' Dennis looked a little embarrassed. Jill turned to Ellen. 'Haven't you heard anyone curse before?'

'Of course I have. Everybody has, but that doesn't mean I like to hear it. A gentleman would never swear in front of a woman he respects.'

The doorbell rang. Jill walked to the window and drew the curtain aside. 'The food's here,' she announced.

'Look, Ellen,' I offered. 'I'll try to remember not to swear when you're around, okay. Now, can we please eat some fuckin' food?'

After the meal, Jill and I bathed together before going out for a few drinks. We were actually giving Dennis and Ellen a chance for some privacy, but I thought the gesture futile. Jill insisted she pay for our evening out and even went so far as to buy scotch. Things were going so well, I took a chance. 'Was Michael your date that night?'

'Of course he was!' Jill grinned sideways at me.

'You've got some nerve.' I grinned back. 'You had me sweating blood, and all the while you were in the same predicament.'

'Yeah, but if I hadn't played the heavy, you'd be writing letters to a girl three hundred miles away and making love to your hand, instead of having the ultimate pleasure of my beautiful body every weekend.'

'That's beside the point,' I countered.

'No, it's not. And what's more, you and whatshername had a session in the hotel that afternoon while poor, dumb Michael got nothing more than a chaste kiss.'

'Poor, dumb Michael!' I laughed, 'He's probably one of the civilians ...'

Jill put her hand gently over my mouth, 'Don't spoil it, Johnson. I wouldn't have done what I did, if I didn't want to keep you for myself.' Her unblinking eyes shone with so much feeling that I felt a completely new emotion. Her hand was still over my mouth and so I kissed her palm. She lowered her hand and leaned over to lightly kiss my lips. It took less than a second before she leaned back, still with the look in her eyes. 'I love you, Johnson.'

My stomach turned and my throat constricted. 'You picked a hell of a time to lay that on me,' I told her. 'I wish we were alone in the flat.'

'We will be.' She smiled, showing the same tenderness as her kiss. 'Ellen has to be home by midnight and Dennis is taking the last train back to Lympstone after seeing her to her door.'

'How do you know that?' I asked.

'I spent a good part of the afternoon talking to them, while a certain someone was asleep. Did you know that you and Jack are Dennis's heroes?'

'Not any more,' I said with a grin. 'My smoking pot and cursing in front of Ellen will leave Jack in sole possession of the hero's cape. Did you see that look on his face? He was genuinely horrified.'

'Don't worry about it. It'll all seem so unimportant come Monday morning. Anyway, don't change the subject. Any girl who has just declared her love for a man deserves a dance. How about it?'

'Dance? I have no idea how to bleedin' dance.'

'Well then, it's time you learned. Follow my directions.'

We returned to the flat around one in the morning. Being the flat's only occupants was akin to being set free. Jill lit some candles and I retrieved the bottle of water she had put in the refrigerator. The lights were turned off and the radio on. We let go of our pretences and defences and loved each other. I think I experienced that night what makes some men go 'over the wall' for a woman.

The next morning I got up early and went to a local store to pick up a couple of newspapers as well some juice, bread, eggs, bacon, and cheese. We spent a long time over breakfast and attempted to finish the crosswords. We were about to return to the bedroom when Jack and Audrey made a badly timed entrance.

Jack went straight to the dining table and started to gorge on the bread and cheese.

'Will you give it a break?' Jill shouted at my oppo. 'Audrey's taking us for lunch.'

Audrey took a playful swipe at Jack's head. 'If you can wait, that is. Stop stuffing your face, you big galloot.'

After Jill and I dressed, Audrey drove us to a country inn in an almost deserted area of Devon. As we got out of the van, she handed the keys to Jack.

'Here you go, lover. I drove here, so you can drive back.'

'Make sure you don't have too much to drink,' Jill told him.

'It's not the drink I'm worried about,' Audrey laughed. 'I've got to keep him away from the food.'

Dennis was already asleep when Jack and I got back to camp on Sunday night, but we woke him to ask if he had enjoyed his weekend with Ellen.

'Did you see her today?' I asked in a loud whisper.

Jack got straight to the point. 'Did you fuck her?'

'Yes. What time is it?'

'Good for you!' Jack gently cuffed Dennis over his ear. 'Did she enjoy it?'

'What? What are you talking about?'

'Ellen. Does she like to fuck?'

'We didn't do anything like that. Besides, what's it got to do with you two?'

'We're just looking out for your welfare,' I said. 'What do you mean, you didn't do it?' Jack sounded disappointed. 'You just said you did.'

'I never said that. I meant I saw her today and I'm gonna see her again next weekend. Will you two leave me alone and let me get back to sleep.'

Comma's training became a full-time effort. Recruit training kept him fit enough to go the three rounds of amateur boxing, so his spare time was devoted to honing his ring skills. He had three PTIs in charge of his boxing career and they planned their routines so one of them was always available to oversee his activities. He experienced shore leave solely through listening to the reports and lies of squaddies. When eating in the mess, he sat at a table reserved for athletes and those on special diets. The only other person to share the table was a discus thrower who represented England and was apparently in training for an international meet.

Boswell's appearances were still too scarce for our liking and various rumours circulated explaining his absences. One speculation was that he had contracted some life-threatening disease. Another had him seconded to some special operation which limited the time he could spend with us. Dusty acted as the squad leader and Stephenson hovered in our vicinity, keeping a watchful eye open. Most of us, however, did feel Boswell had let us down. We did not care what the reasons might be. It became particularly galling to see Willie Wanker always in attendance with G Squad. Whenever Boswell was absent and Stephenson was distant, The Wanker would try to exert his influence over us. One day, he ordered Dusty to have H Squad attach itself to G Squad so that he could drill us as a combined unit.

'You will not give orders to my squad,' Boswell roared at Willie. I had no idea where our leader had come from, but it felt great to hear his voice. 'Recruit Miller, who, as a member of the Parachute Regiment, outranked you, is perfectly capable of doing whatever is required until Sergeant Stephenson or I take over from him. Is that clear?'

I stretched my spine on hearing his voice. My shoulders went back and my chest filled out. I willed my arms to be even straighter than they already were; my thumbs secretly sought the seam of my trousers and then remained fixed in place. I pulled in my chin.

Willie Wanker did not respond.

'Corporal Wilkins, I need you to acknowledge my instruction.'

'Yes, Sergeant, perfectly clear,' the Wanker replied. His face seemed to show no emotion but he must have been seething behind his mask.

When parade finished, Boswell sent us away to change into fatigues. When we reconvened, Stephenson stood waiting.

'What's goin' on, Sergeant?' Pete asked.

'Something that will be explained on another day, Bell. No more questions.'

When we gathered in our hut at night, discussing how to put the world right, we sometimes speculated on what it might be like to have The Wanker as our squad's Drill Instructor. We often mingled with some of the guys in G Squad, but they still had enough squad spirit to never complain to us about their DI. Unlike Boswell, Wilkins did not lead by example. He gave orders with the knowledge he had the power and the right to do so. He was the only corporal we knew of who had a squad of his own and that fact, some argued, could be an indication of the man's capabilities. Could it be he was merely too inexperienced to be favourably compared with our squad's leader? Could Boswell have been similarly inept when he first became a DI?

Keith Blackburn was G Squad's star recruit. He broke records on all courses and earned the begrudging respect of PTIs. Whenever Wilkins was not around, Keith took control of the squad. One day, at the finish of morning parade, Willie left his squad to go and talk to someone on the far side of the parade ground. Two other squads were drilling at the time. Keith detached himself from the ranks, called G Squad to attention and marched them to a part of the parade ground where they would not interfere with the other units, one of which was H Squad. He then stood the squad easy and waited for The Wanker to return.

Their DI had apparently been so engrossed in his conversation, he was unaware his squad had moved until he turned to rejoin them. It took him a moment to determine which squad on the parade ground was his and, after he rejoined them, he covered his embarrassment by verbally attacking Keith. 'Did you move the squad, Blackburn?'

'Yes, Corporal.'

'Who the fuck do you think you are?' he screamed. The attention of everyone on the parade ground suddenly focused on The Wanker. 'I'm the only one that tells this squad when to move.'

'Our position on the parade ground caused other squads to make detours and I thought...'

'You thought. You fucking thought. You're a miserable recruit, Blackburn. I'll do the thinking around here!'

'But you weren't here, Corporal, and I thought …'

'There you go again. Fucking thinking. How can I get it through that thick head of yours that I do the thinking for this squad?'

'I was under the impression that part of our training is to learn to think for ourselves and then act.' Keith then added 'Corporal,' as if it was an afterthought.

The interval between Keith's response and the word 'corporal' was so beautifully timed, it made the rank sound like something that had crawled out from under a snake. Willie Wanker stepped up to Keith and jutted his face forward until their noses were two inches apart. As Keith's nose was at least an inch higher, Willie raised the heels of his boots to make their eyes level. Wilkins held his pace-stick vertically in his right hand, the tip of it seemingly pressing the skin under Keith's chin and causing him to tilt his head back. We couldn't hear what the two said but the NCO slowly lowered his pace-stick and Keith's head came back down until he was again eye-to-eye with Wilkins. The two men looked at each other for a second before Keith performed an 'about-turn' and rejoined the ranks of his squad.

Dusty presented us to the Regimental Sergeant Major, as Boswell was again absent. The RSM was resplendent in his immaculate khaki uniform with rows of medal ribbons, gleaming leather belt and strap. The morning sun reflected off the visor of his cap, making it difficult to see his face and thereby assess his mood. He didn't bother to inspect us. 'Have the men stand easy, Miller.' Permission to stand easy in the presence of the RSM was a rarity, so he got everyone's undivided attention. 'You men have obviously been aware of Sergeant Boswell's absences, and circumstances are now such, that he can no longer continue as your DI. Sergeant Stephenson has agreed to take over the running of H Squad as of today and until the end of your recruit training. Sergeant Stephenson has volunteered to fill this role out of his friendship for Sergeant

Boswell. Do not think for one moment that his magnanimous gesture has anything to do with you sorry bunch of arseholes.' The RSM then called us to attention and nodded to Stephenson, who had made a timely appearance. 'They're all yours now, Bert. God help you and them.' The man actually smiled before he wheeled about and marched away.

Stephenson strode to the front of the squad and told Dusty to fall in. It was the first time we'd seen the man in full uniform and he had a strange air about him. 'Okay, men. This is the other me. I can be a real son of a bitch when I have to wear these uncomfortable clothes, so don't piss me off! You have only a few weeks of training left, so you'll all have your precious Green Berets before Christmas, when you can go home and terrorise the neighbourhood children. Until then, you're going to work hard. Sergeant Boswell is my friend and you are still his squad. I am going to make sure you do nothing to blemish the record of one of the finest Drill Instructors this man's Marines ever had. For instance - Bell!'

'Yes, Sergeant.'

'Don't think I haven't noticed that patch of shit-paper on your chin. If you insist on cutting yourself while shaving, do it from ear to ear and then report sick. That goes for all of you. I want carefully shaved faces every morning. No more rush jobs where you nick yourself or forget your eyelids. Know that you can stand proud when you're out here.' Stephenson looked around the parade ground. We were the only squad left. 'The RSM mentioned that I'd volunteered for this job. Do not misinterpret the reasons. Francis Boswell and I go back a long way together. We were oppos when we were recruits and we've been through a lot of shit together in different parts of the world since that time. You sorry fucks are going to shine for me. When other sergeants see me at the bar in the mess, they're going to remember that the only squad I ever had was one of the best to pass through this establishment. You all got that?'

'Yes Sergeant!' we roared as one.

'Good.' He smiled. 'Any questions?'

'What's the story with Sergeant Boswell?' Pete asked.

Stephenson looked at Pete for a couple of seconds before he spoke. 'This mustn't go any further. What I'm about to tell you is not yet common knowledge and that's the way it has to stay.'

The PTI paused again. His gaze swept the squad as if to impress on every one of us the seriousness of the matter. 'When you passed out from The Depot and went home to tell your friends how many commies you'd already killed, Sergeant Boswell spent his leave in London. One night, he was out for a pint and 'ad to take a drain-off. A faggot allegedly accosted him in the shit house and Francis regrettably gave the man a beating from which he died. Actually, he choked to death on his own blood. Sergeant Boswell is now in London about to stand trial for manslaughter. The shit will probably hit the Sunday papers soon but until it does, you are all to keep your mouths shut.'

'When does the trial start?' Ron asked.

'A week Monday, I think. Maybe the Monday after that. I'm not sure.'

'Why such a big deal, Sergeant?' asked Spike. 'Surely they'll let him off.'

'Not so surely. The prosecution is basing their case on the fact that, as a Royal Marine Commando, Boswell's hands are deadly weapons. The defence is that a man can't leave his hands at home and the trouble came looking for him, not vice versa.'

'How's it likely to turn out, Sarge?' Comma asked.

'Who knows? Even if Frank gets off in the civilian court, there's always the Marines. Then again, a friend of mine in recruiting believes that once details of the story go public, there'll be a rush of guys wanting to join up. Whether or not we want sickies like that is another issue.'

Someone started to ask another question but Stephenson held up his arms for silence. 'Look, guys, we can go round and round with this one. I've given you the facts. The rest is all supposition. You've got to let it drop now and see how things turn out. Anything I hear, I'll pass on to you. Miller, take the squad back to the hut. The first period is shot so you can start today's schedule with the second period.'

Wild questions and statements of support for Boswell filled the air of our hut. Pete capped it by punching the air and shouting 'Boswell's Fairies!' We all joined in and as we jogged to the gym for the next period, we chanted 'Boswell's Fairies', 'Boswell's Fairies' to the beat of our feet. By lunchtime we grew sensible and in the evening we accepted the fact that all we knew was what Stevenson had told us.

The following weekend, Audrey and Jill took Jack and me to buy some acceptable civilian clothes. We still had the clothes bought in Manchester, but Jack and I had worn them so much they were apparently no longer acceptable in discriminating company. Hints about the state of our wardrobe had not been sufficiently embarrassing to cause us to waste our hard-earned cash on new threads and the two women decided to withhold their favours until we bought clothes that would make us presentable. If I was prepared to leave the new duds at the flat, Jill promised to contribute a percentage of the cost. Jack was jealous of Jill's offer but he understood why Audrey couldn't match it. After borrowing money from Bobby, we both got a sports jacket, a pair of slacks, a couple of shirts, a pair of shoes and two pairs of socks. Thankfully, neither woman was particular about men wearing ties. I felt good in the new clothes, but nothing could alter my haircut.

'Don't worry, Johnson, we'll tell everyone you're a film star and your last role required a short back and sides. On the other hand, we could buy you a wig. How would that suit?'

Jack and I dressed in our new clothes and took our dates to dinner at a restaurant that someone had recommended to Audrey. The two women looked beautiful and sexy but the pleasure of seeing them was somewhat dulled when the bill arrived. Jack and I had to endure the embarrassment of pooling our cash. The two women distanced themselves from us by searching their handbags for the tools to make after-dinner facial repairs.

The waiter returned before we had assembled enough cash to cover the bill and a tip.

'Excuse me, Sir.'

'Come back in a minute, will you,' I growled.

'You can stop counting the money, Sir.' I gave him a hostile glance. 'The gentleman at the table by the bay window has offered to pay your bill, Sir.' The waiter gently slipped the silver salver containing the bill from under our pile of money and carried it across the room to where our patron sat with his family.

'Leave a two-quid tip,' I said to Jack as I rose from my seat. I walked over to the table where our middle-aged champion was in the act of paying for our food and drink.

I put out my hand. 'That's very generous of you, Sir. Thank you.'

The man shook my hand. 'Think nothing of it. I was once a poor recruit and someone helped me. In a way, I am returning the favour. Perhaps you'll do the same for someone else one day.'

'I definitely will. Thank you again.'

I let go of his hand, smiled at his wife and two sons and rejoined my friends.

'Pity he wasn't around when you got the new clothes,' Audrey said under her breath.

Jill had another reason for me to get new clothes, or perhaps it was the main reason. The following day, Sunday, I wore the duds for presentation to her parents.

Jack was overjoyed at the prospect of being alone in the flat with Audrey. 'Make sure ya mind yer bleedin' manners,' he joked as we departed.

We arrived at the house around eleven-thirty and I shook hands with Harry and Jill Meadows. The two Jills retired to the kitchen while I went through the obligatory question and answer routine concerning life as a recruit in Her Britannic Majesty's Corps of Royal Marines. Harry had been a Marine during the Second World War and his questions were sensible ones. He had undergone infantry training in Scotland before going to Deal. Small units of men went from the Kent coast to France, where they crept ashore under cover of darkness to blow up a bridge, or a railroad, or otherwise upset the Germans. They used to cycle from their barrack building out of the main gate and down to the beach where they left the bicycles. They were then taken by boat to a spot within swimming distance of the French coast. They often took medical supplies and materiel for the French Resistance. A man might remain on the continent for several days to teach resistance members how to use new equipment or to lead a raid on an important target. Whenever he returned, he would always find his bicycle exactly where he left it and would pedal back to camp.

'Them there Teddy Boys would probably 'ave stolen the bikes, if they'd been around then,' said the man with a grin.

Daughter Jill brought us each a bottle of beer. 'Time to change the subject, fellas. Brunch is nearly ready and Mum and I don't want to hear about life on the ocean waves.'

'Did she say brunch? What's a brunch?' I asked.

'You've never 'eard of brunch?' Harry was appalled.

I shook my head. 'No. Never.'

'Well, you're in for a treat. All sorts of food gets put in the middle of the table. You help yourself to as much as you want of whatever you like. It's a Yankee invention. General Patton, I think. Sort of like a cross between breakfast and lunch. It's a great idea for a lazy Sunday.' Harry carried his own bottle opener on a key chain and he now used it to prise the tops off our bottles. 'Come on, Paul; let's take our drinks to the table.'

The elder Jill placed the last dish on the table as we sat down. There were fried eggs, scrambled eggs, bacon, sausages, mushrooms, fried bread, black pudding, tomatoes, fried potatoes, fried kidneys, kippers, and a huge stack of toast. A trio of bottles containing brown, red and yellow sauces stood in the centre of the table. Next to them were jars of orange and lime marmalades, strawberry and raspberry jams.

I looked at the impressive spread. 'You made all this for four of us?'

'Well, my son David and his wife might stop by.'

Harry quickly asked, 'Where are you from, Paul?'

'I already told you, Dad ... Manchester.'

We stuffed ourselves and made useless conversation until Harry checked his watch, wiped his mouth clean, and got up to switch on the television. His timing was perfect; the introductory music of Match of the Day filled the room. I still ate, but I gave my full attention to the screen every time the commentator's voice rose with excitement. The game didn't feature City, but was still entertaining. The younger Jill decided I had consumed enough food. She invited me to sit in a chair next to her father and produced two more beers before helping her mother clear the table and wash the dishes.

'He was never going to turn up,' Harry advised me.

'Who?' I asked.

'Our bloody son; Mr Bloody Wonderful. Since his promotion to manager of some fancy hotel in Exeter, He thinks he's too bloody good for this family. He refuses to admit his sister has also done well. The wife believes he'll turn up for a meal someday. It'll never happen, not until he has some bloody kids and wants someone ta baby-sit for free.'

Jill brought in two more beers and gave my shoulder a squeeze before she disappeared again. By the time the match was over, Harry had subsided into a noisy nap. Jill re-appeared and whispered we could depart. Mrs Meadows said farewell for both herself and her comatose husband. 'Make sure you bring this young man and his appetite again,' she beamed.

I stopped at the Pig & Whistle and found Jack. The RSM had seen Dusty on Saturday and told him to sign up for an NCO course when recruit training finished. The RSM had promised to send his own recommendation to add weight to the application.

'We gotta run a book on who makes it first,' said Spike. 'What odds do ya reckon we should give on Dust makin' sarge before The Wanker?'

'Might be tough to pay the winners, Spike,' Pete advised. 'We'll be scattered round the bleedin' globe by the time either of 'em makes it.'

'That's the beauty of it,' Spike grinned.

'Yeah, but you'll meet up with everyone again, sooner or later. We're not like the army that 'as more blokes than Boots 'as pills.' After a couple of pints, Pete grew to like the idea. 'Ya know, we could influence matters if we sent a ... a... anon ... an unsigned letter to the right people.'

'Don't even think about it.' Dusty was grinning, but he could see Pete was serious. 'You guys would screw me ten ways from Sunday.'

'See ya nicked yourself shaving again, Pete,' Ron observed. 'You gotta stop doing that. Stephenson was serious.'

'I know, but it's not that easy. Shavin' every day is preventin' the scar from 'ealin' properly.'

'So 'ow did ya get the scar in the first place?' Ron asked.

'It was when we fell offa that bleedin' train.'

'Why don't you go to the sick bay and get a chit excusing you from shaving for a few days?' Dusty advised.

'What am I gonna tell them if they asked me 'ow I got it?'

'We'll think of something,' I said.

'I dunno. I could get anything past the fuckin' SBA; 'e couldn't give a monkey's. It's Stephenson, the RSM an' the bleedin' Adjutant I'm worried about. They think ya must be up to somethin' if ya blink a bleedin' eye!'

'Ya shouldn't't've shaved this weekend.' Jack said. 'Two days mighta done it.'

'Thanks, Jack. Where was you Sat'dy mornin'? 'Sides, I'd never 'ave gotten ashore.'

'What about soaking yer chin in brine? I knew wrestlers who did that with cuts and stuff that kept opening.'

'Fuck off, Jack. What d'ya want me ta do? Wander round with a bowl fulla brine under me chin all day?'

I put in a word for my oppo. 'He's just tryin' to bleedin' 'elp.'

'Yeah, I know. It wasn't all that practical though, was it?'

'Stephenson's not such a bad guy.' Dusty broke back into the conversation. 'I'd take a chance and tell him what happened. Tell him you'll shave round the cut every day, put a plaster over it for morning parade and then ask if he'll let you take it off for the rest of the day. It might not take all that long to heal that way.'

After Monday parade, Stephenson told us he had obtained tickets for the upcoming bouts at which we hoped Comma might win the Combined Services, Southern England, Middleweight Championship. The bad news was that our seats were directly behind the officers and their wives and we would therefore have to be models of good behaviour. As Stephenson was working in the corner for every boxer from Lympstone, he would be able to keep an eye on us. 'Bring your dates,' he said. 'It's a very large building and we'd like to fill it.'

Given that picking up the girls and going to the fights would take a minimum of four rail journeys, Jack and I thought we might hire the screwmobile for the weekend. Unfortunately, business was so good, Bobby had reservations weeks in advance. To make matters worse, he had rented it to someone from G Squad.

Jack was not happy. 'Give over! We're from your own bleedin' squad.'

'Ya shoulda asked me sooner. What am I supposed ta do, wait for you guys to make up your minds? I 'ave a business ta run.'

'Yeah, Bobby. You're makin' our 'earts bleed.'

The rest of the week went by without incident. We didn't hear anything further about Boswell's trial and managed to convince ourselves that no news was probably good news. Pete and Stephenson came to the hoped-for agreement over Pete's chin. Spike got a letter from his father telling him his divorce was finalised.

Autumn weather arrived. On a couple of mornings, when we were the first squad to tackle the assault course, we found frost covered the monkey bars. The first two or three guys had to make sure they got a good grip of the iron rungs. We heard of Allison's apprehension by the civilian police and consequent detention in cells at Portsmouth. Sammy was on a course of injections to cure a social disease he presumably picked up from the lovely Sandra. I thought he might be a little annoyed at her for giving him 'a dose', but he dismissed it as 'an occupational hazard' and so we concluded his bank account must provide him with great satisfaction.

Jack and I had long ago decided we didn't want to waste our time with the Simpson sisters. We had learned where our best interests lay and we ignored their weekly letters.

Orphan Dennis had seen the company commander and asked for permission to marry Ellen. Captain Smithers advised Den that it was too soon for him to be thinking of marriage and, in any case, he should wait until he finished recruit training. Despite Sammy's cruel words about Den's encounter with the lovely Sandra, Jack and I had a heart-to-heart talk with the ex-drummer and asked if was possible that he might have contacted the same disease as Sammy. He went to the sick bay and gave up a sample of his blood to find it bore no trace of whatever ailed Sammy. Our ex-drummer-boy started making plans to wed his sweetheart of three weekends.

Thankfully, Jill persuaded her father to lend her the car for the weekend, so not getting the screwmobile wasn't as inconvenient as we'd anticipated. When we arrived at the naval barracks at Plymouth, we found every other recruit in dress blues. As the event was not high on the list of priorities for able seamen or trained Marines on a Saturday night, men in civilian clothes attracted immediate attention.

'To hell with them,' said Jill. 'You two look fine for this dump.'

It was easy for her to say, but Jack and I were worried we might have missed an order regarding the dress code for the occasion. A matelot took us to our seats in the middle of the row behind the empty officers' section.

'We're in full view of everyone 'ere,' I said. 'Let's get ta the back of this place 'til the front seats fill up or the lights go down.'

'Oh yes, and what are *we* supposed to do?' asked prickly Audrey.

'You come with us, of course.'

'I don't think so. Jill and I have on three-inch heels and our skirts aren't much longer. If you think we're going to come back to these seats when the place is full, you're out of your tiny Marine mind.'

Jill laughed. 'She's right, guys. While we're daintily trying not to stand on anyone's toes, every bootneck and matelot in the place will be watching and waiting for a flash.'

'Yeah, and everyone on this row's going to politely stand up to let us past and then make sure we brush up against them. Is that what you want?'

Jack and I sat and prayed for darkness. Five minutes later the officers, all dressed in their mess uniforms, entered the cavernous hall. Wives and lovers who mostly wore variations of the same black cocktail dress, accompanied most of them. Jack and I received some pointed stares that felt like icy blasts blowing down my open-necked collar.

'Must be saving their blues for Monday morning,' said one young officer.

'They're hardly incognito under those haircuts,' someone's date observed.

Jill squeezed my thigh and smiled at me.

'Do recruits sell their tickets to civilians?' a flabby wife wanted to know.

'What civilians would sport such haircuts, my dear?'

Jack and I remained silent, but I waited with trepidation for either of our feisty companions to direct a comment at someone.

Stephenson climbed onto the ring's apron and put his bucket by the corner post. The first two boxers were still making their way to the ring and the hall remained fully illuminated, allowing the sergeant to survey the crowd. When his eyes found Jack and me, his jaw clenched into a grimace.

The bouts started with the lighter weights and, as the combatants were mainly matelots, we had no particular interest. Stephenson acted as a corner-man in a couple of them, during which time his glance fell on us two or three times. Perhaps he needed to confirm what his eyes had seen earlier.

At the announcement of Comma's bout, we all stood to cheer and applaud our squaddie. After a few seconds, our applause became rhythmic and we started to chant 'Boswell's Fairies ... Boswell's Fairies,' in time with our hand clapping.

Audrey and Jill joined in, 'Boswell's Fairies ... Boswell's Fairies ... Boswell's Fairies.'

Other people were chanting with us, including members of G Squad. 'Boswell's Fairies ... Boswell's Fairies ... Boswell's Fairies.' Some started to stamp their feet to the beat. 'Boswell's

Fairies … Boswell's Fairies … Boswell's Fairies.' Thump thump … thump thump … thump thump.

The officers and their women twisted in their seats to look back at us. A few of the women showed traces of fear. Some of the younger ones stood up to see what was happening and were quickly pulled back down by their socially-aware escorts. One young thing brushed a restraining hand away and joined in, 'Boswell's Fairies … Boswell's Fairies … Boswell's Fairies.'

A woman on the row in front asked her aspiring admiral, 'What *are* Boswell's Fairies?'

Some matelots took up the chant, 'Boswell's Fairies … Boswell's Fairies … Boswell's Fairies.' The noise of the chanting, clapping and foot stomping swelled to a crescendo. Dust rose from the floor. The noise bounced back from the walls. Some of the officers' older women put handkerchiefs to their noses and mouths and turned back to face the ring in an attempt to avoid the clouds of dust.

'BOSWELL'S FAIRIES … BOSWELL'S FAIRIES … BOSWELL'S FAIRIES.'

A senior naval officer climbed into the ring and held up his hands for silence. The noise slowly started to ebb and people retook their seats. The sound of shuffling feet, moving chairs and the re-opening of paper programs took over. Both boxers were now in the ring. Comma stood in his corner, beaming out at the crowd while Stephenson, who was wearing a grin bigger than the Mersey Tunnel, massaged his shoulders.

When the hall became relatively silent, the grey-haired, balding senior officer lowered his arms and spoke. 'We are impressed by the "esprit de corps" displayed by the Royal Marine recruits, especially those of H Squad.' A single voice shouted out 'Boswell's Fairies!' and people laughed. 'However, as I was about to say, the young man from H Squad does have an opponent and I think we all owe it to him to show a little respect. Please. Let's not have another outburst like the one we have just experienced.'

The MC was still in the ring and he started to announce the fight for the second time. When he introduced Comma's opponent, we gave the sailor a hearty round of applause. The man did not seem fazed by the commotion. He lightly hopped from foot to foot, jiggled his head from side to side, and wiggled his shoulders and arms around in an effort to keep warm and loose. At the mention of Comma's name, there was a smattering of 'Boswell's Fairies' before Stephenson raised his arms to quell the cheers.

'Is his name really Sargent?' Audrey inquired.

'Why do you call him 'Comma'?' Jill asked.

'Not now, love. Ask us again later.'

At the bell, Comma rushed across the ring and unleashed a cannonade on the matelot. He aimed his initial punches at his opponent's head, but as the sailor raised his arms to protect himself, Comma switched the attack to the man's ribs. The matelot was so busy trying to ward off the onslaught; he was unable to mount an attack of his own. The referee muscled his way between the two boxers, his back to the sailor. He used both arms to push Comma away and ordered him to a neutral corner before giving the tar a standing eight-count. The matelot had not yet thrown a punch. The referee needlessly wiped the tar's gloves on his shirtfront and indicated the bout should resume. Comma strode across the ring and continued his attack as if there had been no break. He punched the sailor's head, heart, stomach and ribs. His opponent was completely devoid of a defence. The referee waited for about twenty seconds before he again stepped between the two combatants and signalled an end to the fight. Comma had won his first match within two minutes and fifteen seconds of the first round. We stood and cheered. There was some more chanting of 'Boswell's Fairies'. This went on until the MC asked for silence so he could officially declare Marine Sargent the winner of the bout by a technical knockout.

Each bout consisted of three rounds. Rounds lasted for three minutes, with a one-minute rest period between them. Winners of the first series would meet in the semi-finals, with the finals fought on Sunday. There were not enough contestants at every weight level to fill the card and so some boxers advanced to the semi-finals via 'byes' or 'walkovers'. Comma's speedy dispatch of his first opponent ensured he would be fresh for his second bout.

It didn't take long to ascertain who Comma's next opponent would be. Corporal Bronson, a Plymouth-based Marine, boxed in the second series against a sailor also from Plymouth. Bronson was a tall, slim and sinewy southpaw whose left shoulder forever fronted his opponent. His left jab kept peppering the head of the matelot, while his right hand occasionally followed with astonishing speed. He sporadically threw a combination of punches that moved so fast, it was difficult to count them. The man looked to be in his late twenties or early thirties and had the presence of someone with a long history of ring appearances.

Although completely outclassed, his opponent seemed to be unconcerned by the power of Bronson's blows. The Marine danced around the sailor, scoring at will while easily evading the tar's occasional counter-punches. The sailor's frustration grew as Bronson's jabs continually snapped his head back and when the first round ended, the able seaman thumped the top ring rope in anger. The second round was a repeat of the first. The matelot's face turned red from the constant pummelling of Bronson's jab. The man seemed to want Bronson to face him head on and battle on a toe-to-toe basis. With approximately thirty seconds left in the round, the sailor lunged forward in an attempt to land some telling blows on his elusive target. Bronson neatly wheeled to his left and rained a succession of heavier blows on his opponent's head, opening a cut over the man's right eye.

At the start of the third round, Bronson re-opened the cut and the blood flowed freely down the side of the tar's face. The Marine dropped his hands and looked at the referee, expecting a momentary halt to examine the gash. The battered sailor used the opportunity to put everything he had left into a mighty swing at Bronson's head. The Marine saw the blow coming and was able to take it on his left shoulder. Concern for the sailor's welfare vanished, as Bronson vented his anger in a furious attack. He drove the sailor backward across the ring until the ropes prevented further escape. The onslaught against the trapped man continued until the referee managed to catch up with the antagonists. He forced himself between them with arms upraised to signal the bout over.

The four of us bought some cold drinks and took them outside.

'Comma's gonna have some bleedin' trouble with that Bronson,' said Jack.

'How the hell do ya box a man like that?' I wondered aloud. 'All he offers is his bony shoulder.'

'I'd body-slam 'im,' Jack grinned.

The women broke what had been a long silence for them. 'You two are different tonight,' Jill started. 'You're like Jeckel and Hyde. Is this what you're like when you play soldiers?'

'That's right,' agreed Audrey. 'When all that chanting was going on I tried to speak to you, Jack, and you didn't even know I was there. And when your friend was beating up on the poor sailor, you looked almost as frenzied as he did. You scare me sometimes.'

I tried to change the subject. 'Apart from that, are you two enjoying yourselves?' 'You should make the most of it 'cause you probably won't be seeing us for a while.'

'Why not?' Jill asked sharply.

'We think we should've been dressed in best blues tonight,' I said.

''Ad to be,' Jack agreed. 'Did ya see Stephenson's face? 'E looked like 'e wanted to spit nails at us.'

'Yeah, I know. But I never saw anythin' in orders about it. And how come nobody said anythin' when they saw us going ashore in civvies? If there was nothing in orders, how the hell can they charge us with anything?'

'Ever 'eard of 'conduct contrary to good order and military bleedin' discipline'?' Jack grinned wryly. 'They can get us for anything under that catchall.'

'Listen to him!' Audrey said with a shriek. 'Catchall! Have you been reading a dictionary just to impress me, Jack?'

Jack grinned like an embarrassed schoolboy.

'Even that's a bit thin,' I said.

'So what?' my oppo continued. 'It's not like Perry Mason's gonna be around to plead our case.'

'Will you girls forget us, if you don't get to see us for a couple of weeks?' I smiled at Jill.

'Positively.' She leaned forward and kissed me.

We finished our drinks and returned to our seats to watch the semi-finals.

When we saw Comma and Bronson enter the ring, we realized with some dismay that Bronson had a three inch height advantage over our squaddie. The Marine's height and stance meant his reach, especially the left jab, was considerably longer than Comma's. The ring announcer stressed there must be no bedlam such as that which preceded Comma's first fight. Jill and Audrey were annoyed because someone without authority over them wanted to restrain their freedom. Once the MC finished announcing the match, the two women started to chant for our squaddie, 'Boswell's Fairies ... Boswell's Fairies.' A few other women in the crowd took up the chant and soon there were a dozen or so female voices chanting and clapping their hands, 'Boswell's Fairies ... Boswell's Fairies.'

Stephenson looked in our direction and I shrugged my shoulders. His inclined head and raised eyebrows seemed to indicate he believed me responsible for Jill and Audrey. The bell sounded and Comma ran across the ring in an attempt to trap Bronson in his corner. The chant turned to cheers of anticipation. The corporal was surprised by the rush, but he had advanced far enough out of his corner to prevent Comma gaining the hoped for advantage. Bronson wrapped his arms around our squaddie until the referee ordered them to break. Both boxers stepped back a pace before Comma leapt forward and started to rain uncoordinated punches on Bronson's body. There was not one iota of skill in his attack, but it served to fluster the older man. Bronson covered up and allowed Comma to drive him into a corner, seemingly at our squaddie's mercy. As soon he felt the ropes at his back, he wheeled to his right with such speed, that he completely reversed their positions and began to pound his gloved fists into Comma's body. The punches were calculated and hard. Comma seemed unable to get out of the corner and took Bronson's blows for several seconds.

Jill tightly grasped my forearm.

Audrey screamed, 'Get out of there, Comma!'

I saw Comma's jaw muscles harden with resolve and he started to force Bronson backward into the centre of the ring. He was not throwing many punches and was still absorbing a lot from Bronson, but he did back the man up. Jill's fingernails bit into the skin of my wrist and Audrey clamped her teeth on the knuckle of her forefinger. Once Comma had space to work in, he stepped back from his opponent and gained the respite he needed. Bronson happily spent the remaining seconds lightly dancing around the ring, sporadically throwing a jab into his opponent's face. When the bell sounded, Comma returned to his corner where Stephenson berated him. Jack and I exchanged worried glances. We both knew Comma had lost the first round by a considerable margin and wondered what he could do to gain control of the fight.

The bell sounded. Stephenson placed the gum-shield between Comma's teeth and gave his final instructions. Our squaddie stood and the sergeant patted his shoulder as if to propel him across the ring. This time Comma stopped his rush short of his opponent's corner and, as the man came to meet him, feigned a right to his head. Bronson stepped to his right and swung his left arm up and out in an attempt to ward off the blow. Comma drove his left fist into Bronson's side with such force we heard the corporal grunt. The elder man's knees buckled for a microsecond and he backed up to the corner, encouraging Comma to unleash a volley of strikes to his head and body. Again, the wily boxer managed to wheel to his right and extricate himself from the situation. Once he reached open space in the centre of the ring, he regained his composure and again started the deadly move-and-jab style that was so effective. As the jabs continued to land, Comma's face turned red and the flesh around his right eye started to swell. Our squaddie ducked, weaved and bobbed, but he was unable to mount a serious attack on the two-striper. Bronson's left glove seemed to follow Comma's every movement. Like the sailor before him, Comma was starting to show signs of frustration as he realized his opponent was accruing points. It looked as if the only way to win the bout would be by a knockout.

Jill shouted, 'Don't let him fight this way. Get him into a corner again.'

I glanced at Audrey. She sat on the edge of her seat, her mouth wide open, concern etched on her face. In the ring, Comma tried again to launch an attack. Bronson took most of the blows on his upper arm and leading shoulder. Comma stopped in the middle of the ring, noticeably exhaled and dropped his hands to his sides. He looked tired and took a deep breath as Bronson danced from foot to foot, watching him and sizing up the new situation. Comma didn't move. Bronson shot a jab into his face and still he did not move. The NCO cast a nervous look at his corner, as if to ask, 'What's going on here?' He looked at the referee and was told to box on. He threw another jab that was seemingly more of a probe than an attempt to hurt or score. Comma slowly raised his fists and Bronson seemed happier to see his opponent take on a more traditional stance. Two quick jabs landed flush in our squaddie's face. Audrey raised her hands to cover her eyes, keeping her fingers splayed so she could watch what was happening.

Jill started to yell again, 'Come on Comma, *do* something!'

More jabs smashed into Comma's face and he started to bob and weave from the waist, his feet planted on the canvas. Bronson must have thought Comma had run out of energy. A look of renewed confidence appeared on his face and he prepared to finish off his opponent.

'Oh, God, don't let this happen,' Audrey whispered.

Jill silently watched the drama, her nails still digging into my skin. Jack looked over at me with pursed lips. In the ring, Bronson threw three quick jabs to further test the situation. Comma bent at the waist and moved his head and shoulders, trying to avoid the blows that still found their mark. The corporal flicked out a stiff jab and moved in behind it with his right hand. Comma took the left, exploded inside Bronson's reach and started to pummel the corporal with a blur of well-placed and powerful hits. The lanky boxer was completely surprised and he back-pedalled as fast as he could. Comma guided the man into a corner, landing a succession of punches as he did so. Bronson felt the ropes at his back and tried to twist away, but Comma anticipated the tactic and cut off the man's escape route. Trapped by a heavy puncher, Bronson lost some of his reserve and started to fight back wildly. Comma took the opportunity and landed a tremendous right on the corporal's nose just as he was turning to his left. The nose split open to the gristle. Blood flew out, some of it spattering the hair, face and flowery dress of a young woman in the front row, causing her to gag into her gloved hand. Comma pressed his advantage with relentless fury and the referee contorted his neck trying to assess the severity of the cut on Bronson's nose. The bell sounded to end the round and, for one minute, relieved the man of his responsibility.

Bronson's corner-man wiped away the blood and asked that a doctor inspect the cut. The insipid naval officer showed annoyance at leaving his seat, climbed onto the ring apron, and roughly pushed Bronson's head back in order to assess the damage. The bell rang to start the third round but the doctor waved his arms crosswise to indicate an end to the bout. The referee walked to the corner where Comma stood waiting, grabbed his wrist and lifted his arm in the air. Chants of 'Boswell's Fairies … Boswell's Fairies' broke out again, but as Comma crossed the ring to commiserate with Bronson, they quickly died. Jack and I called Comma's name and pumped the air with our fists when he turned to acknowledge us.

'See ya back at camp,' Jack yelled.

The boxers left the ring and everything after that was an anti-climax. We had no interest in the remainder of the card and we left. It was a two hour drive back to Exmouth and we didn't want to return too late. Harry was probably fretting over his car.

After breakfast, I went to the newsagent to pick up the Sunday papers while Jill cleaned the kitchen. When I saw the headlines I knew it was going to be a tough morning. We settled into facing armchairs to read. The Sunday tabloids had fun with the story of the Royal Marine Commando who beat a hapless homosexual to death in the toilet of a London pub. The conservative rags took Boswell's side, saying England would be a better place if all deviants got their just deserts. The liberals thought it might be a good idea if Her Majesty's Royal Marines be kept in some far-flung out-post of the empire, a la French Foreign Legion, 'so England's streets can be safe for the people, no matter their colour, race, creed or sexual preference'.

As the pages that carried the story about Boswell were, in most papers, the other half of the sports section that included a report about Manchester City's win over Preston North End in the FA Cup, Jill and I kept swapping pages.

'Is this your Boswell? The man whose name everyone was chanting last night?'

'Yeah, that's him; our DI.'

'Holy Mother of God. Do you mean to say that I was chanting 'Boswell's Fairies' over and over, while Boswell himself is on trial for killing a fairy?'

'You do have a way with words.' I laughed and crisply flipped my page.

'It's no laughing matter. How could you let me do it?'

'Don't get carried away! All he did was smack a pervert who tried to put the make on him. The fact that the guy later choked to death on his own blood is just bad luck for him.'

She collapsed the pages in her lap. 'Bad luck! Is that what you call it? Bad luck?'

'Of course. The Sarge never meant to kill the poofter, just discourage him from trying to suck on his tube steak. Wouldn't you expect your brother to do the same?'

'No, I would not! I would expect him to walk away.'

'Get real. You 'ave a couple of pints in a pub and go for a drain-off. Somebody in the toilet starts to make advances on you; a pervert who has been waiting just to proposition somebody. That same person could be in the toilet at a football match when a child goes for a drain-off. What then? At least this pervert won't be able to do that anymore.'

'You don't know if he's done anything to a child.'

'No, I don't. But I bloody well know he won't have the opportunity to in the future.'

'And that's it, is it? Let Bosman off?'

'Boswell.'

'Whatever. I hope if you ever face the same situation, you'll walk away.' She reached over, pushed down the top of the paper I was reading and fixed me with a stare. 'Will you?'

'I don't know. What if the person's persistent? How do you know what you'd do in any given situation?'

'I don't think a man would persist if he knew his advances were unwelcome.'

'Maybe not. Nevertheless, the incident did occur in a boozer. What if the bastard was so ossified, he didn't know when to quit?'

'You're reaching now, Johnson.'

'It could happen.'

'I'm not so sure. It's a bit of a cliché, isn't it?'

'What do you mean, cliché?'

'Isn't it what all those who beat up homosexuals say? He approached me in the toilet, your honour. You'd think gay men would've learned to keep the hell away from toilets by now. I would hazard a guess that bullies follow their targets to toilets to beat them up. Anyway, you're leading me away from what I wanted to say. This man gave you the title of 'Boswell's Fairies' that you're all so bloody proud to brag about. Do you think it might be time to let it drop? Imagine if the News of The World were to find out there are twenty-eight recruits down here in deepest Devon who are proud to describe themselves as Boswell's Fairies. His bloody fairies!' she shouted. 'The jury wouldn't even have to leave the courtroom to deliberate on the verdict if they knew about that.'

I gave Jill a long look to see if she might be contemplating turning into little miss reporter. 'Don't you dare!'

'I wouldn't, but someone might. Think about it.'

'Where're Jack and Audrey?' I asked a few minutes later.

'They stayed at a motel last night. Jesus, Johnson, you were there when we dropped them off.'

'I knew that! What I meant was, are they finding their way back here, or do we 'ave to pick 'em up, or what?'

'Or what? We're picking them up. I already spoke to Audrey and she told me Jack wanted to stay there until they absolutely have to leave. He'll call us when they're ready. Apparently, he wants as much time as he can get in the room. They somehow scored the honeymoon suite and as the walls and ceiling are mirrored, he wants to watch himself in action.'

'My oppo! You sure he hasn't got Audrey taking pictures?'

The floodlit motel had not seemed so seedy against the backdrop of night. Jill drove her father's car to the main entrance and I turned round as Jack ducked into the seat behind Jill with a wide grin on his face.

'Man, was I good last night! I looked like a god!' he exclaimed.

'We don't want to hear about it, Jack,' Jill coolly advised him.

'He is so full of it!' said Audrey as she scooted him along the seat and got into the car. 'All he did was watch himself in the mirrors. I could have been a tailor's dummy for all he cared.'

'Give over! You're lookin' at it the wrong way,' said my still-grinning oppo. 'You should think of it as having had the opportunity to be with one of the world's greatest sexual athletes.'

Audrey erupted into laughter. 'Sexual athlete!' she shrieked. 'Should I tell them what really happened?' She gave Jack a kiss on his cheek. 'Have you two seen the papers? Jack was saying the Boswell man is their DI and he's the one that gave them the Boswell's Fairies title.'

'We've seen them,' said Jill. 'We discussed it and agreed to disagree on the matter. It's not something Paul is happy with. His pride is confused.' She squeezed my thigh and I let her words go without comment.

'Yeah,' said Jack. 'It's not news to us, but I never thought there'd be all this shit about it.'

Jill knew a pub on the outskirts of Plymouth where we would meet Spike and Pete for lunch. The upper two floors of the old building had whitewashed walls and black timbers. A creeper grew up the walls. Leaded windows contained occasional stained glass panels. As we arrived before noon, we strolled through the landscaped gardens. At five minutes past opening hour, I guided the women back toward the building. We were crossing the car park when a shiny red Jaguar with Spike behind the wheel pulled in and drew to a halt in front of us. A beaming Pete sat next to him.

'Where's the fuzz?' I asked.

'Very funny. Don't bleedin' stand there. Open the doors for the ladies, y'uncouth bastards,' Spike requested.

Jack and I obliged and were surprised to see two tanned and scrawny women with elaborate hairdos emerge. I guessed they were mother and daughter. The women swivelled on their seats and stepped out, showing off the colour of their underwear. Both wore fashionable, expensive clothing and eye-catching jewellery. Mother's legs were too skinny to go with her big clothing and daughter's breasts too insubstantial for her revealing silk blouse. What kind of sex, I wondered, could our squaddies have enjoyed if the women managed to keep their hair so perfectly groomed? Neither Pete nor Spike seemed possessive of either woman but they did introduce them as Penelope (don't call her Penny) and Patricia (don't call her Pat) Halcombe.

Eight of us entered the hostelry, as mother Penelope called it. Those from the Jaguar headed for the cocktail bar. Jill diverted me from my path to the main bar and we followed them. A tall waiter with a black bow tie re-arranged some furniture so we could sit together and then asked what we wanted to drink. The Halcombes ordered 'gin and French, please'. Jill and Audrey each asked for a medium-dry sherry.

Before the rest of us had time to order some beer, the lofty man advised us, 'I'm sorry, gentlemen, but we only serve half pints in the cocktail lounge.'

Spike stressed the aitch and imitated the waiter's haughty attitude. 'Make it four halves of your best bitter then.'

'What about me?' Pete exclaimed. 'Make it eight 'alves please, or you'll be doin' nothin' but wearin' out the carpet between 'ere an' the bar.'

'Make it twelve 'alves,' Jack told the man.

I amended the order. 'Make it sixteen. Do you need help?'

'Thank you, Sir, but I'll bring the drinks as needed,' said the aggrieved man.

The seating arrangements led me to believe Spike and Patricia were together.

'Didn't see you at the boxing last night,' I said.

'We was there,' said Pete. 'We musta bin on the udda side of the ring.'

'How were you dressed?'

'Same as now, why?'

'Stephenson saw me and Jack in our civvies and nearly had a bleeding coronary. It never occurred to us ta be in uniform.'

'Nobody said nothin' to us,' said Spike.

'Or gave us any bleedin' looks,' Pete added. 'Ya must've imagined it.'

'Give over!' Jack said. 'I saw 'im as well, an' 'e wasn't 'appy.'

'What are your friend's chances today?' Penelope asked.

'I'd say 'is biggest test was Bronson but I've no idea who 'e's up against,' Jack said.

'Me, neither,' said Spike as he twisted around to check on where the waiter was with our drinks. 'Guys 'round us were rabbitin' on about some Percy who 'as no idea 'ow to box, but can lay someone down with one punch, provided 'e gets ta land it.'

'What on earth is a Percy?' an aloof Patricia wanted to know.

'It's short for Percy Pongo and is a term used for someone in the army,' Jill explained. 'Marines believe they're superior to any other branch of the armed services, don't you dear.'

I realized the remark was addressed to me. 'Hey, what's wrong with that? My old man told me – always go for the best. That's why I'm with you.' Jill smiled indulgently, closed her eyes and slowly shook her head. I imagined my Percy Pongo father sitting at a nearby table, tut-tutting.

'And what, pray, do these Percy Pongoes call you?'

'Machines, Royal Machines,' Pete said with pride. 'They reckon we're so disciplined we operate like machines. Getting' paid more than them don't improve relations. On the other 'and, they only sign up fer three to five years while we sign up for nine big ones plus another three as reservists. Our training takes ten months, while theirs is somethin' less than ten weeks. Whenever there's a punch-up somewhere in the world, we go in first and come out last. They ponce around between times.'

Jack returned to the original subject. 'Ya know, Comma didn't exactly show a lotta boxing skill last night, but 'e got clever in the end with that Bronson. I'm not about ta believe what some unknowns say about a bleedin' Percy.'

'Do leave off, Jack. Comma 'ad to fight the way 'e did. It'll be different today, you can bleedin' count on it,' Pete said loudly, his pride redoubled.

The waiter arrived with our drinks. 'Just four halves this time, gentlemen. Four more are being poured and will arrive soon.'

Pete's pride and enthusiasm were so high, he paid for the round, plus an additional half-pint tip. I had envisioned us all taking time and making a scene as we pooled our money. I felt relieved.

Spike and Jack downed their beers in a gulp and told the waiter he could take the empty glasses back with him. 'Save yer soles and the carpet,' Jack said with a smile.

'Do you follow boxing, Patricia?' Audrey asked.

'Not at all. I'd never seen a boxing match before last night. I know my brother was made to box when he was at school, but I never witnessed any of his fights.'

Penelope broke in. 'As I recall, dear, your brother was a very reluctant participant in any sporting event. He must have hated boxing. I'm sure he would have much preferred to be the water-boy.'

'I must say I thoroughly enjoyed the atmosphere last night. I stood and chanted for Pete's friend along with everyone else. It really was quite exciting, 'though I don't think Mother approved of my behaviour, did you, Mama?'

'As long as you don't act like that at the tennis club, dear, I don't see any harm in it.'

'I need another drink,' said Spike. He focused his attention on the waiter's approach with four more halves of best bitter. His date tapped him on the shoulder. 'I'm still here.'

'I know. I'm just waiting for my drink.'

Patricia looked at the back of Spike's head for two seconds, before turning back. 'I've lost track. Where were we? Oh, yes. The chant. Stephen tells me you all call yourselves fairies.'

'Who's Stephen?' Jack asked.

'Me,' said Spike.

'Give over!' Jack laughed aloud. 'Stephen Kielly,' he said slowly, testing it to see if it fit our squaddie. 'Nah,' he decided. 'I'd stick with Spike if I were you.'

Spike blew air down his nostrils. 'Thanks, Jack. I'll try to remember that.' He reached out to the tray. 'Which one's mine?'

'Can I resume now?' Patricia asked, not pleased at the interruptions.

Audrey leaned forward. 'You were talking about fairies. Have you read today's newspapers?'

Jill almost drowned out Patricia's reply. 'Let's not get into that.'

'I had a brief look at The Times this morning, why?'

'Did you see the story about ...?'

'*Audrey*! Let's change the subject, shall we!' She gave her friend a pointed look

Penelope joined the conversation again. 'This is delicious. We must buy a copy of every newspaper on our way home and see what it is that we are not supposed to read. In fact, if I can attract the waiter's eye, I shall ask him if he could procure a newspaper for us.'

Jill gave me a look that said, 'I tried'. I squeezed her hand.

Ten minutes later, our waiter arrived with four more beers. He had The Sunday Express tucked under his arm. He dropped the paper on one table and our replenishments on the other.

Spike paid for the drinks. The headline below the fold announced ROYAL MARINE BEATS MAN TO DEATH. Penelope picked up the paper, scanned the article and then turned to her daughter.

'It seems the man whose name you happily chanted last night is accused of manslaughter and is currently on trial in London. His victim was a homosexual who allegedly accosted him in a toilet.'

'And Boswell's the killer?' Patricia asked.

'Well, we must assume he is innocent until proven otherwise, but yes.'

''E is *not* a killer,' Pete insisted in a harsh whisper. ''E beat up a pervert who accosted 'im while 'e was takin' a leak. The fact the man died later on is not Boswell's fault.'

'Oh, you mean that the man would have died whether or not Mr Boswell attacked him?' Penelope countered.

'Sergeant Boswell.' The words came from between Spike's teeth. 'Look. If a perve puts the make on ya, you 'ave to be allowed to discourage him.'

'By discourage, you mean give a severe beating?'

I was becoming annoyed with the haughty bitch. 'If that's what it takes, yes.'

'Are you still proud to call yourself one of Boswell's Fairies?' Patricia asked me.

'Yes, I fucking am!' I shouted. I got to my feet. 'I am one of Boswell's Fairies. You got that?'

Everyone in the room stared at me. A couple of people had newspapers with them and they started to search the pages, knowing there was a connection.

Penelope picked up her handbag and rose from her chair, 'I think it is time for us to leave. Come along, Patricia.' She looked down at Pete, who had not bothered to stand. 'I take it a Royal Marine can find his way home.'

'We'll take care of Spike and Pete,' Jack advised her.

Penelope turned her full attention to me. 'You will not speak like that to my daughter or me again, young man. We will not tolerate it.'

'Go fuck yerself, lady,' I said quietly.

'Paul!' Jill thumped my leg.

Mother and daughter walked out of the bar, their chins so high, the skin on their throats stretched into furrows.

I looked at Pete and Spike, 'Sorry about that, guys. I didn't mean to screw things up for ya.'

Spike spoke for both of them, 'Forget aboud it. The way things were going, someone was bound to blow sooner or later. We got our use out of 'em. Plus they gave us some bread, so I couldn't care less.'

As I sat, Jill turned to me. 'That last remark was totally uncalled for and could well come back to hurt you.'

'The woman got to me. Anyway, how's it gonna hurt me?'

'If she's the vindictive type, she might just call the newspaper and tell them about H Squad being a bunch of fairies. Not just them, anyone in the room might do it. We talked about this already. You know very well what I mean.'

The thought made me feel sick. So much for the discipline Pete had bragged about. The possibility dawned on the others and we all fell silent. What a fool I'd been. My father tut-tutted again. I finished my last half pint of beer and stood up. 'Come on, let's get back to civilisation and get some good beer at reasonable prices.'

Spike drove Harry's car and Pete rode shotgun. Jack and I sat in the back with our respective women on our laps. During the journey, we learned about Pat and Penny, or Pee and Pee as Spike called them. Both claimed to be married to homosexuals.

'Give over!' Jack laughed. 'What's the chance of mother and daughter both bein' 'itched to a bleedin' faggot? Wouldn't the mother 'ave told her daughter about her own fucked-up marriage?'

'Hey, what the 'ell do I know? That's what they told us. Maybe they said that ta make us feel better about fuckin' 'em.'

'About that. Their hair looked too neat and tidy for a couple of parties who'd supposedly just enjoyed a fuck. Did you actually fuck 'em?'

'Well, not technically,' Pete said with a laugh.

When we arrived at the drill hall I was surprised to see fewer people than the previous night. The support for beaten boxers might have disappeared, but I assumed there would be more interest on the night of the finals. A number of Percies from the Royal Engineers were present to cheer on Comma's opponent. I was glad to see how apprehensive they were about their chances.

Once we were in our seats, Jill whispered in my ear, 'Sorry if I upset you in the pub at lunchtime. Do you still love me?'

'Who said that I loved you in the first place?'

'You do, especially when you make love to me.'

'You mean when we're 'avin' sex?'

'You're a real pain, Johnson,' she said with a smile.

I changed the subject. Her declaration of love unnerved me, but not as much as I thought it might. 'What about those two women Pete and Spike were with? They were a bit bleedin' strange, weren't they?'

'If I married someone who turned out to be gay, I'd be out picking up young energetic Marines myself,' Jill said with a grin. 'What am I saying? I already do that and I'm not even married.'

'You have a way of making a guy feel real good, lady.'

'Oh, come on. I'm not telling you something you didn't know already.'

'Yeah, but I'd conveniently forgotten about it.'

The first two bouts went the full three rounds. Each winner received a cup and a medal signifying he was the champion at whatever weight he boxed. As soon as a rear admiral had made the presentation to the winner of the second bout, the chant started. 'Boswell's Fairies ... Boswell's Fairies.'

Comma entered the ring wearing a Royal Marines tracksuit and no hair. It did not improve his appearance. Comma, or one of the PTIs, must have thought lack of hair would make him look more formidable. He lightly hopped from foot to foot as Stephenson massaged his shoulders and surveyed the crowd. This time, we received no facial recriminations. The chant grew as Comma's opponent climbed into the ring. 'Boswell's Fairies ... Boswell's Fairies.'

If anyone had read the reports of Boswell's trial, it hadn't deflected them from Comma's cause. Comma's opponent, an army engineer, was an older man and, like Bronson, had a face that suggested a lot of time in the ring. The MC asked for silence and I was surprised how quickly he got his wish. Jack must have been surprised, too. His was the only voice to roar out the last 'Bowell's' and 'Fairies' died on his tongue. At least he earned a smile and a kiss from his girlfriend. The MC then announced the names of the men boxing for the 'Middleweight Championship of the Armed Forces, Southern England'.

When the bell sounded to start the bout, Comma made his now customary charge across the ring. His momentum pushed the surprised soldier back into his own corner, where our squaddie rained a storm of blows on his ribs and waist. The soldier put a lot of force into a wild swing that twisted his body and exposed his right side. Our squaddie ducked and stabbed a couple of blows to the soldier's kidneys. The man turned sharply back but Comma's blows continued and the pongo was so busy trying to defend himself, he was unable to land any punches of his own.

The soldier dropped his elbows, allowing Comma to switch his attack to the man's head. The engineer then lowered his head and shoulders and bulled his way to the centre of the ring. Comma again landed a blow to the man's kidneys and the army referee cautioned him. There were a few sarcastic comments from the engineer's supporters.

'About bleedin' time, ref!'

'You just remembered you're not in the bleedin' Navy!'

The referee told the combatants to resume boxing. Comma threw a couple of unanswered jabs at the engineer. It was obvious his opponent did not have much skill and I began to believe the stories about his haymaker. The pongo turned in clockwise circles in the centre of the ring, his elbows tucked into his sides, one fist beneath his chin and the other below it. Comma danced around him, flicking jabs into his face while staying outside the reach of any bomb the soldier might try to launch.

Stephenson was becoming agitated, and he shouted out to Tommy. 'Don't lose the plot, Sargent!' Fifteen seconds later, he called out again. 'Remember your plan and stick to it.'

Nothing changed. Tommy continually tried to sting the man with his jab. When the bell rang to end the round, I couldn't recall one punch landed by the soldier. Between rounds, the referee went to the soldier's corner and spoke to the boxer. Stephenson was very animated in Tommy's corner and I assumed he was trying to impress on our squaddie that he should stick to the fight plan.

The start of the second round was no different from the first, except the soldier was ready for the charge. The man allowed Tommy to reach him and then abruptly turned and pinned our man in the corner. With the situation reversed, the engineer started to pummel Comma's body. Comma merely wrapped his arms around his opponent. The referee shouted for the two to break, but Comma still held on. Realising Comma was not going to break, the referee stepped between the two men and prised them apart. Comma smiled and escaped to the centre of the ring.

The referee again made a show out of his cautioning of Comma. 'When I say break, you must do so at once. If I have cause to caution you again during this bout, I will deduct a point. Understand?'

Comma nodded at the man, all the time looking at his opponent.

The referee motioned that they should resume and said 'Box on.'

The soldier retook the middle of the square and waited for Comma to move within his range. Comma again started to dance around the man, flicking jabs into his reddening face. A few of his punches missed but he remained outside the immobile soldier's reach. The referee stopped the bout again and sent Comma to a neutral corner.

He addressed the engineer, 'I already told you if you don't generate some offence, I'm going to end this bout in favour of your opponent. This is your last warning.' He waved his arms toward each fighter. 'Box on.'

Comma skipped lightly across the ring to meet the Percy. The soldier suddenly charged toward Tommy, his right arm cocked to land what was supposed to be the winning blow. Comma offered his chin but, when the engineer unleashed his haymaker, he quickly ducked, stepped to his left and delivered a crushing blow to the soldier's ribs. The man winced, but he turned to look for another opportunity to land a telling blow. Our squaddie had already set himself for the next shot. As the engineer turned full on, Tommy feigned a right and then put everything he had into a punch with his left. The soldier's right arm dropped to protect his flank and Comma threw caution to the winds. He stepped smartly up to the soldier and commenced to attack the man's head again. The blows were a blur of action that caused The the engineer to back away as fast as he could. Tommy followed him, throwing fewer punches as he became more selective in choosing his target.

The soldier ended his backward motion as he reached the ropes. Still Tommy punched the man with little fear of a response. The referee had seen enough. He pushed his way in front of Comma, signalling an end to the bout. Comma raised his arms in victory and returned to the smiling Stephenson in his corner. After the referee escorted the soldier safely back to his helpers, he crossed the ring and grasped Tommy's still raised hand to signify he was the winner. 'Boswell's Fairies ... Boswell's Fairies,' filled the air. Tommy turned and waved to the knots of his chanting supporters.

As we exited the drill hall and made our way to the car, we heard thunder.

'Nice night for a storm,' said Jack gleefully as he rubbed his hands together.

'You want to drive in it then?' Audrey prompted.

'He can't,' said Jill, 'he's not covered by my dad's insurance.'

'What about Spike?' Audrey asked.

'They're going back on the train,' I advised her.

'No, dummy,' Audrey said with a smile. 'What about the fact he drove after we left the pub at lunch-time?'

'I know,' Jill sighed. 'It never entered my head at the time.'

'Okay, I'll drive,' Audrey offered. 'You drove to the pub, so I suppose it's only fair.'

By the time we reached Exmouth it was eight o'clock. We'd driven through thunder, lightning and torrential rain. Jill and I went to the flat while Jack and Audrey went to the local pub. At nine-thirty, we switched venues. It had stopped raining by the time the pub closed, so Jill and I walked hand-in-hand through the wet streets sharing another joint. We planned our route so that we arrived back at the flat around midnight. Jill was too stoned to drive so Audrey again took the wheel. Jack took the front passenger seat and Jill and I slept in the back.

A frantic shaking of my shoulder awakened me. 'We're stuck on a roundabout.' Jill shouted at me. 'Audrey went to sleep at the wheel. Wake up, for Christ's sake.' I was instantly alert and looked out of the window to see dark-coloured chrysanthemums encircling us. 'The car won't move. You and Jack'll have to get out and push.'

Liquid mud splattered our lower bodies as we half-lifted and half-pushed the car until the tyres gained a purchase. The car suddenly shot forward, leaving Jack and me face down in the flowers and dirt. To add insult to injury, more mud rained down on our backs as the vehicle became temporarily stuck again and its spinning wheels churned up the roundabout's surface. The car then bumped itself onto the tar macadam and the women got out to see what damage it might have sustained. Judging by what they saw in the glow of the street lighting, they concluded the vehicle had not suffered greatly and got back into the car.

Jack and I were about to join them, but Jill stopped us. 'You can't get into the car like that. You're both covered in mud. My dad'll have a fit if he finds crap all over his seats.'

'Give over!' Jack protested.

'What're we supposed ta do?' I asked. 'Walk ta fuckin' Lympstone.'

The women started to laugh uncontrollably. Jack and I exchanged glances to see if the other understood what the cause of the humour might be. We wiped off as much of the mud as possible, but it was not enough to gain us entry into the family car.

'Take off your shoes, pants and jackets,' Jill instructed.

'We're in the middle of a bleedin' street!'

'Oh, come on. It's nearly one o'clock in the morning. There's no one around at this time on a Sunday night. What are you, men or mice?'

We had our clothes in our hands and were about to get back into the car, when I realized the night was getting brighter. A car slowed to pass us, windows down and horn honking. 'Boswell's Fairies ... Boswell's Fairies,' they shouted as they passed.

We piled into the car. 'Follow them,' Jack urgently commanded Audrey.

'Did you see who it was?' I asked.

'No. That's why I wanna follow them.'

'We're not getting involved in any Hollywood-like car chases in *this* car,' Jill informed us. Audrey agreed. 'I have no intention of driving after them,' she said.

'Come ON!' I shouted. 'We could be the ridicule of Lympstone if we don't find out who was in that car and convince them to keep what they saw to themselves.'

'Sorry, fellas. That's the way it's gotta be.'

Audrey stopped the car at the bottom of the hill. 'You two want to get out here, dress yourselves and walk up the hill to your camp, or should we drop you as you are outside the gates?'

'Give over!' Jack shouted. 'Let us get bleedin' dressed 'ere, then get back into the car an' you can drop us off at the gates.'

'You're not wearing those clothes in *this* car!' Jill told us emphatically.

'You've gotta be kidding!' I shouted. 'You can't do this to us.'

'We can and we will. Don't be such a whine, the pair of you. Get out of the car, get dressed and walk the, what is it, a quarter of a mile, to the camp gates.'

Jack exploded. 'We got this bleedin' way by getting' your old man's car outta the mud after Audrey fell asleep! The least you can do is take us back to the camp gates.'

'No problem, Jack. Just as long as you don't mind getting out of the car in your underwear.'

I was horrified. 'You know we can't do that!'

'What's the big deal, here?' Audrey laughed. 'All we're asking you to do is walk the few hundred yards to your camp gates. I've had men walk miles for a date with me and then walk miles back home again. Surely, a couple of tough guys like you can handle this little hill.'

Jack and I got out of the car and put on our damp, mud-caked clothes. Once we were dressed, we started to trudge up the hill. We heard the car turn around and head back to Exmouth, leaving sounds of raucous laughter in its wake.

We walked hurriedly but confidently past the guardroom.

'Hold it, you two miserable-looking objects.' We stopped and turned to face the Sergeant of the Guard. 'What the bleedin' 'ell are you two supposed ta be? Scarecrows?'

We told him of the good deed we'd done, but the man was less than sympathetic and put us on report for being improperly dressed, and for conduct contrary to good order and military discipline. We were to appear before the company commander.

When we saw the problems other guys were having, we felt a little better. As the Commanding Officer had paid everyone's fare to Plymouth, those who used the train thought they should dress in blues. Sammy had been the only man to stay on board. His regime of medication required him to be at the sick bay every morning and evening. The rail-passes were for specific trains and so everyone had returned at the same time. They had detrained at Lympstone station and then trudged up the hill to the camp during the worst part of the storm. Now every man, save for Sammy, Dusty, Ron, Spike, Pete, Jack and me, was busily trying to get his dress blues ready for the next day. Men scrubbed away the white blanco that had run from their belts and into their tunics. Ironing served a double purpose; it dried the soaked uniforms, as well as pressing them. There were irons everywhere. In order to make acceptable creases, guys rubbed a line of soap on the insides of trouser legs before pressing them. We unaffected six helped in any way we could.

Sammy was a trifle reluctant. 'Why should I bleedin' 'elp? I've been on fuckin' board all weekend.'

'So, Sam, didn't you get to dip your wick this weekend?'

'No, arsehole, but my blues are in great shape. You?'

The hut was like a steam bath and the smell of damp serge was inescapable.

Comma had not yet returned and his padlocked locker prevented us from ascertaining if he had worn his blues. Some of the panic was a little overdone, as we were required to be in field dress for the morning parade. However, one never knew what we might have to wear later in the day.

Stephenson marched smartly up to us before we assembled on the parade ground. 'Miller. Assemble the squad on the parade ground for immediate inspection.'

When we were in ranks of three, Stephenson told Dusty to join us. He looked at his watch and then at us. 'You're going to be inspected by the Commanding Officer. The two rear ranks inspect the back of the person in front of them NOW.' He gave us thirty seconds, then, 'About turn. Now, do the same again.' He then had each rank do an 'about turn' so that every man could have his front inspected. The whole procedure took about three minutes. When it was over, the Sergeant relaxed somewhat.

'Congratulations to Sargent on your victory in the boxing over the weekend. I fully expect you to apply for training as a PTI once you've done a tour with a Commando. Where were you, Samson?'

'I'm not allowed ashore on doc's orders, Sergeant.'

'Oh yeah. You still squeezing-up?'

'Yes, Sergeant.'

Stephenson pretended to shiver in the presence of his unclean charge.

'Johnson, Mason?'

'Here, Sergeant,' Jack and I simultaneously called out.

'You can forget about being in front of the company commander this morning. The matter is dropped. Just make sure you never come back on board in that state again. And while on the subject of what state you might be in, what the fuck were you two wearing on Saturday and Sunday?'

'What do you mean, Sergeant?' I asked.

'I mean that just about everyone else in this squad wore their dress blues. How come you two didn't do the same? That includes you, Bell and Kielly.'

'We went ashore early and didn't know how everyone else was going to dress, Sergeant. I didn't see anything in orders about it.'

'There are things in life not covered by company orders. Did it not occur to you, you were attending a special event? That your squaddie might appreciate seeing how many supporters he had in the hall?'

'Yes to the first and no to the second, Sergeant,' I replied for us all. It would have been nice if one of the other three had said something.

'You didn't do anything wrong, other than not think, so I can't punish you. Next time think. Okay?'

Now the other three spoke up. 'Yes, Sergeant,' they chorused.

The CO walked amongst us with our company commander in tow. Neither man bothered to inspect us. However, the Adjutant trailed behind them like a faithful doberman, his piercing eyes checking every one of us. The RSM and Stephenson completed the group. I felt relieved once the inspection group had passed beyond me. It suddenly occurred to me that I could not remember when I had last had a haircut. I took a chance and swivelled my eyes from left to right trying to find the back of Jack's head. If he were tonsorially acceptable, then so too would I be. No one would have said anything about anyone's haircut during the squad's self-inspection minutes before, as it was too late to get it cut. I was unable to find his head and so I waited in trepidation for the Adjutant to pass by my rear. I need not have worried, but it did occur to me that during the last three days I had been adjudged out of uniform, returned on board in a filthy state, and fretted over my haircut. Jack and I needed to smarten ourselves mentally or we would soon be in trouble.

The CO finished his inspection and returned to the front of the squad. 'Good morning. I am happy to see you all so well turned out. My congratulations to you, Sargent, on winning the boxing Championship. You have brought us honour. Now, to a more serious matter. As I am sure you are all aware, Sergeant Boswell is on trial, accused of manslaughter. I realise his predicament is a disappointment for you, and I can assure you that all of us at Lympstone, officers and NCOs, are fully aware of what the loss of your drill instructor means to you. You have handled the situation well thus far and I trust you will continue to do so.' The man spoke as would a parent and my mind conjured an image of the CO with my father, each raising a glass of gin and tonic and saying 'chin chin' to each other. I almost shook my head to clear the vision but I stopped myself and replaced the image with one of Jill lying naked on a bed.

'Sergeant Stephenson assures me you are all well above average in all aspects of your training. Well done. It is not long until the day you will no longer be considered recruits. In the time that remains, I would like to hear from your instructors that you have raised yourselves with an even greater effort, so that future recruits will look back to the men of H Squad as the standard to which they should aspire. However, it has *not* escaped the notice of the Provost staff, duty personnel and your instructors, that your discipline in matters apart from things military has slipped a little recently.' It occurred to me that it was unlikely anyone else in the squad would have visions of their father and the CO together. I was slipping in my efforts to be one of the guys; a regular squaddie. I had to be more careful or Jack would say something.

'No great sins have been committed and people have looked away in deference to the manner in which you have handled yourselves generally. This creeping lack of discipline must stop. Each one of you must take stock of himself. Being proficient in military theory and able to get around an assault course is not enough. You must become men on whom other Marines can depend, no matter *what* the circumstances. You must show you have the character that makes a Marine different from his counterparts in any other branch of Her Majesty's armed services.

'Now, back to Sergeant Boswell. You must not believe everything you read in the press. To the purveyors of yellow journalism, the sensation of Sergeant Boswell's trial is an opportunity to sell more papers, and to that end, some of the truth may become distorted. I urge you to read papers like The Times, The Daily Telegraph or any of the more responsible journals. They will provide a more accurate account of the matter. Whatever the outcome of the trial, you have every right to hold your heads high. Be proud to be a Royal Marine and, in particular, proud to be a member of H Squad. I understand that Sergeant Stephenson has become an honorary ...' The man turned to his Adjutant, 'What's the term, Captain?'

'Boswell's Fairy, Sir'

'Ah, yes. An honorary Boswell's Fairy. I am sure Sergeant Stephenson is extremely proud to have been asked to become a member of such an elite group.' The CO's smile was infectious, but I had no recollection of anyone asking Stephenson to become a fairy. 'However, I want you all to consider the wisdom of continuing with your collective moniker, especially when one considers what is happening in London at the present time. No one will order you to drop the title. It has to be your own decision. My advice to you is that you let the title die through attrition, or non-use.

'There were newspaper reporters outside the camp's main gate for a short time yesterday, and they may well return. None of you is to talk to a reporter. That *is* an order. There will be trucks to take you to Exeter and/or Exmouth at the weekend. Those same trucks will be available to bring you back to camp again. You will find details of this free service in company orders. I am doing this solely to help you avoid questioning by the press. As it is impractical to make the trucks available Monday to Thursday, you are *not* to proceed ashore on those days. Not, that is, until the reporters have gone from our doorstep. You will be advised of the situation through company orders.' He turned to the company commander. 'That all right with you, Charles?'

'Certainly, Sir.'

'Very good.' The colonel turned his attention back to us. 'I will be present to witness your passing-out ceremony. Let us hope all this will be behind us by then. Carry on, Sergeant.'

Stephenson saluted our most senior officer. 'Yes, Sir. Thank you, Sir.'

Twenty-eight of us stood still while everybody else saluted each other and went their separate ways. I relaxed a little before the top man suddenly turned about and retraced his steps. I stiffened. Others scurried back to rejoin him.

The CO walked along our ranks until he stopped in front of Comma. 'Did I congratulate you on your performance, Sargent?'

'Yes, Sir.'

'Good. I wasn't sure. Good job.'

After changing into fatigues, Dusty marched us to the assault course where we found the last two sets of men from G Squad awaiting their signal to start. Tucker looked at our front three. 'Think you can start thirty seconds after the last lot from G Squad and beat them to the finish?' he quietly asked.

Ray, Comma and Dennis grinned their acceptance of the challenge.

G Squad had on their steel helmets and backpacks. We wore fatigues and berets. When 'Dinger' Bell let them go, our three front-runners sprinted off. They caught up with the final trio from G Squad just before they all reached the fifteen-foot wall and were in front of them by the time their feet hit the ground on the other side. They caught a second trio and almost the third as they raced for the finish line. Guys in our second set overtook the last of G Squad's stragglers and finished together with the penultimate trio. The Wanker and some members of G Squad seemed indifferent to the incident. Not so Keith Blackburn. He and a couple of his oppos dropped to the back of the squad as they marched off to the regain tank. They would make sure we didn't witness any failures when we caught up with them.

Not until Monday evening were we able to speak to Stephenson about the money we had won on Comma. He promised to contact the bookie in Portsmouth and let us know when to expect payment.

Jack and I were surprised to each get a letter from our respective Simpson sister. They asked how we were and how we found training before getting to the reason they picked up a pen. The wording was slightly different but Jack and I agreed the two had composed the words together. *It was a shame you had to leave so suddenly the day you came to our home but I understand how daunting the scene must have been. Could we try again? I had planned to give you a little personal attention after the meal and hoped you would reciprocate. I have ached with disappointment since that day and would love to see you again before you leave Lympstone.*

Jack wanted to auction the letters off to the latest squad to arrive at the camp, but I quashed the idea, saying we had to protect Johnny Simpson's name.

On Wednesday night, he handed me ten pounds.

'What's this for?' I asked.

'I sold the Simpson letters,' he grinned.

'I thought that we agreed not to do that.'

'*You* agreed. I told these guys everythin' and that there was no guarantees. They figured they'd write to 'em, sayin' they'd found the letters in some rubbish they'd been detailed to clean up. They'll say they were sorry to 'ave read someone else's mail, but they were so lonely, they couldn't 'elp it. You know Belinda and Dierdre'll fall hook, line and sinker for that shit.'

The next weekend, as we rode through the camp gate in a truck provided by the CO, we waved to the knot of reporters congregated outside.

'See you around, arseholes,' someone shouted to them.

As we sped away, several guys hung onto the tarpaulin frame, leaned out of the back of the truck and gave the newspapermen the 'V' sign.

At the flat in Exmouth, the four of us talked about Dennis.

'Is Ellen as keen on Dennis as he is on her?' I asked.

'Let me put it this way,' Audrey began. 'Every penny Ellen can lay her hands on is used to buy pots, pans, cutlery, crockery, sheets, pillowcases and anything else she thinks they'll need for their flat.'

'What flat?' Jack inquired.

'They don't have one yet. She stores everything in the rickety garage her parents never use. They don't have a car and they haven't seen the inside of their garage for years. I don't know how dry it is in there, but that's up to Ellen.'

'Does Dennis know what she's doin'?' I asked.

Jill joined in the conversation. 'We think so. Ellen tells us Dennis gives her as much of his pay as he can and she puts it into a joint bank account. Apparently, it was opened for the sole purpose of saving up to get a flat when they get married.'

'Married! 'E already got turned down on that request by the CO.' Jack said. 'When da they think they're gonna do it?'

Jill shrugged her shoulders.

'So, what are they doin' this weekend?' I asked.

'I have no idea,' said Audrey, 'but whatever it is, it sure as hell won't involve spending any money. Ellen is tighter than a fish's rear-end.'

'They could be getting married,' Jill suggested.

'Married!' I was beginning to sound like Jack. 'Don't they have to have banns read first, or something?'

'Only if you get married in a church. They could go to a Justice of the Peace.'

'Give over!' Jack interrupted. 'What JP would marry a couple as young as them without checking with their parents or the mob, or someone?'

'I think if they're over eighteen, they can get married without anyone's permission.'

'I'm not sure if Den is eighteen yet.' I said. 'Have they even had sex yet?'

'You are a base bastard, Mr. Johnson,' Audrey told me.

I grinned. 'I know.'

'So, like I said, they can't get married, can they?' Jack seemed genuinely worried.

'We don't know,' Jill said. 'I'm sure Audrey must have told you Ellen is the last person to tell anyone about their life as a couple. She almost bit Paul's head off one day because he smoked a joint and swore in front of her.'

'Why don't you ask Dennis?' Audrey suggested.

'We did. He told us to piss off.'

'Good for him.'

We flipped a coin to see who was to get the bedroom. Jack and Audrey won.

On Sunday morning, I went out and purchased several newspapers and breakfast items. The four of us then gathered around the only table in the flat and ate scrambled eggs on toast while we scanned the pages. Manchester City had won again. The reports of Boswell's trial made us think he was in a lot of trouble. He had no witnesses to give credence to his version of what happened. His girlfriend, the CO and Stephenson had appeared on his behalf as character witnesses. Unfortunately, our DI had not reported the incident in the lavatory to anyone. After visiting the men's toilet, he had returned to the bar, finished his drink, and gone to his girlfriend's flat.

One expert who took the stand on behalf of the prosecution, stated that the beating suffered by the homosexual had been too severe to be purely a rejection of any alleged sexual advance. The victim had suffered several broken ribs, a broken arm, and heavy bruising to much of his upper body and genitalia. The man had died from choking on his own blood. Another expert advised the court that the training and experience of a Royal Marine Commando was such that Boswell's hands were offensive weapons. The testimony of several witnesses established that Boswell had been absent from the bar for approximately five minutes. The trial was to continue on Monday.

At lunchtime, Jack and I went to the local pub while Audrey and Jill took care of some personal business. Once we each had a pint of scrumpy in front of us, I brought up the subject of our coming vacation.

'Ya know, our next leave will be our end-of-training- leave and Christmas leave rolled into on. Feels like we're getting ripped off. Anyhow, what d'ya want to do for the two weeks?'

'Fuck knows.'

'We spent the time up my end of the country last time. You want to be in your patch for this next one? Ya got anybody ya want to see for Christmas?'

'Nah. There's nothin' for me there. I'd be 'appy to stay round 'ere and screw Audrey for two weeks straight.'

'I could go for that idea, but I can't spend two bleedin' weeks with all four of us sharing that miniature flat.'

'Why don't we get Bobby's van and go tourin' round the country? Two of us could stay in a boozer or motel every other night. Take it in turns.'

I wasn't so sure. 'I woulda thought Bobby wants to take the screwmobile with him. He probably spends all 'is leave touring race tracks.'

'Give over! There're no races 'ere in winner! When 'er bleedin' Majesty gives Bobby a free fuckin' train ticket, 'e's gonna use it. 'E'll be 'appy gettin' home for free, gettin' rent for the screwmobile and spendin' all his time in the bookies bettin' on races in Hong Kong, or some such place. *That's* the perfect leave for 'im.'

We approached the girls with our idea that afternoon.

'We'll have to see what holidays we get.' Jill said. 'Plus, our families like to see us. Don't you want to spend any time with your parents and brothers? Let me check with work and home and I'll let you know. The last thing we need is to lose our jobs just before you two go riding off into the sunset.'

'I've not been working long enough at my place to get any time off yet,' Audrey said.

'Quit the lousy job!' Jack exploded, 'What're they paying you, five quid a week?'

Audrey stiffened. 'Nine pounds, thirteen shillings and sixpence, actually. And, besides, I don't want to be out of work.'

'Can't you both put in requests to have off whatever additional time is involved without pay?' I prompted.

We left it at that they would both ask their respective bosses for unpaid vacation time during the coming week.

No reporters milled at the gates when we returned to camp.

On Monday morning, the Company Commander, Captain Briggs, interrupted our lesson on silhouettes of ships, planes et al. He strode into the classroom with sheaves of newspapers under his arm. Tucker called the room to 'attention' with such panic in his voice, the captain gave the man a second glance.

'Thank you, Corporal.' And to us, 'Be seated.'

The officer looked in the instructor's desk, picked up several drawing pins and used them to attach pages from various newspapers to the upper frame of the backboard. Several sheets bore a photograph of guys giving reporters the 'V' sign. Two of them had a headline in very large letters that shouted: 'BOSWELL'S FAIRIES'. Captain Briggs read some of the more sensational parts to us.

'Royal Marine drill instructor, Sergeant Francis Boswell, on trial for the slaying of a homosexual man in the toilet of a London public house, made recruits under his charge call themselves "Boswell's fairies".'

'Royal Marine slayer of homosexual had a fixation with 'fairies'.'

'Evidence unearthed indicating Royal Marine sergeant accused of killing homosexual in London public house has history of homophobic tendencies.'

'Recruits from gay-slayer's squad call themselves fairies.'

'Two Royal Marine recruits, known as "Boswell's Fairies" seen cavorting naked on a Devon road.' When I heard those words I had to stop myself from glancing at Jack, and hoped he had the presence to keep looking to the front.

'Navy to initiate inquiry into homosexual activity in Marine ranks.'

'Is the Corps of Royal Marines a haven for men with homophobic beliefs?'

'Do homosexuals have a place in today's armed forces?'

'I think you now have some idea what our national newspapers are printing in their pages today. We have reached a very sad state of affairs. Can you imagine what Sergeant Boswell is thinking as he reads this? What do you think is going through the minds of everyone involved in this case, whether they are for or against the sergeant?' The company commander stopped speaking and looked around the room. 'Those of you who are recognisable from the photograph,' he turned and indicated the picture of the men giving the 'V' sign, 'will be charged with conduct contrary to good order and military discipline. The same goes for the two men allegedly seen, sans attire on that Devon road. That is, if I ever find out who they are. It is only a week since the commanding officer cautioned you about acting in a manner detrimental to Sergeant Boswell's case.'

Tucker coughed, then spoke up, 'Excuse me, Sir'

'What is it, Corporal?'

'None of the men giving the "V" sign in the photograph are from H Squad, Sir.'

'Are you sure? Let me see.'

The Captain studied the photograph. He turned round to look at someone, and then returned to the black and white picture. 'It seems you are correct, corporal. My apologies to you men. I'm afraid I am guilty of assumption.' The man returned his attention to us. 'Have any of you been approached by a reporter from a newspaper?' Silence. 'I will take that as a collective "no". Good. The CO is considering choosing one of you to front a group of selected reporters. In case any of you are thinking of volunteering for the job, I can tell you now you will be wasting your time. I will let you know who the volunteer is.' Captain Briggs smiled. 'You ought to know by now that to be a volunteer in the Marines is to have been specially selected.' The officer started to take down the pages from the backboard. 'Do not think this matter dead just because none of you appear in this 'photo'.' He waved the unpinned paper in the air. 'If I find any man here has been talking to a reporter, he will experience

such wrath as he has never known.' He assembled his papers
and dropped the pins back into the desk, 'Carry on, corporal.'

'Yes, Sir. Thank you, Sir.'

The Sergeant Major marched me into the office of the company
commander. 'Recruit Johnson, Sir.'

The captain looked at me but was quiet for a couple of
seconds. I wondered if he'd somehow discovered that I was one
of those supposedly seen cavorting on the Devon road? 'I
suppose being commanded to appear before me might be
unsettling but there is nothing for you to be worried about,
Johnson. Having said that, I wish to inform you that the CO and
I have decided you will volunteer to be H Squad's
representative at a press conference to be held in the officers'
mess in,' he swept back his sleeve and looked at his watch,
'forty-five minutes.' I swallowed an abundance of saliva. 'It's
nothing to worry about. Having received a good education and
worked in a bank, you are better acquitted than most of your
squad to handle a variety of questions and give concise answers.
I stress the word concise. It is inevitable that you will be called
upon to give certain opinions. I do not wish to tell you what
your opinions are but I remind you that you are a member of
Her Britannic Majesty's Corps of Royal Marines and I'm sure
you will bear that in mind when voicing said opinions. Do I
make myself clear?'

He certainly did. One wrong word and he'd throw the book
at me. 'Yes, Sir.'

'Good. Any questions?'

'Not right now, Sir. What happens if I need advice during
the conference?'

'Both the CO and I will be in attendance, along with our
Sergeant Major. The RSM and Adjutant may also attend. You
will not be alone and we will do our best to deflect inappropriate
questions or remarks. It will, however, be harder for us to
deflect anything you may say, so keep your wits about you.
That's it. Is your kit up to scratch?'

'Yes, Sir.'

'Good. When you leave my office, the Sergeant Major will accompany you to your hut where you will change into your dress blues. He will then escort you to the officers' mess.

The Commanding Officer started the conference. 'Gentlemen …'

'And lady,' said a lone female voice.

The boss coughed. 'Lady and gentlemen. Welcome. There has been a mixture of facts in articles, reports and editorials in several newspapers regarding Sergeant Boswell and the recruits under his command. Royal Marines past and present and from across the globe are unhappy at some of what they've read, and thus we've decided to allow you to speak to one of the recruits from Sergeant Boswell's squad. You have all been given a fact sheet containing Marine Johnson's personal details. He will now answer your questions.'

The first man to speak introduced himself by name and said he was from The News of The World. 'I think we can dispense with this *fairy* story,' he said as he screwed up the fact sheet and dropped it to the floor.

Another laughed, then said, 'A one-time bank employee! Looks to me like a misfit recruit for a misfit sergeant!'

'My life …'

Thankfully the CO intervened. 'I have arranged this conference for the benefit of the press. If you insist on insulting Marine Johnson, I shall call an immediate halt to the proceedings. I trust I make myself clear.'

The same reporter asked the first question. 'I understand from a Marine Carling that you and your squad-mates call yourself fairies. Would you like to comment on that?'

I had never heard of the guy. 'There is no Marine Carling in my squad.'

'Perhaps not, but he knows all about H Squad.'

'Look,' I paused to gather my thoughts. 'Sergeant Boswell wanted to make H Squad the best he'd ever commanded. To that end, he gave us the tag 'Boswell's Fairies'.' Flash bulbs exploded and several reporters raised their hands and voices. I surprised myself by being so calm. 'He believed,' I shouted above the din, 'that defending the tag would make us tougher.'

A few men laughed. The female looked at me with half-closed eyes.

'Did it ever occur to you that, by calling yourself a fairy, you were inviting the attention of homosexuals?'

'No, Sir. I understood we were inviting ridicule and would have to defend our honour and the honour of the squad. Sergeant Boswell gave us the name to make us better Marines. It became a badge of honour for all of us.'

There was laughter. 'A badge of honour?'

'Do you think your sergeant is homophobic?' another reporter asked.

'No.'

'Do you know what a homophobe is?' asked another.

'Yes. Someone who hates homosexuals. Holds a grudge against them.'

'Did the cap fit?'

'I don't think so?'

'I used to be in the army, young man,' said a man with the educated accent of an officer, 'and it was common practice to denigrate homosexuals. Is it the same amongst recruits in the Royal Marines?'

'To a degree, yes.'

'So,' the same man pushed, 'how do you know what was playful denigration and what was homophobic diatribe?'

'In my opinion, Sir, it was all done in fun.'

'Oh, it's fun to treat homosexuals as lesser mortals, is it?'

My mouth opened to say 'yes', but the CO saved me.

'Recruits are generally teenagers who are full of life and ready to laugh at almost any perceived humour. The case you are trying to make would be relevant to most young men whether in the military, or not. Next question.'

'Were you a member of The Queen's Squad?'

'Yes, but so is everyone who passes out at Deal. If we had a king, it would be The King's Squad.'

'Which Queen is that?' the man from News of The World wanted to know.

'I beg your pardon, Sir?'

'Never mind.'

The CO spoke up again. 'One more snide remark will signal the end of this press conference.

'Do you think Sergeant Boswell gave the squad the identity of fairies so they would seek out homosexuals and beat them up?'

'No, Sir.'

'Are you a homosexual?' another reporter asked.

'No, Sir.'

'Are there any homosexuals in H squad, or do you know of any in another squad?'

'No, Sir.'

'Is the wrestler homosexual?'

I knew I had to keep my cool, but it wasn't easy. 'No, Sir.'

'Has Sergeant Boswell ever made any sexual advances to you?'

'No, Sir!'

'What about anyone else?'

'I've never heard of anything like that, Sir.'

The press conference lasted for about an hour, but mostly consisted of the same questions asked in different ways.

After the press conference, I told Jack about Carling and he and I went looking for the mouthy man. Unfortunately, G Squad were practicing their pass-out parade and we were unable to make contact with anyone until lunchtime. By then, Carling had appeared before the CO. When G Squad 'passed-out', Carling was not amongst them. I had reason to dislike the bastard, but I still empathised with him. After ten months of recruit training, he missed getting his Green Beret by less than two weeks.

Jack and I spent a few days worrying, but we never heard another word about our muddy misadventure. We concluded whoever called out to us that night regretted reporting the incident to the press and wanted to keep their heads down. Perhaps one of them had been Carling.

We spent the weekend with Audrey and Jill. The Sunday papers were not as sensational as we had feared, though The News of The World could not decide if Boswell was a homophobe, a repressed homosexual, or both. Editorials in a couple of other papers suggested H Squad had a homophobic Drill Instructor. Another pointed out that military life was very different from civilian life and that no comparison should be made between the training of one of England's finest fighting units and life at Winchester, Eton or Harrow. (Jack said those places were full of queers, anyhow). However, the general tone of all newspapers was condemnation of our sergeant's actions. I wondered if being a member of H Squad was something that would haunt all of us throughout our military life.

To me, Boswell was perfectly justified in doing what he had done, but I wondered if being a Marine had changed my outlook. Would I view matters differently were I still working in the bank? I tried to assess how my former workmates might see the case, and did not like my conclusion. I wondered how my father might feel, but decided not to call and ask. Jill and Audrey wanted Boswell locked up and Jack and I learned not to discuss the matter in their presence. The media anticipated the trial's end during the following week.

Although Jill refrained from talking about Boswell, she did wrap her arms around my neck and kiss me. 'A misfit recruit, huh? I've a good mind to call that reporter up and tell him what a great fit you are for me.'

Our girlfriends obtained the requested time off work, so the four of us would be able to spend our two weeks leave time together. Bobby was reluctant to hire out the screwmobile, but Jack eventually convinced him he would probably parlay the money we were paying him into a sizeable amount, once he invested it on the right horses. The women made lists of what to take with us. Both wanted to see their families and so we put aside two days. Jill pressured me into writing to my family, asking what day they would like to see the four of us (I could sense my father's peptic ulcer react) but, other than that we could go anywhere. The three dates were to be confirmed by next weekend. The women also made a rule: there would be no screwing in the screwmobile.

'Give over!' Jack shouted. 'Why do ya think it's called the screwmobile? Are ya telling me we'll only be able to screw every *other* bleedin' night?'

'I'm not saying any such thing,' Audrey replied. 'I'm just saying that Jill and I have agreed that there will be no sexual activities in the area in which we all have to live for two weeks. Besides, who knows what has gone on in that thing? It makes me shudder just to think about it. It will be up to you two to figure out where that stuff can comfortably take place.'

'That stuff?' I laughed. 'Is that what you call it, that stuff?'

'Well, it's better than some of the descriptions you two use. We know you don't want to call it making love. Until you come up with a more acceptable description, that stuff'll have to do.'

G Squad no longer existed and we were the senior squad at Lympstone. In two weeks, we would be presented with our Green Berets and recruit life would be over. As senior squad, we were prepared for ten days of serious inspections of our turn-out, our hut, lockers, weapons, everything. However, parade on Monday morning was normal enough until the CO, Adjutant, RSM, and assorted others left the parade ground.

Stephenson then asked Dennis, 'Why're you looking so fuckin' 'appy, Potter? You dip your wick this weekend?'

'Something like that,' Dennis grinned.

Stephenson gave him a satirical smile. 'Well, I've got somethin' that's gonna bring you back to earth. In a manner of speakin', that is. We are gonna learn how to get out of a moving vehicle today. You can all appreciate, I'm sure, that during an ambush, drivers don't like to stop to let a few expendable fairies tiptoe to the ground. They'll slow down some, depending on how much the driver is shittin' 'imself. When that happens, you people bail out the back. Seeing as how 'Er Britannic Majesty thinks so much of your fairy arses, you're gonna get to learn how to do this without the inconvenience of havin' any live rounds whistlin' around your flappers.' He zeroed in on Pete.

'Looks like you already sustained a wound, Bell. What happened? Cut yourself shaving again, did you?'

'Yes, Sergeant.'

'I thought you'd taken care of that problem.'

'I did, Sergeant. Trouble is, the healed skin is slightly raised an' I got another nick this morning.'

'You know what that means don't you, son.'

'Yes, Sergeant.'

'Two hours of extra drill tonight. Then that's it. You are the senior squad. Senior squads do not get extra drill. You're supposed to be fuckin' perfect. What all you fairies are supposed to get from this time forth, is fuckin' experience. Extra drill is for the arseholes who just stepped off   Civvy Street.' The sergeant rubbed his own chin as if empathizing with Pete. 'Forget the extra drill. I cannot have members of my senior squad turnin' up with all the stupid fucks that're still wet behind the ears, but for Christ's sake, get your arse down the sick bay and tell them I want your face fixed. An' that goes for the rest of you. I want everything that's wrong with any of you fixed today. Go to the sick bay, go to the tailor shop, go to the barber shop, go for a shit, go do what's gotta be done. You are the senior squad! You will look like it and you will act like it!'

While we were waiting at the motor pool, Dennis came over. 'I guess you guys figured out me an' Ellen got married.'

'Give over! What the 'ell possessed you to do that?' Jack asked aggressively. 'The CO tells you to wait until we pass-out and you disobey a direct order two weeks before the event. Are you completely fucked up, or what?'

I joined the attack. 'If you were gonna get bleedin' married anyhow, why bother askin' for permission? Like Jack just said, you've now disobeyed a direct order.'

'Who's gonna know?' Dennis smirked.

'Are ya gonna live in barracks as a single man when we move on from 'ere? What about married fad's pay? Ya gonna give that up? If ya do apply fer benefits, you'll 'ave to show 'em the marriage certificate and that'll tell 'em when you got 'itched. What 'appens if they check to see if you were given permission?'

'You guys worry too much. I'll just tell 'em we thought that Ellen was preggers and it was better to disobey a direct order, than to have the child born out of wedlock.'

'Born out of wedlock! Who's feedin' ya these lines, Dennis? The bleedin' baby won't be born within the next two weeks, will it? In any case, why wouldn't you 'ave told the CO about this slight complication?'

'I dunno. Maybe I didn't want anyone to think Ellen got preggers before she was married.'

'You're on thin ice, Dennis,' I said. 'You shoulda waited the two weeks. That's all it was, two fuckin' weeks!'

'Wait a bleedin' minute.' Jack held his hands up. 'Is Ellen preggers, or not?'

'Of course not!' Dennis' face reddened. 'We only got married this weekend! Ellen and I believe you shouldn't have sex unless you're married ...'

'Give over!' Jack exploded. 'What was that you 'ad with bleedin' Sandra?'

'That was a mistake.' The red intensified. 'Anyway, nothin' 'appened.'

'Are ya telling' me ya got married just so you could fuck?'

I could see Dennis was considering taking a swing at Jack. I held up my arms in an attempt to calm the situation. 'Tell me you talked about a future and kids and all that stuff,' I almost pleaded with him. 'You surely did not decide to commit the rest of your life to someone just so the two of you can enjoy each other's bodies.'

'Of course we 'ave plans. She'll be going with me wherever we go when we leave 'ere.'

'That's not a plan for a marriage, Dennis. That's just a plan for taking your sex partner with you when you leave.'

'You know ...' Dennis was temporarily lost for words. Then he found them, 'Why don't you two go fuck yourselves. Ellen and me're different from you lot.'

We got into the trucks and set out to the grassy flatland where we were to risk our lives and limbs. The greatest fear was we could get back-squadded because of a broken arm or leg. Stephenson assembled us and explained the procedure. The roll was almost the same as the one we perfected in unarmed combat. The difference was we had to roll to the side so that any trucks following in convoy didn't drive over us. Moreover, by rolling to the side, we would hopefully be rolling towards any cover that might exist.

'We'll give you one demonstration only, so make sure you pay attention.'

We stood clear of the dirt path and waited while one of the trucks took the three NCOs away from us, made a 'U' turn and came back. As the vehicle went past, Stephenson came roaring out of the back of it and made the perfect roll, which brought him to a standing position right in front of us. Next came Bell, then Tucker. The three men gave us breathless smiles.

'See. It's easy. The blood-curdling yell was purely for effect and is optional for today. Some people find it easier to do their first roll if they're screaming like a banshee. Just remember, there'll be situations in the future when you'll 'ave to perform this move quietly and so it might be a good idea ta get used ta doing it that way. Do not be put off by the fact the truck is moving. It'll only be going about twenty miles an hour. Your grandmother can probably walk faster than that, can't she, Pearson?'

'On a *good* day, Sergeant,' said Bobby with a grin.

'Okay, first ten in the front truck with me, next nine with Corporal Bell in the second truck and the last nine with Corporal Tucker in the third truck.'

Jack and I were in the first truckload. As the vehicle set off, we were less than reassured to see a Royal Navy ambulance park behind a nearby copse.

Jack turned to Stephenson. 'Can we get another demo, Sarge? I don't think I've got it down right.'

'Too late, Mason.'

As my turn came to bail out, I grasped the side of the truck with my right hand and lowered myself down and to the side.

'For Christ sake, Johnson,' Stephenson yelled. 'Those behind you are gettin' nervous with all these rounds whistling about.' I felt his boot in my back. 'Get the fuck outta here.'

My backpack took most of the impact. I rolled away and forward at the same time but was unable to bounce into the standing position the NCOs had so easily attained. Rather I turned over a couple of times and ended up spread-eagled on my back, staring up at the sky. However, I was not hurt. The other two trucks went by and I stood well back from the path to avoid flying bodies and limbs.

Stephenson re-assembled us. 'The good book says you only have to do one of those. However, some of you,' he looked at me, 'performed like pregnant nuns, so we'll do it again.' He grinned. 'I know you all had such fun you want to do it again anyhow. Am I right?'

We all laughed. 'Yes, Sergeant.'

'I just knew you were going to say that.'

We each did two more rolls; one from the left and one from the right of the truck.

We spent the rest of the day on the rifle range.

'Do us all a favour, will you, Samson? Tempted though you might be, you will refrain from blasting any four-legged friends to kingdom come, won't you?'

'Of course, Sergeant. I wouldn't think of 'arming a defenceless animal. Is there any chance Corporal Tucker will be taking a stroll across the range, Sergeant?'

'Not unless I send him out to retrieve you, Samson.'

The sandwich woman arrived around lunchtime. I purchased three bacon-dripping rolls and a pint of tea.

'That shit is disgusting,' said Jack, pulling a face.

'I know, but it tastes so bleedin' good. Here, try it.' I offered him the roll.

'Give over. I'll stick to me beef drippin' butties.'

During the rest of the week, the education officer (it was the first time we'd heard of such a person) was to test us on the theory we'd learned. We would also pass-out on the assault, endurance, and Tarzan courses. However, after completing each course, we would fire at targets and have the number of missed shots added to our time over the course to establish a final score.

After completing the assault course, Sammy said he couldn't understand why he missed all ten shots at the paper Russian soldier charging toward him. Spike, who was shooting next to Sammy, saw the marker count thirteen hits on his target. He thanked Sammy for his generosity.

'We make a great team,' said Sammy.

The company commander was supervising the tests and was not amused. He decided Sammy would go over the assault course again and shoot at what now had been clearly defined as *his* target. He further decided to subtract Sammy's new score from the thirteen to ascertain Spike's final score. That did not go down well with Spike who elected to again go over the course and shoot at his own target.

Without the handicap of anyone in front of them, they finished in excellent time and ran over to the firing range to shoot ten rounds at their targets. Unfortunately, or fortunately, everyone had forgotten each man needed ten more rounds. Corporal Tucker hastily found the additional ammunition. Sammy and Spike inserted the rounds into their magazines and took up firing positions. Their breathing had returned to normal and so Spike got a perfect score while Sammy missed the centre of his target once. The company commander frowned on the situation but allowed the scores to stand.

On Wednesday, Comma broke the endurance course record made just two weeks previously by Keith Blackburn.

That evening, a rumour went around the camp that Sergeant Boswell had been cleared of manslaughter, but found guilty of assault and given a suspended sentence of three years' imprisonment. Dusty went to the Sergeant's Mess and asked to see Stephenson. He returned to the hut with confirmation of the rumour. The case now closed, I suddenly realised the sentence was justified and I had been guilty of bias myself in arguing that what he did was acceptable. Jill had been right all along. I had fought Boswell's corner to justify my admiration of the man. Some of the guys in the hut cursed the system of justice that could find Boswell guilty of anything. Thankfully, Jack agreed with me, while Pete and Spike took the other view. In bed that night, I realised I would be happy when our training ended, the squad disbanded and the now sour idea of Boswell's Fairies was over and done with.

Thursday saw us on the Tarzan course. It went well for everyone except Paddy Phelan. In order to get a fast score, Paddy decided not to use his legs and feet to get a purchase on the first rope. He hauled himself hand over hand to almost the top but then lost his grip and started to slide. He managed to get the rope twisted behind his right knee and over his ankle before standing on it. However, friction had burnt and blistered his skin. He wrapped his most painful hand in his jungle hat and still managed a passable time for the course. He missed eight shots on the range but still squeaked in under the 'fail time'. Thankfully, he would not need any great effort from his hands for a few days.

On Friday, we drilled in the morning and cleaned our kit in the afternoon. At lunchtime we were happily surprised to find some good food in the galley. Sammy even ran back to the hut to tell all who skipped lunch they should change their minds. While we ate, a victualing sergeant asked if we enjoyed the food.

'How come it got good all of a sudden?' Jack asked him.

The man smiled. 'There's been a change in management.'

'Pity you couldn't have changed the management some time ago,' I said.

'Yeah, well, better late than never, eh?'

'Maybe, but we've all spent a fair bit of money in the NAAFI.'

The man shrugged his shoulders and wandered to the next table.

Jack and I worked on our kit until we thought it was perfect. Our three NCOs came to the hut during the afternoon and we asked Stephenson to inspect us.

'You two think your kit's in order, do you?'

'Pretty much, Sergeant,' I replied.

He stepped to my locker and ran his fingers along the top. They came away clean and he moved to the shelves.

'Your toothbrush isn't firm enough to ensure two months' effective use and your toothpaste tube has been squeezed in the middle.'

'Come on, Sarge. You're reaching now.'

'Not really. Anyway, you did ask. There could be a coup in some African country today and you'd be in the air within hours. You wanna get pyorrhea. You cannot run to a fuckin' quack or a tooth fairy in the middle of a desert or a jungle. I'll grant you the toothpaste thing is a bit ridiculous, but some officious young lieutenant might pick you up on it.'

'Okay Sarge. I get the message. I'll keep an unused toothbrush in my drawer to be ready for any such emergency.'

He smiled, then turned to Jack. 'Marine Mason. What can I find wrong in your space?'

I noticed we were no longer addressed as 'recruit'.

'Nothing, Sergeant.'

'Now, you know better than that, don't you?' Jack kept quiet. Stephenson continued, 'I take it your silence means you are learning, Mason. Everyone's locker always has something amiss. Look at these items suspended from the clothes rail here. It should be civvies on the left, uniforms on the right. You have the separation of civvies and uniforms, but then you've got uniforms hanging on either side of your greatcoat. Looks like a fuckin' toast rack in there. Hang 'em in order of length. Did you hear what I told your oppo about the dentistry department? Would *you* pass that one?'

'No, Sarge.'

Stephenson went to talk with some other guys and we started to squeeze toothpaste up the containers and curl the ends of the tubes.

Corporal Bell smiled as he approached us on our return. 'Pain in the arse, all these regulations, aren't they?'

'Fuckin' ay,' agreed Jack with a grin. 'Hey, what's the story in the galley? Food was pretty good at lunch time.'

'The victualing officer was arrested for selling food supplies to a couple of restaurants in Exeter.'

'Give over! The bastard was selling our food ta the civvies?'

'Yep. Postie Simpson, too. That must be 'ow 'is two charming lickhisallsorts are able to put on those enormous spreads for every guy they want to impress. Some was even sold to the Officer's Mess when they were having a party. That's how it all came to light. By the way, you two still see those parties in Exmouth?'

'Audrey and Jill? Yeah, why?'

'Are they still friendly with Potter's wife?'

Jack couldn't stop himself. 'Yeah, why ...' Then he blushed at his gaffe.

Bell grinned, 'Don't worry about it. We all know. He hardly kept it a secret. Went around telling everyone, or asking for advice on different shit. I just wanted to say, well, you two being friends with him an' all, don't fuck up his head. He's still naive when it comes to the opposite sex and there are some who believe that's 'ow it's supposed to be when a young couple first get married. I understand his wife is pretty much the same.'

'Worse,' I told him.

'Yeah, well, like I said, the kid's in love, so don't you guys put the mockers on him. Okay?'

'Us?'

Stephenson clapped his hands three times to get everyone's attention. 'Okay guys. Monday is the thirty-mile march. I know I don't have to tell ya to leave off the booze this weekend. Make sure you take a good dump on Sunday and get rid of all that excess weight. Be back on board early and get a good night's kip. Make sure your kit is ready on Sunday night so you can just buckle it on come the dawn. By the way, I spoke to the book in Portsmouth. The money'll be here come Monday morning. He was just waiting for someone to come this way to deliver it.

You'll all get whatever is yours after the march. Any questions?'

The NCOs left and Jack and I went to the NAAFI for new toothbrushes.

We went ashore early on Friday night and turned up at the girls' flat without having given them an advance warning. Both had just returned from work and were sharing a pot of tea.

'Quick, Audrey, call up those cute civvies we met and tell them we can't see them 'til next week.'

'You do that an' I'll break both yer legs,' Jack warned.

'Is that both of Audrey's legs or are you including me in that threat?' Jill sweetly asked him.

We all laughed and Audrey lit a joint. After a couple of deep tokes, she passed the grass to Jill. 'What's it to be tonight, then?' she asked, holding her breath so as not to release any of the smoke from her lungs.

'How much money've you got, Johnson?' Jill asked in similar fashion.

'A few quid. Why?'

'Let's go to the mirrored motel room where these two had so much fun,' she said as she retained the smoke in her lungs and passed the joint to me.

'Fun? Fun?' Audrey shrieked as she exhaled. 'This lunk spent the whole time admiring himself.'

Jack smiled at the memory as he leaned toward me and stretched out his hand for the joint.

'That was your problem,' Jill released some of her smoke. 'Johnson here is going to spend the night admiring *me*. Aren't you, lover?'

'Providing you put on an admirable performance, shweetheart.'

I inhaled the words until my chest could expand no more.

Audrey kicked Jack lightly on his shin. 'Come on, stud. Hand it over.'

'I guess you two heard about Dennis and Ellen.' The words rushed out of my mouth with the smoke I'd held in my lungs.

'Yeah. It's a shame though. Poor thing can't tell anyone about it, except us. A girl should be able to shout it from the rooftops when she gets married. Instead of that, she's living at home with her parents and keeping her marriage a secret. The two of them are staying at a motel this weekend, but as her parents insist she be home by midnight, poor old Dennis will have to sleep alone in the wee hours. If it wasn't so sad, it'd be funny.'

Both women knew of the Boswell verdict. 'God knows, he must have had a hard time growing up in the Gorbals with a name like Francis,' Jill mused. 'That'd make a man a good fighter.'

Audrey nodded. 'That, and requiring a bunch of recruits in his charge to call themselves Fairies, would surely give a psychiatrist plenty to think about.'

Jill and I booked into the newly named Reflections Motel and then went in search of sustenance.

My licentious companion grinned at me. 'Make it light, Johnson. I don't want you to be hampered by a full stomach.' We ended up buying a bottle of wine, some fruit and three different cheeses.

I was munching on apple and cheddar when Jill started another of the heavy conversations that numbed me. 'So, Johnson, what does the future hold for us? You going to leave me with a couple of fond memories or did you have something else in mind?' She couldn't be asking me to marry her. She'd already told me she planned to marry a civilian. 'Will I ever see you again after our two weeks' holiday? Or will you march off to the tune of "A Life on the Ocean Wave", leaving me with a tear in my eye as I wave a white handkerchief at your departing back?'

'I thought you had designs on marrying a civilian, someone who was going to provide you with all the trappings of suburbia.'

'I did say that, didn't I? Things have changed, Johnson. I've fallen in love with you. What about you? Do you love me?'

I took my time to select a chunk of cheese. 'Well, yeah, I guess I love you, but you never know where I'll be posted. I might leave for Singers or Aden in a month's time. Who the hell knows?'

'We can get to that stuff later. I'm still on the subject of your emotional commitment to me. Never mind with the "yeah, I guess I love you" shit. Grow a pair and tell me whether I'm just a girl you've enjoyed some good times with, or tell me you love me. Which is it?'

I started a smile but saw the intensity on Jill's face. I killed the humour in my eyes and wiped an imaginary crumb from my lips. 'Shit, Jill. You're a real fuckin' pain. Yeah, I love you, but …'

'That's all I need for now, Johnson. No ifs, ands or buts, as they say. I am prepared to stay here or follow you wherever you go. I'm not asking you to marry me or make any promises about our future, but as long as I'm part of your life, I want to be an important part.'

'Come on, Jill. Enough of this heavy shit. I thought we came here to use the mirrors.'

'I got you here so we could talk, Paul. The mirrors'll come later. I know you think life is a game with the rules constantly changing to suit whatever takes your fancy, but I won't put up with it. Don't we, I mean you and me, mean more to you than that? I came here tonight primarily to tell you I love you and care for you. I want to be your friend and your lover.'

'Come on, Jill. You already *are* my friend and lover.'

'Let me finish. You will never find another woman like me. Don't let me go or fade away, because sure as eggs are eggs, you'll live to regret it. Now, I've got that off my chest so you can stop looking so crestfallen. Anyone would think I'd just said goodbye instead of telling you of my undying love. Put the cheese down and take off your pants. Try and demonstrate to me those feelings you find so hard to put into words.'

I smiled with relief.

'No, no, Johnson. Tonight you'd better make love to me. I can enjoy a fuck with anyone.'

On the train back to Lympstone, I told Jack how close Jill had come to giving me an ultimatum over the level of my emotional commitment. 'Did Audrey say anything to you?'

'Give over,' he said. 'She knows better. Fuckin' parties always want to spoil things by changin' 'em. Why can't they be 'appy with the way things are? They knew we'd be gone after we finished training. That was part of the deal. I mean, they fuckin' date *us* at weekends and civvies during the week.'

'That's right. Jill even told me at the start that she planned to end up marrying a bleedin' civvy. Now she says she's changed her mind. She thought Audrey might be layin' the same shit on you.'

'Like I said, she knows better.'

'So what're we gonna do? Spend our leave with them and then say goodbye?'

'Why not?'

'I dunno. Seems a little 'arsh after all we've been through together.'

'Give over!' Jack said. 'If we 'ang around and make fond fuckin' farewells, someone's nose'll get bent out of shape and then we'll get called everythin' from a pig to a dog. Parties are like that. Come on, you know what I mean. When we get to Pompey, we'll send 'em some flowers or summat.'

We arose at five Monday morning, ate a light breakfast, and rode in trucks to the starting point of our march. Nobody appeared to be hungover or otherwise ailing. We were dressed in fatigues and carried full gear, including tin hats and rifles. Stephenson, Bell and Tucker would march with us while the company commander witnessed the event from the seat of a Land Rover. Pete and Spike took first spell as front traffic markers while Jack and I did the same at the rear. Getting the job early in the march had to be better than doing it later, when fatigue might set in.

We set off at six-thirty, loping along the level road at a leisurely pace. Jack and I had to keep our eye on what happened on the road behind us. Thankfully, only one car and a tractor appeared while we were the back markers.

My tin hat bounced on my head and I continually tightened the chinstrap to keep the movement to a minimum. I wore a cap-comforter to ease the bounce, but the woollen skullcap was only partially effective. The three NCOs wore their white and red gym outfits. They ran up and down the side of the squad, constantly calling out the cadence. They even ran backwards for a spell so they could keep an eye on us.

After about ten miles, we left the macadamized roads and broke into smaller groups as we jogged over the moors and through fields and woods. I took my rifle off my shoulder and carried it in a horizontal position in my lowered right hand. The cessation of its bouncing on my back was a relief. Jack set a faster pace, which was a welcome change. Moving as a squad, especially when we were the rear traffic markers, had been an uncomfortable tempo. The NCOs had spread out in an attempt to watch the whole squad and we saw them infrequently. The Company Commander seemed to have disappeared.

Red flags marked the course. We passed Sammy, Dennis and Sergeant Stephenson. Sammy's crotch was dark with sweat and he seemed to be struggling.

'You okay, Sam? 'asked Jack.

'Nothing for you two to worry about. Just make sure you finish the course,' said Stevenson. 'Fourteen miles to go, Samson,' he said to Sammy. 'If you quit now, you'll be back-squadded and have to do it again in two weeks' time. And think about your oppo, while you're at it.'

The ground became relatively flat and the two of us moved along without a problem. We jogged past Ron and Dusty who had taken off their packs and were lying on the ground, smoking a cigarette, with their feet propped up against a tree trunk.

Dusty shouted to us, 'You two should stop and get your dogs in the air for five minutes. It'll take miles off them.'

I didn't want to speak for fear of changing my breathing pattern, but I couldn't ignore them. 'Thanks, but we're in a groove now and don't wanna stop.'

I looked at Jack and he nodded his assent.

'Okay. Just remember to stop at a time that's convenient for you both.' Dusty may have said more, but we were past them and the bouncing of my tin hat, the thudding of my boots and the harsh noise of my breathing drowned out any sound. Four paces to breathe in, four paces to breathe out. Inhale, exhale.

Jack and I kept a distance between us, making sure not to bump into one another and so alter the pace. My head was hot, but if I removed my cap-comforter, the banging of my steel helmet would increase dramatically. My feet seemed to move without me knowing it. My breathing was harsh but steady. I knew what my body was doing but I was not conscious of causing it to happen. On and on we went; four steps per inhale and four steps per exhale. I even began counting the bounces of my helmet to make sure it stayed in the same cadence as the rest of me.

We returned to the hard surface of a road, the flatness of which made it even easier to jog along. I had no idea how much further we had to go. We didn't speak. We just kept putting one foot in front of the other and pounding along the course. I fell into a sleep-like trance for a few miles, my legs striding under me without effort. Bell's voice woke me with a start.

'Wake up, you two. You'll get yourselves killed running on the roads in that state.'

I looked at Jack who grinned at me, causing spittle to trail from the corner of his mouth. A little later, we passed Tucker.

'Keep it up, you two. Only about three miles to go.'

Only three miles!

We rounded a wooded area and found a hill waiting for us. Shit! Jack gave me a look as if to say 'Give over!' A quarter of the way up we slowed to a walk. My legs suddenly seemed to be made of rubber and our pace slackened. I managed to adjust my breathing to keep pace with my legs but I was fearful of losing any semblance of rhythm. I wondered if it was time to take a five-minute break. Jack had pushed ahead and was now twenty yards in front of me. He looked to be progressing well and I didn't want to be the one to call for a break. I found some fresh energy and increased my stride and pace in an effort to catch up with my oppo. As we neared the top of the hill and the ground started to level out, the rubbery feeling gradually left my legs. I caught up with Jack as we crested the rise and the two of us started to jog down the easy side. However, the pace became too hurried and I thought I would lose my balance.

'Hang on, oppo!' I called out.

Jack slowed the pace and we were walking again by the time we reached the bottom. I had completely lost my rhythm and I assumed Jack was in the same condition. My movements were becoming a little awkward and so I called for a five-minute rest. We walked to the side of the road and found a spot near a tree. Both of us removed our helmets and sweat-soaked cap-comforters, laid our rifles and packs on the ground, and eased ourselves down beside them. We leaned our feet on the trunk.

My throbbing head cooled and the blood drained from my legs. I almost fell asleep again, but the sound of squeaking brakes from the Land Rover pulling up on the road next to us brought me back to reality.

'Come on, men. You have just a mile and a half to go. I'm surprised to see you taking it so easy when you're almost at the finishing point. Hot tea and food are waiting for you.'

I got to my feet like an old man and achingly put my gear back on. The first few steps were difficult, but as we pressed on I got back into rhythm and jogged to the finish.

About a dozen guys who had finished ahead of us were wolfing down sandwiches and tea. Jack and I unbuckled our belts and allowed our packs and pouches to drop to the ground. An unknown Marine asked for our names and I was instantly irritated with him. We took off our tin hats and cap-comforters and leaned our rifles against our packs. The effort to extract my tin cup from a side pouch seemed to be unreasonably difficult. Both of us made for the tea canister that sat on the tailgate of a truck. The hot, sweet tea tasted wonderful and the new management at the galley had made roast beef, ham, and chicken sandwiches with trimmings. I took one of each and wondered what the change in the galley staff would do to the private entrepreneur and her mobile kitchen. Two more men arrived and we left the food area so they could help themselves without us being in their way. We strolled over to the Land Rover where an unknown man was recording everyone's times.

'How'd we do?' Jack asked. 'Johnson and Mason.'

'Uh, five hours and twenty seven minutes. Green and Sargent were the first in. They did it in four hours fifty-five.'

The last squaddies to arrive was the quartet of Sammy, aided by Dennis and talked in by Dusty and Ron. Stephenson arrived behind them. Dark stains marked the crutch of Sammy's trousers, his armpits, and his shoulders where the webbing had rubbed against his shirt. The man was in obvious pain. Ron unhooked Sammy's belt, Dusty lifted his gear away and Dennis helped his oppo to the ground. Ray and Comma asked Jack and me for our mugs and then took four measures of the hot tea to where Sammy lay.

A while later, as everyone prepared for the ride back to camp, Sammy asked for help in getting to his feet. Once upright, he started to undo his trousers and see what damage he'd sustained.

'Leave it, Samuels. That's an order. If you take those trousers down now you'll be in a worse state when you have to pull 'em up again. Maybe that'll teach you to take the time to rinse the fuckin' soap outta your clothes in future,' Stephenson told him.

'Come on, Sarge. I'm bleedin' 'ere.'

'Do as he says,' Ron advised. 'Here, let me help you onto the back of the truck.'

Dusty and Ron linked hands and made a sling to lift Sammy up until his feet were level with the floor of the truck. Hands reached out, grasped Sammy's outstretched arms and levered him inside.

'Jesus fuck!' he winced as he sat down.

By the time we arrived at Lympstone, most of us were feeling fine. We unpacked our gear and brought everything back up to inspection level. The truck took Sammy round to the sickbay where a Sick Berth Attendant gave him some cream to put on his badly chafed and bleeding inner thighs. Dennis had to run down to the sick bay to get Sammy's locker key and thereby allow the rest of us to take care of his gear. The SBA wanted Sammy to stay in the sick bay overnight but he was merely a matelot and our tough little squaddie had no trouble in declining the offer.

The following day we were to take some written tests, but a night march was on the agenda for Wednesday. Stephenson came to the hut to see if everyone was in good shape.

'You gonna be up to that, Samuels?'

'I'll make sure I am, Sergeant.'

'That's the spirit. Tell you what. If you can stand a little pain, there is a way of clearing up that mess on your thighs quickly. You game?'

'Absofuckinlutely, Sergeant.'

'Good man. All you have to do is pour after-shave all over yer thighs. Shit'll clear up quicker than you can say Jack Robinson.'

Sammy went to the NAAFI and purchased a bottle of 'Old Spice'. The curses he yelled out when the liquid ran over his thighs, under his armpits and onto his shoulders were so loud, a couple of guys from the next hut came to see if there was trouble.

'You smell like a fuckin' brothel,' Pete observed.

'Hey, if the cap fits ...' Spike added.

Sammy said it was only a slight discomfort to march in his blue serge trousers the following morning. Wednesday night, he told us, would be a doddle.

On Tuesday, we all passed our final hut, bathroom, kit, and locker inspections. We practised marching for our Thursday pass-out, which must have hurt Sammy, and in the evening returned some of our gear. It felt good to start packing. Jack and I obtained our railway tickets from the company office and exchanged them for cash with a couple of guys in K Squad. They hailed from a town near Manchester and planned to use them to go home and see their girlfriends one weekend. They seemed not to mind that the return station was Portsmouth. 'We'll get 'em changed at the ticket office.'

I tried to talk Bobby into giving us the keys for the screwmobile so we could pack our gear into it, but he preferred to hold on to them until we gave him money.

That night, Stephenson gave us the proceeds of our wager on Comma. 'Sorry it took so long, guys, but the timing's pretty good when ya think about it.'

Eleven of us picked up thirty-two pounds each while Bobby picked up sixty-four.

'That's a far cry from the fifty you said you'd wagered, Pearson,' Stephenson reproached him.

'I thought I said I would *win* fifty pounds,' Bobby retorted

'Yeah, that could've been it,' the sergeant said with a grin.

The squad leader had news of Boswell. 'Someone from the Advocate's Office has made an appeal on Sergeant Boswell's behalf. In the meantime your man has to stay at Portsmouth until Her Majesty's pleasure has been established.'

Now we had money, Jack and I got the keys to the van. We stowed gear not needed until we arrived at Portsmouth in the vehicle, and I was happy to know I wouldn't have to hump my kitbag and suitcase on and off trains and busses for the next two weeks.

On Wednesday evening, trucks took us to an area on Dartmoor where we were to begin the night march. The ten miles didn't give us pause. Sammy was not even worried about his thighs. The main idea was to see if we could find our way from one map point to another in the dark. We split into three groups and set out for three different destinations. So confident were we of completing the course with ease, our main concern was to keep our clothing and equipment as clean and dry as possible. Our group decided to 'leap frog' home. We determined the route by use of map and compass and then half the party set out for a specific land or sky mark. The second half watched the marchers and checked a compass to ensure the group travelled in the right direction. The first party then stopped and the second party caught up to them.

Everything was going to plan until we stepped into a bog and sank to our shins in mire. We'd thought frost would give us a firmer surface. When we realized we were going to have to launder our clothing and give our boots a good polish, we increased our speed.

Once back at camp, we had plenty of time to launder our fatigues and clean our boots. The clothing would dry overnight and be ironed and packed in the morning. Our dress blues and khaki battle dress would be on hangers in the screwmobile. We needlessly recleaned our battle dress, parade boots, khaki webbing and brasses in readiness for our pass-out parade.

Guys talked about what they would do while on leave. Some fantasied about going to their local pub on New Year's Eve wearing the Green Beret and khaki battle dress with the Commando dagger on its sleeve. Others planned to attempt death by fornication. Some wondered if their girlfriends still considered them their boyfriends.

'Didn't you write to her, then?'

'Fuck, no. Write?'

'So you could be dead, for all she knows.'

'Yeah, I suppose. What a great surprise for her when I turn up.'

'The bleedin' surprise might be on you.'

'Nah! The cow loves me. She'll 'ave bin waitin' for me to come back and give 'er the best Christmas present she's ever 'ad – me.'

One guy, who had received a 'Dear John', intended to 'kick seven buckets of shit' out of the old girlfriend's new boyfriend. Dusty reminded him of Boswell's predicament and urged the man to let matters be. Three guys wrote 'Dear John' letters to women they had been dating in Exmouth and Exeter.

'I'll post it on Friday, so she'll still come an' see us pass-out,' said one.

Sammy went to the bank of telephones outside the main gate to discuss how Sandra was faring with her arrangements for the move to Portsmouth. Comma went to the gym to get the name of the PTI in charge of boxing there. The Fairies were disbanding. Everybody made different arrangements; not only for their leave, but what lay beyond. It was possible some of us would never see each other again. The Corps allegedly tried to keep oppos together, but no-one else.

As we entered the galley, we heard the bugler play the 'fall in' for morning parade and it felt good to know I didn't have to be there. For our last meal at Lympstone the chefs allowed us to eat whatever was on the hot plates, knowing there was no one left to follow us. Jack and I had made it to the galley early and had collared steaks not eaten by those on special diets. For the first time in my life, I ate steak, eggs, grilled tomatoes and fried potatoes for breakfast. When we had gorged ourselves as much as we dared, we went back to the hut to iron and pack fatigues laundered the night before and visit the bathroom. We carefully donned our battle dress and inspected each other. It was the last time we would wear the black beret with the red patch.

Stephenson, Bell and Tucker arrived at the hut looking very impressive in their uniforms. Could we possibly look the same, save the medal ribbons?

We lined up in ranks of three and Stephenson marched us past the recruits' huts, the company office, and along the road to the parade ground. As we turned the corner by the company office, we heard the unexpected music of a band on the parade ground. They must have trucked in the band from Plymouth for us. As we neared the parade ground, 'Colonel Bogey' changed to 'A Life on the Ocean Wave'.

'Fuckin' ay,' someone said.

'Quiet!' Stephenson ordered.

I stretched my body as high as it would go. The small of my back straightened and my chest went out. I tucked in my chin, drew back my shoulders and turned my arms into metal rods. I drove my heels into the concrete and knew everybody else was doing the same.

Stephenson brought us to a halt in front of an almost empty mobile-reviewing-stand. There were a few spectators, but people were hardly queuing to get a seat. We stood easy and everyone made one last inspection of the men around him. The three NCOs walked among us, chatting and checking our uniforms. The band, having got us onto the parade ground, had fallen silent. We waited for Dinger Bell to report officers making their way toward the parade ground.

Stephenson returned to the head of the squad. 'H Squad, attennnnnnnntion!'

Twenty-eight boots made a single sound.

The band started to play background music. Stephenson marched smartly up to the Commanding Officer and saluted him. 'H Squad ready for your inspection, Sir!'

The colonel returned the salute. 'Thank you, Sergeant.' He proceeded to make his way along the front row, his entourage trailing behind. He stopped to say something to every man. The Adjutant and Company Commander also spoke to a majority of the guys. The RSM and Stephenson mostly smiled and nodded their approval.

We were immaculate. The whole squad had been to the barbershop and been cursed at for turning up 'gang-handed'. Some guys had paid the tailors' shop to press their uniforms.

'Marine Johnson.' How did the CO know my name? 'Did you find any of the training here difficult?'

'Yes, Sir. I'm surprised the instructors convinced me to do some of the things I've done.'

'Yes,' the man smiled. 'They do have a way. We do that to men in the Royal Marines. Wish you still worked in a bank?'

'No, Sir!'

'I understand you are going to Portsmouth to await further posting. My advice to you is to do a tour with a Commando and then look to specialise in something when you return. No need to rush things. Good luck to you wherever you go. Perhaps I'll have the honour of commanding you again someday.'

'Thank you, Sir.'

The Adjutant was next. 'Good work, Johnson. Keep it up. Always remember, it is a general rule that if you are proud of yourself, others will be proud of you and proud to serve with you. Those who have no pride in themselves are the ones most likely to screw up. Not something you want to happen when you are in a tight spot. I'm on my way overseas in about three months. Perhaps we shall meet again. I sincerely hope so.'

The Company Commander seemed at a loss for words. As the Colonel was still talking to the man next but one to me, he had nowhere to go and so he turned to the RSM to cover his apparent embarrassment. When the party moved forward, the man smiled at me. 'Keep up the good work, Johnson.'

To the next man the Company Commander said, 'Got your railway ticket to take you home, have you?'

The retinue having passed me, I let my mind wander. So, what do you think, Father? Is it a mark in your book that I now wear the Green Beret? I had received a letter from him telling me he was taking the family to Australia for Christmas. He didn't ask what I was doing, so I probably wasn't a mark in any book he kept. The day allotted to see my folks on our two-week calendar, was now free. I was a little disappointed, as I would have liked to introduce Jill to them. Jill. I didn't want our relationship to be over just because I was moving to Portsmouth. On the other hand, how long would I be there? I might be sent to a Commando within a couple of weeks and that would mean spending eighteen months in the Yemen or Singapore/Borneo. Jack said he had no qualms about walking away from Audrey, but I wasn't convinced. He'd told me some weeks ago that, after being bundled around most of his life, he liked the idea of a constant girlfriend. He'd never say it, but what he really liked was the specific attentions of Audrey. We would have to sort things out in the coming fortnight.

The inspecting group stepped up to the reviewing stand.

The Adjutant spoke without the aid of a microphone and it was difficult to catch every word. 'In the Second World War, men were selected from various military units and sent to Scotland to form a special force, a Commando to combat the enemy. For our purposes, the word Commando comes from the Boer wars in South Africa. Small units of Afrikaans caused great problems for larger English forces and earned their begrudging admiration. Baden-Powell formed the Boy Scout movement because of his regard for the Afrikaans. Back to the men in Scotland. As they were from different units, they all wore different headgear and the Green Beret was introduced for unifying purposes. By the by, after 41 Commando acquitted themselves so gloriously in Korea, General Eisenhower commanded a similar unit be formed in the US. Accordingly, a US Army Special Forces unit, better known as the Green Berets, came into being, ably assisted by John Wayne. Being awarded the Green Beret is a distinction of which you can be justifiably proud. Well done men!'

He then called on each man to march to the stand and receive a handshake and the hallowed headwear. We would take the faux-metal badges from our black berets and put them into the Green Berets once we returned to our hut.

The band played the Marine hymn. Having presented each of us with the new part of our uniform, the CO gave a quick speech. 'Well done, men! You should have pride in yourselves. The courses you have completed are amongst the most demanding in the world and have turned you into men of whom Her Britannic Majesty is justifiably proud.' He paused and swept his gaze over us. 'On a different note, you must not allow Sergeant Boswell's misfortunes to affect you. His unfortunate circumstance has nothing to do with you … is not a reflection of you … or you of him.' He paused again. 'There is a well-worn saying that is still true, especially in a force as small as the Royal Marines: "There is a Field Marshall's baton in every man's knapsack." For those of you who aspire to greater things, it is a saying worth noting.' His gaze swept over us again and he smiled. 'That's it men. Enjoy your leave and then report promptly to wherever you have been assigned to start life as a Royal Marine Commando. Good luck to you all!'

***

Peter Lingard

Glossary

AWOL – absent without leave

Bootneck – Royal Marine

Brekkers – breakfast

CSM – company sergeant major

DSO – Distinguished Service Order

Dead chuffed – very happy (chuffed = happy)

DI – drill instructor

Dip in – be lucky

Dip out – be unlucky

Drain off – urinate

Fash – worry (Scotland)

Flappers – ears

Geordie – someone from the Newcastle area

Gong – medal

Heads – toilet/bathroom

Irish pennant – stray piece of lint, cotton, et al

Johnnies – condoms/prophylactics

Leatherneck – US Marine

Made up – happy/pleased

NAAFI – Navy Army Air Force Institute

Oppo – opposite number/one half of a solid friendship

Partie – naval slang for a female

Plonker – penis

PTI – physical training instructor

SBA – sick berth attendant

Scouse – someone from Liverpool

Skiving (off) – avoiding

Strides – pants/trousers

Vits – food (victuals)

Wets – drinks (usually beer or scrumpy)

Acknowledgements

To Mary for telling to pick up the pen.

Chas Eeles who gave me my first guidance and encouragement.

Phoenix Writers who listened, advised, and even said they liked it.

To all the magazines who published my short stories and encouraged me.

Sylvia Karakaltsas

Greg Hill

Toph Welch

Stu Reedy

Nicole Hayes

Stephanie Doyle

About the author

When a youngster, Peter Lingard told his mother many fantastic tales of intrepid adventures enjoyed by him and his friends. She always said, 'Go tell it to the Marines'. When he asked why, she said, 'They've been everywhere and done everything, so they'll want to hear about what you've been up to.' Of course, Peter joined the Royal Marines as soon as he was old enough. He later worked as an accountant and a farm hand. Peter lived in the US for twenty-five years and owned a freight forwarding business in New York.

Look for further books about Paul and Jack to be published in the future.

www.ingramcontent.com/pod-product-compliance
Lightning Source LLC
Chambersburg PA
CBHW030623110726
47901CB00002B/283